STAR WARTZ

Also by Patrick Tilley

STAR WARTZ

TALES OF ADVENTURE
FROM THE RIMWORLD

Patrick Tilley

ORBIT

An *Orbit* Book

First published in Great Britain in 1995
by Little, Brown and Company

Copyright © Patrick Tilley 1995

The moral right of the author has been asserted

*All characters in this publication are fictitious
and any resemblance to real persons, living or dead,
is purely coincidental.*

A CIP catalogue record for this book
is available from the British Library.

ISBN 0 1 85723 320 4 (HB)
ISBN 0 1 85723 333 6 (TPB)

Typeset by
Hewer Text Composition Services, Edinburgh
Printed and bound in Great Britain by
Clays Ltd, St Ives plc

Orbit
A division of
Little, Brown and Company (UK)
Brettenham House
Lancaster Place
London WC2E 7EN

To Barbara
in appreciation of her unwavering support
during the years of the Amtrak Wars and,
more especially, during the aftermath
when words failed me.
A friend indeed.

Chapter One

If you were to wake up on what, to all intents and purposes, seemed a perfectly normal Tuesday and found yourself caught up in a bewildering series of events which left you watching not one, but two suns sink into a golden sea on a strange planet several million light-years from home, you would probably think it rather extraordinary.

In your astonishment and wonder, you might even – after a precautionary glance over your shoulder – be moved to mutter something along the lines of 'Bugger me . . .'

Twenty-nine-year-old Andrew Webber was about to experience such a day.

Andrew, who was trying to establish himself as a freelance journalist, had found himself in some extraordinary situations during a chequered eight-year stint with the military but, as he shuffled downstairs to pick up the morning mail, he had no inkling that he was about to be lured across the threshold of a magical device that would sweep him through Time and Space towards an epic adventure on the far side of the galaxy.

But then, how could he – how could anyone – have imagined such a thing was even possible? Especially in Catford. For, despite the undoubted charm of its location and inhabitants, this South London borough has never been regarded as the epicentre of other-worldly encounters.

And what makes it even more amazing still is that Andrew was one of the thousands who bought a vacuum cleaner from Hoover and never managed to get the promised airline ticket to Florida.

Clutching a fistful of junk mail, Andrew made his way to the

1

small kitchen, filled the electric kettle and ripped open the first envelope. It contained a glossy invitation to borrow money from one of the main clearing banks. All it took was a telephone call to a toll-free number. The photograph featured a young couple – husband gaping joyously with the receiver to his ear while his wife squeezes his arm excitedly as the honey-voiced operator portrayed on the facing page agrees to lend them £5,000.

What the brochure didn't include was a picture of the same couple a week later, sitting prematurely-aged on their no-deposit, interest-free sofa, as the realisation that they had to *pay back* the five grand plus another two and a half thou in interest started to sink in.

The second envelope included yet another smarmy invitation to apply for an American Express Gold Card. He always found it mildly insulting to read he had been chosen as 'one of the select few' when he was always late in settling the monthly statements on his existing credit cards. Didn't they run any checks at all?

Andrew toyed with the idea of using the £10,000 overdraft facility to fly off to somewhere like Thailand and stay there until he died of pleasure or the money ran out but sanity prevailed as the kettle came to the boil. He made himself a cup of tea and sat down at the kitchen table to examine the remaining envelopes.

The first two were from Reader's Digest and Britannia Record Club. No need to open those. The next was from a charity called Sense. It contained a sweet-smelling sachet of *pot pourri* and an appeal for £15 to provide a deaf-blind person with a 'day of achievement'.

Letters like this always made Andrew feel bad. He didn't have fifteen quid to spare and he'd already squared his social conscience by sending the odd cheque to ChildLine. They had obviously passed his name on as a soft touch because, a short while later, appeals from the World Wild Life Fund for Nature, the Royal Society for the Protection of Birds, the Muscular Dystrophy Trust and SCOPE started dropping through the letterbox. Finding himself unable to throw such letters away,

Andrew did the next best thing. He tucked them behind the clock on the mantelpiece to be dealt with later. They were still piling up and Andrew was now reaching the point where he was going to have to get a thinner clock or a wider shelf.

He inhaled the fragrance leaking from the plastic sachet, slipped it back in the envelope and set it aside. The last envelope, made of recycled grey paper, had been mailed from Prague and bore the usual trigger words:

IMPORTANT COMMUNICATION.
RUSH DELIVER. OPEN AT ONCE.

Andrew opened it, convinced he already knew what it contained – an invoice for at least £400, payable to a company in Liechtenstein. In return for this princely sum, his name and fax number would be included in a forthcoming international fax directory.

Yeah, sure, pull the other one . . .

He was right. It was an invoice, and once again they'd printed out his name, address, fax number and occupation. Only this time, the amount he was required to pay for a bold-face entry in *The Galactic Fax Directory* was $10,000.

Andrew frowned. *Galactic* fax directory? What next? He read the invoice again and decided it was an elaborate hoax. But in contrast to the previous invoices he had received from the nebulous world of fax directory printers, this one was boldly stamped: SEND NO MONEY! YOU NEED ONLY PAY WHEN YOU RECEIVE YOUR COPY. The line below read: 'Supplied on five 1000-gigabyte laser discs.'

Andrew was intrigued. Computer technology was developing at bewildering speed but he hadn't heard of any manufacturers who were marketing CDs capable of storing that much infor-mation although, clearly, if you were going to compile a list of all the subscribers that might at this moment be orbiting upwards of one hundred billion solar masses, you would need something pretty hefty.

This notion, plus the fact that someone was trying to flog copies of a galactic fax directory, led him to think he might be

3

able to concoct a modest inside-page filler that he could place through a bloke who worked for the *Mail*. Andrew had yet to make his debut in the national press. Up to now, his published work had consisted of articles and test-firing reports in the pulp mags bought by gun buffs and survival nuts.

He scanned the invoice again. In the bottom left hand corner was a printed invitation: For further information please contact Olympic Marketing Enterprises (UK) Ltd, 4 Shadwell Court, London W1. Andrew checked the location in his A to Z; Shadwell Court was one of the maze of streets near Berwick Street Market in Soho.

He dialled the number given on the invoice. The phone rang and rang. Just when Andrew was about to hang up, a bright sing-song voice responded. 'Olympic Marketing Enterprises. My name is Morr-reeeen. How can I help yeww?'

'Uh, yeah . . .' Andrew cleared his throat. 'I've just received an invoice for a bold-face entry in your *Galactic Fax Directory*. The thing is, it's for rather a lot of money – '

'I know.' Maureen's voice was full of concern. 'I can't see many people paying that much, can you? Though of course, as it says on the invoice, you don't have to pay nothing till you get your copy so, I mean, you do see what you're getting. And it is on thirty-day sale or return. If you don't like it, you can always send it back.'

'It doesn't say that on the invoice.'

The melodic intonation was replaced by a nasal whine. 'Oh, dear! You sure? Bloody printers! They always get summink wrong, don't they?' The songbird returned. 'Sorry about that.'

'That's okay,' said Andrew. 'And that's not what I really rang about.'

'So how can I help yeww?' sang Maureen.

'Well . . .' began Andrew, trying not to sound too tentative, 'I'd like to find out a bit more about, err, y'know . . . what's in the directory.'

'There's not a lot I can tell you,' said Maureen, liltingly. 'It's just a list of names, addresses and phone numbers.'

Andrew wondered where she'd acquired the knack of making

4

an ordinary sentence sound like an entry in the Eurovision Song Contest. 'Yeah, I know the sort of thing. I've got the one put out by British Telecom. But this one's called the *Galactic* Fax Directory.'

Maureen's voice flattened. 'That's nothing to do with me. I'm just employed to answer the switchboard. Well, I say switchboard but between you and me it's just like the one phone, really. See, we don't get all that many calls because were just, y'know, the local agents.'

Andrew warmed to her candour. 'So where's the head office?'

'Dunno. I just answered an ad in the paper a few weeks ago. Some bloke phoned me up, asked me a few questions, then gave me the address of this place and posted me the keys. I've been here a couple of weeks now but nobody's turned up.'

Andrew's interest quickened. 'Bit odd isn't it?'

'Depends,' said Maureen. 'Tell you one thing – '

'Yeah? What's that?'

'The money's good.'

'Glad to hear it. But the thing is – ' He paused then asked: 'Can you spare a moment to talk to me? I don't want to, err, y'know – interrupt anything.'

Maureen giggled. 'Talk all day if you want. There's bugger all going on here.'

'Right.' Andrew adopted a persuasive tone. 'Well, see, I'd like to be in this directory that Olympic Enterprises are putting out, but I'm still a little confused.'

'About what?'

'The title. *Galactic Fax Directory*. See, an *International* directory would contain all the fax numbers of all the countries in the world – '

'Yeah . . .'

'But the word "Galactic" comes from "Galaxy" which for most people means all the stars in the Milky Way. Not just Earth and the planets in our solar system but billions of stars and God knows how many planets – some of which might support intelligent life.'

5

'You ain't half got a lovely voice,' said Maureen. 'Anyone ever tell you that?'

'Uhh, no. Thanks, err – but what I'm trying to say is, if this really is a *Galactic* fax directory, some of those planets which may or may not be out there would have to have telephones.'

'Yeah, I see what you mean,' said Maureen. 'Which is daft, isn't it, I mean, when you come to think about it. 'Cause if they 'ad phones and suchlike, they'd've been in touch, wouldn't they?'

Andrew laughed. 'They might even want to buy a few copies of your directory. The thing is – and please believe me when I say I'm not trying to get anyone into trouble – if there aren't any fax numbers for little green men in your directory then Olympic Enterprises is committing an offence under the Trades Description Act.'

There was a long silence. 'Hello? Maureen? You still there?'

'You're not from the Customs and Excise are you?'

'No. I'm a journalist but I'm not planning to do an exposé or anything. I'd just like to find out what's going on. D'you remember those ads announcing cash awards for the worst contribution to music last year? Everyone thought it was a hoax but it turned out to be for real. I thought this could be something similar . . . I dunno . . . a publicity stunt set up by one of the cellular phone companies maybe.' Andrew paused then asked: 'Are you sure there's no one I can talk to?'

'Ooo-err, um, hang on a minute . . .' Maureen sounded distracted. Her voice became fainter as she covered the phone and spoke to someone in the office: She came back on the line. 'My boss has just walked in. Can I ring you back?'

Andrew gave her his name and number then made himself another cup of tea and found a place for the latest charity appeal on his crowded mantelpiece. He picked the phone up on the first ring.

'Mr Andrew Webber? It's me, Morr-reeeen, Olympic Marketing Enterprises.'

'Great. Thanks for calling back. Everything all right?'

'Yes, fine. Talk about coincidence – you phoning and Mister

6

Potemkin dropping in like that. So listen, I've had a little word like, to sort of explain things. Where are you calling from?'

'Catford. SE6.'

'Ooh, that's a bit of luck. I live in Sydenham. D'you know Perry Hill?'

'Yes,' said Andrew.

'Go clubbing, do you?'

'If I've got a partner. Err, about Mr Potemkin – '

'Oh, yeah. He said if you care to join him for lunch, he'll be pleased to answer your enquiries. Can you make it over here for one o'clock?'

'Yeah, no problem.' Andrew's mind went on a minor binge of speculation. Potemkin . . . there was talk of the Russian mafia moving into Europe. Was the *Galactic Fax Directory* a scam set up by a bunch of disaffected *apparatchiks* from Star City . . .?

'Hope you like Greek food.'

'Love it,' lied Andrew. If lunching with Potemkin turned out to be a wild goose chase, there was always the chance of pulling the lovely Maureen.

'Good. Okay, one o'clock at the office then,' tinkled Miss Melody. 'We're on the first floor above Chico's Sandwich Bar. Door's on the left-hand side, name's on the bell – all right?'

'Terrific. Thanks. See you.'

Shalimar carefully removed the lightweight headset to avoid ruffling her elaborate coiffure and swivelled her chair round to face the shadowy figure whose vast bulk filled the doorway behind her. When she spoke, there was no trace of 'Maureen's' South London accent and she bore absolutely no resemblance to the mind-picture Andrew had formed of her during their conversation. 'I didn't believe it would be that easy to get him on the hook.'

Constantine Parnassus chuckled. It was a deep, resonant sound that came rumbling up from the depths of his enormously fat body. 'He's intelligent, imaginative, resourceful and reasonably honest. Young men like that are born to exploited by people like me!'

A Dravidian clerk, one of hundreds employed by Parnassus, entered after knocking politely, handed him a sheaf of accounts then bowed to Shalimar and left. Parnassus flipped through them with a practised eye. He had the kind of brain that could study a profit and loss account and hold a conversation at the same time.

'Besides, I'm about to offer him the greatest adventure he will ever have in his whole life! Where's the harm in that?'

'My thoughts exactly,' said Shalimar.

'And why am I asking such questions?' continued Parnassus. 'I'm an incorrigible, deceitful rogue. It's the secret of my staggering success. I have no need to justify myself. Especially to you.'

'Absolutely not.'

Parnassus completed his inspection of the accounts of one of his many enterprises with a happy sigh. 'Is the shuttle Earthed?'

'Yes.'

'And we have the correct time slot?'

'Yes.'

'We can't afford any slip-ups.'

'There won't be any. Go and order lunch.'

Parnassus floated off. Despite his bulk he was light on his feet, thanks to the anti-grav harness which reduced his weight to a manageable ten stone. Shalimar checked with Transportation. They confirmed the connection with Shadwell Street was in place and on stand-by mode. When the target entered the unit, it would automatically go on-line and the transfer would be made.

Shalimar rose and walked out onto the marble-tiled verandah. The twin suns that breathed life into the Rimworld had begun to overlap. Palladia, the planet which was one of her employer's many abodes, was about to enter another of its cool seasons. She thought about the number of light-years that separated her present location from Andrew Webber's flat in

Catford and mentally calculated the approximate cost of the long distance call.

It was just one of many Connie had been making over the last few years. Fortunately, he had found a way to tap into the British Telecom network and by some fancy fingerwork on the computer, he'd fixed it so they were also footing the bill as part of their operating costs. He figured that with the money they were making, they'd never notice and if they did detect a fall in profits, they'd just lay off more staff.

The man was a genius. Shalimar adored him.

In time – if he could forgive Connie for what was about to happen – Andrew Webber would come to love him too.

☆ ☆ ☆

Arming himself with a pocket tape recorder and reporter's notebook, Andrew put some milk out for Kelly, a feline vagrant who had decided to move in with him, secured all windows, double-locked his front door and boarded the first of two buses that would take him into central London.

At this mid-morning hour the top deck was almost empty and he was able to secure his favourite seat at the very front on the left hand side from where he could scan the shops and other places of interest on both sides of the route.

As a young boy, Andrew used to exercise imaginary control of the bus by pressing the three screws set along the bottom edge of the front window frame. One to start, one to stop and one to ring the conductor's bell. He played this game until the age of twelve when he became aware that his favourite seat was also the ideal perch from which to study the staggering variety of busty substances on parade below.

From that moment on, each journey became a voyage of exploration; a quest for the perfectly-filled 40D cup. Okay, so it's not the Holy Grail but, hey – we all have to start somewhere.

Chapter Two

As careful readers of Chapter One have already deduced, we are not alone. Sentient beings – which, in this context, means any life form with the brain and hand coordination required to instantly switch off any tv programme hosted by Jeremy Beadle – exist elsewhere in our galaxy.

That's the good news. The bad news for fans of E.T. and anyone who likes to attend sf conventions dressed up as an alien is that there aren't any. The beings out there came from Earth and they look like us.

And that's not all. Despite being millions of years ahead of us on the evolutionary ladder, they are still prey to the same irrational instincts and often get completely rat-faced on their equivalent of a Saturday night.

Incredible? Not really. How long did it take the present generation of *homo sapiens* to swap his stone axe for a pump-action Winchester, plant a flag on the moon and launch Voyager on its epic voyage through the solar system? The latest guesstimate by the experts is five hundred thousand years but their calculations assume that present-day humans developed from ape-like hominids. *Homo erectus.*

We didn't.

Our present civilisation began when Earth was revisited by a bio-engineering task force around 35,000 BC. Compared to the Age of the Dinosaurs that's just a blip on the space-time continuum. Their sublease on the planet ran for one hundred and sixty *million* years. And here's the kicker – when they emerged during the Triassic period some two hundred and twenty-five million years ago they were treading in the footsteps of our predecessors.

10

Atlanteans.

Now some of you may have a problem with that word. At the back of your brain there may even be a warning bell sounding a 'Dingbat Alert'. Every sensible person knows that the belief in the existence of previous civilisations has long been regarded as the kind of wacky idea eagerly embraced by people who use green typewriter ribbons, keep pet crystals and swap the serial numbers of flying saucers at Mind and Body Festivals.

Not any longer. Put all your preconceptions on hold and check out the following facts from the **Now It Can Be Told Department**. Make of them what you will. And remember – you read it here first.

Fact One: The Atlantean civilisation – from which Connie and Shalimar are descended – wasn't the first. That's why the stories of gods and other magical beings are engraved so deeply on the human psyche. Every myth, every saga, every creation legend contains a irreducible grain of truth. We were here before, and before that and before that. And before that we were somewhere else.

Fact Two: The scientific theory that the building blocks of life came from outer space is correct but they didn't arrive molecule by molecule on the backs of meteors. They were shipped in. This was a big operation. When the terraforming crews completed their task of making the air fit to breathe, a new batch of specialists from LifeCor stepped off the ferry, clutching their duty-frees, to run the computer programs which would be used to generate plant and animal life forms and control their evolution. Which explains why there is no missing link because –

Fact Three: *Homo sapiens*, the ancestor of modern man, did not drop off the evolutionary branch from which the primates are still swinging. We were here right at the beginning – several geological eras before Lucy's forebears had the operation that enabled them to stand up on their hind legs and walk along the Rift Valley. The fishes, the reptiles, the birds, the mammals came *after* Man. We were part of the design team – which goes a long way to explaining the dominance of vertebrate species.

11

Fact Four: Despite the six hundred million year gap that separates us from our proto-ancestors the physical similarities are quite remarkable. Pre-Palaeozooic Man ('Preppies') would not attract more than a cursory second glance if we passed a group of them in the lobby of the United Nations building in New York. Being olive-skinned, perfectly formed but only four feet tall, it would be easy to mistake them for a bunch of well-behaved schoolkids from somewhere on the Pacific Rim.

So the inevitable question that now arises is: what happened to these civilizations that preceded our own? Simple. They were destroyed by large lumps of rock lobbed at us by an unseen hand from the depths of space. Cosmic Kissograms – like the one that closed down the very first real-life Jurassic Park.

Bad news if you were a Tyrannosaurus Rex but good news if you happened to be a small mammal trying to find a quiet ecological niche to raise a family in.

You've all seen the size of the hole in Arizona and heard about the disastrous effect it had on the environment. That was a small one; the earlier arrivals varied in size from the Isle of Wight to Western Australia. Some small consolation can be drawn from the fact that the big ones only crash-land every few million years or so but each time Planet Earth takes a hit, it tends to ruin everybody's social calendar, regardless of whether you have reached the ultimate state of peace and harmony by eliminating the genetic defect that causes haemorrhoids or have still got the skin off yesterday's dinner wrapped round your tool kit and spend your spare time decorating caves with palm prints.

Fortunately, not everybody waited for the sky to fall in. At some point towards the end of the Mesozoic era, Connie's distant ancestors got word that another granite Valentine addressed to Gaia was on its way. Since they were already into space travel and had tried, without success, to re-colonise Mars, they slipped the key under the mat and headed off for pastures new.

It made sense in more ways than one. The genetic pro-gramme for reptilian development had gone haywire. The dinosaurs were getting bigger and nastier and air traffic controllers were going prematurely grey trying to avoid collisions between Air Atlantis shuttles and giant pterodactyls.

So why, you ask, didn't they just shoot 'em down? Simple. It's a question of professional ethics. When you've been given the job of running a Life Project you don't kill off your creations; you correct any undesirable trends by modifying the program. Unfortunately, there were so many lines of dodgy code in this particular batch of software, tinkering with it only made made worse.

Evacuation was the only answer.

Not everybody left, of course. In any society there are always some who rubbish doom-laden scenarios. And they invariably prove to be right. On several occasions in our own century charismatic seers have led their followers up onto one of the high places to await Armageddon and Eternal Salvation. The fatal day passes. They wait patiently for another week or so while their leader struggles to invent some plausible explanation, then down they all come to be rubbished by the media and branded as dickheads by the rest of us.

The Atlanteans who stayed behind were able to pursue their agreeable lifestyle for another million years or so before the predicted collision occurred. The original forecast which had triggered the lemming-like rush to evacuate the planet was now entirely forgotten by the public at large. The few experts with access to the ancient records (and who had actually bothered to read them) either dismissed the possibility or thrust it firmly to the back of their minds.

The look on their faces as they slowly realised that the small luminous object, which they had assumed to be a returning spaceship filled with crestfallen wanderers was, in fact, a tumbling misshapen lump of rock the size of Venezuela can only be imagined.

The legendary city of Atlantis was vaporised as the asteroid landed with the deadly accuracy of an ICBM and punched a hole nine miles deep into the Earth's crust. Atlanteans living in other settlements perished in the geological holocaust

13

unleashed by the impact and all trace of their civilisation was wiped off the face of the Earth.

So don't waste time looking for it. What remains of this so-called golden age is out there amongst the stars.

As Andrew is about to discover.

His second bus journey ends at Piccadilly Circus. He walks a little way up Shaftesbury Avenue, turns left up Rupert Street and heads north across Brewer Street, into the bustle of Berwick Street Market.

Shadwell Court, Maureen the songbird from Sydenham, and the mysteries of Olympic Marketing Enterprises (UK) are now just a short step away.

Andrew checked his watch. He had half an hour to kill before his appointment with Parnassus. He stopped at a second-hand record stall run by a girl with a neck tattoo, black Egyptian-style eyeliner, matching lipstick and net mittens, Max Wall tights, oversized biker jacket and boots. The only cranial hair she possessed was a beaded forelock. Her shaven skull was hidden under a Paddington Bear hat.

She turned a pair of expressionless grey eyes onto Andrew, took a deep drag on a prison-style roll-up then continued her conversation with a neighbouring stallholder.

Andrew flicked carefully through the first box of LPs. He was looking for a copy of 'What's Going On', the all-time classic album by Marvin Gaye, but since the stock appeared to have been thrown together at random, he had to trawl through everything on offer.

In the process, he came across several other albums that recalled the highs and lows of his own life. It was amazing how music could bring it all back even when you had forgotten the tune. Just a few bars of a melody was enough to trigger total recall of a long forgotten moment; not just what happened but how it felt. As fresh and as painful as the first time around.

Andrew riffled mechanically through the last box and drew another blank. He hesitated over a James Brown album then decided against it. He could always come back later. He looked at his watch. Time to move on.

☆   ☆   ☆

At five minutes to one, Andrew paused outside the side entrance to Number 4 Shadwell Court. The lunchtime queue at Chico's Sandwich Bar had spilled out onto the pavement. Andrew adjusted his tie, checked the state of his fingernails, drew a deep breath and pressed the bell labelled 'Olympic'. The other three label slots were empty.

'Olympic Marketing Enterprises.'

The voice was unmistakable.

'Oh, hi – Maureen? It's, uhh . . . Andrew Webber.'

There was a buzz as the lock was released.

Andrew pushed the door open. It closed smoothly and firmly behind him as he climbed the stairs. The hallway had a vaguely shabby air and the carpet underfoot was not new. To his right, on the first floor was the door to Olympic Marketing Enterprises (UK). A sign read: RECEPTION/ENQUIRIES PLEASE ENTER.

Andrew ran his fingers back though his hair, braced himself to meet the lovely Maureen, knocked and went inside.

The office was empty. The desk which, presumably, was occupied by the Sydenham songbird was completely bare except for a telephone and a computer terminal. There was not a scrap of paper anywhere.

From the condition of the hallway, Andrew had half expected the Olympic set-up to be equally seedy but the office furnishings, from the lustrous floor covering to the illuminated ceiling, looked exceedingly expensive – like a set from a sci-fi movie.

But where were the actors?

The heavy bronze-tinted window glass cut out all exterior noise. The only sound came from the computer terminal on what he assumed was Maureen's desk. Thinking there might be some revealing data on display, Andrew moved round to take a closer look. The top of the range Apple Power PC was running

15

a fractal screen-saver. The moving patterns were suddenly replaced by the following words:

MESSAGE FOR
MR ANDREW WEBBER
WE ARE SORRY NO ONE WAS HERE TO MEET YOU
PLEASE TAKE A SEAT IN THE MAIN OFFICE
AN ESCORT WILL ARRIVE SHORTLY
TO TAKE YOU TO YOUR LUNCH APPOINTMENT
WITH CONSTANTINE PARNASSUS
THANKYOU
(PRESS KEY A THEN ENTER TO ACKNOWLEDGE)

Andrew did so. The screen-saver pattern returned. He glanced towards the curved glass wall and door that separated the second room from the reception area and was struck by its odd appearance. It had no corners. In fact it wasn't really a room in the conventional sense. It was a windowless circular chamber about fifteen feet across, illuminated by a ring of recessed lights set around the edge of the ceiling – and there was a similar ring of what looked like circular air vents set into the floor.

Its odd appearance, plus the mystery of how Maureen could have spoken to him over the door-phone without being there, prompted Andrew to examine the interior before entering. In the middle of the chamber stood a high-backed charcoal grey leather and chrome chair. The sort of £875 plus VAT kind of chair you'd expect to find the top executives of privatised water companies sitting in.

Next to it was a sleek office desk that was obviously part of the set. Lying on its charcoal grey top was a six inch-thick computer print-out bound between sky blue covers. That was all. No telephone, no blotter or pen set, no time-wasting executive desk toys.

Andrew brought his nose close to the glass and cocked his head to read what was written on the cover.

It was the *Galactic Fax Directory*. Volume 1. Aaa-Azz.

Thrusting his misgivings aside, Andrew entered the chamber.

Even if this turned out to be a hoax, the print-out had obviously been placed on the desk for him to look at while waiting for his escort to arrive. The Galactic Fax Directory was, after all, the primary reason for his being there.

The curved door closed noislessly behind him. He sat down in the high-backed chair. The padded leather moulded itself to his back and thighs. A soft, yielding, almost lascivious embrace.

Andrew closed his eyes briefly, ran his hands along the arms of the chair and imagined himself making earth-shattering decisions. Yes, this was definitely an empowering piece of furniture.

He dismissed the daydream, swivelled the chair towards the desk and leant forwards to pick up the bound volume. Both hands passed through the right and left hand edges and met in the middle. He blinked and tried again. Same result. The print-out looked quite solid and convincingly real but at the same time was completely insubstantial. He laid his palms on the desk while he thought things out and found that wasn't real either.

But there was no doubting the chair. Andrew passed a hand through the desk top several times then sat back to consider the situation.

A hologram. That's what it was. He remembered seeing an item about the latest developments on a *Tomorrow's World* programme. But who would want to install a hi-tech piece of wizardry like this above a sandwich bar in Soho? And why?

As his mind framed the question, his ears registered a smooth swishing sound. He turned his head in time to see two curved, floor-to ceiling wall-panels slide from hidden recesses on either side of the glass partition. Before he could react, the leading edges meshed together, sealing the chamber from the reception area beyond.

Without thinking, Andrew reached out towards the desk to steady himself but of course there was nothing to grip. And the desk, or rather the image of the desk and the elusive volume of the fax directory had now vanished. The swishing noise was replaced by a powerful humming noise and, with a sudden flash,

17

the ring of lights on the ceiling were joined to the circular vents on the floor by iridescent pillars of light.

Fuck me, thought Andrew. What's all this about? It was totally bewildering but strangely familiar – like stepping through the tv screen into an episode of *Star Trek*.

He sank back into the chair and gripped the arms. He was not easily scared but caution suggested it was the safest place to be. No point in trying to kick his way out. The humming sound changed pitch, rising to a shrill whine that set his teeth on edge. The curved walls of the chamber surrounding the pillars of light seemed to dissolve. And now Andrew started to feel that he was dissolving too.

He gripped the arms of the chair, arched his head back and strained every muscle and sinew in a desperate attempt to retain his sense of being. His last conscious thought was the realisation he was disintegrating – quite painlessly – into sub-atomic particles. Chico's Sandwich Bar and the comparative safety of Shadwell Court seemed a million miles away.

It was slightly more than that. Several thousand *trillion* is nearer the mark but since astronomical distances of this order don't fall within the compass of our normal, everyday Earth-bound existence, the exact number needn't concern us. Sufficient to say that Andrew reached his destination a millisecond after losing consciousness.

It was, by any measure, an amazing scientific and technical feat, made possible only thanks to the unwitting assistance of London Undergound. Constantine Parnassus had not only tapped into British Telecom, he had somehow managed to get the shuttle terminal in Shadwell Court plugged into the power lines that fed the electrified rails running into and under the capital.

The massive surge of current required to catapult Andrew towards the Rimworld blew power relays right across the system, bringing tube trains to a halt on the Central, Circle, District, Northern, and Piccadilly Lines; from High Barnet to Morden and from Epping to Ealing Broadway.

Since it was a regular occurrence, the stranded commuters

heaved a sullen sigh and waited for the normal lousy service to be resumed. Management blamed the lack of investment and Her Majesty's Loyal Opposition blamed the government.

No one, not even the engineers who eventually got the system back in working order, suspected that the man who had spoiled everyone's day was an overweight corporate raider from the far side of the galaxy.

☆   ☆   ☆

Andrew's eyes fluttered open. He remained seated and slowly spun the chair through three hundred and sixty degrees. The pillars of light that had ringed the chamber had vanished – and so had the two sliding wall panels which had sealed the only escape route. The reception area was once again visible through the curved door and glass surround but the windows in what had been the outside wall of the building in Shadwell Court now reached from floor to ceiling and the street outside had been replaced by an elegant arched colonnade.

Andrew stood up, walked to the glass door, and gazed at the view. The colonnade enclosed a polished marble verandah. Beyond its edge, a beach of almost pure white sand stretched out of view on either side and ran down to meet the gently lapping waves of a turquoise blue sea. In the sky above were two overlapping suns.

This is a dream, he thought. I don't know what's happening but none of this is for real. It can't be.

He gazed at the sea again. The waves weren't moving. It was like looking at a video after pressing the 'Pause' button only, in this case, the picture was pin sharp. He pushed open the glass door, walked across the reception area and stepped out onto the verandah.

A tall, slim, elegant woman with the figure and grace of a top super-model leant against one of the columns with her back towards him. She wasn't moving either.

Andrew approached the woman. She was almost seven feet tall, and had the profile and coiffure of the ancient Egyptian Queen, Nefertiti. The resemblance to the painted head – one of

19

the priceless treasures unearthed by archaeologists – was amazing. She wasn't moving and she wasn't breathing either.

A statue, decided Andrew. One of those amazingly life-like wax sculptures similar to those fashioned by Allen Jones – some of which appeared as props in the milk-bar scene in Kubrick's *A Clockwork Orange*. Her green unblinking eyes stared off to the right. He turned his eyes and looked in the same direction.

Just a few feet along the verandah a table stood next to a white reclining chair. On the table was a small blue bottle. An old-fashioned tie-on buff luggage label was knotted round the neck.

Drawn by this curiously familiar object, Andrew moved across to the table and picked up the bottle. The label bore a two-word message: 'DRINK ME'.

This is pure Alice in Wonderland stuff, he thought. He turned the label over and found more instructions:

WHEN YOU HAVE SWALLOWED

THE CONTENTS OF THIS BOTTLE

SIT DOWN AND RELAX

YOU WILL COME TO NO HARM

WHEN YOU WAKE UP, MY ASSISTANT

WILL BE THERE TO WELCOME YOU

I LOOK FORWARD TO OUR LUNCH

YOURS ETC

CONSTANTINE PARNASSUS

Andrew was somewhat disturbed at the thought of swallowing several cc's of an unknown substance. Still, what the hell? If this is a dream, what harm can it do me?

Uncorking the bottle, he took a precautionary sniff. Peppermint. He swallowed the contents in two gulps and lay back on the sun-lounger as instructed.

Within a few seconds he felt incredibly sleepy. Everything went black. His brain and body were filled with a tingling sensation then, just as his subconscious mind was beginning to panic at the thought of being entombed for ever, he woke up and was startled to find someone looking down at him.

20

It was the statue.

She smiled and extended a slim, delicately-boned hand. 'Hallo, Andrew,' she said. 'My name is Shalimar. Welcome to the Rimworld.'

He stood up and took her hand. It felt real but the situation didn't. If this actually *was* an alien world, would this woman *really* be speaking English? That kind of thing only happened in the movies.

Andrew accepted Shalimar's silent invitation to follow her along the verandah. He glanced towards the sea. The waves were moving now, toppling over and merging with the line of foam that ebbed and flowed over the pale undisturbed sand.

Andrew tried to figure out what was different about this particular beach scene. And then it came to him.

No seagulls.

And no litter either.

His thoughts turned briefly to Catford and he wondered how long it would be before Kelly grew tired of coming home to an empty dish and found herself a new home.

SIDELIGHTS ON THE RIMWORLD by 'FIZZ'   No.1
JOURNEY TO THE STARS
The ultimate package tour from Hell

Nowadays – as readers of the main narrative will have grasped – if you have the right connections, it doesn't take forever to reach the Rimworld. But none of the present hi-tech, time-warping wizardry was available when the Atlantean evacuation fleet left Earth in search of a new home. They had to take the long way round.

Estimates as to the amount of time they drifted through the galaxy vary wildly. Two or three million years . . .? Frankly, it all happened so long ago, nobody gives a toss. But we can safely say it was long enough for the succeeding generations of travellers to get heartily sick of the whole enterprise. When you are searching for somewhere to live, it really is quite amazing how many stars are just solitary suns with bugger all going round them.

And when you do find a planetary system, the planets are either too big, too close or too far away from the sun which may, itself, be too new or too old. And you can guarantee that anything which looks about right, gravity-wise, turns out to be a swirling mix of molten lead and erupting volcanoes or has got an atmosphere as thick as custard below which lies an endless swamp of semi-frozen sulphuric acid.

The prospect of continuing this fruitless search for another two million years caused morale to plummet. The majority of the evacuees retired to bed and plugged themselves in for the Long Sleep on the hibernation deck, leaving skeleton crews of stiff upper-lippers to navigate the ships, watch the radar and monitor the life-support systems.

Then the miracle happened.

A star-mapping technician aboard one of the ships was working late processing a batch of photoprints showing sections of the surrounding galaxy. His seven-year old daughter wandered in to see when he was coming back to their quarters. He put up a game on one of the computers terminals for her and carried on working.

The girl, Tanzibar Cremona Panglossian (the only person on this voyage to make the history books), became bored with the game and began to draw on the back of one of the print-outs. Reaching for another, she was about to turn it over onto its blank side when her eye was drawn to the pattern of stars. With the uncluttered perception that only children possess she saw something that caught her interest.

Tanzibar began to draw lines between some of the stars, linking them in the same way you connect the numbered dots in a cheap children's puzzle book. When her father completed his work and returned to collect his daughter, he was understandably annoyed that she had been drawing over his work. His anger faded to amazement when he discovered that the linked star pattern contained a three-line cryptic message which read:

Underneath the words was a large wiggly arrow pointing to the left.

After studying the star pattern containing the message at some length, the fleet commander set up a tv conferencing link with the other ships' captains and steering committees. There was an old saying that 'Man's destiny was written in the stars'. The question was – could this quasi-philosophical concept be extended to include the doodlings of a seven-year-old?

Opinion was evenly divided. In the end, the fate of Mankind and our galaxy was decided by the toss of a coin. The fleet turned left and sailed off in the direction indicated by the arrow.

To many, this new journey seemed to be another interminable wild-goosechase. On and on they travelled, hope fading then rising again as Tanzibar Panglossian deciphered further messages from the latest star-prints such as 'DOWN A TOUCH' . . . 'RIGHT A BIT' . . . and 'SLOW DOWN, NEARLY THERE'.

The evacuation fleet drew nearer and nearer to the edge of the Milky Way galaxy. Behind them lay the incandescent core around which the billions of other stars rotated. Ahead of them, the dark emptiness of deep space, broken here and there by scattered points of light; other galaxies, unimaginably distant from their own.

On either side of the fleet, the stars thinned and fell behind, until only one remained on the forward vision screens. A binary star, set on the outermost rim of the galaxy. Two suns, revolving round each other, raying light and warmth on a planetary system that was utterly unique.

The Rimworld. A ring of planets circling the twin suns. One thousand, four hundred and seventy-six Earth-type globes of varying size – strung out at different intervals along the same orbit like a brightly-coloured necklace of beads.

The Atlantean fleet circled the first planet they came to and

23

made a thorough inspection of the cloud-flecked surface. Below them, blue oceans lapped the shores of continent-sized land masses and island archipelagoes. Streams tumbled down the sides of snow-capped peaks, rivers cut through deep gorges and snaked lazily through lush forests, feeding into huge lakes and through deltas to meet the sea.

On a wide golden beach, five hundred miles long, the view-ingscopes found something else. Another message – spelt out in white stones which read:

EXTENSIVE PROPERTY OFFERING UNPARALLELED
OPPORTUNITIES FOR ALL TYPES OF DEVELOPMENT
COMPLETELY UNSPOILT SURROUNDINGS
MOUNTAIN AND SEA VIEWS. HOT & COLD RUNNING WATER
LARGE AREAS OF MEADOWLAND SUITABLE FOR CULTIVATION
AVAILABLE FOR IMMEDIATE OCCUPATION

The entire evacuation fleet landed without further hesitation. The planet was promptly christened Dun Roamin' and an alehouse named The Wanderers Rest was built on 'Long Beach', using the stones which had been set out in the sand. Its opening was marked by a month-long surf-and-barbie bash to celebrate their safe arrival.

Sadly, the person who made this all possible didn't get to the party. Tanzibar Cremona Panglossian, who was seven when she discovered the first 'star message', expired before the landing.

Since no one else in the entire fleet was capable of deciphering the hidden words, she had only been able to take short naps on the hibernation deck. The last leg of their marathon journey across the galaxy had taken three thousand, seven hundred and fifty-two years. While the bodies of her fellow travellers had remained frozen in time, Tanzibar had been constantly revived to interpret star patterns. The task consumed every year of her Atlantean life span. With her eyesight fading and now incredibly frail, she died at the age of five hundred and eighty-four – two days before the fleet went into orbit around Dun Roamin'.

A monumental statue of Tanzibar at the age of seven was erected near The Wanderer's Rest but it disappeared when the alehouse was knocked down to make way for a resort hotel and leisure complex. No one protested. When your life can last for up to six hundred years it takes a real effort to remember everything you yourself did and saw, without overloading your brain by trying to recall what happened in the millenia before you were born.

And that, basically, is how Constantine Parnassus came to be where he is today. Obviously a lot has happened on the Rimworld in the last two hundred million years but – as old AJP Taylor used to say – that's history.

The only thing worth mentioning is that Atlanteans – who were ten inches taller than their Pre-Palaeozooic ancestors – have gradually increased in stature. Their average height is now six feet three inches which, with the increased 'Westernisation' of their features, due to cross-breeding with imported blood-lines, makes it possible for them to move amongst us without attracting the slightest attention.

And they do. Connie is not the only one with Earth connections. People from the Rimworld have been dropping in to carry out minor adjustments to the programme, and do the odd bit of shopping, since Sumerian wine merchants started keeping their accounts on clay tablets.

The visits are supposed to be strictly low profile but not everyone plays by the rules. On several occasions in the past this has affected the outcome of certain historical events.

More recently, since the UFO-manic days of the fifties, certain 'incidents' have been sensationalised by rags like America's *National Enquirer* and Britain's *Sunday Sport*. Both have grabbed market share on the back of shock-horror headlines such as: **RAPED BY ALIENS! 12-HOUR KIDNAP ORDEAL** followed, in this case, by an exclusive interview with a cocktail waitress from Mud Creek, Indiana, who claimed she was dragged aboard a spaceship, stripped naked and surgically probed by seven immensely tall silver-suited aliens when, if the truth were known, she was agreeably seduced with the aid of several margueritas then comprehensively shagged on the back seat of a skimmer by a

25

smooth-talking spacejock wearing a Klingon party mask from K-Mart and a fluorescent johnny.

It's not exactly the way one would expect representatives from another star-system to behave but let's face it – they're only human.

Chapter Three

Constantine Parnassus flicked open a serviette the size of two tea towels, tucked one end into his collar, and smoothed the white expanse of linen over his chest and belly.

The picture that came into Andrew's mind was of Russ Abbott dressed up as a grotesquely fat Pavarotti playing goalkeeper to the strains of *Nessun Dorma*. But, even at this very early stage of their acquaintance, Andrew was aware that the man he had been taken to meet was more than an overblown Bacchus.

Three waiters moved with balletic grace around the table, setting a variety of wonderful Mediterranean food before them. A fourth poured out a selection of wines for Parnassus to approve.

Andrew used the moment to take another look at his surroundings. He and Parnassus were seated in solitary splendour under the central dome of a white-walled taverna which appeared to be geared solely to meeting the needs of his host. Tall green plants with fern-like leaves stood in glazed pots on the tiled floor; arched windows along one wall gave a view of the turquoise sea. Canned bouzouki music drifted out of hidden speakers.

Shalimar sat at a smaller table nearby. She had been served a salad dish and a glass of what could have been tonic water but her chair was turned towards her employer. It was clear that her primary task was to answer whatever call Parnassus might make upon her. Like most long-limbed girls, she sat with her legs crossed and calves entwined.

Andrew envisioned them wrapped around his neck and

wondered what it would be like to make love to a lithe willowy beauty twelve inches taller than he was. Probably like wrestling with the contents of a broom cupboard.

A voice jerked him out of his reverie. 'Eat!'

Parnassus jabbed a fork at him then set about the meal with gusto. Each huge mouthful was washed down with great gulps of wine. He rolled his eyes, muttered appreciative comments and almost swooned with delight as he sampled each new delicacy.

Within a few minutes, he was three courses ahead of Andrew who was still sampling the different varieties of taramasalata.

'Something wrong with the food?'

'No,' said Andrew. 'I'm, uhh – still trying to get my bearings.' He paused, then added: 'No, that's not true. What I'm really hoping is that all this is some kind of hallucinatory experience.'

'It isn't,' said Parnassus. Eating and speaking were two of the other things he could do at the same time.

'Or maybe I'm lying in an intensive care ward – in a coma – after being hit by a truck as I was leaving Berwick Street Market.'

'You weren't.'

'But . . . being here – wherever this is – doesn't make any sense,' insisted Andrew. 'I mean, I haven't grasped all the details of Einstein's Theory of Relativity but from the little bit I do remember, it's just not possible to be in Soho at five to one and on a world with two suns at quarter past.'

'The fact that you are here is proof that it *is* possible,' said Parnassus. 'But don't waste time trying to make sense of it. It could drive you insane. Just accept it as a new reality.'

'Easier said than done.'

'Don't argue, just eat and let me do the talking.'

Andrew shrugged. Sure, why not? Dream or no dream, coma or no coma, this was all good copy for a would-be writer. If he was able to remember any of it when he woke up, there might even be a book in it. Someone else in his position might have been frightened but Andrew, who had faced incoming fire without shitting his britches, was not easily intimidated. In

28

fact, considering what was supposed to have happened, he felt strangely relaxed. He sampled one of the dishes in front of him. The contents were unfamiliar but they were really quite tasty.

'Let me tell you something about myself,' said Parnassus. The transfer of food from plate to mouth barely faltered as he launched into a potted biography. 'There are several interglobal corporations with bigger balance-sheets but I am, unquestionably, the richest private individual in the known universe. You would do well to bear that in mind before making any major decisions about your future career.

'How have I achieved this pre-eminence? With the aid of an IQ of two hundred and thirty, a plausible manner, a large degree of low cunning and a mountain of borrowed money which, due to my unrivalled flair for business and financial acumen, has never had to be repaid.

'How is this possible, you ask? I'll let you into a little secret, Andrew. Offshore investments. Billions of pounds, francs, deutsch-marks, dollars, yen – you name it – all converted into gold and silver bullion, platinum, tin and other precious metals and transferred back here from our modest little *pied-à-terre* in Shadwell Court.'

'I'm sorry,' began Andrew, 'But I've got to interrupt. I know some pretty dubious lending went on during the boom years of the eighties but are you seriously telling me there are banks and investment houses daft enough to loan money to someone who lives on another planet?'

Parnassus tried to look contrite. 'I've got a confession, Andrew. They didn't know my real address – and I feel rather bad about this – they were not immediately aware I was plundering their cash reserves.'

'You were in London . . .?'

'London, New York, Paris, Frankfurt, Zurich, Tokyo – if a place smells of money, I've been there. I've been milking cash from Earth since the middle of the nineteenth century.'

'That's not possible – '

'It is. Out here, on the Rimworld, human beings have a far longer lifespan. I come from a family of financial free-booters.

29

One of my ancestors led the team that made off with the treasure of the Templars – which explains why that was never found – and way before that, another bunch landed in Egypt and stole almost everything worth taking from the tombs of the Pharoahs.'

'So it wasn't local grave-robbers . . .'

'They came later – like the jackals after the lions have feasted. All they got were the leftovers.'

'I don't believe you.'

'It's true, nevertheless. When we have more time you must visit my private museum of antiquities.' Parnassus laid down his fork; a sure sign he had something important to say.

Shalimar stifled a yawn. Having sat through many previous performances, she knew exactly what came next.

'I too have achieved some notable successes – and I'm not telling you this because of any need to boast but because I want you to know that I'm the kind of person who – when he makes a commitment – can deliver the goods. Who will back you up all the way – right, Shalimar?'

'Absolutely . . .'

Parnassus toyed with his fork but resisted the impulse to eat. 'Now, Andrew . . . you're something of a military history buff. Do you recall the Bolshevik Revolution? 1917? The storming of the Winter Palace?'

'Yep . . .'

'And later, the massacre of Tsar Nicholas and his family?'

'Yep . . .'

'You're looking at the man who emptied their Swiss bank account. A fortune in gold bullion.' Parnassus beamed like the Cheshire Cat. 'You didn't know it went missing, did you? Very few people do. It's one of the most closely-kept secrets in the Swiss banking system. Their business would collapse if the truth ever leaked out. After World War Two, I found a way to link the names with the numbers and winkled out gold and treasure stashed away by the Nazis. I'm the brains behind every major electronic banking fraud – including millions from BCCI – '

30

'Ah, so that was you too. Did you get a buzz from ruining the lives of thousands of small depositors?'

Parnassus admonished him with a raised forefinger. 'Andrew, give me some credit, please. I never touched those funds. I just siphoned off the laundered drug money.'

'Any other masterstrokes?' asked Andrew.

'Just one which might bring a smile back to your face. I'm the only man who ever managed to swindle Robert Maxwell out of several million pounds. Does that restore me somewhat in your estimation?'

'Only if you plan to pump some of it back into the pension funds he raided.'

Parnassus picked up his fork. 'For someone so young, you have a very cruel tongue. When you get to know me better you will discover I am not entirely without principles.' His mouth became crammed with food as the fork regained its natural rhythm. 'And that on rare occasions, I've allowed sentiment to cloud my better judgement.' Parnassus washed down the food with wine and invited Andrew to speak. 'Okay. Your turn. Fire away.'

'Well, there is something I've been dying to ask. Why me?'

Parnassus answered with a jab of his fork. 'Good question.' He chewed on another mouthful with the relentless jaw action of a caterpillar munching its way through a mulberry bush then emptied his wine glass and held it out at arm's length.

One of the white-coated waiters appeared and refilled it instantly.

'I'm going to be totally up front with you, Andrew. You were not my first choice.' Parnassus sampled a dish of dessert, found it not to his liking and loosed a stream of abuse in a foreign tongue.

Another waiter materialised and bore the offending dish away. Parnassus drank some more wine, savoured the bouquet then said: 'In fact, you were not even on the original short list.'

Emboldened by the contents of his own glass, Andrew said, 'So, in fact, you actually intended to bugger up someone *else's* life.'

31

Parnassus dismissed this with the philosophical shrug of a man used to having ingratitude heaped upon him.

A third waiter brought a new dessert dish. Parnassus took a trial spoonful, nodded approvingly then aimed a stubby finger at Andrew. 'Let me tell you about the space-time shuttle.'

'Is that how I got here?'

'On a wing and a prayer would be nearer the mark. This "Beam me up, Scotty" stuff is not as easy as it looks. In the early days it was used to ship machine parts. Know how long it took to perfect the system to handle live freight? Four thousand years.' Parnassus expelled a derisive burst of air. 'Dynametrix – the corporation that was developing the technology – spent ten billion dollars just trying to deliver a Party Tub of Southern Fried Chicken from their research lab to a space station orbiting overhead.'

'That's a lot of chicken.'

'Yeah, well, that did include the cost of the terminal on board the spacestation.' Parnassus consumed the rest of his dessert, pushed the empty dish away, snapped his fingers then made a Churchillian V-sign.

Shalimar placed a large trimmed cigar between his raised fingers then lit it with an oversized match. Parnassus disappeared briefly in a cloud of smoke then emerged as Shalimar fanned it away.

'Cuban,' said Parnassus. 'I only smoke the best.'

Andrew wondered why people who had mastered time-travel were still using matches then decided it was a fashion statement. He set about finishing his plate of stuffed vine leaves.

Parnassus pulled on his cigar with the aplomb of Michael Winner. 'They went bust, of course.'

'Who?'

'Dynametrix. My family bought the plant and patents.'

Andrew eyed his host. The layers of fat made it hard to guess his age, but his face was still plump and youthful and his brow was barely furrowed. A hairy Telly Savalas without the menace.

'A real bargain.' Parnassus moved the cigar to and from his

mouth with extravagant arm gestures. 'Mind you, we didn't get everything. They'd made some disposals just before they went through the floor, but we walked off with the only working prototype of the shuttle and the technicians who put it together. Cost us the equivalent of twenty-four billion pounds sterling.'

'Seems a awful lot to pay for a Party Bucket of Southern Fried Chicken,' said Andrew. 'Would've been a lot cheaper to have it hand-delivered.'

Parnassus cocked a pistol finger at Andrew. 'Very good.' He raised his voice. 'Did you hear that, Shalimar? Our young friend has a sense of humour. I like that.' He pulled on his cigar. 'Forget the chicken. The shuttle you came in was developed from that prototype.'

He drank some more wine. 'The Dynametrix publicity handout called it "The miracle of matter-transfer". Know why? Because if it works it *is* a fucking miracle. The whole kit and caboodle has to be constantly re-tuned for each jump otherwise you're liable to arrive at the other end looking like something painted by Picasso.'

The prospect caused Andrew to swallow hard. 'Is that what happened to the other guy?'

'The other three. You were the lucky one. The guy before you . . . nyughhh!' Parnassus waved the memory away.

'So . . .' Andrew's time in the Gulf had inured him to scenes of violent death but the ghastliness Parnassus had hinted at was so bizarre, he had to steel himself before framing the question. '. . . what did you do with them?'

'I had them cremated. They were dead.'

Andrew lowered his knife and fork. 'You lured me into your office – '

Parnassus laughed. 'Yeah, that nonsense with the Galactic Fax Directory really got you going, didn't it?'

' – knowing that I might be killed in transit?!'

Parnassus adopted a pained expression. 'Andrew! What are you getting so worked up about? You live in Catford! You walk down dark streets. You cross busy roads with two-way traffic. Large airliners weighing hundreds of tons fly overhead on their

33

way to London Airport. You're in mortal danger every second of every day!'

'That still doesn't give you the right to mess around with other people's lives!' Andrew threw down his serviette and jumped to his feet. 'I can't believe this! Three people are dead because of this crazy set-up, I've been kidnapped and . . . and you expect me to act like nothing has happened!'

Parnassus flapped his hand in a calming gesture. 'Andrew, please! Sit down. I appreciate how you feel – your sense of moral outrage does you credit. No, I mean that sincerely. But let's try and keep a sense of proportion.'

Andrew appealed to Shalimar. Her eyes said 'Please'. He plonked himself down on his seat and adopted a brooding expression. It was important to let her know he wasn't a pushover.

Parnassus spread his hands. 'Just let me put you straight on a couple of things. First: I've ridden that shuttle dozens of times. If our relationship is to have a future, you must believe I would never expose anyone to a risk that I was not prepared to face myself.'

'But I wasn't asked!' cried Andrew. 'You made that choice for me!'

'Second: Nobody was murdered. The first three guys applied for jobs with Olympic Enterprises.'

'What as – corpses?'

'No – soldiers of fortune. And don't interrupt unless you have something serious to say. Unfortunately they died in transit on their way to the job interview. But – and no doubt you may be pleased to hear this – they were covered by our special travel insurance arranged through one of Lloyd's top underwriters.'

'He must be regretting doing business with you . . .'

Parnassus let this pass. 'Your life was also covered for half a million. But I would like to point out that you were not "kidnapped". Correct me if I'm wrong, but I'm under the distinct impression that you were invited to have lunch with me.'

34

'Well, yes – '

'And you accepted the invitation.'

'Yes, I suppose I did but – '

'Andrew, there is no "suppose" about it. I admit I may be guilty of a minor subterfuge – '

'Oh, is that what you call it?!'

Parnassus turned to Shalimar. 'He's got spirit too. Don't you just love him?' He switched back to Andrew. 'It's really quite simple. You *assumed* we would be lunching somewhere in Soho. If we'd given the exact location you'd never have come.'

'Too bloody right,' said Andrew. He sank back wearily. 'I still don't get it. There must be ten million people in and around London. Why the hell pick on me?!'

'Your military background. You've packed a lot of experience into the last nine years. Not every young man manages to join the Air Force *and* the Army.'

'I was thrown out of the Air Force.'

'Yes, for unauthorised low flying.' Parnassus adopted a colourless official tone. "In that he severely jeopardised his own safety, that of the aircraft and the general public, and showed a reckless disregard for official regulations and flight procedures" was how the charge read. Correct?'

'I got carried away.'

'Killing several sheep in the process.'

'I didn't kill any sheep. I just singed a few with my jet exhaust.'

'Andrew! According to the local paper, eight Welsh breeding ewes grazing on a hillside near Capel Curig ended up as roast lamb!'

'Rubbish. You can't believe anything you read in the press. I should know, I'm a journalist.'

'I think you'd like to be,' said Parnassus. He glanced across at Shalimar. 'Still some way to go on that front, I believe.' He silenced Andrew with a raised hand. 'But it's not your writing skills that interest me. It's your taste for danger, your ability to pilot an aircraft, your training as a Marine Commando plus the two years you spent with the SAS.'

'It's all behind me. Done and forgotten. I'm a civilian now.'

'You've only been a civilian for the last eight months, Andrew, and you go shooting on the range at Bisley every other weekend with two other ex-soldiers called Gary and Mike.'

Andrew's eyes moved from Parnassus to Shalimar then back again. 'How do you know so much about me?'

'We do our homework.' Parnassus drew on his cigar until it glowed brightly then filled the surrounding air with smoke. 'Tell him, Shalimar.'

'Your name first came to our attention when we were collecting background material on another possible candidate. Cameron Bannister.'

'Not Major – '

'Yes, your ex-battalion commander.'

'Oh, God,' groaned Andrew. 'Was he one of the . . .?'

'No,' said Shalimar. 'We dropped him off the list when we found he was about to get married. Where possible, we prefer to enlist the help of single, unattached men with no close dependants. You, for instance, were brought up by an aunt in Shropshire following the death of your parents in a charter jet crash on the island of Tenerife.'

The plane had strayed off course while descending through cloud and had slammed nose-first into the island's 12,000-foot peak. The memory of the shock he'd felt when the news came through momentarily froze Andrew's brain.

Shalimar, reading his face, said: 'I'm sorry. I didn't mean to cause you any distress.'

'No, that's – that's okay but . . . where do you get all this stuff?'

Parnassus replied with an expansive wave. ' "Knowledge is Power", Andrew. It's been the recipe for my success. Knowing more than other people and knowing it before they do. My people are able to access any database anywhere on Earth. We cruise the global information highway twenty-four hours a day; in fair weather or foul, we trawl the deeps of cyberspace. Credit card transactions, bank accounts, e-mail conversations you

36

may have preferred to remain confidential. If it's stored electronically, it's ours for the taking.'

Shalimar took over. 'We know, for instance, that you own an Apple Quadra 840 AV purchased, with the aid of your NUJ card, at a generous discount and that you're running MicroSoft Word and their Flight Simulator – '

'Plus pirated editions of X-15, Strike Commander, Desert Assault and Chuck Yeager's Air Combat World War Two.'

'What's that got to do with anything?'

'It shows you have a sneaky side,' said Parnassus. 'Which is good. Adds an element of unpredictability. I hate working with Boy Scouts.'

Andrew placed his knife and fork together and pushed his plate away. So that was it. They had finally reached the bottom line. 'Let me get this straight. Are you offering me a job?'

'In a manner of speaking.' Parnassus started to waggle his hands around each other as if sorting through an invisible sock drawer. Given his forceful personality, it was a curiously evasive gesture. 'I'd like us to be friends, Andrew. And as a mark of our friendship, I'm prepared to set you up in business on your own.'

Andrew eyed his host. 'You're a self-confessed swindler with criminal ancestors going back to the year dot. What on earth makes you think I'd want to be friends with someone like you?'

Parnassus produced another pained expression. It was one of a range he practised regularly with the aid of a mirror. 'Andrew, you are Prog knows how many trillion billion miles from home, the cash in your pocket is worthless, and you are stranded on a strange world about which you know nothing and from which you can never escape without my assistance. Please don't play hard to get.'

Andrew thought this through then glanced at Shalimar. This time her eyes said: 'Say Yes'.

'What sort of business did you have in mind?'

'Well . . .' The hands started to circle again. 'It would involve a certain amount of travelling.'

'Whoa, wait a minute!' said Andrew. 'This had better not have anything to do with double glazing.'

'Of course it hasn't!'

'Or insurance.'

'No! No! We're talking high adventure here! You'll be the captain of a spaceship – trading with other worlds! Fighting off pirates. Evading the forces of an oppressive authoritarian regime!'

It sounded like the preamble to a computer game. Andrew did his best to keep the conversation on a serious note. 'But I don't know anything about spaceships.' He threw up his hands. 'I don't even know where I am!'

Parnassus waved dismissively. 'That's not a problem. We have accelerated learning systems. Shalimar will take care of all that.' Parnassus pulled the serviette from his collar and threw it on the table. 'So – do we have a deal?'

Andrew laughed. 'I'm sorry. I'm trying really hard to get my head around this but . . .' He sighed and tried again. 'There's too many things that don't add up. All this talk about space-ships and other worlds. If you've got ships then you must have people who can fly them. Bringing me here to do their job doesn't make any sense!'

'Oh, but it does,' said Parnassus. 'It does. Think back to the moment you stepped out of the shuttle. What did you see?'

Andrew reacted warily. 'Is this a trick question?'

Parnassus sighed. 'Andrew, I've got a string of meetings this afternoon and several important business decisions to make besides this one. Just tell me what struck you when you walked out onto the verandah.'

'The waves weren't moving – and neither was Shalimar. It was like walking through a still picture.'

'And then what did you do?'

'I saw the blue bottle on the table with a label tied to it – '

'Instructing you to drink the contents – '

'Which I did – '

'Then you lay back on the lounger and . . .?'

'When I woke up, Shalimar was standing over me.' Andrew's eyes connected with hers. 'She wasn't a statue after all.'

'Merely statuesque,' said Parnassus. 'And the waves were crashing on the shore.'

'Yes . . .'

'And as a result, was your curiosity aroused in any way?'

Andrew shrugged. 'Didn't really have time to think about it. The moment after I got back on my feet, I was on my way to meet you.'

'And now that you've had lunch?'

'I'd say it was just one more strange incident in what is turning out to be a day to remember.'

'I think you're being deliberately obtuse.'

'Yeah, it's what's called a wind-up. But I would like an explanation.'

'Here on the Rimworld, we not only live longer, we also live at a slower speed. Metabolism – d'you know what that means?'

'Yeah, it's the complex of physical and chemical processes involved in the maintenance of life.'

'Very good. And it's also the speed at which those processes function. Your metabolic rate is much, much faster than ours. Picture a highway and imagine Shalimar as a Reliant Robin driving flat out on the inside lane.'

'I'll try . . .'

'Well, you wouldn't be a turbo-charged Porsche Carerra overtaking in the outside lane, you'd go past her like a low-flying jet that's just broken the sound barrier.' Parnassus leaned forward to add emphasis to what came next. 'Compared to you, in terms of distance travelled, she would appear to be almost stationary. *Verstehen?*'

'Of course,' said Andrew. 'Which is why nothing seemed to be moving. My eye and brain was like an ultra high-speed camera running at a thousand frames a second.' He paused, wrestling with the next piece of the conundrum. 'Was Shalimar able to see me?'

'Only as a fleeting blur. At Earth speed you're almost

invisible. Neat, huh? In certain situations that can give you a real edge.'

Andrew nodded. 'Yeah, so that stuff I drank slowed down my metabolic rate to match yours – but from what you've just said, I gather it's not permanent.'

'No, it'll last you ten days. But you won't need to carry little blue bottles around. We'll give you a supply of booster pills. Just pop one when you start feeling hyper. Shalimar will explain how to recognise the symptoms.'

Andrew eyed her once more and wondered if the promised briefing sessions were going to include some 'hands-on' experience. This time, her eyes gave nothing away. It suddenly occurred to him she might be telepathic. In which case he'd probably blown it.

'Anything else you want to know?' asked Parnassus.

'Yeah, if your metabolic rate is way below mine, how did you manage to get around London?'

'Simple, I was on speed. It's a drug that has the opposite effect to the stuff you drank. The formula has been in my family for generations. Could make a fortune by putting it on the market but I'd lose the edge it gives me over the competition.'

Andrew nodded understandingly but there were so many new concepts coming in at all angles he needed more time to take it all on board. 'You mentioned setting me up in business . . . with a spaceship.' He could scarcely believe the words were coming out of his mouth.

'Yes,' said Parnassus. 'You can pay it back in instalments once you start earning money.'

'Doing what?'

Parnassus answered with another vague gesture. 'Whatever comes along. You'll soon learn the ropes.' He drained his coffee cup and stood up. 'Must go. What's your answer, Andrew? Are we going to give this a whirl or what?'

'I don't seem to have a lot of choice.'

'That's true. You don't. But if you approach this situation with a positive frame of mind, you won't regret it. I promise.'

'Okay, I'll give it my best shot.' Andrew thrust out his hand

40

and had to grit his teeth on discovering that Parnassus had a grip like a gorilla.

'Now that we're friends and business partners, you can call me Connie, okay?' Parnassus moved towards the exit. Since he had still not released his grip, Andrew was obliged to follow. 'I may not see you before you leave, but I'll be in touch. Oh, uh – almost forgot – you'll be operating under an assumed name. Shalimar will fill you in.'

Andrew began to feel bewildered again. They reached the door. The waiters and kitchen staff were lined up to bid their patron farewell. Parnassus released Andrew's hand and gave him a fatherly pat on the shoulder. 'One last thing – just to put your mind at rest – we've arranged for someone to tidy up the loose ends of your Catford existence. The milk's been cancelled along with your order for the *Radio Times*. The rent's been taken care of and, uh – we've found Kate a new home.'

'You mean Kelly . . .'

Parnassus aimed an enquiring glance at Shalimar. 'Kelly. . .?'

'The cat. Kate is his girlfriend.'

Parnassus dismissed the mistake with an airy wave. 'Are we doing anything about her?'

'No need,' said Andrew. 'She blew me out last week after some bloke at work gave her a spin in a brand-new Cavalier.'

Parnassus gave him a final consoling pat. 'There'll be others, Andrew. There'll be others. You are about to have the time of your life – and this is where it begins.'

The assembled staff bowed as he swept out of the taverna in a Demis Roussos-type robe with a floor-length hem that contained enough material to make a tent for a troop of Brownies.

Andrew, who had been introduced to Parnassus when his host was already seated at the table, was amazed to discover how light he was on his feet. He moved so smoothly, he could have been on wheels. The existence of anti-gravity devices was one of the many things Andrew had yet to discover.

He turned back to find Shalimar's lustrous green eyes fixed upon him. 'So . . . it's just you and me then . . .'

41

'Yes. Over the next few days we'll be spending a lot of time together. You have a great deal to learn.'

Could be worse, thought Andrew. Play your cards right and you might be in with a promise. He pictured the Page One headline the *Sunday Sport* would run on his return: I SHARED TORRID LOVE-NEST WITH ALIEN BEAUTY. It was a pity he hadn't brought his camera. A few juicy snaps would have drawn bids from *The News Of The World* and *The Mail on Sunday*.

Shalimar smiled inwardly. Young men were so transparent. She gave the waiters a regal nod and led Andrew out of the taverna.

As they reached the corner of the colonnade, she paused and turned to face him. 'There's something I think I should say to you, Andrew.'

Oh, gawd, he thought. Here it comes. She *is* telepathic.

Shalimar switched on a melodic South London accent: 'On behalf of Olympic Marketing Enterprises, I would like to welcome yewww to Palladia, one of the many planets that make up the Rimworld.'

Andrew could not contain his astonishment. 'I don't believe it! You? Maureen . . .?'

Shalimar became herself again. 'I thought you should know before we went any further. You've been fed enough lies for one day.'

Chapter Four

In the two weeks following his lunch with Parnassus, Andrew spent the greater part of each day lying in an assimilation 'tank,' absorbing a mass of data about the Rimworld.

Clad in an electronic version of a wet-suit and wearing an advanced model of the video-helmet that engineers in Britain and the USA were currently developing to explore the computer-generated worlds of virtual reality, Andrew had been plugged into a massive audio-visual database which fed a staggering variety and amount of information directly into his brain in three-hourly doses. Imagine yourself attached by a drip-feed to a full, all-singing, all-dancing set of the *Encyclopedia Britannica* and you'll get the picture.

One of the drawbacks of living in our solar system is the distance you have to travel between the planets. It takes months to get to Mars, years to get to Jupiter, even longer to reach Saturn and as for the last two bum-freezers, Neptune and Pluto, you might as well not bother. Once you get past Mars there's nothing you can live on anyway and even if you could rig up a life-support system, the planets are so enormous, their force of gravity would glue your feet to the ground.

None of these problems were encountered in the Rimworld. All the planets were habitable, with a gravitational force ranging from plus to minus five per cent of Earth-g; all of them shared the same orbital path and there were one thousand, four hundred and seventy six of them travelling in a anti-clockwise direction around the two suns at the centre of the system.

Once they had got their bearings, the first settlers had

christened these stellar twins Bilgharzi and Bengharzi which, in ancient Atlantean, meant 'The bright one on the left' and 'The other bright one'. Over the millenia the inevitable abbreviation occurred and nowadays, even in the driest cosmological databases, you will find them listed as 'Bill and Ben'.

Since they rotate around each other and are indistinguishable in size and colour to the naked eye, the one on the left is always called Bill regardless of which planet you are on. In effect this means that when observed simultaneously from two points on opposite sides of the system, Bill is Ben and Ben is Bill and both are on the right – or left – at the same time. This terminological inexactitude – which 99.9% of the Rimworld has never lost any sleep over – tends to drive the more pedantic astronomers round the twist but that's how it is.

We all have our cross to bear.

Besides having two suns, the rotation of the Rimworld system was vastly different to our own. The Earth completes its journey round the sun in 365.25 days but the chain of planets that make up the Rimworld are much farther away from their two suns – which is just as well because they are both are 5.64 times larger than Sol. Our own round trip is a doddle compared to the enormous distance the Rimworld planets have to travel to complete one orbit. To be precise, it takes 365.25 Earth-years – one of the many curious coincidences with which this story abounds.

This sounds an incredibly long time, and it is, but if you happen to be in the business of publishing calendars and diaries, you can make an absolute fortune.

The only problem with a year that has 133,225 days is that annual events such as birthdays and New Year parties take a long time to come round. Not that this bothers them. When it comes to high-days and holidays, Atlanteans are even worse than Spaniards who – as everyone who has ever tried to phone them during business hours knows – are constantly inventing significant events that require them to take the whole day off. The mere fact that Tuesday begins with a 'T' (or in their case 'M') is reason enough to send the Pablos, Manuels, Juanitas and Conchitas crowding into tapas bars and dancing through the streets.

Andrew learned that neither Christmas nor Easter appeared on the Rimworld calendar. Their two hundred million plus years of history had been totally untroubled by religion. Given the mayhem, murder and misery inflicted on our own world by competing belief-systems in the last two thousand, he was inclined to view that as a blessing.

He also gained an insight into 'Prog knows'; the cryptic phrase Parnassus had uttered over lunch. This was the Atlantean equivalent of 'God knows'. Prog was shorthand for The Programmer; the Mysterious Being without whom nothing would exist.

Atlanteans believe – no, that's the wrong word; 'belief' carries the notion of 'faith' which, taken to extremes, can lead to all kinds of manic behaviour. Let's start again. Atlanteans *accept* that everything within the universe is part of an interactive computer game of cosmic proportions designed and being run by The Programmer.

The game has a unique feature: there doesn't appear to be any point in playing it. It is, of course, an adventure, a quest in which the player encounters a series of obstacles or challenges which have to be overcome by making one of several choices on offer. It is only as the player progresses that he or she begins to understand that the point of the game is discovering *what the game is about.*

There are lots of alternative strategies you can employ to avoid the life-threatening encounters that come at you from all sides but even if you reach the highest level and score the maximum number of points, the game can still end without the player ever unravelling the final mystery that is locked in the secret heart of the game. The key which unlocks the final door is an answer which you have only one chance to provide, *without knowing what the question is.*

Sounds impossible but the word is, it can be done.

Andrew decided that life back on Earth was a bit like that. You got to make a few choices, press a few buttons, but you

45

couldn't change the rules or the final outcome. Maybe these Atlanteans were onto something. They all saw themselves as players and potential winners. They didn't think of themselves as victims, or view life as cruel or unjust; Life just *is* what it is – a way of passing the time.

The thing that had surprised him most about the Rimworld was the all-pervading influence of money and the commercial dominance of an interglobal enterprise known as 'The Corporation'. In the absence of religion, making money had become the creed. In this scheme of things, the Corporation wielded the power of the Vatican in one of its more repressive phases.

Andrew had yet to find out if this was true. The learning programme he'd been put through was a 'Parnassus Production'; The World According to Connie. And in this scenario The Corporation was trying to enforce its own set of rules and regulations throughout the Rimworld while he, as the valiant champion of free trade, was determined to ignore them. In his eyes, they were the enemy.

Time would tell, decided Andrew. He would make up his own mind on that score. But having reconciled himself to the idea that he was fated to be part of the Rimworld until further notice, he had begun to give some serious thought to what he now knew of its history.

Back home, in the brief moments when he had considered what society might be like millions of years from now, he had imagined everyone would be dressed in long flowing robes and curly silver wigs and looking VERY SERIOUS – like Marlon Brando and Susannah Yorke playing the parents of Superman. Anybody who has been reared on a diet of sf films knows with absolute certainty that – unless they're watching an episode of *Red Dwarf* – people from advanced civilisations rarely ever smile and they never break wind.

The Atlanteans, who in the course of their long existence had been there, done it, and had buried the T-shirts in a time capsule, already knew this. In past ages they had used mind-expanding drugs, recited tantric mantras, had internalised their

46

sexual energy so that each orgasm bounced off the seven chakras like a pinball then blew their brain through the top of their skull like an exploding firework, had explored their higher selves, had become at one with the cosmos – not once but several times over – and had discovered that *it was all incredibly boring*.

Once you become a luminous crystal being, you float above this shimmering plain with a host of other luminaries contemplating the infinite wonder of creation for the rest of eternity. The mind that once animated your physical brain is now linked to everyone else's and your collective consciousness is filled with one single, endless thought which is so ineffably sublime it cannot be expressed in words.

That's it. Nothing else happens. It doesn't get less infinitely wonderful or more infinitely wonderful, it just stays the way it is; absolutely perfectly infinitely wonderful – for ever and ever and ever.

Faced with such a daunting prospect, it's hardly surprising that the Atlanteans decided to rejoin the party downstairs. All this exploration-of-the-higher-self shit had led to another very important discovery: *ultimate enlightenment is the death of comedy*.

In a nation of telepaths, the one thing you cannot be is a stand-up comic because the audience knows the punchline before you start to tell the joke. In fact, you don't *have* an audience; the whole town tuned into your entire act while you were at home rehearsing in front of the mirror and decided to save themselves the price of admission.

A lot of people are dismayed to find that the natural world seems to be one vast charnel house. Weeds choke flowers to death, trees elbow each other out of the way in the race to grab the light, leaving the weaklings to wither in their shadow; every living thing, humans included, feeds on the weaker species beneath. Darwin was wrong about our descent from the apes but his 'survival of the fittest' theory was right on the money. Genes are born fighters. They are the archetypal duckers and divers; programmed to adapt to changing conditions in order to

47

function at maximum efficiency and – above all – to survive. That is their whole raison d'être – and it's why we are still around.

Down here, we say: 'Life is a struggle'; out on the Rimworld they say: 'Struggle *is* Life'. Once survival is assured, permanent and effortless, once life becomes a breeze, a society – composed of any living organisms – becomes effete. Without constant challenges, terminal boredom sets in, the moral and physical fabric weakens, entire species become extinct, whole civilisations come crashing down – and we've got the ruins to prove it. It wasn't only the Greeks who lost their marbles.

During their lengthy spell on Earth and throughout the history of the Rimworld, the Atlanteans went down this route several times. Just as the tide ebbs and flows, their civilisation advanced to the edge of extinction then retreated into an equally dangerous period of chaos from which the survivors emerged to begin another upward climb.

Sometimes there were only a handful – which explains why they haven't colonised the entire galaxy. And, as Andrew now knew, the present Rimworld only left the starting-blocks some twenty thousand years ago. But, with each succeeding wave, the overpowering desire for progress was gradually brought under control.

Atlanteans came to understand that the technological development which underpinned progress did not have to follow an exponential curve. It could be a series of steps in which each significant advance (the vertical line) was followed by a period of stasis (a much longer horizontal line) in which the impact of each new invention or process was evaluated and fully absorbed.

Andrew, who had collected a B+ in A-Level History, knew the Egyptian and ancient Chinese dynasties had both managed to damp down progress because they ran things with a firm hand from the top down. Inventing new ways to do things in a society whose ruling classes regard the old ways as being absolutely tickety-boo is as provocative as carrying a protest placard in Tiananmen Square and just as dangerous.

Had the step'n'stasis method been applied to our own era, the modern world would be radically different. Instead of a bewildering transition from horse-drawn stagecoaches to space flight in less than two hundred years, railways would have reigned supreme for five hundred years before the motor car came on the scene, to hog the roads for five more centuries before the advent of powered flight.

Whether this would have been a good thing, Andrew couldn't say. It would, at the very least, have made life less chaotic. But he was sure about one thing – which no doubt came from his years with the military – much of the confusion in today's society arose from the fact that there were too many choices. It would be interesting to discover what difference – if any – this controlled approach to progress had made in the day-to-day life of the Rimworld.

There was another segment of the learning programme that Andrew, as an ex-pilot and soldier, found equally interesting. Tactile sensations – which in real-life would have come from operating equipment and being at the controls of a car or a plane – were fed into his memory, so that when the moment came for him to be 'launched' into the Rimworld, a wide range of objects including space and ground vehicles would be instantly familiar.

He was also given a deep memory-set to back up his assumed identity. Shalimar had offered him a short list of names to choose from. All of them looked pretty awful but since he had to pick one, he settled for Andiamo Cartahaynyar; Andiamo because it was the closest to his own name and because the current fashion of abbreviating the more unwieldy Atlantean surnames meant he could introduce himself as Andi Carta, regardless of what was printed on his smart ID card.

His identity was fake but the card, apparently, was the genuine article. That was the good thing about working with a criminal genius. Parnassus was into everything and could get his hands on anything, unlike Andrew, who had signally failed to get his hands on Shalimar.

Not that she was unfriendly. They had shared a table every

49

evening in Connie's private taverna, had walked side by side along the beach and watched the two overlapping suns sink into a sea of molten gold. But that was it. No hand-holding, no accidental body contact, no lingering glances full of Eastern promise. Genuine interest, yes, but allied to a professional detachment. Medical specialists are good at this kind of thing. During the consultation they beam in on your case, give every appearance of listening to what you say and you leave thinking you've established a caring, one-on-one relationship. Five minutes later, they sail past you in the corridor without the slightest glimmer of recognition, leaving you standing there with a frozen half-assed smile and feeling like an absolute prawn.

Working with Shalimar was a bit like that. During the debriefing sessions that followed each trip in the tank, she was warm, companionable and concerned as she talked him through the subject checklist then, when she was satisfied he was making steady progress, the light would go out of her eyes as if someone had thrown a switch and she would walk off just as abruptly to relay the news to Parnassus over a video-link.

Connie liked to keep up-to-date with all his investments.

During the rest periods of the second week, Shalimar took him for several test runs in a skimmer – a vehicle with the same capability as the flying police car in *Bladerunner*. Settling himself into the driver's seat, Andrew found he knew the position and function of all the controls. The smell of the plastic and metal interior was instantly familiar – so was the *feel* of everything – and he was not even surprised by this; the assimilation programme had even implanted the sensation of having flown the vehicle many times before.

The first brief flight enabled Andrew to get an overview of his immediate surroundings. The shuttle terminal and the taverna were part of a luxury retreat Connie had built on an otherwise virgin island which he had named Hesperides. It was one of a chain known as the Hedjukhayteen Archipelago which, in its turn, was located in a semi-tropical region of Palladia. The resulting lush foliage, white beaches and abundant sunshine

50

recalled pictures Andrew had seen of the smaller unspoilt islands in the Caribbean.

With Shalimar acting as tour guide, they explored Connie's private paradise and some of the islands nearby. They all had palm-fringed beaches straight out of a Bounty commercial and any number of romantic settings that were so perfect, it was a shame to waste them. They glided over deep purple falls, and leafy garden walls but when the stars began to twinkle in the sky, she always broke the spell with a brisk reminder that it was time to go back in the tank.

Andrew, who reckoned he could lay on the boyish charm that Jeff Bridges displays on the silver screen and pull anything that was fanciable, could not believe it.

Part of his problem lay in the fact that he had absorbed too many screen fantasies, including the fatuous Top Gun romance between Tom Cruise and course instructor Kelly McGillis, who, from the air combat-babble she was paid to deliver, clearly knew even less about pulling eight-g than she did about pulling a pint of Best Brew.

Andrew did briefly consider that Shalimar might be spoken for – might even be the plaything of her employer – then dismissed the idea as a physical impossibility. The image of her slim body conjoined with a hot-air balloon version of the Michelin Man was just too grotesque. There was, he decided, only one reason for his failure; despite the subtlety he had employed, his intentions were still too clodhoppingly obvious for someone of her evident intelligence and sophistication.

The possibility that Atlanteans might assign a different order of priority to sex between consenting adults, or have other methods of achieving fulfilment simply didn't occur to him. In the end, Andrew did what a man usually does when the chances of achieving a leg-over situation drop below zero. He decided his behaviour was quite pathetic, that the whole idea was totally naff anyway and that there were better ways of passing the time.

Which was true.

On his last night in the tank before leaving the island of Hesperides and the planet of Palladia, Shalimar gave him a surprise going-away present. When he was hooked up and locked down, she inserted a special Sensoramic CD into the play-deck. Like they say on tv cookery programmes, it was one she had prepared earlier.

Instead of another briefing on the Rimworld, Andrew found himself drawn into a see-me, hear-me, feel-me, mind-blowing sex session with an image of Shalimar that was more realistic than the real thing. It was absolutely incredible. *She* was absolutely incredible. Abandoned, voracious, insatiable, the willing slave to his desires; the embodiment of every erotic fantasy he had ever had since the first stirrings of puberty.

The experience left Andrew bathed in sweat, rubber-kneed and completely knackered. He tried to rise but his fingers were unable to grip anything and he had the distinct impression the balls had been removed from his scrotum and replaced with two red-hot lumps of Phurnacite.

Seeing his predicament, Shalimar rose from her seat in front of the control monitors and helped him out of the tank. It was a couple of minutes before he was able to straighten up.

'Are you okay?'

The tone was one of cool, professional concern – not the voice of someone who had just given their all.

'Yeah,' gasped Andrew. 'Jeezuss! That was just fantastic! Boy!' He caught his breath. 'I know we don't have any time now but does this mean that one day we're gonna get to do it for real?'

Shalimar smiled. 'This is as good as it gets, Andrew.' She pressed a button to eject the CD and handed it to him. 'Something to remember me by.'

Andrew hesitated. 'Are you sure? I mean this is – '

Shalimar placed the CD in his hand and closed his fingers round it. 'Don't worry. I've got plenty of dupes. I give copies to all my friends.'

☆   ☆   ☆

Bright and early on the following morning, they ate breakfast together in the taverna – cappuccino topped with a sprinkling of powdered chocolate and fresh-baked croissants with butter and strawberry jam on the side. Andrew found it hard to believe he was so far from home. The meal passed in almost total silence. Andrew was still tongue-tied by his last trip in the tank and also a little ashamed. What a tosser you are, he told himself. When you're swept into an adventure on the far side of the galaxy, you don't kick off by trying to shag the hired help.

Talk about letting the side down.

Shalimar, on the other hand, seemed to be mildly amused by the whole episode and not in the least judgemental. But was that how they did it out here? By exchanging Mega-Sex CD's?

Too late to ask questions now . . .

On Shalimar's signal, Andrew drained his coffee cup and followed her out of the taverna. They used an electric cart to cover the half-mile stretch to the octagonal hard-stand where the skimmer had been parked.

In its place stood a larger, chrome yellow craft with a cluster of rocket exhausts and two rows of retractable wheels. In shape, it was what you might get if you used a morphing programme to turn a de Lorean into a school bus then stopped halfway through and used Adobe's Photoshop to replace the side windows with a couple of circular viewports. It was an SSV – a space shuttle vehicle.

The multi-layered entry door was raised. Shalimar invited Andrew to mount the built-in steps then followed him aboard.

Compared to the craft's external dimensions, the passenger compartment behind the cockpit was smaller than you might have expected. Four Club Class airline seats with five-point safety straps were ranged on either side of the wide aisle. Mounted on the centre-line behind them and occupying 25% of the available floor space was an extra-luxurious double-width chair designed to accommodate someone with a monstrously large bum.

Andrew realised he was about to ride in Connie's personal space-limo. He swept his hand around the interior. 'Want me to sit anywhere special?'

53

'Yes, up front with the pilot. It will be a good opportunity to show us that some of the things you've been learning have actually sunk in.'

'Don't worry.' Andrew tapped his head. 'It's all stored away up here. Every last delicious detail.'

If she got the message, it didn't show. 'When you dock at the spacestation, present your ID at the passenger enquiry desk. They will give you the card-key to a numbered locker. You will find your baggage inside. It contains the basic items you will need on the voyage plus the outfits you chose last week. I hope they fit.'

'This one does.' Andrew indicated the up-market jumpsuit and blouson he had been given to wear after the lunch with Connie. Beautifully made, using a soft, lightweight synthetic cloth that didn't seem to crease or absorb dirt, they were the kind of casual clothes you could imagine buying from Ralph Lauren's town-house shop in New York – assuming, of course, you had the money. It was a relief to discover he wasn't expected to waltz around in figure-hugging flannel underwear like Captain Kirk.

'Well, if you do need anything else, there's a shopping mall on the spacestation and you can buy stuff on the spaceliner too. But don't go too crazy – '

'I know,' said Andrew. 'The excise men are out to gouge you for all they can get.'

The pilot put his head round the door. 'Time to go.'

'Okay.' Shalimar backed towards the entrance. 'Take care. Enjoy the trip. Keep taking the pills.'

They shook hands. 'Will I see you again?' asked Andrew.

Shalimar shrugged as she withdrew her hand. 'Que sera, sera.'

'How come you know the words to a Doris Day song?'

'Another time, Andrew.' She walked down the steps and stood clear as they retracted into the hull of the SSV and became part of the floor. The outer door closed and the pressure seals inflated. She raised her hand in farewell as his face appeared in the small circular viewport.

54

Andrew entered the cockpit and settled into the left hand seat. When he looked out of the window, she had gone.

☆ ☆ ☆ ☆ ☆ ☆ ☆

SIDELIGHTS ON THE RIMWORLD by 'FIZZ'   No.379
SPACE TRAVEL
With 500 years to pay, going places was never easier

If you visualise the planets that make up the Rimworld lying like a necklace of coloured beads on the black velvet cushion of deep space, it will be obvious that transit from one to the other is a relatively easy matter.

In theory, all you have to do is board a spacecraft and aim for the stars. When you reach the point where you can float your coffee cup down the aisle for a refill, you heave to. Then, as the world you left behind glides away along its predetermined path and grows ever smaller, you settle down and wait for the next one.

It's like standing outside Green Park tube station waiting for a mid-morning Number 14 bus to Fulham. Half an hour goes by and nothing happens then four come along all at once.

That's how it is with the planets of the Rimworld. The beads on the necklace are not equally spaced. Some of the worlds orbit in solitary splendour, others are bunched together like lads with empty glasses in front of a Party Keg of Allbright's, but sooner or later – if you had the patience to sit there throughout one bi-solar year – they would all pass by.

In practice, of course, it works somewhat differently. When interworld travel moved out of the exploratory phase and became a business moving goods and people, it did not take long for the Atlanteans to get organised. The planets of the Rimworld are now linked by two scheduled services. The Cirkadian and the Arkadian Lines. The Cirkadian line travels in a clockwise direction around the far- or dark-side of the chain of planets; the Arkadian Line travels anti-clockwise, on the near- or bright-side.

Imagine a big clock dial and place yourself on the figure six.

55

It is obviously quicker to fly Cirkadian to any point on the left-hand side of the dial between six and twelve since your chosen planet will be moving round towards you as you move towards it.

On the other hand, if the world you wanted to reach is on the right-hand side – between one and two – then you would travel sunny-side up with Arkadian Spaceways, aboard their flagship SS Narayana for instance, on which Constantine Parnassus had, with his usual foresight, made a prepaid non-refundable reservation for a single berth in order to secure the maximum discount.

Chapter Five

Three months after soaring into the sky above Palladia to catch the spaceliner Narayana, Andrew was now nearing the end of the first stage of his journey through the Rimworld.

Parnassus had promised him adventure. Well, I suppose journeying through space along the chain of planets that make up the Rimworld *is* an adventure of sorts, but so far the experience had been like being stuck on a P&O cross-channel ferry which, having sailed from Harwich, had proceeded to stop at every port in Western Europe from Cuxhaven to Cadiz.

The spaceliners didn't land on the planets; the costs in fuel alone made it prohibitive and many of the vessels – which had been assembled in offworld yards – weren't designed to use runways or set-down pads. The planets served by the Cirkadian and Arkadian lines (and not all of them were) had large spacestations, parked in solar orbits, directly above their north pole.

These stations, which were the permanent residence of many of the people who worked there, were like floating airport terminals from where STVs ferried passengers to various destinations on the planet below. Some of these craft were mass-transit vehicles run by the equivalent of bus companies; the smaller ones – spaceflight versions of taxicabs – were usually owned by the pilot.

Several passengers had warned Andrew against using these spacecabs even though the prices touted for a particular journey might sound tempting. The owner-pilots were unscrupulous, sometimes desperate individuals who did not hesitate to rip off unwary travellers. Worse still, any travel insurance policy became null and void once you stepped into one of these vehicles because many of them were not properly maintained.

It sounded like good advice. Andrew hadn't actually purchased any travel insurance – in fact, the thought of doing so had never entered his head. Although he gave every outward appearance of normality, Andrew was still dazed by the rush of events and the flood of new information that had been poured into his brain. And despite having accepted that the world about him was real – no matter how bizarre or jokey it might seem – he had not, prior to that moment, considered he could actually be in danger of losing his life.

It was a sobering thought. And one that had already occurred to Constantine Parnassus who, with his customary grasp of the financial realities, had taken out a policy on Andrew's life with himself as the named beneficiary for a sum fifty times greater than his initial outlay on JERICHO – the code-name for the master-plan in which Andrew was the key player.

Prior to leaving the island, Shalimar explained that a substantial sum of money had been deposited in a bank account bearing the name of Andiamo Cartahaynyar – Andrew's current alias. The bulk of the money was to be used to buy a second-hand spacefreighter and to meet the intitial start-up costs – fuel, provisions and a crew.

That was the purpose of this trip to Buena Vista, the spacestation above the Rimworld planet of Zhannandor.

Shalimar had made it sound so simple but even though Andrew had learned a great deal about the present Rimworld, he did not feel he had been adequately briefed about negotiating his way through the money maze.

What he would have liked was some additional advice on wheeling and dealing from his villainous benefactor but none was forthcoming. After their lunch date in the taverna, Connie had flown back to Mount Olympus, the spaceship which was both home and head office of his multifarious business empire, leaving Andrew to be dropped, well and truly, into the deep end.

He couldn't even pick the brains of fellow-passengers. Shalimar had stressed the importance of not revealing his true identity or his links with Constantine Parnassus and Andrew had pledged never to do so. He had also been instructed not to disclose his reason for travelling to Zhannandor to anyone who was not officially entitled to know. If pressed to give a reply, he was to say he was looking for 'business opportunities'. As for general conversation, he had the deep memory-set of 'Andiamo' to fall back on.

Andrew could have avoided trouble by spending the entire journey cocooned in a hibernation unit but that option was not available on the cut-rate deal Connie had chiselled out of Arkadian Spaceways. Besides being the most expensive way to travel, it was also the dullest. Andrew was glad to have been given the opportunity to mix with and observe the other passengers; to experience at first hand some of the sights and sounds that had been force-fed into his brain.

Thanks to the learning programme, he was able to relate to his surroundings without looking like a bewildered rubber-neck but as the voyage progressed he realised that there were still some disturbingly large gaps in his education. Gaps that also occurred in the given memory of the alter-ego that was riding piggyback on his own. Perhaps Parnassus intended him to fill in the gaps himself as he went along. It could be a test to see how resourceful he was.

At this precise moment, there were about nine hundred passengers on board but the number varied with each stop as people disembarked and others got on. Excluding special charter flights, the Cirkadian and Arkadian liners would dock at a particular spacestation once every ten weeks. Hardly the peak-time, three-minute landing pattern operated by Heathrow Airport but Andrew was still amazed at the number of people travelling round the system and by the fact they could afford to do so. Because it wasn't cheap.

Meaningful comparisons between pounds sterling and the plethora of Rimworld currencies were simply not possible but the shortest journey between two adjacent planets cost at least half the average annual wage. The price of Andrew's ticket was a smidgin less than a spacelines cabin attendant would earn in fourteen years – pre-tax; a sum that would have taken a lifetime to repay. And that didn't include the in-flight meal service or entertainments.

He soon discovered that for most of the people on board the question of repayment didn't arise. Space travel in the Rim-world was rather like travelling First Class on British Rail. When the ticket inspector comes round you find that, apart from the Japanese and ageing Americans, three out of every four suits are British Rail executives travelling on free passes. It was the same situation on the SS Narayana. Most of the people on board were techicians or executives employed by the Corporation.

Given that Connie viewed them as the enemy, it was not surprising that Andrew had been urged to keep a low profile.

Enemy or not, his fellow passengers were remarkably well dressed. Shalimar had failed to explain exactly how Andrew came to be kitted out with a range of clothes that bore the hallmark (if not the label) of Ralph Lauren, but he would not have been surprised to discover that Connie was masterminding some shady scheme to pirate the best ready-to-wear designs from the fashion capitals of Planet Earth.

Kate, his last girlfriend, was an editorial assistant on *Cosmo* and had brought home enough issues for him to spot people wearing clothes that could have come from Armani, Calvin Klein, Donna Karen, Katharine Hamnet and Rifat Ozbek. Those particular names were familiar because they were the designers Kate was constantly crooning over. Even at this distance, he still found it hard to believe someone with her tastes could have transferred her affections to a dweeb who not only drove but had actually *bought* a Cavalier SRi.

Taken as a whole, the passengers were also a good-looking bunch. This had been his first impression on docking at the spacestation above Palladia. Averaging six feet in height, with mainly light olive to coffee-cream complexions, Atlanteans were a blend of Caucasian and sub-Asian stock; broad shoulders combined with slim graceful bodies, well-boned faces but with the cragginess smoothed away, large, expressive almond eyes – blue, green, brown in a range of tints plus a marvellous tawny-gold, and full sensuous lips that recalled the sculpted head of Tutankhamun.

Andrew's lips were not as ripe as Tut's but he was not mean-mouthed either. And thanks to his mother, who was of Anglo-Indian descent, his skin was a pale olive brown and his eyes, while not large, had dark lashes which some women confessed to being attracted by. These features, added to his height and build, allowed him to pass unnoticed among the other passengers and, provided he kept to the script, it was highly unlikely that anyone would guess he was from Earth. Shalimar had told him that the Corporation accorded a high priority to the detection of unregistered imports. Anyone who was not tagged and part of the taxbase was regarded as a threat to the system and the penalties for non-disclosure could be severe.

The possible dangers of being unmasked were quickly forgotten once he had entered the departure lounge on the space-station. Joining the travellers waiting to board the SS Narayana, Andrew made the pleasurable discovery that – in contrast to Shalimar's well-rounded but modestly-proportioned silhouette – the majority of female passengers were endowed with truly scrumptious bazongas. Some of the more spectacular examples made the top-heavy stars in Russ Meyer's epics look positively anorexic.

There was, in other words, plenty to look at.

Given his fascination for the fuller female figure, it was somewhat surprising that Andrew should strike up an acquaintance with a young woman by the name of Kelly Mandell. Of less than average height (she measured five feet nine inches) she was attractive without being either pretty or beautiful and had a boyish figure – which is the polite way of saying she had breasts like two poached eggs on a board.

Kelly – who had made the opening move across a dinner table – was a perky, intelligent, self-assured, pain-in-the-ass who claimed to be a fully-qualified ship's navigator. Since

Andrew's cover story as Andiamo Cartahaynyar included the fact that he had a space captain's ticket, Kelly had decided to regard him as a deckmate and from that point on had pestered him to reveal his future plans.

Andrew, mindful of the need to keep *shtum*, had brushed her questions aside but she was so persistent he was driven to give her the cold shoulder. The relationship might have ended there if Andrew had not blurted out something he would later have reason to regret.

After the final rebuff, Kelly had glared at him fiercely with her pale gold eyes then, as she turned away Andrew found himself saying, 'I had a cat called Kelly.'

The woman who turned back to face him was a different person. The anger had melted away. 'You had a cat?'

'Uhh, yeah – well . . .' It was the colour of her eyes that had triggered the remark. Why the hell couldn't he have kept his mouth shut?

'I thought you came from Tyrenia.'

Tyrenia was the home planet of his alias, Andiamo Cartahaynyar.

'Uhh, yeah . . .' Andrew was now winging it.

'But they don't have cats.'

'Err, no – '

'In fact, they don't have animals of any kind.'

'No, that's right,' admitted Andrew. Having to be two people at once was proving a lot harder then he thought.

'So where did you get the cat?'

Andrew realised he was sinking deeper and deeper into a quicksand of deceit. 'Well, I obviously picked it up somewhere, but now that you ask, I just . . . can't remember. When you're flying an offworld trader you're in and out of so many places . . .'

Kelly nodded like a silver screen DA who has just spotted a fatal admission from the defendant. 'I see. You can't remember where you got the cat but you do remember its name.'

Andrew decided to laugh it off. 'Hey! C'mon! Ease off! It was a joke! It was just the way you looked at me – the colour of your eyes. It just . . . came out that's all. I never had a cat – okay? You just reminded me of one.'

If Andrew thought he was in the clear, he was wrong.

Kelly eyed him thoughtfully, then said: 'How old are you, Andi?'

'Twenty-nine.' At least that was the truth.

'So how do you know what a cat looks like?'

Andrew tried to hide his bafflement. 'Hey! What is this – the trial of the century?!'

'The Public Access Channels haven't carried any data on animals for the last two hundred and fifty years. The only people who know what these creatures look like outside of the Genetic Research Institute belong to banned organizations.' She looked around to see if anyone was eavesdropping. 'Are you a – ?'

Andrew cocked an angry finger. 'I don't belong to anything, Mandell! I'm not interested in any kind of protest shit. And if you are, I don't want to hear about it.'

Kelly smiled. 'I might be trying to track 'em down.'

'Yeah? Well, either way your secret's safe with me.'

She didn't press him further, but Andrew was conscious of the fact that his unguarded remark had left a big question mark hanging over his cover story. As far as he could tell, Kelly did not pose any particular threat but he couldn't quite understand why she had fastened onto his off-the-cuff remark about cats.

What the hell was there to get worked up about?

Shalimar had explained that a long time ago, the ruling councils of the Rimworld had decided that the pooper-scooper was incompatible with their vision of an advanced society. As a result of their deliberations, all domestic animals and a large number of other non-food-bearing species were gradually phased out over the next two centuries. They did not become extinct. The genetic codes for each species were carefully preserved in special units. The fish, white-meat birds and flesh-bearing ungulates that met the strict hygiene and health standards imposed by the Corporation's food safety inspectors were farmed on just two hundred of the Rimworld planets.

63

Given the total number, this may seem to be a very small proportion but all the planets grew their own leaf, fruit and root crops and – according to the learning programme – a significant percentage of Atlanteans preferred a vegetarian diet but, in keeping with their relaxed attitude to life in general, this was not taken to extremes.

During the rest of the trip to Buena Vista, Kelly Mandell made no further reference to animals of any kind and she stopped hassling Andrew about what he planned to do when he got there. The fact that she was also travelling to the same destination rang a small alarm bell but he brushed his suspicions aside. Taken in small doses, she was amusing to be with.

If you wanted to avoid someone, the SS Narayana was big enough to lose yourself for days at a time on one of several decks. Unfortunately, it still wasn't big enough to avoid the second person who had decided to batten himself on Andrew.

At the fourth stop down the line, he had had the misfortune to run into Larsenik Vindhooklammersdorp – shortened on his business card to 'Lars Vindhook'. Whoever named him Larsenik knew a thing or two. This guy was pure poison.

A plump, white-blond, shambling hulk of a man in a baggy safari suit, Vindhook was one of those people who regarded everyone he met as a friend-for-life and was instantly on first name terms even when his overtures were being met with a blank wall of indifference. Such people cannot be rebuffed, they turn aside insults, they overwhelm you with armour-plated bonhomie. If you were to run them over with a steamroller they would still think you didn't really mean it.

As soon as Lars heard the words 'business opportunity', his eyes lit up. Lars – an entrepreneur looking for co-investors – could not wait to tell Andrew his Big Idea. In fairness, it should be said that Andrew was only the first. By the time they reached Buena Vista. Vindhook had buttonholed every single person on the SS Narayana – not once but several times.

The big idea which Vindhook was peddling was this: he was going to open a restaurant called The Longship whose frontage would feature the dragonheaded prow of a Viking sailboat. The interior of the restaurant would be decorated in the style of a Viking banqueting hall where patrons would feast on reindeer steaks, seal cutlets, salmon and sea trout, washed down with Kvasir (a specially-brewed ale of legendary potency). All these delights would be served up by big girls – and from the curving movement of Vindhook's hands, he meant very big girls indeed – dressed as flaxen-haired Viking maidens.

The mystery of how he knew anything about Norsemen was never satisfactorily explained. Andrew, who always did his best to avoid saying anything that might extend their conversation, didn't ask.

It wasn't the worst idea in the world but having heard it once was enough to exhaust any excitement the proposition might have contained. But Vindhook felt the need to describe it in every detail right down to the dimensions and thickness of the floor tiles and he was constantly embellishing the original concept. He even had a two-hour video containing detailed fly-through 3D renderings created with a drawing programme for which he had supplied the voiceover and also appeared as a fully-animated figure on screen.

The man could clear a crowded lounge in ten seconds flat by simply appearing in the doorway. No one was spared, not even the crew. Passengers outbid each other in a desperate attempt to secure one of the remaining hibernation units and when these were full, locked themselves in their cabins and had their meals delivered by stewards. It wasn't even safe for them to venture out at night. Vindhook was so excited by the sparkling originality of his business proposition he was unable to sleep properly and would prowl the deserted corridors. The crew grew rich by selling duplicate keys to utility and store cupboards into which people would throw themselves when warned of Vindhook's approach.

There was even a petition – to which Andrew added his name – asking the captain of the Narayana to eject Vindhook at the next docking station, by force if necessary, and a collection was started with a view to refunding the unused portion of his ticket.

The alternative was to find some pretext to have Vindhook thrown in the brig.

Since the captain was already getting a cut of the bribes being offered to his crew by desperate passengers, he declined to take any action. Boring people to death on an extended space voyage was not an indictable offence or grounds for imprisonment. It was not even regarded as a public nuisance. Faced with this rebuff, the aggrieved organisers of the petition retired to mutter darkly amongst themselves and plot ways of luring Vindhook onto one of the emergency escape rafts and casting him adrift.

With Zhannandor drawing ever closer, and the Buena Vista spacestation now visible on the display screens as a bright point of light suspended three hundred miles above its surface, Andrew had begun to take a sunnier view of Vindhook and was actually looking forward to waving him goodbye. The feeling of pleasurable anticipation this thought engendered was shattered by Kelly Mandell with the news that Vindhook planned to be right behind them as they walked down the disembarkation ramp.

And she wasn't joking.

☆   ☆   ☆

A melodic bing-bong preceded the honeyed tones of the synthesised female voice that had been part of Andrew's life over the last three months.

'Arkadian Spaceways are pleased to have brought you safely to Buena Vista Space Terminal. Any passengers bound for Zhannandor who have not made preparations to leave the SS Narayana should do so now. Disembarkation will begin in approximately one hour, when the docking phase has been completed.'

Andrew carried his baggage into the main passenger lounge and set it down on one of the banquettes near to where Kelly Mandell was punching down the badly-packed contents of a bag in an effort to close the zip.

'Want any help with that?'

66

The answer was delivered through clenched teeth. 'Nope. I'm doing just fine!'

The phantom announcer came back on the air. 'Passengers leaving the SS Narayana at this point should ensure they have all their cabin luggage and personal effects, together with their onward travel documents. Arkadian Spaceways does not accept responsibility for unregistered items found on board following our departure from this station.'

Kelly Mandell had still not managed to close her bag. Andrew decided to let her get on with it. Having worked out alongside her in the ship's gym, he knew she was physically and mentally equipped to handle bigger problems than a jammed zip fastener. Mizz Mandell was one of those females who didn't look to men to get them out of trouble.

His heart sank as Vindhook appeared at his shoulder. Andrew always thought there was something odd about people whose lashes and eyebrows were several shades lighter than the surrounding skin.

'So, this is it. Pastures new.' The periwinkle blue eyes radiated unalloyed, irrepressible goodwill.

'Yup.' The man was either a total innocent or had the hide of a brain-dead rhinoceros.

'Are you catching the Main City shuttle today?' The question was addressed to both of them.

Kelly, who was still wrestling with her bag, didn't even bother to look up. 'Haven't decided yet.'

Vindhook, who would not have recognised a rebuff even if it was delivered with a sledgehammer, accepted this with a nod. 'I see . . . because I was wondering, as we are all newcomers, if we could keep in touch when we get to town. As you know, I'm planning to – '

' – open a restaurant. Yeah, you already told us.'

'And showed us the video,' said Andrew. He held up a hand as Vindhook reached in his top pocket. 'No, keep the cards. You already gave us a stack.'

'Good. Pass them round. Of course, the place must be gutted and completely redecorated. Everything will change except the

67

address. I'd really like you to be there when we open. Bring as many people as you like. On the first night, all the food and drink will be on the house.'

Andrew tried to put some enthusiasm in his voice. 'Sounds great, Lars. I've never been one to turn down a free meal but, the thing is – I'm not planning to visit Main City. Buena Vista's as far as I'm going.'

'I hear it's a good place to pick up a ship.' Kelly finally managed to close the zip on her bag. 'The yard here has some real bargains.'

Vindhook brightened. 'Oh, are you buying a ship? I'd be more than happy to hire you to bring in regular shipments of – '

'Too late, Lars. I'm already under contract.' That was true at least. 'Anyway, I'm not here to buy a ship. I'm just picking up a ride.'

'Where to?' asked Kelly.

Andrew aimed a finger at her. 'Didn't we decide a while back you were asking too many questions?'

'There's no need to be so defensive. I only asked where you were going?'

'Well, wherever it is, there's only room for one.' Andrew treated them both to a parting smile and hooked his baggage straps over both shoulders. 'It's been great knowing you both. But this is where we go our separate ways.'

Although there were still forty minutes to go before the docking procedures were completed, a large untidy queue of passengers had collected by the forward exit door of the main lounge. Andrew infiltrated a standing group and dropped out of sight by sitting on the arm of a chair in the hope of avoiding further contact with Vindhook. As hopes come, it was fairly slim. Once the Reindeer Man locked onto someone, he was harder to throw off than a heat-seeking missile.

The sight of these Atlanteans crowded up against the exit door with their cabin luggage brought a smile to Andrew's face. This was just like the end of any flight back home. Despite the request to remain seated, and the pointlessness of standing when there was nowhere to go, the aisle was always jammed by people with itchy feet – and Andrew was always amongst them.

Although millions of years of evolution set him apart from his fellow passengers, the discovery that the inhabitants of the Rimworld were still unable to subdue the impulses that led to outbursts of impatience was somehow reassuring. They might travel dizzyingly large distances, at unimaginable speeds in spaceships bigger than the tower at Canary Wharf but they hated having to hang around waiting to board or disembark from a flight even when – as in this case – it had taken months to get where they were going.

Ashkelon Ishkenazi, a kinetic psychologist who first achieved fame by producing an elegant mathematical formula which explained why the outward journey to anywhere always seemed to take longer that the journey home, conducted a long-term study of this stress-related condition using a research base of ten thousand vacationers.

He found that when a subject left his dwelling place carrying a suitcase containing holiday attire, time seemed to slow down in inverse ratio to his rising expectations. This made a delay of even a half an hour almost unbearable. Ishkenazi also discovered that if the subject was wearing sunglasses, a novelty hat and a brightly-coloured shirt, i.e. the clothes he (or she) would normally wear *once they had arrived at their chosen destination*, then the rising impatience curve became exponential and went completely off the chart.

Ishkenazi called this condition *premature anticipation* and, in a paper he later presented to a symposium on time and emotion, he gave it the clinical name of *Polytouritis*.

☆   ☆   ☆

Andrew set down his flight bag and handed his ID card to one of the ten immigration controllers manning the inspection desks. Vindhook was two lanes over to the right. The

69

controller plugged the card into a reader-unit connected to his computer terminal. Andrew's three-view portrait and the name, occupation and personal details of Andiamo Cartahaynyar came up on the colour screen.

The controller's eyes flicked back and forth from the screenshot to Andrew's face. He had seen the same expressionless look before. Disconnected but not missing anything.

'Are you planning to apply for residential status, sir?'

'No, just passing through. I plan to stay on board Buena Vista.'

'Okay . . .' The Controller punched some keys. 'A four-week Visitors Visa will cost you one thousand Cords.'

Cords were dollars issued and backed by The Corporation – a universally-accepted currency rather like American Express Travellers cheques.

'Fine. Book it.'

The Controller entered the transaction on his keyboard and the amount was automatically deducted from Andrew's credit balance – the details of which were held in the ID card's data chip. Microscopically small in size but with an enormously large memory.

The controller handed Andrew his ID. 'You're allowed one extension. After that you'll require a Temporary Resident Visa. They are five K a month.'

'Thanks,' said Andrew. He slipped his ID back into its wallet, picked up the flight bag and moved on through. It was nice to feel wanted.

The baggage retrieval hall in the Buena Vista terminal could have been in any ultra-modern airport back home. The overall style and cleanliness reminded Andrew of the time he spent in transit at Singapore on the way back from a short stint with HM Forces in Hong Kong. And the general scene was what you'd expect to find after the arrival of a holiday charter – a hundred or so passengers waiting to retrieve their luggage.

Andrew had not been allowed to carry off the two heavy zipper-bags he had brought into the main passenger lounge. A

70

steward had taken them from him to be unloaded down a separate conveyor. Having resigned himself to the usual long wait, he emerged from the frosty encounter with Immigration and was pleasantly surprised to find his luggage was already circulating, along with heavier items dredged from the Narayana's hold. He grabbed the only trolley available and loaded his stuff onto it.

Kelly Mandell elbowed her way through the crush, snatched a long heavy bag from the carousel and heaved it onto Andrew's trolley. 'Mind that for me, will you? Gonna see if I can grab one of these for myself.' She broke off as she caught sight of someone. 'Oh-oh, here comes the Reindeer Man. I'll catch up with you in the Customs Hall!'

She dived back into the crowd, skipped across the carousel and was lost from view.

Anxious to avoid any eye-contact that Vindhook might take as an invitation to mingle, Andrew put his head down and wheeled his luggage smartly into Customs.

A dozen uniformed officials stood behind two long low counters on opposite sides of the hall. On Buena Vista, there was no Green Channel and no allowances. Now that the Corporation had taken over the running of all the major space-terminals, excise duty was levied at every conceivable opportunity.

Andrew wheeled his trolley into position behind a passenger who was in the process of repacking his luggage, then craned his neck in an effort to see where Kelly Mandell had got to. He caught a glimpse of a dark, tousled head of hair bobbing along in a group of taller travellers. His eye then fell upon Lars Vindhook who beamed with delight and waved happily.

Convinced Kelly was about to join him, Andrew moved quickly into the now vacant space and unloaded all the bags onto the counter, spacing them out to deny Vindhook any opportunity to move in beside him.

The Customs officer, whose ID tag identified him as Blake Severnoax, asked for Andrew's name and keyed it into the small

71

terminal mounted on a pillar behind the counter. The data which had been fed in at the Immigration Desk came up on the screen.

Severnoax's gaze moved from the screen to the line of bags then onto Andrew. 'Business trip, sir?'

'Yeah, in a manner of speaking.' Andrew's eyes were still searching the oncoming crowd but the tousled head of hair belonged to someone else. Kelly had vanished.

His eyes returned to the Customs man. 'I'm planning to stay on Buena Vista until I can catch a trader out.'

'And these bags contain your personal belongings. You did not purchase anything on route on which duty might be payable.'

'Nope.' Andrew looked for Kelly one more time then came back to find a pair of grey eyes boring into him. 'You can check my card if you want to – every purchase I made in the last three months is listed on my charge account.'

'I actually have those details on the screen, sir. Did you make any acquisitions with hard currency?'

'I don't carry cash.'

'Very wise, sir. And you are not carrying any prohibited items – a list of which you can see on the video-board behind me.'

Andrew glanced casually over the list without actually reading it. 'Nope. It's just clothes, personal items and mementoes, a few data disks and that's it.'

'Right, sir. I wonder if you'd like to start by opening this bag.' Severnoax laid his hand on Kelly Mandell's zipper-bag.

'Uh, no. That doesn't belong to me. These are mine here.'

'Are you sure, sir? This one has the same baggage claim number as these three – which you admit *are* yours.'

'No, no, no,' insisted Andrew. 'Lemme take a look.' He compared the plastic tags fastened around the strap handles. They were all identical. He frowned at the Customs man. 'There must be some mistake.'

Severnoax sounded concerned. 'It's even got one of your

72

name tags attached to the zip.' He turned it round for Andrew to examine. Andrew took one look then reached for his flight bag. The name tag was missing. Removed by someone with sticky fingers. But how did she get hold of the extra baggage label? And why?

He began to feel uneasy. 'Look, I don't know what's going on here but that's not my bag, no matter what the label says.' He pulled out his ID card and thrust it at Severnoax. 'My baggage claim numbers were entered when I checked in at Star Point.'

The Customs man plugged the card in, entered the appropriate recall code and studied the result. 'Mmm, well, sir – according to this, you checked in all four items.' He swivelled the unit around to let Andrew see for himself.

'This is crazy,' muttered Andrew. 'How many times do I have to tell you?! This is not my bag. It belongs to a woman pa – '

'Yes, I'm sure there's a simple explanation, sir. In my experience, there always is.' Severnoax signalled another Customs officer to join him. 'So if you'd be good enough to open it.'

Andrew zipped the bag open, expecting to find female attire of some sort. What came out were several items he distinctly remembered packing the night before they were due to disembark. And carefully wrapped up in waxed paper, inside more of his own clothes, were four menacing pieces of hardware. They were all several light-years ahead of anything issued to any army in Europe or the USA, but Andrew didn't have to be told what they were.

Weapons . . .

They were right at the top of the list of banned items along with explosives, ammunition, poisons and dangerous drugs.

The passengers at the counter on either side of Andrew edged away nervously as two Spaceport Security men came up behind him and pinioned his arms. A plastic ribbon lock was quickly fastened around his wrists then, without warning, a hood was dropped over his head.

73

'No need to be alarmed, sir,' said one of the men. 'Just standard procedure. But we would ask you not to struggle. It tends to upset the other passengers.'

They led him away.

I'm going to kill her, thought Andrew.

Chapter Six

Once inside the holding unit, the hood and wrist-tie were promptly removed. Andrew was then obliged to strip and submit to a body search which included having an optical probe stuffed up his backside. He was then given a lightweight disposable coverall which smelt of antiseptic and espadrille-type slip-ons made of the same material.

His ID card had been taken away to be given what one of his examiners referred to as 'a Deep Seven'. Whilst waiting for its return, Andrew answered all questions by sticking to his cover story and repeatedly denied all knowledge of how the weapons – which lay accusingly on the table in front of him – came to be in his luggage.

While this interrogation proceeded, the clothes he'd been wearing, the remaining contents of the four bags and the bags themselves were minutely examined at a nearby table. The search turned up two identical padded yellow garments resembling flak-jackets but with two straps that went between the legs like a parachute harness. The jackets raised a few eyebrows but nothing was said and nothing else of an incriminating nature was found.

It was at this point that Andrew's interrogator got a call on his portable vidiphone. He plugged in the earpiece, nodded at the miniature picture of the caller as he got the message then told Andrew to dress and ordered his luggage to be repacked.

A few minutes later, Captain Krevassar, the SDO who had conducted the brief, formal proceedings which specified the offences for which Andrew was being held and his rights as a defendant, entered the room with Severnoax and a senior

Customs officer with five gold rings round each sleeve and a peaked cap loaded with scrambled egg.

Everyone jumped to attention – including Andrew. After eight years in uniform, it was a reflex action.

Krevassar ordered his subordinates to leave the room then handed Andrew his ID card. 'I'm sorry about this, Commander. We had no idea. But then – how could we?'

Andrew frowned. 'Commander . . .? What is all this?'

'The Navy should have tipped us off.'

'Navy . . .?' Andrew's frown deepened.

'Of course! Yes!' said the senior Customs officer. 'Secret mission!'

Andrew eyed each of them in turn and tried to give the impression he knew what they were talking about. This was obviously a case of mistaken identity but, if it meant he was out from under, he wasn't going to spoil the illusion.

Krevassar winked. 'Don't worry, sir. Our lips are sealed.'

Andrew nodded solemnly and played it off the cuff. 'Good. If word of my presence here was to leak out, it could jeopardise the entire operation.'

During this increasingly surreal exchange, Customs Officer Severnoax busily repacked the four weapons in their waxed paper outers then slipped them and the two yellow jackets into the long zipper-bag. He now loaded all the bags onto a spaceport trolley.

'This way, sir,' said the senior Customs officer. He held open the door.

'Good luck, Commander, uhh – I mean . . .' The good Captain bit his lip.

'Mr *Cartahaynyar*,' said the senior Customs officer. He ushered Andrew out with a respectful nod then signalled Severnoax to follow with the trolley.

☆ ☆ ☆

Exiting through a door marked CUSTOMS PERSONNEL ONLY and controlled by a push-button security lock, Andrew found himself in the Arrivals Reception area. He paused to survey the scene, unaware that Kelly Mandell was watching all exits from the restaurant gallery above – and had been doing so for the past hour.

She saw Andrew wheel the trolley over to a two-tiered line of luggage lockers. He placed all four bags inside one of them then closed and secured the door by withdrawing the keycard.

The manner of Andrew's reappearance raised some interesting questions. The fact that he had emerged at all confirmed her earlier suspicions that he was not who he claimed to be but, if he *was* an agent, why hadn't he reported her to Spaceport Security? Her picture should have been on every tv screen by now. Did the fourth bag – the one she had dumped on him – still have the guns inside? Kelly, who believed she had learned enough about 'Andi Carta' to guess how he would react to being set up, had a hunch they would be. That was why she had taken such a huge gamble. But if she was right – if the shipment *had* got through – how was she going to get it back without being trapped into revealing her own undercover mission?

Down on the main floor, Andrew turned away from the lockers and headed towards an illuminated sign marking the location of a bank and bureau de change.

He was aware of the upper galleries but had purposely avoided giving them anything more than a cursory glance. If she's watching me, he thought, she'll be wondering if I still have the guns. Since she was clever enough to set me up, she'll have found a way to bypass customs control so it won't be long before she makes contact. Which puts me in the driving seat, because I have something she wants and the goons running this place have all but told me I'm fireproof.

From his time in the sim-tank, Andrew knew the Navy was the elite enforcement arm of the Corporation and, as such, inspired the same awe and deference among the lower echelons as the Liebstandarte Adolf Hitler, the Fuhrer's personal SS division.

Nice one, Andy . . .

For the moment, he was happy to profit from the situation. The possibility he might have to pay for this subterfuge seemed

77

a distinctly unthreatening prospect. Andrew, it must be said, shared the very British attitude towards distant lands peopled by foreigners with funny-sounding names. He found them hard to take seriously. At the back of his mind there still lurked the idea that – if he ever reached the point in this crazy adventure where he was in really serious danger of losing his life – he might still wake up.

Andrew stepped through the automatic doors into the bank. A large 3D logo on the wall was surmounted by the words BANK-COR; underneath, was the legend: A DIVISION OF UNITED SPACE DEVELOPMENT CORPORATION. There was a line of customers in front of all six counter clerks. Andrew tagged onto the shortest only to discover he had unerringly chosen the same queue as Lars Vindhook. Before he could slink away, the Reindeer Man gave him a bright-eyed, waggly-finger wave then let the next three people move past in order to be next to his 'friend'.

'Did you get everything sorted out?'

'More or less,' replied Andy. He made his voice sound flat and tired to discourage further conversation.

'It was so upsetting the way they marched you away – with that hood and – '

'Yeah . . .'

'That girl, you know, uh – Kelly Mandell – she was looking for you earlier.'

'Good . . .'

'I told her what I'd seen. She seemed really worried.'

'She's got a lot to be worried about,' said Andrew.

Vindhook stepped forward to take his turn, heaved a bulging sealskin bag up onto the counter and popped it open. It was stuffed to the brim with wads of banknotes – which explained why it was secured by a chain to Vindhook's left wrist.

The female bank clerk eyed the notes and greeted him with a plastic smile. 'Welcome to Bank-Cor. How may I help you?'

'I have two million Skandavian Trolls I wish to change into Corporation dollars.'

78

The smile lost some of its plasticity. 'The Skandavian Troll . . . one moment, sir.' The clerk used a keyboard to call up some information on her computer terminal. 'Ye-eess, that's an unlicensed currency.'

'Unlicensed?!' squeaked Vindhook. 'Since when?!'

The clerk, who had been taught how to avoid answering customers, tapped some more keys, studied the result then said: 'I'm afraid I need to consult my supervisor before proceeding with this transaction.'

Vindhook sighed heavily and looked over his shoulder. 'Sorry about this hold-up. Can't understand what all the fuss is about.'

Andrew shrugged. Vindhook turned away and began to arrange the top layer of banknotes in his bag into neat rows.

Andrew let his gaze wander and noticed two men at an automated service point. Their gaze was focused on Vindhook. The elder of the two whispered what seemed like instructions to his taller younger partner who then left the bank.

Through the glass front of the bank, Andrew saw the younger man go into a huddle with two more guys who were inspecting the racks of a nearby video store. Andrew had a feeling something was going down and that it might involve Vindhook who was, once again, being studied by the grey-haired man.

Andrew gave the man a hard-eyed stare. When he realised he was also being observed, the man shifted guiltily and pretended to study the video board listing the bank's customer services.

The clerk returned to her seat at the counter. 'Right, sir. Subject to a satisfactory ID check, we can take one hundred thousand Trolls at the rate of fifty to the dollar – '

'Fifty!? That's – '

' – and a second tranche at one hundred to the dollar.'

Vindhook exploded. 'One hundred!!??'

The clerk remained ice-cool. 'The best rate we can offer on the remaining one million three is one thousand Trolls to the dollar.'

The news brought forth a bull-like bellow of pain. 'But that's

79

absolutely outrageous!' Vindhook appealed to everyone in earshot. 'How can these people be allowed to do this!?'

Any protest about the Corporation's banking strategy was clearly a lost cause. Vindhook's appeal drew the same mute, pitying glances you'd get if you were to stand in an out-of-town shopping mall on a Saturday afternoon, proclaiming the world could be saved by the love of Jesus plus a wholesome diet of tapioca and senna-pod tea.

The clerk adopted a crooning note, the sort you might use when calming a sick child. 'We *are* trying to help, sir. We don't have to change your money. The Skandavian Troll is not a recognised trading currency – which means its value cannot be guaranteed by the Corporation.'

'Bunch of crooks!!' Vindhook slammed the bag shut. 'What am I going to do? I have come here to start a business! I have builders to pay, staff to hire – '

'He's opening a restaurant,' said Andrew helpfully.

The clerk changed from nurse to businesswoman. 'In that case, sir, you no longer have a problem. We can arrange a cash advance secured against your property. And this leaflet shows how the Corporation can help you with long-term finance at very attractive rates.'

'Hnarrhh!' snarled Vindhook.

'However, I must draw your attention to the cautionary paragraph on page 12. If you fall into arrears on the repayments, your property and your personal liberty may be at risk.'

Vindhook snatched the leaflet from the clerk's hand, tore it into several pieces, threw them into the air then grabbed his bag and stormed out of the bank.

The clerk turned her plastic smile on for Andrew. 'Welcome to Bank-Cor. How may I help you?'

Andrew produced his ID card. 'I'm expecting a fairly large sum of money to be credited to my account. It was being wired to this branch. Could you check to see if it's come through?'

'Certainly, sir.' The clerk took his card.

Andrew looked across at the automated service point. The grey-haired man had gone. He twisted round to look through the glass front of the bank but was unable to spot Vindhook amongst the crowd moving through the arrivals area.

☆ ☆ ☆

Vindhook was there however, pivoting on his heels and staring into space as he tried to decide how to overcome this unexpected blow to his lovingly-crafted business plan.

'Excuse me . . .'

Feeling a tap on his elbow, Vindhook looked down and saw a personable grey-haired man holding out a business card.

Vindhook accepted it. His chubby face brightened as he read out the printed message: 'M.I.T.Wurlitza, Licensed Currency Dealer.'

'I was in the bank a little earlier,' explained Wurlitza.

'Bank!? Hnnhh! Gangsters!'

'The Corporation's out to screw everyone, friend. And things ain't getting any easier. But if you're looking to unload your Skandavian Trolls, I may be able to – '

' – help? Ahah! Wonderful! I – ' Vindhook broke off as he was jostled by three passers-by.

Wurlitza seized both his arms as if to steady him. 'Hey! Why don't you guys watch where you're going?!'

An instant later, a concealed blow rendered Vindhook half-senseless. As his legs buckled, two of his attackers, Steel-Eye and Hot-Roxx, caught him by the arms. The tall young man – known as Shades – walked ahead of them towards the Men's Room, waving curious onlookers aside. 'Out of the way, please! This man's not feeling well!'

M.I.T.Wurlitza cast a casual glance around the arrivals area. Satisfied that no one looked as if they were about to raise the alarm or intervene, he sauntered after his crooked companions.

☆ ☆ ☆

Inside the bank, an inexplicable impulse made Andrew turn his head just as the counter clerk was about to speak to him.

81

He caught a glimpse of two men marching a rubber-legged Vindhook towards the Men's Room. Just ahead of them was the young guy who had been talking to Old Grey Hair.

Andrew was faced with a difficult split-second decision. He could either let someone he heartily disliked meet the fate they so richly deserved, or do the right thing – and probably live to regret it.

'Be right back!' He made a placatory gesture to the counter clerk then hurled himself towards the automatic doors and was almost knocked senseless as they failed to open.

A bank adviser left her desk and helped him up off the carpet. 'Sorry, sir, it's a security precaution. The doors do not operate to allow egress unless you approach them at walking pace.'

Andrew threw off her helping hand and peg-legged out of the bank, rubbing his right kneecap. He was just in time to see the three muggers hustle Vindhook into the Men's Room.

A notice on the door read: CLOSED FOR EMERGENCY MAINTENANCE. SERVICE STAFF ONLY. It was one they had stuck up ten minutes earlier. They had also disabled the security camera inside.

Wurlitza, realising Andrew's appearance on the scene signified trouble he would rather avoid, swerved away from the door and took cover behind a holographic display of travel goods.

Andrew burst through the door of the Men's Room and made a rapid assessment of the situation before weighing in.

Steel-Eye and Hot-Roxx held Vindhook down with his head over the washbasin by the end wall and were landing what looked like painful kidney punches. Shades was trying to get a bolt-cutter onto the chain securing the bag of money to Vindhook's wrist but the Reindeer Man kept on jerking his left arm free. He was a lot stronger than his flabby exterior suggested and was proving difficult to hold down.

The three muggers registered Andrew's arrival but evidently did not view it as a good enough reason to give up on their quest for some easy money. Hot-Roxx, who was pinned between

Vindhook and the back wall, cried 'Keep still, asshole, or we'll cut your friggin' hand off!' He hit Vindhook twice behind the ear to make sure he got the message.

Vindhook went limp. Hot-Roxx aimed a finger at Andrew as he took a step forward. 'If you don't get lost, I'm gonna flush your brains down the toilet!'

Steel-Eye seized Vindhook's left arm with both hands and held it down on the counter. Shades quickly severed the chain. Hot-Roxx grabbed the bag of cash. Steel-Eye, reacting to Andrew's arrival, let Vindhook fall to the floor.

Realising the bolt-cutters held by Shades could do some serious damage, Andrew floored him with a sweeping side-kick to the knees but before he could take him out of the game, he was set upon by Steel-Eye and Hot-Roxx.

Although not a born streetfighter, Andrew had undergone some bruising combat courses in the Army. Two aggressive lager-louts would have been no problem but these two weren't drunk, they knew their stuff and they kept getting back up. Shades was also up on his hands and knees and reaching for the bolt-cutters. Andrew managed to stamp down hard on one wrist – a move which slowed the young man's return to the fray.

Vindhook, still on the floor, hooked a foot round Hot-Roxx's legs, causing him to crash down on top of Shades. Andrew, who had just sent Steel-Eye reeling backwards with a chest-high heel-kick, spun around, stomped Shades in the balls, grabbed a handful of Hot-Roxx's hair and slammed his head against the marble counter before they could disentangle themselves.

'Look out!'

The warning from Vindhook came too late to deflect a bone-jarring kick to the shoulder as Steel-Eye came back yet again. The force of the blow sent Andrew sliding across the floor and head first into the wall. Before he could recover, a second kick on the nerve centre of his left thigh reduced the chances of getting back on his feet. The third blow to the head might have done some really serious damage but it landed off target thanks to Vindhook, who saved the day with several wild swings with the bolt cutter – one of which clipped Steel-Eye's ankle. Huffing and puffing with pain, the mugger grabbed the bag of cash and hobbled towards the door.

'Thanks . . .' Andy hauled himself to his feet. 'You okay?'

'More or less.' Vindhook crawled out from under the line of washbasins and slumped against the back wall. 'How about you?'

'Don't ask,' winced Andrew. 'Keep an eye on these two. If they move, hit 'em. Hard.'

'Where are you going?'

'After your money!' Which wasn't true. Andrew didn't give a toss about the money. He wanted to get even – preferably by inflicting a great deal more pain than he himself was then experiencing.

From the restaurant gallery, Kelly Mandell saw one of the muggers exit from the Men's Room carrying Vindhook's bag. Having witnessed the original covert assault, and Andrew's entry on the scene, it wasn't hard to guess what had happened. The White Knight was clearly in need of some assistance – and that could only improve her chances of getting a free ride.

Exiting from the Men's Room, Steel-Eye adopted a normal walking pace and caught the eye of Wurlitza who was hovering nearby. They had done this often enough to know what came next. As Steel-Eye slipped away through the thinning crowd, Wurlitza stepped forward to block the door and collided with Andrew as he burst out. They both went down in a heap. Andrew tried to untangle himself. Wurlitza grasped at his jacket in an obvious effort to delay him.

'Now wait a minute! What the heck d'you think – '

Andrew wasn't in the habit of hitting grey-haired men but he was angry, he was hurting and this man was the cause of it all. He seized the neck of Wurlitza's shirt, punched him out with three short sharp blows then stepped over him to continue the pursuit.

In the Spaceport Security Control Room, the loss of

picture from the Men's Room had been reported to Video Maintenance who had added it to the ever-growing list of service faults. There are people who fondly believe that the future will be an electronically-controlled paradise, programmed to repair itself, but it ain't ever gonna happen. Ten thousand years from now it will still be easier to find God than a reliable plumber.

The assault on Wurlitza had been picked up by the cameras covering the Arrivals Hall and watched with interest. Normally, the nearest three-man Rover Patrol would have been despatched to restore order and arrest any wrong-doers and, in fact, a team had been alerted then put on hold by Captain Krevassar who entered the Control Room in time to see Andrew flooring Wurlitza. Believing this could be part of a covert Navy operation, Krevassar judged it better not to interfere.

Andrew, on the other hand, would have been more than happy to see some law and order arrive. Shades and Hot-Roxx, bruised, bloody and feeling deeply aggrieved, had wobbled back onto their feet and were clearly intent on inflicting some lasting damage. With only one fully serviceable arm and leg, he was now regretting his involvement. If he didn't put these guys down quickly, they'd be all over him. He called up his last reserves of energy and went for it.

'The guy's good,' observed one of the screen-watchers.

'But he's tiring,' said another.

'Yeah,' mused Krevassar. 'I don't think the Navy's going to win this one.' He switched on his headset and spoke to the unit he had put on stand-by. 'Rover Eight, we have three men brawling in the Arrivals Hall, and – '

'Hold on, sir,' said another screen-watcher. 'The other two bad guys are heading towards the escalator. I think that woman at the top may be planning an intercept. Camera Eight-Three-B.'

Krevassar focused on the screen. 'Stand by, Rover Eight.'

Nursing a swollen jaw, Wurlitza paused at the bottom of the escalator in the hope of seeing Andrew get a good kicking.

Steel-Eye ascended, clutching Vindhook's two million Trolls to his chest. As he neared the top, Kelly Mandell stepped into view with a cheerful smile and started down.

'This is the up-escalator, lady'

'Really?' Loosing a shrill *kai*, Kelly executed a jump-kick that caught Steel-Eye under the chin and sent him arcing backwards through the air. The crunching noise his body made when it landed made the startled spectators wince. Vindhook's bag landed close to where Wurlitza was standing. As Steel-Eye travelled back up the escalator feet first, Kelly seated herself on the moving handrail and slid past him, gathering speed as Wurlitza decided to take the money and run. With both feet extended, Kelly shot off the rail like a speeding bullet and caught him bending.

Wurlitza hit the floor nose first.

Halfway between the foot of the escalators and the Men's Room, the untidy and uneven slugfest between Andrew and his two opponents was reaching crisis point. Staggering back from a heavy punch, Andrew collided with someone coming from behind. He turned to parry any blows from this new quarter and was confronted by Vindhook's bag.

'Here – ' Kelly thrust it against his chest. 'You take care of that, and I'll take care of these two.' She launched herself like a high-kicking whirling dervish at Shades and Hot-Roxx.

Kapow! Whamm! Hai-ii! Yaaahh!! This girl was straight out of a Bruce Lee movie. Except this wasn't play-acting. Bones were being broken here. A gathering crowd of spectators applauded as Shades and Hot-Roxx went down. The Rover Eight security team moved in to collar Wurlitza and the fallen duo while another unit unblocked the up-escalator and brought Steel-Eye down on a stretcher.

Captain Krevassar pushed through the crowd. 'Well done, sir. Would you like a medic to check you over?'

'No, I'll be okay,' gasped Andrew. The pain in his ribs made it hard to breathe. 'An icebag'll bring these lumps down.'

Krevassar turned to Kelly. 'That was quite a show, ma'am. Am I to understand that you, err – ?'

'Yes,' said Kelly. 'I'm with him.'

Krevassar nodded and tapped the side of his nose to show he knew how to keep a secret. 'What about these four men, sir? D'you want us to keep them until the, uh – ' Kevassar just managed to stop himself blurting out the word 'Navy' ' – your, uh, people can take them into custody?'

'Just charge 'em with attempted robbery with violence,' said Andrew. 'All I was doing was helping a friend.'

It was the wrong word to use when Lars Vindhook was in earshot. Catching Kelly's warning glance, Andrew turned and was enveloped in a sweaty bearhug with the bag of money still trapped against his bruised chest. He used the last of his strength to force Vindhook away by thrusting the bag in his face.

The Reindeer Man kissed it then hugged it tenderly. 'Wonderful! My dream is still safe! How ever can I repay you?'

'Forget it. And don't squeeze me again – okay?'

Vindhook had a flash of inspiration. 'I know! Free meals at my restaurant whenever you're in town. For life! For both of you!'

Andrew wanted to tell Vindhook that his mere presence on the planet was sufficient reason never to pass this way again but chose to remonstrate with him instead. 'I put those two guys on the floor, Lars. Why didn't you make sure they stayed there like I said?!'

'They slipped out when I went into one of the cubicles.'

'What the hell were you doing in there?!'

'I was feeling sick. All this violence . . .'

'Hey, now! Don't tell me how bad *you* feel!! I've just had the shit kicked out of me! If Kelly hadn't turned up when she did . . .'

'Yes!' Vindhook beamed at them both. 'We make a great team, don't we? I really think the three of us should stick together.'

Andrew, barely able to control himself, thrust a trembling finger under Vindhook's nose. 'You've got your money, Lars. Now get out of my face and stay out of it. I don't ever want to lay eyes on you again. Understand?' He turned on his heel and walked towards the bank.

Kelly caught up with him. 'I think you've hurt him.'

'Not as much as I'd like to. And speaking of people with brass necks, you've got some nerve, haven't you?'

'I saved your ass, didn't I?'

'Yeah – and thanks to you, I almost got it busted back in Customs. That was really neat, the way you dumped that bag on me. You've got some explaining to do, lady.'

'They let you through, didn't they? I'd say *you've* got some explaining to do.'

'I don't have to tell you anything,' snapped Andrew. 'But if you want your bag back, you'd better start talking.'

'Okay, but not here. I'll meet you in Main City. Promise. C'mon. Gimme a break.'

Andrew entered the bank with Kelly tugging at his jacket. 'Get the hell offa me!'

'Andi, please! I'm going to miss the shuttle.' She sounded desperate. 'Look – just give me back what's in the bag and I'll get out of your hair. For ever.'

Andrew lowered his voice as they approached the counter. 'The bag is in a locker and it's gonna stay there until I get a proper explanation. You know civilians aren't allowed to carrry weapons. You could be looking at ten in the pen – maybe more.'

'Andi . . . I gotta have that bag.'

'Then call Security.'

'Scumball,' hissed Kelly.

The same counter clerk greeted Andrew with another well-rehearsed smile.

'You were checking my transfer account. Name of Carta-haynyar'

'Ah, yes, sir. The present balance on your current account is three point seven five million Cords.'

Corporation dollars. The top-rated currency.

Kelly's jaw dropped. 'What've you been doing to earn that kind of money?'

'None of your business.'

88

'Would you like to make a withdrawal, sir?'

'Yes.' Andrew reeled off the figures Shalimar had given him. 'One point five mil. In cash cards. Four 250 Ks, three 100 Ks, three 50 Ks and five 10 K's.'

Kelly's mouth was still open as she watched the clerk authenticate the cash cards. Andrew pretended to take it all in his stride. It wasn't too hard. Since he had no practical grasp of Rimworld currencies or the earning power of its inhabitants, 3.75 million Cords meant little or nothing.

Kelly tugged at his jacket. 'What're you going to buy – a trader?'

'How many times do I have to tell you? It's none of your business!' Andrew took the cards from the clerk with a smile that said 'Thank you' and turned from the counter. 'So would you please let go of me?'

Kelly trailed him out of the bank and watched him as he worked out which way to go. 'So you're not going to give me my bag . . .'

'There's one thing you should know about me, Mandell,' said Andrew. 'I don't like being taken advantage of. On the other hand, I have a forgiving nature. So if you feel like talking, leave a message at the Passenger Information Desk.'

Kelly watched him walk away. 'You're a mean, heartless sonofabitch!'

Andrew swivelled round to face her but kept on walking. 'Does that mean we're through?!'

Kelly waited until Andrew had turned his back, then produced the keycard she had pinched from his jacket and waved a smiling goodbye with it. Dear old Andi was going to go ballistic when he found out he'd been had. It was a pity she couldn't be there to watch.

Vindhook ambled over with his luggage piled high on a trolley. 'Do you know yet if you will be catching the shuttle?'

'Yes,' said Kelly. 'Just gotta get my bags. They're in that line of lockers over there.'

89

SIDELIGHTS ON THE RIMWORLD by 'FIZZ' No.4626
DRAMATIC ART, LITERATURE AND ENTERTAINMENT
Something old, something new, something borrowed, something blue

Given the fact that the top-selling book in the Rimworld continues to be Irvin Thrushbuglers *A Thousand and One Ways To Make a Million* (now in its 19,000th edition) followed by his second blockbuster *You've Made a Fortune, Now Invest it Wisely*, it is not really worth discussing the work of any other modern author.

In the talking-book field, a firm producing unabridged tape-cassette versions of pornographic literature under the label 'Sounds Obscene' has carved a profitable niche in the market. Purchasers of the firm's offerings are now free to abuse themselves with both hands while listening to such gems as Annanas Ninja's *Leonie the Pig Fondler* and Markweeder Zhardonnay's vintage offering, *The Blue Nun*.

Television is currently dominated by stolen programmes relayed by a chain of particle accelerators. Almost every programme ever made on Earth can be seen on one of the four hundred Rimworld Channels; the decision to screen these terrestrial offerings was entirely pragmatic. As one network chief remarked: 'Why spend money producing our own crap when we can pick it up for next to nothing?'

Some of the more ancient dramatists continue to excite controversy. Villyum Shaggesbeer, who penned such classics as *Omlette, Henry The Filth*, and *Alpha-Romeo and Juliette-Bravo*, is back in the news again. Tradition holds that Shaggesbeer wrote his plays to amuse his patron, Knurloff Scouserampton but now a noted scholar and researcher, Gravitas Spondulix, claims that the plays were actually written by Freda, Scouserampton's pet chimpanzee, and that Shaggesbeer, far from being the literary giant his supporters claim, was merely the man employed to clean out her cage.

As might be expected, this has outraged Shaggesbeer scholars since it appears that Spondulix's claim is based solely on the suspiciously large number of times the word 'banana' appears in the texts. Defending his thesis, Spondulix cited numerous examples including the famous line from MacBroth, 'Is this a banana I see before me?' and the romantic comedy entitled, *All's Well That Ends With a Banana*. The jury is still out.

Chapter Seven

Within half an hour of leaving the bank, Andrew found himself gliding through space aboard a private shuttle with a firehouse red and white paint job, masses of chrome trim and a rear cluster of completely redundant fins. Their outlines were so familiar, it was hard to avoid the suspicion that someone must have raided the parking lot of a Cadillac main dealer sometime during the mid-fifties.

The shuttle belonged to a second-hand spaceship dealer operating out of the BuenaVista station and bore the following legend in bold type on each flank:

HONEST JOHN T FFASTBUKK

OFFERS THE BEST DEAL ON USED SPACESHIPS

THIS SIDE OF ETERNITY

The accommodation sections of the craft had also been decorated in the same flamboyant manner, reminiscent of some of the luxury steam yachts featured in *Hello* magazine. Lit by miniature crystal chandeliers, the stateroom – which could seat a dinner party of twenty – was furnished with white leather and mock zebra-skin upholstery, gold lurex-flecked carpeting and moulded wall panels in some kind of mahogany-type veneer, hung with an eclectic display of framed images ranging from paintings of cowboys, cattle and covered wagons from the Texas school to the decadent S&M fashion plates by Helmut Newton.

Andrew decided against asking how they came to be there but it was clear that there was a great deal more to discover about the connection between Earth and the Rimworld. What

Connie and Shalimar had told him was only the tip of what was turning out to be a very large and increasingly mysterious iceberg.

The purpose of the flight was to view the fleet of used spacecraft that were moored in Ffastbukk's floating parking lot. Some two dozen ships of varying shape, size and condition were ranged in two lines, stretching away from the spacestation. Several of them had chipped paintwork and missing hull panels.

Ffastbukk took these defects in his stride. 'As you can see, some of these need a few cans of touch-up paint – but they are all runners and covered by the Honest John Straight Dealing No Small Print Guarantee.'

Andrew, who stood next to Ffastbukk on the viewing deck under a frameless teardrop canopy, nodded sagely. Men with prizefighter's knuckles, sharp suits and gold bracelets were using the same patter to flog late-reg cut'n'shut Cortinas all over South London.

He clutched the handrail firmly. The view of the spacestation, the world below and the stars beyond was exhilarating and terrifying at the same time. The canopy was so clear, it was like standing in a car with the top half of your body out of the sun roof. He knew it must be safe but he was still seized by the irrational fear that they might be sucked into space at any moment.

Ffastbukk continued his pitch. 'And, of course, with our rapid stock turnover, we have other models coming in all the time . . .'

At the end of the first line was a strangely familiar shape. It grew larger as they approached, completely dwarfing the previous ships. Honest John's shuttle hovered beneath its bulk like a minnow under a pike. Andrew stared in wonderment. It was a real-life version of the Starship Enterprise. Not exact in every detail but close enough to fool anyone but the most devoted Trekkie.

Andrew raised a hand to point at the ship then dropped it against his mouth, forefinger hovering uncertainly. He had to be careful what he said. 'The starboard engine pod's missing.'

'Yeah, that's why we're letting it go for nine point nine billion,' said Ffastbukk. 'A real bargain . . . but a little over-sized for anyone starting up as an independent.'

'Just a little . . .'

'Let's see if we can find you something smaller.' Ffastbukk told his pilot to take them down the second line. They paused above a shabby spaceship. The letters painted on the hull had mostly worn away but from the fragments that were left you could see they had once formed the word 'NAVY'.

'How about this one?' asked Ffastbukk. Onboard freight capacity is only five-K cubic but it'll haul a full string of boxcars. In fact, I'll throw in ten just to get you started.'

Andrew ran his eyes over the ship as the shuttle circled round it. 'Hmmm, a fleet tug . . . T-40 GD. The Navy stopped using those about twenty years before I was born.'

He blinked as a mild electric tingle surged through his brain. Where in hell did that information come from? It wasn't part of the 'Andi Carta' cover story, and it didn't connect with any-thing he'd learned in the sim-tank.

Andrew became aware of Ffastbukk's voice . . .

'But built to last! That's the original paint job. The ident letters have worn off but they weren't part of the factory finish. Check it out. No sign of corrosion anywhere!'

'Yeah, the T-40 hulls were good. It was the drive units . . .' Andrew dried up. It was happening again! How did he know all this?

Ffastbukk waved the problem away. 'Been totally rebuilt. As good as new.'

'Hardly a selling point.'

'Rebuilt, reconditioned and retuned – giving one hundred per cent increase in performance. You'll be able to get point five Lux out of this baby.'

'Till she burns out.'

Ffastbukk had an answer for that too. 'She's guaranteed for the whole period of the warranty. Five years peace of mind for ten per cent of the purchase price. That includes parts and labour. Repairs can be effected at any Honest John dealership, which can be found on every accredited spacestation through-out the Rimworld.'

'Do they do call-outs?'

Ffastbukk side-stepped this one. 'And of course, all our ships come with a full service history and a set of interactive video-disks showing every detail of the structure and onboard systems.'

'So how much are you asking for this tub?'

'Three point nine five . . .'

'. . . million Cords . . .'

Ffastbukk moved up a gear. The chance of unloading this turkey was too good to miss. 'That includes the ten boxcars and the warranty! Prog-nosis! That alone is worth nearly four hundred K!' An expert in reading faces, Ffastbukk knew he had to play another card. 'And being an ex-Navy man myself, I'll throw in six recycled fuel cells. The first three million miles are on me!'

Andrew nodded thoughtfully. He had no intention of buying the T-4O but he wanted to see how far he could push it. 'I've got to admit it, John. I'm tempted. But what makes you think I was in the Navy?'

Ffastbukk greeted the question with a keen-eyed glance. 'I'm a good friend of the head of Station Security. Captain Kre-vassar.'

'I see . . .'

'The Corporation doesn't like me selling ships to just any-body.' Ffastbukk shrugged. 'If I was to cut a deal with someone who had a criminal record they could close me down. So, to cover myself, I try to get some background on anyone who walks in through the door.'

'Can't blame you.'

Ffastbukk grimaced. 'Trying to run an independent outfit these days is no joyride – and it's getting tougher all the time.'

'So everyone tells me. Still, business can't be too bad if this shuttle's anything to go by.'

Ffastbukk brightened. 'That's right! The question is – are you going to help me pay for it?! Where were we?'

'You just threw in six recycled fuel cells.'

'Still not enough, huh? Okay, on top of all that, I'll ferry your crew up here and clear the paperwork with the port authorities.' Ffastbukk paused. 'Uh, I take it you do *have* a Captain's ticket?'

'Are you kidding? I'm A-rated for hyperspace!' Once again, Andrew's brain was filled with the same electrifying tingle. He gripped his forehead and tried to analyse what was happening.

And once again, Ffastbukk's voice cut across his mental confusion. 'Wow! A time-jockey. I've heard about 'em but you're the first one I've ever done business with! This is a great honour. No, it really is.' Ffastbukk pumped Andrew's hand. 'And to mark the occasion, I'll cut another two and a half per cent off the top.'

'I appreciate the gesture, John – but I don't have three point nine five mil – or anywhere near it.'

Honest John's smile faltered but didn't fade. 'It's Andi, isn't it?'

'Yes . . .'

'Come this way . . .' Ffastbukk led Andrew down into the stateroom and pressed a hidden buzzer.

A dark-haired woman, in a short red and white dress that fitted like a second skin, glided into the room. Imagine Rita Hayworth, Cyd Charisse rolled into one with the combined busty substances of Jayne Mansfield and Anita Ekberg stuffed into one bra. Andrew was instantly, totally and hopelessly smitten. Back home it was something that happened quite regularly – sometimes twice in one week.

'Imelda! This is Andi. Get him a drink!' Ffastbukk slid a fatherly arm around him. 'I've got some good news for you, Andi. We offer the lowest cost finance in the known universe. See what's printed on my card? Read it out for me. I enjoy hearing it. Makes me feel good.'

Andrew took the offered card. "Honest John T Ffastbukk. Nobody offers more for less."

'Great picture of me, isn't it? Check out the other side.'

96

Andrew turned the card over. ' "Not just a good deal – a friend for life." '

Honest John gave him a one-armed hug. 'That's the bottom line, Andi. And that's what I'm ready to be. "A friend in need." Are you ready to accept a helping hand?'

Imelda brought Andrew a glass of amber liquid. As their eyes met, he got an unmistakable message. This wasn't the only stimulant on offer. He raised his glass to them both then took a sip. The glass contained whisky and soda. Another mystery.

'You're a heck of a guy, John. But I don't want to get into debt. I've seen what happens when . . .'

That tingle again. How did he know what happened? Was his mind playing tricks – getting its wires crossed because of all the information that had been pumped into him? Or had Parnassus used those sessions to plant something he didn't know about?

Andrew's mind jerked back to the present as Ffastbukk gripped his shoulder and oozed sincerity.

' "Debt" is a not word we use around here, Andi. We prefer to call it "creative financing".'

'Call it what you like. What I need is a ship I can pay for in one hit.' Andrew took a huge swallow of whisky to steady his nerves. Something very strange was happening. The words were coming out of his mouth but somebody else inside his brain was doing the talking.

Ffastbukk lifted Andrew's glass from his hand and passed it to Imelda for a top-up. 'Be up front with me, Andi. Exactly how much are we talking about?'

'One point seven five max. But out of that I have to buy provisions and post the usual advance for the crew.'

'Provisions are no problem,' said Ffastbukk. 'I can get you cut-throat rates. And forget the crew advances. I know guys who will pay you just to get off this planet!'

'Whoa! Ease up! I'm not shipping out with a bunch of dope-heads and drifters!' Back came the tingle. It was the ghost rider talking again.

97

Imelda brought back Andrew's freshened drink and handed it over with a smouldering look. He had to make a conscious effort to listen to what Mr Sincerity was saying.

'You're forgetting what it says on the card, Andi. Honest John does not stiff his clients! There's nothing on the lot I can let go for one point seven five but I'm going to make a few calls to see if we can help you cut a deal.' He beckoned forward Miss Bosom of the Year. 'Look after this young man, Imelda. Just be a little while – okay?'

Ffastbukk exited. Imelda steered Andrew over to a corner couch, curled up beside him and slid her right arm along the back cushion behind his neck. Her long fingers began to gently massage his far shoulder. Andrew dragged his gaze from the monumental breast-works and looked into her glowing, honey-coloured eyes.

Imelda edged closer. 'I think I'm going to like you, Andi. May I touch you?' She placed her left hand on his thigh without waiting for a reply.

Whatever's wrong with the Rimworld, you certainly can't complain about the women, thought Andrew. In fact, if I had to create a future world, this is just how I'd imagine it.

And maybe I am . . . maybe I am . . .

☆   ☆   ☆

Constantine Parnassus sat at his desk on a raised platform in the middle of a vast cargo hold; one of several contained within the hull of the SS Mount Olympus. As long as a football pitch and four storeys high, the hold had been converted into an open plan office with several galleries linked by escalators and moving walkways. Imagine Tyneside's Metro Centre – or any other modern galleria – crossed with one of the glossier currency trading rooms and you'll get the picture.

There was one missing ingredient. Computers. The only terminal – a vidcomms/multi-media machine was on Connie's desk. A large desk, of ample proportions to match his prodigious girth, from which he could survey row after row of desks running away into the distance, manned by a small army of clerks from the Indian sub-continent, scribbling away, surrounded by piles of paperwork.

The chair Parnassus sat in could swivel, enabling the master to snack at a table to his left that was constantly replenished with his favourite dishes, wines and strong black coffee. The rear of the platform was taken up by a low conference table, surrounded on three sides by excessively comfortable armchairs, while to his right, there was a second, smaller desk where Shalimar could be found when she was not occupied with business elsewhere.

She was there now, regulating the flow of papers being brought up to the platform by an unending line of clerks for Parnassus to accept or reject. A fairly speedy process since Connie's brain could crunch figures faster than a 586 DX2 running at 100 megaherz whilst chewing his way through an eight-course meal and – at this moment – holding a conversation with a colleague over a scrambled line on the far side of the Rimworld.

Honest John T Ffastbukk . . .

Parnassus signalled Shalimar to send the waiting clerks back to their desks then beckoned her to listen into his conversation with Ffastbukk's screen image. She circled his desk and stood behind the terminal, out of view of the video camera that framed Parnassus.

'So how can I help you, John?'

'I've got a customer here who might be of interest. The guy's got one point seven five mil in his pocket and he's looking to buy a trader. At that price I don't have anything that moves – and he has some moral or philosophical objection to forward financing.'

Parnassus pushed an overloaded fork into his mouth. 'So why call me?'

'Didn't anyone ever tell you not to speak with your mouth full?' demanded Ffastbukk. 'Just put that fork down and listen. This is important.'

'I'm sure it is, John. So is eating. It's part of my personal war on want. But since you insist . . .' Parnassus laid down his fork

99

with a heavy sigh. 'You've got the next thirty seconds to whet my appetite.'

Ffastbuck leant forward confidentially. 'According to my contact inside Buena Vista Security, this guy's Navy but he's travelling on a civilian ID. There was some problem in Customs so they ran a Deep Seven. Turns out he's a Commander.'

'Hmmm . . . unusual for someone of that rank to leave the service.'

'My contact doesn't think he has. That suggest anything to you?'

'Yes. How thoughtful of you to call me on a secure line. Anything else?'

'Yeah. He claims he's A-rated for hyperspace – but I don't think he meant to tell me that. It just sort of . . . came out.'

Parnassus raised his eyes to meet Shalimar's. 'What's the name of this customer of yours, John?'

'Security couldn't tell me. Even with a Deep Seven search, there was a lot of stuff they couldn't get at without some seriously high-level access codes. But he's travelling under the name of Andiamo Cartahaynyar.'

Parnassus glanced up at Shalimar again. 'I'm glad you called me, John. This ties in with several things I'm involved with right now. I'll call you back when I've had time to work out how best to handle this. In the meantime, make sure this gentleman is kept entertained. And have a nose around – see if you can find something for one point seven five mil. And John – '

'Yes . . .?'

'This timely gesture will not go unrewarded.'

'That's good enough for me, Connie. You've always been more than generous.'

'And I shall be so again, John. We'll speak soon.'

The screen went blank as Parnassus ended the call. He sighed heavily, picked up his fork, pushed the food around on his plate then put the fork down again. Shalimar resumed her seat. He swivelled round to face her.

'How could there have been a problem with Customs? What

100

on earth was the boy doing to make Buena Vista Security run a Deep Seven?'

'I have no idea. We could ask Ffastbukk to fish a little deeper but . . . that might send the wrong signals.'

Parnassus nodded. 'I'm really not happy about this. "Daniel" shouldn't have surfaced yet. What d'you think could have happened?'

'I don't know the answer to that either,' said Shalimar. 'Some word sequence must have accidentally triggered the recall mechanism. It's a risk we've always known about.'

'Yes, but it's far too soon. It could ruin everything. All those years of planning and patient effort. All that money! It hardly bears thinking about . . .' Connie toyed with his fork. 'D'you think we should pull him back in for reprogramming?'

Shalimar shook her head. 'No. He might not be able to take a second mind-dump. And there's no guarantee that it will hold any better than the first. But if "Daniel" is leaking out of his subconscious, it's going to leave him very confused.'

'Ye-eess . . . that's what I'm afraid of. I just wish I could decide what's the best thing to do.'

Shalimar eyed her employer. 'You could always tell him the truth.'

Parnassus threw his head back and roared with laughter. When he finally subsided, he wiped away a tear and gazed at her fondly. 'My dear girl . . . I know you like him, but I don't think we need to do anything quite as drastic as that!'

☆   ☆   ☆

Ffastbukk returned to the stateroom to find Imelda laying some heavy charm on Andrew. 'Ah, you're hitting it off. That's good.'

Andrew, hugely embarrassed at being caught in semi-flagrante, pulled away from Imelda and jumped to his feet.

'Relax. She's all yours. Now listen, I've made a few calls and got some promising leads on some ships that may fit the bill.'

'Oh, marvellous – '

'But it's gonna take a few days to follow them up. So, Imelda – are you listening to me?'

101

'Yes, John.' Imelda rose obediently and pulled her dress back onto her shoulders then smoothed her skirt down over her long golden thighs.

Ffastbukk did not seem in the least put out. For all the emotion he displayed he could have been watching her open a shorthand notebook. 'Okay. I want you to take Andi over to the Spaceport Hotel and check him into our hospitality suite. You're to stay there and look after him till I call. Whatever he wants, make sure he gets it. You understand?'

'Yes, John.'

Andrew felt his ears redden. 'John – that's not really – '

Ffastbukk cut him off. 'Andi, please! We keep it for entertaining clients. Compliments of the house. Don't worry, it's all tax deductible.'

'I appreciate that, but even so – '

'Is Imelda the problem? Is that what's bothering you?'

'Heck, no!' It seemed an incredibly tactless question to ask when she was standing there. Her eyes met his. Andrew tore his gaze away. 'She's amazing but – '

' – why am I doing all this?' Ffastbukk slapped Andrew's shoulder. 'We Navy men have to stick together, Andi. Okay, we may not have a ten-figure deal this time around but the way I figure it, you're a good investment.'

On his way back to the luggage lockers, Andrew discovered that the keycard had disappeared from his pocket. Imelda left him fretting and fuming and went off to get help. Andrew could scarcely believe that Kelly had had the moxey to pick his pocket. But why not? he asked himself. Given the other stunts she'd pulled he should have realised that she had only come to his rescue in order to set him up yet again.

Imelda returned with a spaceport employee whose photo-ID tag indentified him as Muskagee Willikers.

'Ah, great. D'you want me to describe the luggage I put inside?'

'That won't be necessary, sir. The fact that you're a client of

Honest John is all the proof I need.' Willikers produced a pass-key and opened the locker. 'Hmm. I see you believe in travelling light.'

'What?'

Willikers stepped aside and invited Andrew to take a look. All the luggage had gone – not just the long zipper bag. The only items that remained were an electric toothbrush, a pair of boxer shorts and a folded piece of paper.

Murderous thoughts rose from the depths of Andrew's mind. 'I don't believe this! Why is she *doing* this to me?!'

'Woman trouble?' enquired Imelda.

'Yeah, but not the kind you're thinking of. It's just some goof-ball who . . . Nyaghh!' Andrew cut it short with a fly-swatting wave. 'The crazy bitch has stolen every proggin' thing I own!'

Imelda looked inside the locker. 'She left the essentials. What's in the note?'

Andrew fished it out and read it aloud. 'Sorry, couldn't wait for you to see reason. If you want your luggage, I'll be at the Hotel Serafinto in Main City. If not, they'll have a forwarding address.' Andrew scrunched up the note, threw it on the floor then collected his toothbrush and boxer shorts.

Willikers shut the locker. 'I'm sure you have every reason to be angry, sir, but it is my duty to warn you that the dropping of litter draws an automatic on-the-spot fine of two hundred dollars.'

'What? Ohh, yeah . . . sorry.' Andrew retrieved the mangled piece of paper. When he straightened up, he found Willikers tapping figures into a Newton-type notepad.

'If you will just let me have your ID card, sir . . .'

'You can't be serious!'

'Andi – just give him the card.'

Andrew handed over his ID card to have two hundred Cords subtracted from his credit account.

'Thank you, sir.' Willikers nodded politely and left, leaving Andrew close to boiling point.

'I'm going to kill her – and this time I mean it.'

103

'Aww, c'mon, relax,' crooned Imelda. She linked arms and led him away. 'Once we've booked into the suite, I'll run you a hot tub, pour you a stiff drink and when you've had a long soak, I'll give you a deep body massage to work off that aggression. Think you can handle that?'

The prospect took the edge off Andrew's anger. 'Yeah, I s'pose we could give it a try.'

'And afterwards, you can put in a call to Main City and straighten things out.'

'Okay, but . . .' The thought of having to talk to Kelly instead of throttling her rekindled his anger. '. . . I mean, to leave me with just one pair of shorts!'

'Buy yourself some new clothes.'

'I've got three bags full of new clothes!'

'Then we'll get the hotel to detox what you're wearing,' said Imelda soothingly. 'They run an express round-the-clock service.'

'Great – and in the meantime?'

The question drew a mischievous smile. 'I guess we'll just have to stay in bed.'

☆   ☆   ☆

It took two days for Parnassus to decide how to handle this unexpected threat to his master plan and another day to make the necessary arrangements which included a suitably generous 'gesture' to Ffastbukk.

When receipt of the agreed amount popped up on the office computer, Ffastbukk slipped out between two appointments and rode the walkway to the Space Hotel. The desk clerk greeted him with a familiar smile.

'My secretary booked a Mr Cartahaynyar into the hospitality suite. Are they in the hotel?'

'They are indeed, sir. Apart from Room Service, nobody's been allowed through the door since they arrived three days ago.'

Ffastbukk nodded. 'Can I use that phone?'

The Desk Clerk slid it across the counter. 'If you could explain that we'd like to change the sheets and clean the – '

'Sure.' Ffastbukk punched in the room number. After a short delay the receiver was lifted at the other end. Someone started to speak but broke off before they could complete the first syllable. There was some clinks and clunks and muffled sounds then Andrew finally came on the line.

'Room three-oh-five. Sorry, I, uh – dropped the phone.'

'Andi? John. Don't start anything you can't finish in two minutes. I'm on my way up.'

Ffastbukk rapped three times on the door to the suite, waited for a moment, then let himself in with his passkey and paused in the hallway, listening for some sound of movement. 'Anybody home?!'

A couple of minutes passed then Andrew threw open the door to the bedroom and walked towards him, pulling a hotel bathrobe around his naked body. Tousle-haired, unshaven and bleary-eyed, Andrew looked like a man who had been comprehensively seen to.

Ffastbukk swallowed a smile. 'Kept you busy, huh?'

'Where did you find her, John?' Andrew's voice was cracked with fatigue. 'She never stopped. I just couldn't keep her off me!'

'Oh, yeah, of course.' Ffastbukk frowned and snapped his fingers. 'I forgot to tell you about the zapper.' He headed towards the bedroom.

Andrew followed. 'The what . . .?'

Imelda – who made no attempt to cover her naked body – sat on the bed amid the crumpled sheets, her long legs folded gracefully. The abundant mass of dark hair cascaded down over her shoulders towards her mouth-wateringly large breasts.

Ffastbukk reached in the top drawer of a storage unit and pulled out a black handset like a tv-remote. He turned towards Imelda and smiled. 'Time for bye-byes.'

'Aww, John, please! I was just beginning to enj – '

Deaf to her entreaties, Ffastbukk aimed the remote at Imelda and pressed a button. A pencil-thin ray drew a glowing red line between the remote and Imelda's forehead. Her eyes rolled upwards, her body convulsed wildly for a brief instant then she collapsed onto the bed with one hand hanging limply over the side.

Andrew stood there, struck dumb, mouth agape.

Ffastbukk placed the zapper in his hand. 'The red one marked "Cancel" is the off-switch.'

There was even a 'Pause' button. Andrew stared at the control unit then at Imelda's inert body. His anger flared as he came back to Ffastbukk. 'Are you telling me I've spent the last three days shacked up with a machine?!'

'Of course not! She's a G-Two.'

'What the fuck is that?!'

'It's shorthand for Genetically Engineered Task-Oriented Replicate. They're tailored to perform specific functions. Imelda's what they call a "love-bunny". She's part of a pre-production run farmed out for field trials. Got her for next to nothing.'

'But that's terrible!' exclaimed Andrew.

'Who for? Imelda? She loves giving people a good time. Don't tell me you didn't enjoy it.'

'That's not the point, John.'

'Oh, I see. You feel cheated because you didn't win her over, is that it? You must be "old Navy". Fun-loving but strait-laced. Not too many of them around these days.'

Once again that troubling reference to the Navy . . .

Andrew covered Imelda's body with a sheet. 'I just hate the idea of programming people.'

'Get real, Andi. The idea of building a female robot that would be ready and willing to fuck your brains out whenever you pressed the "On" button was never more than an engineer's wet dream.'

Andrew nodded. 'So who was it dreamed this up?'

'Some division of The Corporation. They're into all kinds of stuff these days.'

'Unbelievable . . .'

'Yeah – but they won't be on the market until they fix the bugs. The G-Twos are designed to perform a narrow range of tasks but sometimes the brain locks itself into a closed loop.

When that happens, they tend to, uh . . . overdo what they're doing.'

'Which is why they come with an off-switch.' Andrew smoothed the hair away from Imelda's face and placed the zapper on the bedside unit. 'Unreal, John. So . . . what news on the ship?'

'It's looking good, Andi. There are four grounded traders up for sale in Boot City. They're going cheap but you'll need a bucket of cash to boost one of 'em back into orbit. Rocket fuel is available at the local spacepark.'

Andrew nodded. 'Boot City . . . where is that?'

'It's a free-port on the far side of Zhannandor. It's where all the trading crews hang out.'

'D'you know who owns these ships?'

'No. But there's a woman in Boot City who's got the inside track on every deal that's going down. She also runs a bar where everything's on tap. And I mean everything. It's called Sadie Moon's. So grab a shower and pack your toothbrush. She's expecting you.'

☆ ☆ ☆ ☆ ☆ ☆ ☆

SIDELIGHTS ON THE RIMWORLD by 'FIZZ'   No.1513
PEAKS OF PERFECTION Mammifacturers now set to make inflated profits

Many observers of Western society who witnessed the orgy of bra burning that heralded the reawakening of the feminist movement will have been nonplussed by the record number of women currently booking into private clinics for breast-enhancements. From the frequent references in the main text to excessively large bazongas, readers will gather that women in the Rimworld are driven by the same desire to improve upon Nature.

Once Rimworld surgeons cracked the weight problem by buttressing the silicon inserts with small anti-grav pads, beauty knew no bounds. Forty-inch busts soon became the fashionable norm but swimsuited finalists in regional beauty contests were

107

soon breasting the tape with chest measurements of fifty to sixty inches

Driven by the media, it was inevitable that someone would push the technology to its limits. That distinction fell to Cherry Chinchilla, a novelty dancer, who became the first woman to possess a one hundred inch bust. Unfortunately, whilst performing in a night club on Ozzymandyass, the anti-grav pads failed. The ensuing collapse cracked several ribs and caused a double fracture of the pelvis. At the time of writing, her claims against the clinic and the makers of the anti-grav devices for grievous bodily harm are being vigorously contested on the grounds that, at the time Mizz Chinchilla was given her record-breaking breast implants, she did not disclose her intention to attach tassels to her nipples and cause them to rotate in opposite directions.

Chapter Eight

Starting with the purchase of a shoulder bag, Andrew picked up a few essential items, including two changes of underwear, in the Buena Vista shopping mall then headed towards the Passenger Information Desk. On the way he passed a line of large illuminated posters and was stopped in his stride by what, at first glance, appeared to be a life-size, full-length picture of Darth Vader, the villain of the *Star Wars* movies.

But he was wrong. When he looked again, he saw that the poster was advertising a movie-length episode marking the return of a television series called *Star Wartz*. The lettering above the cloaked figure actually read 'Darft Veda' but otherwise, the image was remarkably similar to Lucas' creation.

Andrew, now thoroughly intrigued, inspected the poster from top to bottom. The cloaked and booted figure stood on a rock against a black and red holocaust-type sky. He wore the familiar deep-brimmed W.W.1 German steel helmet with a drain cover masking his face, but Andrew could now see that the helmet had two downward-pointing bull's horns on either side, surmounted by two Mickey Mouse-type ears which served as radar dishes.

On the bottom right-hand corner of the plexiglass frame someone with a felt pen had scrawled, 'Underneath this cruel disguise, this man is wearing lipstick and ladies' underwear.'

At the Passenger Information Desk, a smiling girl gave him the bad news. 'I'm sorry, sir. Shuttle flights to Zhannandor are timed to meet incoming spaceliners.' She consulted a computer screen. 'The next departure – Flight Z-257 – is on the first of the next quarter. Twenty-one days from now.'

'Stagnation!' fumed Andrew. Atlanteans tended to draw their expletives from their twin obsessions, money and hygiene, with particular emphasis on the end products of the digestive process and bodily decay in general. In a society untouched by religion, the concept of Hell and Damnation were totally meaningless. To have used unfamiliar terms like 'Goddamm' and 'Holy Shit' would have immediately aroused people's curiosity. He had already had one narrow escape when Kelly had fastened upon his careless reference to cats.

'I can't wait that long,' continued Andrew. 'Is that the best you can do?!'

His bad-tempered response failed to dent the smile. 'There are always a number of space-limos for hire, sir. Independent operators. But Arkadian Spaceways do not officially recommend their use or offer any guarantee of safe passage. If you have any doubts about using this mode of transport or need further advice, you should consult the Buena Vista Transit Authority, the regulatory body responsible for issuing licences to the owner-pilots.'

'Yeah, okay, I get the picture. Some of the other passengers warned me about this on the way here. What's a one-way ride going to cost me?'

'That's entirely up to you, sir. Employees of Arkadian Spaceways are not allowed to give any additional guidance in this matter.' The clerk aimed her smile at the next customer.

Andrew treated her to a jaundiced look but it was entirely wasted. He checked the overhead signs and set off towards the docking bays. Ten yards from the counter, a shifty-looking man fell into step beside him. 'You looking for a ride, mister?'

Andrew, whose body was still bruised from his run-in with the three muggers, was in no mood to be accosted by someone who (a) looked totally untrustworthy and (b) had the darting eye-movements of a shit-house rat. He kept walking.

The tout skipped one pace ahead then spun around and led the way back-first. 'You heading for Zhannandor?'

'Piss off!'

'Hey, hey, go easy!' The tout produced an official-looking

110

card and held it up for inspection. Andrew glanced at it briefly and decided it was a fake. 'I'm a registered commission agent. I can get you the best deal on the best limo to any destination.'

Andrew stopped dead in his tracks and squared up to the tout. 'I said "Piss off!" You flyblown piece of shit! Ya hear me?! Get out of my face! And if I catch sight of you again while I'm on this station, I'll call Krevassar in Security and have you airlocked!'

The tout paled and backed off, hands raised. 'Hey, no need for that, mister. Just trying to earn a crust. Don't worry, I'm outta here!' He turned tail and moved quickly away.

Andrew stood there feeling almost as shaken as the tout had been. He had been trained to meet trouble head on, but on the whole he liked to think of himself as easy-going. Like almost everyone, he was subject to sudden outbursts of irritation, but this was different. He hadn't just brushed this guy off, he had savaged him verbally and had come perilously close to attacking him with murderous intent.

What had made him think of calling upon Captain Krevassar? And why had the tout paled at the threat of being 'airlocked'? Once again someone else's words had sprung from his mouth.

The silent question that had been gnawing at him since the troubling exchange with Ffastbukk resurfaced. Was this latest outburst from the 'ghost rider' a further sign that Parnassus had screwed around with his mind? Or was this new, vicious edge to his anger merely a side-effect of the 'decelerant' pills he was taking to keep in step with the Rimworld?

An adverse chemical reaction, while not exactly good news, was at least curable and certainly not as worrying as the alternative. Andrew hated the thought of not being in control of his own body but it was too late now. He could only go forward, deeper into this mad adventure. At some point down the road he would discover who was doing what to whom and then – when he understood the game and his role in it – he would be in a position to turn the tables and make a break for freedom.

111

Freedom . . .

People talked about it, dreamt about it, went to desperate
lengths to achieve it yet, in the end – this side of death – was
anyone ever really free? Was anyone – even the richest, most
powerful person in the world – ever totally in control of their
lives?

Out here in the Rimworld, people didn't torture themselves
with such questions. The Programmer took care of all that.

☆   ☆   ☆

As Andrew stepped into the shuttle docking bay, twelve space-
jocks homed in on him like blowflies on a juicy dag. There could
have been more. There was no time to count them or make
himself heard. He was literally besieged by two rings of rough-
looking faces, all talking at once, with more than a hint of
desperation. Amidst the clamour, several voices came through
loud and clear.

   – **Looking for a ride, John? This way! Three months to pay!**
   – I'll put you on the ground, safe and sound!
   – *Forget the rest, I'm the best!*
   – **Book with me and your luggage goes free!**
   – Wanna fly a new rig? Step this way!
   – *Don't listen to him! It's a tin bucket!*
   – **Fully pressurised cabin! No suits!**
   – Me too! Yours for ten K and a free ride into town!
   – *Nine seven fifty!*

The undercutting started in earnest with each cabbie low-
ering their bids by amounts ranging from one to two hundred
dollars. Each reduction drew a torrent of abuse from those who
had just been undercut mixed with equally foul-mouthed
appeals for solidarity in the face of Andrew's naked exploitation of the market.

It was like being trapped in the middle of the trading floor
of the futures market in Chicago on a particularly frantic
day.

Seven seventy!

Three hundred Cords lower than the previous bid. The abuse

peaked and focused on the culprit as Andrew raised a hand to signal his approval.

– **Pus-bag!**

– Bogey-Head!

– *Dick-licker! What're you tryin' to do?!*

– **Run us all into the fuggin' ground?!**

The butt of their collective scorn elbowed his way towards Andrew. 'The name's Westering. We got a deal, or what?'

'Okay, you're on.'

'You'll have to suit up. Got a problem with that?'

This news raised another chorus of jeers.

– **Congratulations!! You just bought a ride on the Flyin' Barbeque!**

– Yehh! You'd better double your insurance!

– *Wanna see a vanishing act? Ask to see his licence!*

'Just sour grapes,' said Westering. 'She's sound – and I just got new papers.'

'Okay. But before we go, does the seven seventy include a free ride into town?'

'Hey! C'mon!' cried Westering. 'I'm committin' financial suicide here! A zip-rail ticket to Main City is fifty Cords. You gonna gouge me for that?'

'Wait a minute! I want to go to *Boot* City!'

Westering's eyes popped open. 'For seven point seven K?! Forget it! I wouldn't fly you there for twice that much!'

The small crowd of space-jocks started to melt away. With the prospect of a ride vanishing fast, Andrew had no choice but to raise the stakes. 'All right, all right! Hold it, guys! Eight twenty-five . . . eight fifty . . . eight seventy-five!'

It was enough to halt the exodus but nobody met his eye.

'Hey! What is this?' Andrew raised his voice. 'You wanna work or not?!'

No response. They just stood, talking amongst themselves.

'Okay, okay! Nine big ones! We're talking three zeros here! Nothing.

Andrew, realising he was over a barrel, tried to contain his annoyance. 'Nine fifty . . . nine seven five!'

113

Several of the space-jocks turned back towards him as greed overcame caution.

'Nine eight five! Nine nine five! Ten K!' Still no takers. Andrew turned on his heel. 'To hell with it! I'll wait for the next Mass Transit!'

'It won't take you to Boot City!' shouted one of the jocks.

'And twenty-one days at the Buena Vista Hotel's gonna cost a lot more than a limo ride!' yelled another.

Andrew swallowed his pride and turned back to face the cluster of grinning faces.

'Ten two fifty . . . ten five!'

Now it was like a poker game. The spacejocks watched each other like hawks as the bid neared an acceptable figure.

'Ten five fifty! Ten six – '

' – fifty! Done!' A mean-eyed, muscular but curvy crewcut blonde stepped forward, leaving three other space-jocks with their mouths half open. 'No cards, cash up front.'

'No problem,' said Andrew.

'Paid your Departure Tax?'

'When I left the hotel.' Andrew held up the magnetic card that would allow him to pass through the relevant control points. It had cost him a thousand Cor-dollars.

'Then you got yourself a ride.' The blonde slapped Andrew's hand to clinch the deal.

A wild-eyed dude with a major outbreak of face jewellery and with his name and cab registration number tattooed on his shaven head stepped forward. 'She's rippin' you off, man! I'll take you for ten straight!'

'Too late, pal,' said Andrew.

'So go shove it, Flap-Jack!' The blonde raised a middle finger, then grabbed Andrew's arm and steered him down the docking bay.

Stepping through an airlock door, Andrew found several small STVs parked in a row. The blonde space-jock led him towards a wedge-shaped limo with the words 'Randy McRabbit's Hutch' painted on the nose section. It had a curved underside that grew into two airplane-type fins set on

114

either side of the rocket-motors at the rear end, and stood on a tricycle undercarriage, which raised the belly some eight feet off the ground. Entry was via a hatch and extending ladder just ahead of the two rear sets of wheels.

It all seemed a bit primitive but Andrew decided it was too late to back out. The blonde looked like a girl who would cheerfully break the legs of difficult customers. He nodded to the nose section. 'Unusual name . . .'

'Yeah. The guys gave it to me.'

No need to ask why, thought Andrew. The hardness of her chiselled face and strong neck was immensely attractive. Add in her muscular build, breasts like Viking helmets, a waist that looked slim enough to strap into a dog collar, plus thighs that could press metal, and you ended up with a pretty amazing package.

One that you unwrapped at your peril.

Back on Earth, she would have been an overnight sensation on ITV's *Gladiators*, a million-seller bedroom poster pin-up, and the nation's adolescents would have been in grave danger of damaging their eyesight.

'So what's your real name?'

'Sharandarella Mingemungar.'

'Randy's better,' said Andrew. He climbed aboard ahead of her and took a look round as she wound up the ladder and sealed the hatch. The four-seat passenger section was tidy but the seat covers were threadbare and the paintwork chipped.

As she stepped past him towards the cockpit, he handed her a wad of Cor-dollars – part of a pile he'd drawn out at the hotel cash desk when settling his account. 'Ten six fifty . . .'

Randy stuffed it somewhat carelessly into a side pocket of her bomber jacket which she then took off and threw onto one of the seats. She hadn't even bothered to close the zip.

'Aren't you gonna count it?'

She eyed him with a faint smile. 'You don't look like the kind of guy who'd short change a working girl.'

Definitely not, thought Andrew. But after three days with

115

Imelda he was in no condition to prove it. He followed her up to the cockpit. 'Okay if I sit up front? I'm in the biz.'

'Yeah, all right – but no flying lessons. This ship's not state of the art so we'll be riding a roller-coaster on re-entry and it's gonna feel like an oven in here.'

'Anything else I should know about?'

'Landing at Boot City has its problems – but we'll deal with those when we get there.'

Andrew watched with casual attentiveness as she pulled the tank top down over her skin-tight trousers, smoothing it over a hard, flat stomach. She had wonderful arms and shoulders with great muscle definition; strong but not beefy.

'Why did everyone fade away when I mentioned where I wanted to go?'

'Not everyone likes to earn their money the hard way.' Randy fastened her seat harness and began to run through the pre-flight systems check.

'Is that the best you can do? I've heard it's a free-port and a little rough at the edges – but what exactly goes on there?'

'I just fly the limo, Mister. I don't do guided tours. You'll find out soon enough.'

A squat, multi-wheeled robot unit topped by flashing lights, approached the limo, locked on and towed it nose-first towards the main airlock from where it would sail into space then curve gently towards the planet below.

Andrew strapped himself into his seat, took a mental vow of silence, and got ready to ride.

Zhannandor was a reddish-brown planet covered with random swirls of rose-coloured cloud. The land masses were separated by large areas of dark green water. The planet was orbited by a small moon which, in turn, was orbited by a tiny moonlet – like a mandarin orange being circled by a pea.

Andrew braced himself as the space-limo encountered the thin upper layer of the atmosphere and skipped along it like a flat stone across the surface of a pond. The drag effect lowered the speed of re-entry, reducing the heat generated by the friction between the air and the limo's hull. The viewports were lit by a fierce red glow as the ceramic tiles on the nose and underside became incandescent.

The limo started to judder. A searing, ripping noise grew into a roaring hurricane that built up and up into a thunderous, ear-splitting crescendo and now the red glow surrounding the limo was pierced by darting flames. The cockpit became suffocatingly hot. Each breath seared the back of his throat –

'Hang on!' yelled Randy. 'We'll soon be through!'

Andrew had sat through a re-entry sequence in the sim-tank but it was a long way from the real thing. In his mind's eye he could see the ceramic tiles starting to melt, being ripped away, exposing the metal skin beneath. He could see it glowing white hot, disintegrating layer by layer; soon it would burn through the inner pressurised skin . . . sucking all the air out . . . leaving their unprotected bodies –

The juddering ceased, the flames vanished and they were suddenly embraced by a blissful silence. The air in the cockpit became easier to breathe as the overworked cooling system regained the upper hand. They dropped swiftly towards the layer of clouds in a glide pattern that would take them halfway round the planet away from the sunlit side towards a night landing at Boot City.

Randy flipped several switches and made radio contact with the ground. 'Boot City Tower, this is Hotel Queen Two Niner One Niner incoming from Buena Vista Terminal. Altitude five-zero thousand descending on the Blue Channel glide path for a roll-out landing. Please fix and advise. Over.'

There was a slight pause before the ground controller responded. 'Hotel Queen, this is Boot City Tower. Maintain Blue Channel approach. You are clear to land on Runway Two Seven. Do you require escort and secure parking?'

'No thanks, Boot City. This will be a touch and go. Off-loading one passenger. Can you organise a pick-up?'

'Affirmative, Hotel Queen. We now have you locked on the

117

screen and looking good at one-five-zero miles from the outer marker, altitude four-five thousand feet and descending. Are you picking up our approach pattern and gradient markers on your flight display?'

'Affirmative, Boot City. We are now lined up on Two Seven and coming down the hill.'

'Boot City, listening out.'

Randy put the craft on autopilot, lowered and locked the undercarriage then sat back with a breathy sigh. Her firm brown shoulders were beaded with sweat. She mopped her cleavage then jiggled the curved neck of her tank top to let some air in.

Andrew caught her eye. 'This "touch and go"? Am I to understand we are not going to come to a complete stop?'

'Yep, that's right. I'm gonna let her roll to the end of the runway, then swing around and head for the sky.'

'Ah, great . . . so what do I do – jump off the back?'

'Something like that.' She grinned as she saw his reaction. 'Relax. Nothin' to it.'

At Boot City Field, the lights fixed to the descending rows of masts that made up the boundary array flicked on, followed by the blue lights on either side of Runway Two Seven. Air Traffic Control was laying out the welcome mat.

Over at the fortified terminal building, all the approaches were floodlit and constantly monitored by surveillance cameras. A wide, heavy security door began to open upwards, releasing a widening band of blazing light. Inside, four powerful vehicles gunned their motors.

In the darkness beyond the far side of the runway, sleeping figures stirred in the uncut grass. Heads poked from under threadbare blankets, eyes turning skywards. The blue runway lights gave their unkempt, unwashed, unshaven faces a ghostly pallor.

A thin man with sunken cheeks and hollow eyes rose onto his hands and knees, saw the terminal building coming to life then pointed to the bright light hanging low in the sky. 'Somethin's comin' in!'

118

His immediate neighbours passed the news on to those further away. 'A ship! A ship's comin' in!'

The darkened field erupted into feverish activity as a ragged army of grey-faced hitchers rose from the grass and began to pack away their meagre possessions. Some, with less to carry, were already moving towards the far end of the runway.

The welcome they were planning was a little less friendly.

Over at the terminal building, an armoured cab with big rear wheels and heavy-duty roll and bull bars roared out of the secure garage towards the battery of approach lights at the far end of the runway. It looked as if it had driven straight off the set of a Mad Max movie. The cab had an open roof, armour-plate with hooded slits instead of side doors, venetian blind front and rear windshields and lots of headlights protected by heavy metal mesh.

An instant later, three other vehicles of similar design, with spiked fenders, shark-toothed side-rippers and blood 'n' guts paintwork, thundered after him. Soon all four were jostling for lead position – ramming, skidding, fish-tailing, side-swiping. A murderous, mindless demolition derby. Twenty seconds later, the first cab out had emerged the winner. The other three were lying belly up; one was on fire.

The victorious cab turned onto the runway, positioned its front wheels astride the white centreline and gunned its motor. A look in the rearview mirror confirmed that Randy's space-limo was on its final descent. The landing light clusters on the undercarriage legs blazed like falling stars. The cabbie, Lead-Boot Waxmann, hit the gas and got ready to ignite the first of three rocket boosters.

As the space-limo floated over the boundary array, Andrew and Randy saw Waxmann's cab appear from under their nose and shoot down the runway.

Randy fisted Andrew's shoulder. 'Okay! There's your ride! Go for it!'

Up in the control tower, the duty staff held their breath as Randy flared her descent, skimmed over the speeding cab with just a few feet to spare, then touched down with her main wheels

119

on either side of it. Waxmann fired the first booster to keep pace with her higher landing speed and hold his position beneath the belly of the ship.

Andrew was standing on the steps as the hatch opened. With the slipstream tearing at his clothes and the ground rushing past at one hundred miles an hour, it was a white-knuckle moment. Below him was the open roof of the armoured cab. The crash-helmeted driver signalled to him to drop down into the space behind his seat. Barely two feet separated the bottom of the hatch from the roof of the cab but it looked a lot further.

Just as Andrew was about to make the death-defying leap, the cab braked and fell back to avoid an oil drum that came rolling across the runway, passing diagonally between the limo's main wheels, missing the last set of tyres by a whisker. The move left Andrew hanging onto the left handrail with his legs flailing in the air. He tried to grab one of the steps to haul himself back up but only managed to get his fingers onto the front edge. Meanwhile his right hand was starting to slip down the rail.

This is great, he thought. In about three seconds, I'm gonna fall off these fucking steps, hit the ground at ninety miles an hour then get run over by a steel-plated truck doing a hundred. He wondered about trying to limit the damage by performing the para's landing roll and decided it wouldn't make much difference.

With one last desperate effort, he let go of the step and managed to get his arm across another, three rungs down. It gave him enough leverage to heave his rear onto the bottom step and get a better grip on the handrail but before he could breathe a sigh of relief, the limo jerked and bumped over something on the runway.

The impact bounced Andrew off the ladder just as the cab slid back into position. His feet landed on the bonnet, and the cab's forward speed toppled him head-first through the roof of the cab.

Waxmann spoke to Randy via the bar mike in his helmet. 'The John is home and dry. Go, sweet bird. It's time to fly!'

120

Andrew collapsed untidily into the rear of the cab as Waxmann hit the brakes, dropped back clear of Randy's limo, then burned off an inch of rubber with a fancy high-speed U-turn. Shaken and bruised, but with nothing broken, Andrew clambered out of the back and dropped into the spare front seat as they bounced across the grass towards the terminal.

'You okay?' enquired Waxmann,

Andrew bit down hard on the pain. 'Yeah, nothin' to it.' He strapped himself in and put on the crash helmet offered by the cabbie.

At the far end of the runway, the ragged army of hitchers were building a ramshackle chicane using more oil drums and beams of decaying wood. They weren't trying to wreck the limo, they were just trying to slow it down or – better still – bring it to a temporary halt so a lucky few could force their way on board. But there were too many people with the same idea – desperate to get a free ride to anywhere. A sprawling fight broke out as the strong attempted to drive the weaker elements back into the darkness.

Randy had already closed the belly hatch, but she had to keep her ground speed high to prevent any hitchers from leaping onto the undercarriage or snagging it with deadweights that would force her to stop. There was always the danger that their frantic attempts to hitch a ride might damage the limo, even wreck it, along with her future. The prospect of what could happen if she was unable to keep up the payments didn't bear thinking about.

She saw the blue-lit figures milling about on the runway ahead and the litter of objects. Realising there were too many to swerve round, she hit the mainwheel brakes and fired the retro-thrusters. It was something she'd hoped to avoid. To replace the two rocket packs in the nose would wipe out more than half her profit for this run.

Unlocking the right set of main wheels, Randy cut the retro-thrusters and wrenched the nosewheel into a left turn but her forward speed was too high. Smoke poured from all three sets

121

of wheels as she skidded down the runway in a series of ground loops. She swore out loud and braced herself as the limo continued its sliding spin towards the makeshift snare thrown up by the hitchers.

With a series of hollow metallic booms and the splintering crack of snapping wood, Randy's limo slid backwards into the barrier. She opened her eyes and quickly checked the under-carriage read-outs. Hydraulic pressure, stress and load factors were all green. Nothing was broken. The read-outs for the hull were green too. The 'Hutch' was still in one piece. But there was no time to waste. Now that the limo had been stopped, the weaker hitchers had rallied and were surging back towards the runway and throwing themselves into the mêlée.

It was crazy. Even if she consented to give some of them a ride, she could only carry eight at the most. But once the hatch was open, the rush would be so great, the limo would never leave the ground again.

She heard an ominous drumming sound. The hitchers were beating the hull with wooden staves. Out of the side port she saw people dragging beams onto the runway to bar the way forward. It was now or never. She set the liquid fuel pumps for maximum thrust and fired the four main rocket engines.

Over on the grass by the terminal, Waxmann had slowed down to let Andy stand up to watch the action through the open roof. He was just in time to see the limo slide tail first into the barrier. Seconds later, the struggling mob closed in around it and started banging on the hull.

He felt driven to do something. 'Isn't there anyone we can call? Where's Airport Security?!'

'Don't worry about it,' said Waxmann. 'She does this stunt three or four times a year.'

'Can't the city do something about these guys?!'

'Don't need to,' said Waxmann. 'The boundary traps keep the numbers down and those that do get through end up killing each other.'

What the hell kind of a place have I landed in now, thought Andrew. In the same moment that question formed in his mind, a huge tongue of flame and billowing clouds of glowing orange smoke erupted from the rear of Randy's limo. The crowd of hitchers scattered in all directions. The blast of flame from the rocket nozzles ignited the residues of oil and vapour in the drums and sent them bouncing and rolling in all directions.

Andrew felt like cheering as Randy sped down the runway, lifted off, then stood the limo on its rear end and went up like a rocket in a thundering rolling wave of sound. For a moment or two it was like standing under Niagara Falls. As the reverberations died away she became a tiny shooting-star with a thin, bright orange tail. Andrew watched until the sky closed around her and as she disappeared, Zhannandor's moon lifted its large pale face over the horizon, followed by its tiny neighbour.

It was a spectacular departure. At the far end of the runway, the more pugnacious hitchers were still slugging it out against the dying flames from the burning drums. Their dispirited companions had melted away into the darkness; back to their foxholes in the grass to wait, with ever-diminishing hope, for the next incoming flight.

Andrew slumped down in his seat.

Waxmann gunned the motor. 'Satisfied?'

'Yeah, let's hit the road.'

Breasting a rise on the almost-deserted freeway, Andrew caught his first glimpse of Boot City and its glittering skyline. The architecture was a curious mix. Las Vegas crossed with the South Bronx. A space-age frontier town glitzed up with neon. Islands of light surrounded by dark alleys where the night people lived. People with furtive eyes who only emerged after sundown. People with a single driving impulse: to score whatever they needed to get themselves through one more day.

Waxmann dropped through several gears as they neared the city centre and cruised along to let Andrew get the feel of the place. The street scenes reflected what Honest John T Ffastbukk had forgotten to tell him about Boot City. The cabbie had been more helpful. Its three major activities were gambling, drinking and sex, with crimes against the person and shady deal-making competing for fourth position.

They turned off the main street into the exotic forecourt of the Hotel Maracariba. Water spilled over the edges of layered pools. One-legged pale blue flamingoes stood amongst a lofty forest of floodlit greenery.

Andrew gazed up at the glittering frontage. 'I wanted Sadie Moon's.'

'I know – but the lady said to drop you here.'

'What lady?'

The cabbie shrugged. 'The lady who called the spaceport. If you want the bar, it's five blocks down the street.'

Thinking the 'lady' must have been Sadie Moon, Andrew paid him off without pursuing the matter further. 'Is it safe to walk?'

The cabbie grinned as he pocketed the money. 'Yea. Just obey the golden rule. Don't ever carry more'n you can afford to lose!'

Andrew climbed out of the cab and watched it drive away. As it vanished in the downtown traffic, he realised he had arrived without his newly-acquired luggage. Shit! He had definitely looped the shoulder strap around his neck before going out of the hatch . . . it must have snapped when he was struggling to hang onto the steps of Randy's limo. Which meant his two new sets of clean underwear were lying on the runway at Boot City Field . . .

Terrific. What a great way to end the day.

Andrew entered the lobby of the Hotel Maracariba. The decor matched the flashy exterior. The lounge area on the right was full of colourful characters, some drenched in sequins and sporting gaudy feathers. They looked like a bunch of revellers who'd just flown in from a carnival in Rio.

Andrew's entrance had not gone unnoticed. A handful of sumptuously-appointed semi-naked hookers homed in, plus a man with slicked-down hair anxious to take him to the best card game in town and another who – as far as Andrew could make out in the general clamour for his attention – seemed to be offering him sex with any animal of his choice.

Andrew told them all to fuck off and made his way to the reception desk where a man whose lapel tag read 'Under-Manager' greeted him with a trained smile. 'Welcome to the Maracariba, sir.'

Given his dishevelled appearance, bruised face, scuffed knuckles and total lack of luggage, Andrew found it hard to believe any swanky establishment would let him through the door but it was that kind of town.

'I'd like to book a room. With a view if there is one.'

'Certainly, sir – and your name?'

'Andiamo Cartahaynyar.' Andrew handed over his ID card for processing.

The Under-Manager slid the card through the reader and studied the result on the screen with some surprise. 'We already have a premium suite booked in your name, sir!' He took a hotel passcard from a holder and laid it on the counter with Andrew's ID. 'Four-oh-eight. And there's a video-message for you. The booths are over there.'

As he traversed the lobby, Andrew's eye was caught by a large illuminated board advertising forthcoming events to be held in the hotel's conference suites. One group, calling itself the Happy Easter Society, was offering a 'spiritual experience' to anyone willing to let themselves be nailed to a wooden cross.

He entered a call-booth and inserted the passcard. As the call connected, the hotel's name and logo was replaced by the smiling face of Kelly Mandell.

'Hi! What kept you? The drinks are on ice, the bath water's running and your luggage is on the bed. Come on up!'

Andrew entered the lift, bashed the fourth floor button with the side of his fist, and rode upwards with murder in his heart.

Chapter Nine

Andrew used the hotel passcard to unlock the door to Room 408 and kicked it open to announce his entry. Finding no one in sight, he slammed it shut to vent his frustration and strode into the lounge section of the large suite.

A verandah with potted greenery and flowers lay beyond a curtained wall of glass. The lounge itself was furnished with deep armchairs set around low tables with a dining area to one side, a fully-stocked bar, a wall-sized HD-tv screen and a music centre playing something that could have been written by Brazil 66.

Two half-open doors gave a glimpse of bedrooms beyond. From one of them came the sound of a shower running.

Andrew walked in and surveyed the room. Items of clothes were scattered over the floor, on chairs and the king-sized bed. Filling his lungs, he marched over to the bathroom door, and yelled at the top of his voice. 'Mandell?!!'

The shower continued to run.

Andrew hammered on the door until it stopped. He stepped back, breathing hard through pinched nostrils and mentally rehearsed the tirade he had prepared on the way up.

Kelly Mandell emerged from the bathroom clad in a hotel bathrobe and a towel turban. Her skin glistened with droplets of water. 'Boy! I'm so glad you made it! I was worried you might not get the message I left for you in Main City.'

Andrew's jaw was clenched so tight he could barely get the words out. 'I didn't go to Main City.'

Kelly, who was about to mop her face with the collar of the bath robe, paused and smiled disarmingly. 'Then I guess this must be what they call Fate.'

Andrew stepped towards her. 'Really? Where I come from it's called taking a goddam fucking liberty! Fate?! Huh! Just what d'you think you're doing, Mandell?! You dump an illegal arms shipment on me, you steal my luggage and now you're making hotel reservations for me! Are you out of your fucking mind or what?!!'

Kelly began to mop her face. 'I knew it. You don't like the room. No problem. We can easily get something bigger.'

A savage note entered Andrew's voice. 'This has gone far enough.' He lunged towards her.

Kelly sidestepped leaving him grasping empty space. 'Uh-uh! Violence is not the solution.'

'Maybe not – but it'll do till I think of something better!' He made another grab. Better judged, this time.

Once again she eluded him, tore the towel from her head and adopted a textbook karate position. 'I really think you should cool down, Andrew. If you beat the shit out of me you'll feel really, really bad.'

Andrew adopted a similar stance. 'You think so?'

'I know so. In fact, I guarantee it. And if I put you in traction – which is what'll probably happen – you'll feel even worse. So what I suggest is – have the bath which is now running and which you obviously need and then, when you're feeling more relaxed, why don't we talk this whole thing through?'

Andrew dropped his hands. His initial rage had faded in the face of her colossal cheek. He was still seething but was having a hard time trying not to smile. 'Just let me get one thing straight. How long have you been staying here?'

'Three days. But don't worry, we have separate bedrooms.'

'But the suite is reserved in my name . . .'

Kelly smiled sweetly. 'Well, you're the man with the money.'

'Which means I can throw you out whenever I choose.'

'You can, but you won't.'

Andrew shook his head in wonder. 'I don't think I've ever met someone who was so sure of themselves.'

'That's what makes me so exciting to know.' Seeing his sour reaction, Kelly dropped the light touch. 'If you really wanted to

127

put the knife in, you'd have turned me over to Security while we were on Buena Vista.'

'Yeah, well, maybe I felt I owed you one.'

His reply brought back a smile. 'Since when did the Navy start handing out favours?'

That word again. And that troubling feeling. Whispering echoes at the back of his mind. 'I think you've got me mixed up with someone else.'

'Sure.' Kelly pointed to the second bedroom. 'Your gear is in there. Grab a bath and some fresh clothes. I'll call room service and order supper for two. After watching you for three months on the Narayana I think I know what kind of food you prefer. And while we're eating it, we can swap case-notes.'

Andrew nodded. Since he never hit women, even when direly provoked, he badly needed to assuage his anger by releasing a stream of verbal abuse. But he kept silent. Ms Mandell really thought she had it all figured out. He'd met girls like this before and knew there was no point in arguing. You endured their company until you discovered the chink in their armour then, at the right moment, you slipped the knife in and totally destroyed their self-confidence.

Yes. He would enjoy that.

Over supper, they touched lightly on a range of subjects which included a review of some of the other passengers they had met on the SS Narayana: Ratti Dikkenburra, producer and film director of *Closing Counters*, a tear-jerking drama charting the demise of a huge department store – Skwaleed Zlumfladd, an immensely rich property developer – Harbinjer Gladdtydingz, ex-newscaster and chat-show host, famous throughout the Rimworld for his televised fireside homilies on the redemptive nature of conspicuous wealth – Yovill Zummerzett who had made a career out of being a racial stereotype and was now able to command huge fees by pandering to the prejudices of the makers of hard-hitting social documentaries – and last, but not least, Nikellodion Mellodion, composer and lyricist, whose current megahit was graced by a chorus line which ran:

'Shimmee-Sham, Jimmee-Jam
Shimmee-Sham-Shimmee
Jimmee-Jam, Shimmee-Sham
Gimmee Jam Jimmy'

By prior agreement, neither Kelly nor Andrew invoked the name of Lars Vindhook. Based on past experience, Andrew had come to believe that whenever you talked about someone you never wanted to see ever again, they always turned up on your doorstep or rang in the middle of your favourite tv programme.

Andrew gave a lighthearted account of his white-knuckle ride with Randy and Lead-Boot Waxmann, and recited a few episodes from the Andi Carta cover story. It was hard to tell how much of it she believed.

Kelly pushed her coffee cup away, placed both elbows on the table and folded her arms. From the determined set of her jaw, it was clear the time for straight talking had arrived.

'How much longer do I have to wait before you ask me why I used you to smuggle those weapons through Customs?'

Andrew shrugged and feigned a total lack of interest. 'The last time I tried to find out, you disappeared with my luggage. So rather than go through all that again, I thought I'd wait until you were ready to talk. This seems as good a place as any. From what little I've seen of this town I've got a feeling that the Corporation isn't in charge of law enforcement.'

'They wouldn't dare show their nose around here.'

'So why don't you start by explaining how you came to be carrying unlicensed guns in the first place.'

Kelly thought for a minute then said: 'My father designs weapons for the Corporation – '

'You have bio-parents? You weren't cocooned?'

'No. I'm a Fast-Track-Nine.'

In the same way that the animal kingdom had been sidelined, the Rimworld authorities had taken the task of child-rearing out of the hands of adults. The far-reaching decision had been

129

taken in the last millenium by social scientists who shared Philip Larkin's caustic view of parenting. Conceived in vitrio, the fertilised eggs were grown to term in artificial wombs then transferred to cocoons where they grew to maturity, emerging at the age of twenty-one, literate, numerate, imbued with a strong sense of civic responsibility, the work ethic, the ability to form positive relationships and a first class degree in something useful like computer programming.

Bio-parenting was limited to the favoured few and the resulting offspring, reared like Earth children, tended to regard themselves as a cut above everyone else. It wasn't surprising she was so insufferable.

'He must be a pretty important guy,' said Andrew.

'He is. Earns big bucks. But we didn't see eye to eye over some of the items they were asking him to dream up.'

'So basically, you put my future on the line because you behaved like a spoilt brat over some domestic upset and decided to leave home.' Andrew was quietly pleased to see he had annoyed her.

'I may be on the small side but I'm not a juve! I'm a fully-qualified astro-navigator with a Plus-One rating from Trade-Cor and eighty-two million miles on the log!'

'Bully for you.' TradeCor was the commercial shipping arm of the Corporation. The official merchant navy carrying goods between the planets of the Rimworld.

'And I did not just "walk out". This was a matter of principle.'

'Oh, I see,' said Andrew. 'You've got principles, so it's perfectly okay to break the law by the illegal carriage and importation of stolen weapons and using an innocent party to help you do it.'

'It's *Corporation* law, Mister. It may be only a matter of time but they don't own the Rimworld yet.'

Andrew decided to push it a little further. 'That's an interesting interpretation of the rulebook. So . . . I've fallen into the hands of an over-privileged revolutionary. What d'you plan to do with the guns – start an armed uprising?'

'No, I'm gonna sell 'em! The stuff in the bag is so new it

hasn't even been issued for service trials. Should be worth a small fortune.'

'Oh, now I get it, said Andrew. 'You're a *gunrunner* with principles.'

'Will you stop sneering at me?! This is a one-off thing, okay? I just needed to raise some money to keep me going.'

'Until when?'

'Until I get a job. I'm saving up to buy a ship.'

'You already had a job with TradeCor.'

Kelly sighed with exasperation. 'When's it going to sink into that thick skull of yours?! I don't *want* to work for the Corporation – in fact, I'm against everything it stands for!'

'Join the club,' said Andrew. 'But who the hell did you think you were going to sell them to? Civilians aren't allowed to own firearms except by special licence – and they are only issued to people living off-world.'

'Like traders . . .'

'Yeah. And even if you were judged fit and proper and could afford a permit, you can only buy a weapon that's been declared obsolete.'

'You're forgetting where we are. Why d'you think I came to Zhannandor? The people here aren't as particular about the rules as you seem to be.' She appraised him keenly. 'How come you know so much about it anyway?'

Good question. Andrew said the first thing that came into his head. 'Natural caution. If you're gonna shell out close on two million Cords to set up as a trader, it pays to read the small print.'

Kelly took this on board with a thoughtful nod. 'Natural caution? Hmmm . . . there wasn't much of that on display when you rushed in to rescue the Reindeer Man.'

Leaving him to reflect on this annoying contradiction, she got up, went over to the bar and brought back two glasses filled with a concoction that recalled the smell and taste of apricot brandy.

Keeping her eyes down, she stroked the sides of the glass with her two forefingers and said: 'What would you say if I were to tell you that you've been lying to me since we first met, that your name is not Andiamo Cartahaynyar and that you've never set foot on Tyrenia?'

Andrew tried to stay cool as she raised her eyes to his. 'I'd say "Don't change the subject". I'm still waiting for you to explain why you dumped those guns on me."

'It's because I figured you were the only person who could get them through Customs for me. And I was right, wasn't I?'

'Yeah'. Andrew continued to stonewall. 'I still can't understand why they let me go. On the other hand, maybe they believed me when I said I knew nothing about them. Maybe they've been onto you all the time and are just waiting for you to make a sale before they pounce.'

It was intended to unsettle her but it didn't work.

Kelly drank deep then pointed the glass and a forefinger at him. 'They let you go because they discovered the same thing as I did when I stole your ID card one night aboard the Narayana and ran a Deep Seven. The feedback says you're Navy, Mister. With the rank of Commander.'

Again that strange tingle. 'I see – and are you now going to tell me my real name?'

'I didn't have the codes to unlock that information. And I've got a hunch Buena Vista Security didn't get past that point either.'

'You're right, they didn't. That's how I got through. They seemed to think I was on some kind of secret mission.'

'Maybe you are. But maybe it's one the Navy doesn't know about.'

Andrew laughed. 'Make up your mind!'

'I'm trying to. In fact, I've been trying to figure you out since you boarded the Narayana at Star City. Despite what it says on your ID, you are not Andiamo Cartahaynyar. The card will clear you through normal security checks and commercial transactions but the substrate data lists you as a Navy Commander. It even has the data channel security blocks that can only be accessed by Navy codes. And yet you keep denying the connection.'

132

'That's 'cos there isn't one. I can't explain how that stuff got on my card. It was only when Customs handed me over to Buena Vista Security I found out that running a Deep Seven allowed people to access another level of highly confidential data. How come you were able to run one?'

'I used the setup on board the SS Narayana. Borrowed a passcard from one of the Signals officers and let myself into the Communications Centre.'

'You mean you picked his pocket.'

Kelly smiled. 'Just one of my many skills. That's why I'm such useful person to have around. But let's get back to your ID. Providing you have the right equipment and know the drill, the bio-data on Cartahaynyar, your alias, is easy to insert. But as far as I know – and I speak as someone who's at the cutting edge of deception – no one has ever managed to forge a Navy ID that will pass a Deep Seven search.'

'Really?'

'Yes. There's only one way it could be done. You would have to insert the fake bio, service record and your pictures onto the Navy's CORE computer using fake input dates then trick the computer into treating it as a bona fide official record – and that's impossible! It can't be done!'

She obviously didn't know about Parnassus.

Andrew made another attempt to wriggle off the hook. 'I'm sorry but . . . I've completely lost track of what this is leading up to.'

His heartbeat quickened, his mind began to race. Thoughts and images tumbled over one another, merging into a rushing, roaring, giddying stream.

'What this is leading up to,' said Kelly, 'is the fascinating question as to who you really are, "Mister C", and what you are up to. That careless reference to cats was very revealing but my curiosity was aroused long before that. There's something about the way you speak, and the strange words you come out with. Something that's . . . that's not quite ri – '

With his heart now pounding like a jackhammer, Andrew leapt from the table, rushed into his bedroom, fumbled in his

133

cast-off jacket for the current packet of decelerant pills, popped one into his mouth, dashed into the bathroom and swallowed it with the help of some water. He leaned on the washbasin and closed his eyes. The pounding eased and the giddiness faded as the pill brought him down to speed.

Kelly was watching him closely as he walked back out and resumed his seat.

'Sorry about that. Thought I was going to be sick. Where were we?'

'I was saying there are things about you that don't add up.'

'Really? I can't imagine why. Maybe you're getting your sums wrong.' Andrew tried a friendly smile. 'How about another drink?'

Kelly fixed him with a hard, piercing stare. 'Forget the drink. You're hiding something and I want to know what it is.'

Andrew decided to come on strong. 'Know your problem, Mandell? You don't listen. I've made it clear more than once that I don't like you prying into my business.' He stood up. 'If you're not happy with the way things stand, pack your bags and find someone else to give you a free ride.'

Kelly got up and walked around the table to confront him. 'I've heard about people like you. Nothing that made much sense, just wild talk, rumours, speculation. But you're one of them, aren't you? From beyond the Rimworld.'

Andrew raised his hands in surrender and laughed off the suggestion. 'Get a grip on yourself, Mandell. I'm just a guy who came here to buy a trader.' He backed slowly towards his bedroom.

'And I'm prepared to believe you.' Kelly cornered him in the doorway. 'So here's the deal. We get the ship, you hire me as navigator, and I won't voice my suspicions to anyone else. How does that sound?'

It sounded terrible but Andrew had no wish to extend their conversation. Alarmed by her constant probing, he wanted to put a door between them before he made any more blunders. 'We'll talk about it in the morning. I'm going to bed.'

She looked genuinely surprised. 'Bed? What're you talking about? This town's just waking up!'

'Well, I'm going to sleep.' He started to close the door.

Kelly blocked it with her foot. 'You can't. We have to meet with someone.' She checked her time-bracelet.

'Who?'

'A guy I ran into yesterday. Owns a trader and is looking for a quick sale. Cash. Sounds interesting.'

Andrew relaxed his pressure on the door. 'What's his name?'

'Ganzwayko. Finnee Ganzwayko. I checked the ship's papers. They look genuine.'

'Did you run 'em through Central Registry?'

'Of course not. The guy's a Star Raider. Once you buy a licence you're in hock for the duration. The trading licence is just the start. The Corporation will hit you for annual increments, operating taxes, ship certification . . . they'll bleed you dry, then encourage you to take out a loan to stay afloat and repo the ship when you can't make the payments.'

'Seems a strange way to do business.'

'Not at all. TradeCor wants to be the only outfit moving goods around the Rimworld. They can only achieve that by eliminating the competition.'

'By using the Navy to stop and search.' A brief dizzying tingle flashed through Andrew's head. This time it made him shiver.

'All they need to do is find one loose nut and you're left holding an enforcement order for a complete refit. Two loose nuts and you're on tow to the scrapyard.'

'Yeah – ' Andrew wondered why he knew this. He couldn't remember it being part of the learning programme. ' – but if they catch you trading without a licence – '

'The trick is not to get caught. It heightens the sense of adventure.' She searched his face. 'You look like a man who's suddenly gone off the whole idea.'

'No. I'm still ready to give it a whirl.' Andrew pulled on a bomber jacket and checked his cards were safely stowed in an inside pocket. 'Let's go.'

135

'Great. I said we'd meet him in – '

'Sadie Moon's. Yeah, I know.' He led the way to the main door of the suite.

Kelly looked stunned as she stepped into the passageway. 'How did you . . .?'

Andrew made it up as he went along. 'I didn't come all this way to look for my luggage, Mandell. I've already talked to Sadie about this guy and he's not even top of the list. D'you wanna walk or drive?' He watched her mouth flap open and shut.

It felt good to score.

Built on several different levels, with balconies surrounding a high-ceilinged central area with exposed beams, and with a host of nooks and crannies and stairways running off in all directions, Sadie Moon's was like a wildly extravagant film set built inside the huge James Bond sound stage at Pinewood Studios, crammed with a colourful cast of extras and fanned by soft laser beams of every hue.

Architecturally, it looked as if it had been put together by a team of art directors who weren't on speaking terms with each other. Hollywood Western saloon bar and bawdy house motifs had been thrown together with elements from Egypt, Greece, Imperial Rome, the gilded luxury of France's Sun King, fairytale Bavarian baroque and the geometric modernity of the Bauhaus. It was, in sum, a classic combination of no-expense-spared glitz and the epitome of bad taste. A splendidly vulgar, velvet and vinyl, flocked, fretted and filigreed, chrome and cut-glass chandeliered, ornamentally plastered Palace of Varieties.

Passing through the front entrance, Andrew and Kelly were almost blown off their feet by a hurricane-force blast of sound. The pounding beat being pumped out of stacked banks of speakers was strong enough to loosen teeth. The floor shook, glasses bounced, the chandeliers shivered and jangled like maddened Tibetan wind-chimes about to self-destruct but the crowd on the dance floor and the g-stringed go-go girls on the various bar counters seemed oblivious of the dangers to life, limb and their back molars. Just on its own, the ear-splitting mega-decibel output was barely tolerable, but it was matched by the noise generated by the other revellers – drinkers, bar-girls, gamblers and spectators who had to shout increasingly loudly to make themselves heard above the music and the din that they and their neighbours were making.

Andrew stayed close behind Kelly as she threaded her way through the festive throng towards a cluster of high-backed drinking booths where she had arranged to meet Finnee Ganzwayko, the Star Raider with a ship to sell. They found him seated next to a bimbolino in a white-blonde cascade-style acrylic wig. Her long slim arms were draped adoringly round his neck. Two of his cronies and a couple of bar-girls were also at the table, hooting and guffawing at what Ganzwayko was saying. To judge from the way they lurched and rolled, all six had been drinking heavily.

The laughter died and all eyes fastened on Andrew as he and Kelly reached the table. In a bar full of dubious characters, Ganzwayko won the prize as the man most likely to steal your wallet, cut your throat, rape your wife, pillage your home and sell your children into slavery. Massively-built, paunchy, bearded and wearing an eye-patch, he looked like a space-age Long John Silver. The only thing missing was the wooden leg. The bimbolino parked against his shoulder was clearly pitching for the part of the parrot.

'Finnee Ganzwayko?'

The shifty eyes sought out Kelly Mandell and drew a nod of confirmation. They flicked back onto Andrew. 'You Carta-haynyar?'

'Yeah. I understand you have a ship for sale.'

'That's right. D'your partner show you the video?'

Andrew gave Kelly a sharp-eyed glance but she was too busy muscling in.

'I ran it for him in a pay-booth on the way down here.'

Ganzwayko's eyebrows interrogated Andrew. 'So . . . you interested?'

137

'If the price is right.'

'Siddown . . .' Ganzwayko dismissed his two drinking pals and the bar girls with a brusque gesture. The bimbolino eased herself off his shoulder, took a graceful sip of her drink, adjusted her neckline and greeted Andrew and Kelly with a self-conscious smile as they sat down inside the booth.

Sadie Moon appeared in person with a tray of drinks. Sadie was a six-foot tall, voluptuous brunette charmer with a Mae West torso, Ann Miller legs, and a cleavage you could lose an arm in. The gold rings she wore on all four fingers of each hand were heavy enough to use as knuckledusters and she had a four-inch deep choker set with a king's ransom in diamonds, rubies and sapphires. Andrew had never seen anyone wearing their entire bank balance before.

Sadie set down the tray. 'Compliments of Honest John.' She pinched Andrew's cheek then sampled his muscle tone. 'Nice to see you here, honey. When you've tucked the kid up in bed, why don't you and me get better acquainted?'

'Great idea,' said Andrew, relishing Kelly's displeasure. 'Soon as we wrap up this bit of business, I'll stick her in a cab back to the hotel.'

'I'll book one now,' said Sadie. 'Don't let Finnee put one over on you.' She patted the back of Andrew's neck and left.

'Overblown bag,' hissed Kelly. 'I can't believe you'd want to go with something like that!'

Andrew ignored her and addressed Ganzwayko. 'So . . . this ship of yours . . .'

'The Dragon Lady . . .'

'If we agree a price, when can I see the real thing?'

'Anytime you like. She's parked at Boot City Field.'

'And she's still in one piece?'

'Absolutely. The crew stayed on board – to guard her.'

'Dedicated bunch of guys . . .'

'They're probably safer than we are,' said Kelly, fending off a passing drunk.

'Look, just shut it, okay? I'll do the talking.'

She shrugged. 'Sure. Go ahead – partner.'

Andrew bit down hard then said: 'The thing is, this ship of yours is so old, she should be drawing a pension.'

'But she's still a runner. And she comes with a full crew – ' Ganzwayko caught Kelly's eye, ' – except for a navigator. The onboard computer is a MIDAS-20-25-100. No sense of direction.'

'That's right,' said Andrew. Again that tingle. 'I've never seen one outside a museum.'

'True. The 25-100's a real collector's item. Find the right buyer and you could pocket a bundle.'

'But right now, I'm the buyer and – '

Ganzwayko cut in. 'I didn't include him in the sale price.'

'Him . . .?'

'Tarqueen.'

Andrew, appalled by the prospect of roaming through space in the company of an over-the-hill electronic entity that was also in the grip of a sexual identity crisis, exchanged glances with Kelly. Her eyebrows indicated the ball was in his court.

'Yeah, well, with or without Tarq – I mean the 25-100, the asking price is way too high. My, uh, partner, tells me you want two point seven five million Cords but it's gonna cost me close to half a mil to get her off the ground and into orbit. Best I can offer is one point five.'

Finnee Ganzwayko looked disappointed. The bimbolino, who still had not been introduced, was devastated. Ganzwayko glared at Kelly accusingly. 'Thought you said he had the money!'

Kelly squirmed uncomfortably and kept her eyes down. Andrew couldn't resist putting the verbal boot in.

'I'm sorry if my partner misled you. She's always shooting her mouth off, but the fact is she has nothing to do with the financial side of the business. One point five mil is my best offer.'

'Then we don't have a deal,' said Ganzwayko.

The bimbolino tugged at Ganzwayko's sleeve. 'Oh, Finnee! Ain't we ever go'n see the back of that ol' Dragon Lady?! How much longer is that rusty bitch go'n stand in the way of our dream of happiness?!'

Ganzwayko's voice turned syrupy. 'Hush, now, Lindy-Lou! The Lady maybe old'n a little creaky but she's still lickety-spit from stem to stern.' He slipped an arm around the bimbo's shoulder. 'I promised Lindy-Lou we'd settle down and raise chickens on Laguna.'

She sniffed back the tears. 'There's this farm – '

'With space for a million birds – '

'Free range. The chicks are just adorable. Cute li'l' fluff-balls that grow real fast. D'y'ever taste real meat?'

'Never touch it,' snapped Kelly.

'Well, I tell you, honey. There are people out there who'd die for a taste of Southern fry. D'y-know what you can get for oven-ready birds these days? We're gonna be mega-rich, ain't we, Finnee?'

Ganzwayko placed a fond finger on the end of her nose. 'I certainly hope so, my little chickadee!'

'Well, if it doesn't work out,' said Kelly, 'You can always keep snakes.'

Andrew glanced at her. The gooey-ness exhibited by the pair opposite was obviously not to her taste.

'Snakes?!' cried Lindy-Lou. 'Uuu-yerrch!'

'They come from eggs too – and the skins fetch a real high price.'

'Is that so?' said Ganzwayko. 'How d'you raise 'em?'

'Simple. You just feed 'em on chickens.'

Lindy-Lou stared at Kelly with a puzzled frown, glanced at Andrew then turned to Ganzwayko. 'Finnee . . . I believe that pint-sized puddle of shit is tryin' to make a fool o' me.'

'Now why would she do that, melon-pie? Girl's only tryin' to be helpful.' Ganzwayko patted her hand then gave Andrew a hard-eyed glance. 'You a gambling man?'

Andrew was not – which was why he was surprised to hear himself saying: 'I play the odds now and then.'

'Then how does this strike you? The ship's worth three mil and I'm not taking a penny less – '

'Oh, Finneeeeee!'

'Hush now, Lindy-Lou. This is men's talk!' His eyes never left Andrew's. 'If you put down the one point five . . .'

'Ye-ah . . .'

'I'll play you for the other half. Cards, toss of a coin, throw of a dice – you name it.'

Andrew felt Kelly give him a warning poke in the ribs. He ignored it. 'And if I lose . . .?'

'I keep your money and you get a free ride to our next port of call. What d'you say?'

'I'll let you know when I've looked over the ship.' Andrew glanced at Kelly Mandell. She had her head in her hands.

'Feel free,' said Ganzwayko expansively. 'Uh – how d'you plan to pay me?'

'In Cords. Corporation dollars.'

'Can't use 'em, friend. Need unlicensed currency. Something the Treasury Department can't get their hands on. I'll take two mil of anything you can find.'

Andrew nodded. 'I'll see what I can do.' He stood up, grabbed the back of Kelly's collar and hauled her off the seat. 'Come on, kid. Time you were in bed.'

☆   ☆   ☆

Andrew and Kelly were still arguing when they burst into the lobby of the Hotel Maracariba.

'I don't want to know how slim you think my chances are! It's my money and if I choose to gamble it away, then that's what I'm gonna do!' He cut her off with a jabbing finger. 'And another thing, partner! Just quit trying to row yourself into this deal. I don't need you or your advice – '

'I set up the meeting with Ganzwayko, didn't I?'

'I already knew about Ganzwayko! Just stay the hell out of my way!'

'Yeah, yeah, yeah, okay. So when do we look over the ship?'

Andrew halted, placed a hand on her chest and loomed over her aggressively. 'I don't seem to be getting through to you. You're not invited. I don't want to be in the same hotel as you, I

141

don't even want to be on the same planet! And as for being on the same ship, you can forget it! It ends right here!'

Kelly's eyes narrowed. 'I hope this doesn't mean you're trying to renege on our deal.'

Andrew brought his face closer. 'There is no deal, Mandell. Ship or no ship, I'm leaving here without you.'

Kelly stayed on an even keel. 'I'm sorry to hear that. The last thing I want to do is turn you in – '

'Turn me in – ?'

' – but if you're not going to give me a ride out of here I'm gonna have to go for the reward to make ends meet. They pay big money for people like you.'

Andrew decided to call her bluff. 'Really? What's so special about people like me?'

'You're from another star system. From the planet called Earth.' She stopped his protest. 'It's okay, you don't have to come clean with me. Once the guys in the white coats go to work on your brain, they'll get the whole story – including the names of the people here who are bankrolling your mission.'

Andrew searched her face. 'You're talking rubbish, Mandell.'

'Sure. That's why you're going to give me the helm of the Dragon Lady. And you won't regret it. We make a great team.'

'You think so?'

'I know so.'

'I'll think about it.' Andrew hated being backed into a corner. Kelly trailed him to the reception desk. The night clerk looked up expectantly. 'I'm told you have a self-drive aircab service . . .'

'That's correct sir. From the roof of the hotel. You'll require a current flying permit. If you're planning a one-way trip, the cabs have an auto-return program.'

'Great . . .'

'And I should perhaps warn you that journeys are restricted to a radius of one hundred miles from this location.'

'No problem,' said Kelly. 'It's just a round trip to Boot City Field.'

'Keep outta this,' growled Andrew.

'Only trying to help.'

'Well, don't. Just button it. Okay?'

The night clerk continued smoothly. 'Provided you are going to the terminal or the security space park, there should be no problem.'

Kelly elaborated. 'The onboard navigation system only accepts the coordinates of locations in approved areas. Sensible precaution, really. There's some bad people out there.'

Andrew mastered the desire to throttle her. He turned back to the clerk. 'Thanks . . .'

Kelly flashed her hotel passcard. 'Any messages for 408?'

The clerk checked his terminal. 'Yes, Madam. There's a videogram from a Mr Lars Vindhook. He checked into the hotel a couple of hours ago.'

Andrew went cold. 'He's as hard to get rid of as you are.'

Kelly gave him a calculating glance. 'I wonder if he's changed his Skandavian Trolls?'

Andrew leant on the counter and dropped his head like a bull waiting for the *coup de grâce* from the torero. 'No, not that. I can't face it.'

Kelly looped an arm through his and led him away towards the lifts. 'You don't have to. I'll take care of it while you check out the Dragon Lady.'

'I'm not sure about this . . .'

'Listen! He owes us both a favour. Don't worry, I know how to handle him. All he needs is warmth and understanding. Something you don't seem to know a great deal about.'

Andrew relented. 'Okay, but don't overdo it.'

'Trust me. I know that goes against the grain but – ' Kelly grinned as they entered the lift ' – given what I know, what choice have you got?'

Andrew gave her the evil eye. 'I wouldn't celebrate just yet. And don't think this means you can – '

' – take advantage of you? How little you know me.'

The lift stopped at the fourth floor. Kelly hit the button to

143

hold the doors open. 'You gonna rest up or take the cab out to the field?'

'I'm too full of uppers to sleep. I'll go out to the field.'

Kelly stepped out of the lift and called back to him: 'You'll love the crew. Great bunch of guys!'

The doors closed, leaving her with the last word. The lift went on up, carrying Andrew towards the air-cab station on the roof. He closed his eyes, thought about the jam he had got himself into and prayed he would wake up back in Catford.

There was a soft ping. He opened his eyes. He was still in the lift, with three more stops to go.

☆　☆　☆　☆　☆　☆　☆

SIDELIGHTS ON THE RIMWORLD by 'FIZZ'　No.1748
COCOONS
Child-rearing from conception to maturity

A passing reference to this method of birthing was included in Chapter 9. An Earth-parent with a family now of marriageable age, whose heart still beats faster at the patter of tiny footsteps and warms to those soft-focus memories of innocence would probably be appalled at the thought of a world without children. But it does have its advantages – far too numerous to list – but which include the elimination of the two and four a.m. feeds, disposable nappies, the need for deafening music when doing homework, all emotional traumas associated with rebellious adolescents including the threat of drug abuse, the sleepless nights engendered by your daughter's inexplicable desire to jump into bed with the biggest creep in the neighbourhood, and the need to buy them designer-label trainers; a pair of which cost as much as a week on the Costa del Sol.

Children are not like birds. They do not fly the nest. They are like the cats and dogs you give a home to, except that these lovable little bundles live up to six times longer. Not only have you got them and their problems for life, they are liable to harangue you on your deathbed for not leaving them adequately provided for.

Cocooning had a double benefit. Once adults were freed from the domestic duties associated with parenthood, women were able to pursue worthwhile and rewarding careers and because they were born sterile – like their male counterparts – were able to enter emotional relationships free from the threat of an unwanted pregnancy. It also enabled men and women to associate with people *they actually liked* instead of having to be nice to a motley collection of cousins, uncles, aunts and other blood relations they couldn't stand the sight of.

Likewise, the emergent young adult entered the world without having to suffer any of the psychological damage that could arise from inadequate parenting. More importantly, being born without parents eliminated the tiresome duty of having to visit a pair of irrelevant wrinklies every Christmas which, given the present average Atlantean lifespan of three hundred and fifty years, could be equated with the humungous prison sentences handed out to serial killers in the USA.

Only without remission.

There appeared to be only one flaw to being born without parents; there was no one you could take your dirty laundry to at the weekend, have it washed and ironed for nothing *and* get a free meal.

Although some liberal-minded readers may find the practice of cocooning creepily reminiscent of *Brave New World* eugenics, the process did not result in a population of mindless, robotic clones or a goose-stepping master-race.

While certain basic elements were fed into every embryo, each cocoon-reared adult had its own individually-tailored formative education programme complete with memories and personality quirks. No two ERICS (Extended Rearing and Induction Cycle) were ever the same but – like any other high-tech enterprise – things could (and quite often did) go wrong.

The problem could lie within one cocoon, a faulty batch or a complete production cycle. Two examples will suffice.

In the very early days when the life-support systems went down, wiping out the whole production cycle, one of Parnassus'

145

ancestors saved the day with a quick trip down the Time Tunnel to Lower Saxony.

Posing as a health inspector, he persuaded the town council of Hamelin that every child under ten should be removed under his supervision to a place of safety nearby while his colleagues moved in to help the adult population deal with the plague of rats; all costs to be borne by the Prince of Saxony.

The townspeople, whose tight-fisted refusal to stump up the cash for a decent sewage system had led to the present infestation, grabbed the offer of a freebie and lined up to wave as the health inspector, gaily dressed and playing a pipe, led a dancing procession of children across the River Weser and into legend.

The team of rodent operatives never arrived and the children never returned. (The crippled boy who lived to tell the tale was a later emendation.)

A more recent computer cock-up resulted in a production batch of quantity surveyors emerging completely tone deaf and with an incurable prediliction for heavy metal music.

The outcome was not a total disaster. The five most afflicted Erics formed a band called 'Renal Failure' and the remainder became roadies, tour managers, T-shirt vendors, fan-club organisers and to this day still form the appreciative core of any audience.

☆　☆　☆　☆　☆　☆　☆

SIDELIGHTS ON THE RIMWORLD by 'FIZZ'　　**No.1749**
BIO-PARENTING
An alternative but more expensive option

Whilst child-rearing by cocoon was judged to be eminently suitable for the ordinary inhabitants of the Rimworld, it was not employed by the ruling and managerial elite. The same kind of people who, in Communist Russia, used to be called the *nomenklatura*; the restaurant queue-jumpers and hard-currency shoppers.

Nobody in the Rimworld had ever had to undergo the

material privations experienced by the Russians under that particular regime but the corrupting effect of power is universal and eternal, and the individuals who ordered the affairs of the Rimworld exhibited the same, understandable desire to maintain the status quo and endeavoured to do so by dynastic succession.

This involved two life-partners (usually but not always of the opposite sex) raising and educating their offspring to which they were directly and genetically related. The process which was initiated at the point of conception and continued after delivery of the infant at the age of nine months was known as bio-parenting. To distinguish such children from the mass of Erics, they were listed in official documents as Fast-Track Nines and each one was expected to carry the dynastic name forward into the next generation.

Since the perfecting of the artificial womb, no human female has been expected or obliged to carry an embryo to term within her own body but a growing number of small, highly vocal protest groups who have united under the inter-global banner of PRAM (Planned Return to Active Motherhood) are now demanding the right to do so.

Chapter Ten

Before leaving the roof of the Hotel Maracariba, Andrew filed his flight plan with the tower at Boot City Field. A short while later, he was circling above the three trade ships in the secure space park. The Dragon Lady was the only one still on her feet. The other two rusting hulks were flat on their bellies and were unlikely to fly again. Beyond the thirty-foot high double electrified fence and the mined 'death' strip, the dark expanse of the unguarded field was lightened here and there by the flickering camp fires of the beleaguered hitchers.

The Dragon Lady, warned of his approach, turned on the floods that illuminated the landing pad on top of its hull. Andrew switched the cab into hover mode and let the onboard computer handle the touchdown.

Opening up one of the gull-wing doors, Andrew stepped out onto the rust-streaked hull and was met by a big, grizzled, knuckle-hard spacer.

'Andi Carta?'

'Yeah.'

'Pug Shilton. First Mate. Welcome aboard.' The greeting was sealed with a bone-crushing handshake.

Leading the way towards an open airlock, he invited Andrew to descend the ladder first. On reaching the bottom, Pug pressed a button on a control panel to close the roof hatch. Nothing happened.

'Well, dock my dangler and call me Doris! It was working fine this morning.' He pounded the panel several times with the side of his fist.

Andrew stepped back as sparks flew from the rear of the

panel, followed by wisps of smoke and the smell of burning plastic.

Pug hit it once more then pressed the button again. This time the hatch closed but rather than demand too much of the system, he climbed back up the ladder and locked it manually. 'This tends to be kinda temperamental,' he said, without the faintest hint of embarrassment. 'But don't worry, we'll get it fixed.'

Andrew nodded then followed him through the inner airlock which Pug did not attempt to close. They proceeded along a narrow service corridor. Several panels on the cable ducting were missing. Ahead of them, a section of flexible pipe hung in a loop at shoulder height.

Pug hooked it back into place with a regretful sigh. 'Meant to do that before you got here . . .'

'That's okay. I'm expecting a few loose ends.' Andrew surveyed the peeling walls of the corridor and found himself saying 'Coat of paint wouldn't hurt.'

'Paint? Hah! The old bird needs a major refit! Twelve years I've been on board. Patching her up . . . best I could.' Pug picked up a fallen inspection panel and clipped it back into place. 'Still . . . beggars can't be choosers. If you and your partner could afford something better you wouldn't be here.'

'Partner . . .?'

'Kelly Mandell.'

Andrew stepped in front of Pug, forcing him to halt. 'Let's get this straightened out before we go any further. Mandell is not my partner. She's just a hired hand with an oversized mouth. If I close the deal – and it's a big "IF" – I'll be in sole command. Got that?'

'Sure. That's fine by me.'

'Good. Okay . . . it's obvious that the Dragon Lady is no gold plate special but just give me the bottom line. Will she fly?'

'If I speak to her nicely, yehh. Getting her off the ground will be the tricky bit but once we hit zero-g she'll be fine.'

They resumed their progress towards the bow of the ship.

149

'Is this your way of telling me she doesn't have an anti-grav field generator?' Once again the words rolled off his tongue, catching Andrew by surprise.

'This is Class Eight trader, mister, not a Navy frigate.' Pug snorted. 'Hnnhh! Do we have an anti-grav field generator . . .! Think we'd be sitting here if we had?!'

'Well, now you mention it, why are you sitting here?'

'Because the skipper ran out of money and ran the ship dry. Set her down here with ten seconds of fuel in the tank. We've been using the last few drops running the lights and the on-board systems.'

'And with no money you couldn't dock at Buena Vista.'

'Course not. And the skipper couldn't park offstation and slap a "For Sale" notice on her because Honest John has the sole franchise and the scag pockets forty per cent of the asking price.'

'And he doesn't trade at the bottom end of the market.' Andrew stopped as they encountered a leaking steam pipe. 'Is that, uhh . . .?'

'Serious? No, a five minute job. It's on my list for tomorrow.' Pug ushered Andrew into the accommodation section. 'That crook Ganzwayko hasn't spent a cent on her since he came aboard nine years ago. Had this dream of buying a chicken farm.'

'Yeah, I heard . . .' Andrew followed Pug down two flights of metal stairs.

'But he could never stay away from the booze and the bar-girls.'

'I'm told he also likes to gamble,' said Andrew.

A scratchy, crackling noise came from a smouldering junction box. Pug grabbed one of the cables and pushed it further into the box until the crackling ceased then fanned the smoke away. 'Gamble? Huh! The man'll bet on two bugs crawling up a wall. I've lost count of the number of times he's thrown the ship in the pot!'

'But he's never lost it . . .'

'He makes damn sure he doesn't,' growled Pug. They turned

150

off the stairs into a passageway with cabin doors on either side and worn treadmats underfoot.

'You mean he cheats . . .'

A voice with a familiar lilt said: 'An' why wouldn't he? Given half a chance, the sharks and twisters in this town'll steal the eyes right out of your head!'

Andrew turned to find a big, red-cheeked, cheerful-looking man half-hidden behind an open cabin door.

Pug introduced him. 'Moses Muldoon. Systems Engineer and Chef de Cuisine.'

'Interesting combination,' said Andrew.

'I do one for love, the other for money. You have a hungry look about you. Can I fix you somethin'? No? Then tell me this – is that Finnee offering to take half the money and play you for the other half?'

'Yes, he is,' said Andrew.

'A word of advice. Don't play him at cards. He's murder.'

'So how come he loses money?'

'Cos they're all dealin' off the bottom! But Finnee now, he's a *lucky* cheat. He may lose most of his shirt but he always comes back with the tail-end.'

'I'm glad you told me.'

'D'you mind tellin' us what the lyin' scuzzbag is askin' for the Lady?'

'Three mil.'

'Worth every penny!' exclaimed Muldoon. 'She's a fine ship an' we'd all be proud to serve with you. Is that not so, Pug?'

'Yep . . .'

'Glad to hear it,' said Andrew. 'Apart from the hitchers outside the wire, I can't imagine anyone with a clean ticket who'd want to crew this rustbucket.'

Pug Milton and Moses Muldoon exchanged glances and looked extremely hurt. Andrew glanced into Muldoon's cabin. A violin and bow lay on a table. It seemed a neat way to change the subject. 'D'you play the fiddle?'

Muldoon stood on his dignity. 'I'd be ashamed to be Irish if I couldn't.'

151

Andrew nodded mechanically. He would have given any-thing to know how an Irishman came to be on board a grounded trader but knew he couldn't ask without betraying his own Earthly origins. There was only one safe question: 'Ahh, so . . . where are you from?'

Muldoon looked puzzled. 'Connemara. Where else?'

This is getting crazier by the minute, thought Andrew. He changed course yet again. 'So, uh – apart from you two, there's – '

'Two engineers,' said Pug. 'Chilli and Gumbo.'

'Do they bunk down in this section?'

'No. In the Fire Department. It's what they call the engine room,' explained Pug. 'But as it's the middle of the night, I'd – '

' – rather not wake them. Okay.' Seeing they were still upset by his use of the word 'rustbucket', Andrew tried to lighten the mood. 'Any stowaways?'

'Just me.' The cultured voice had no lilt but the faint accent was unmistakable.

Andrew turned to find a handsome, grey-haired man at his shoulder. His face radiated intelligence and a sense of humour. He gave a slight bow as he offered Andrew his hand.

'Jean-Luc d'Aramitz.'

'Uh, the ship's doctor,' explained Pug.

'I see. Well, it's good to have you aboard, Doc – but how come you're not on the crew list?'

Aramitz spread his hands apologetically. 'I can only suggest our good captain chose to forget I was here. We, ahh . . . have had our differences of late.'

Yeah, thought Andrew. And I've heard that Medecins Sans Frontières sends medics to some out-of-the-way places but that still doesn't explain what a French doctor is doing aboard a Rimworld trader. One more question he couldn't demand an answer to without giving himself away.

He turned to Pug. 'So – what's next?'

Pug appeared unsure of the question. His eyes flickered from Muldoon to Aramitz then back to Andrew. 'Uh . . . the bridge?'

This turned out to be more like the cramped and crowded

152

cockpit of the Millenium Falcon than the wide-open glossy nothingness that characterised the bridge of the Starship Enterprise.

As Pug and Andrew entered, sensors linked to the onboard computer system detected their presence. The main screen quickly filled with a psychedelic fractal design that changed shape and colour at bewildering speed.

'Hallo? Anyone there? May I know what's going on?' The voice had a throaty, velvety quality. The kind of voice which, had it been attached to a person of the mincing persuasion carrying a placard demanding the right to bugger sixteen-year-old boys, would have tempted Andrew into running them down with a tracked vehicle then reversing back over them to fully register his disapproval . . .

'It's me,' said Pug. He leaned towards Andrew and whispered. 'Tarqueen . . .'

'At this time of night? Are we in mortal danger? In durance vile?'

'Just showing someone round.'

'Just any old someone? Or someone I should know?'

'The name's Andiamo Cartahaynyar, Tarqueen. I'm thinking of buying this ship.'

The designs and colours on the computer screen mirrored Tarqueen's excitement. 'Well now, that really is the most wonderful news. I can tell so much about a person by analysing their voice prints. Ganzwayko was such a pig, whereas you are young, clean-cut – '

Pug cut him off. 'Save it, Tarqueen. We've gotta be moving on.'

The voice became peevish. 'Yes, of course. Don't mind me. I'll just book into the Heartbreak Hotel.' The soft, velvety tone returned. 'Nice meeting you, Andi. I can't wait to get better acquainted.'

As they exited from the bridge, Andrew caught Pug's eye. 'Well, one thing's for sure. If I buy this ship, he's gonna to have to go.'

☆   ☆   ☆

153

Landing back on the roof of the Maracariba, Andrew booked the cab out for another trip then took the lift down to the fourth floor.

On letting himself into the suite, he found the lights had been turned down low. He walked through to the darkened lounge. It was empty, and Kelly's door was closed. Entering his bedroom, he discovered a helmeted figure sprawled across his bed. Andrew turned up the lights. The paunchy body of a man lay squeezed into a virtual reality total sensor suit similar to the kind he had worn in the sim-tank on Palladia. A sheaf of wires ran from the front of the suit to a chest-high box of electronics on a wheeled trolley. The power light was on, but the programme run-time indicator was zeroed.

Andrew raised the visor of the helmet. The face mask underneath hid everything except the pale glassy, unseeing eyes and the white-blond eyebrows.

It was Lars Vindhook.

'Oh, it's you. Thought it was Room Service.'

The yawning voice belonged to Kelly. She stood in the doorway in a crumpled T-shirt that only just covered her torso. Her left hand clutched the collar of a bathrobe that trailed on the floor behind her.

'What the hell's been happening here?!'

Kelly pulled the bathrobe around her, hiding a decent pair of legs in the process. 'Don't worry, I got your money.' She moved across to the bed and closed Vindhook's visor. 'In fact, I got such a good deal, you'll feel like kissing me.' She caught Andrew's look. 'Just a figure of speech.'

'I hope so.' Andrew waved towards the inert body of the Reindeer Man. 'Why the suit?'

'Vindhook wanted me to sweeten the deal by letting him get inside my pants. I managed to persuade him that a mega-sex CD would deliver more than I ever could.'

Andrew laughed in disbelief. 'You . . . have got a sex CD?'

'Of course not.' Kelly hit the eject button on the wheeled console to eject the CD. 'I borrowed the one that was in your bag.'

154

Andrew caught the CD as she flipped it across the bed like a frisbee. It was the one Shalimar had given him. He was seized by a wave of helpless anger. 'This is outrageous!' he thundered. 'You let this unspeakable piece of blubber . . .' Words failed him. He waved the CD feebly. '. . . screw this . . . close . . . friend . . . on MY BED?! How could you DO such a thing?!'

Kelly raised her eyes to the ceiling. 'Oh, come on! Get real, Andi! And stop jumpin' on my bones! Nobody DID anything to anybody. It's just a bunch of electronically-induced sensations! This Shalimar, whoever she is, will never know! That's the great thing about sex CD's. You don't have to be there!'

Andrew had encountered something similar back on Earth while stationed near Hereford during his time with the Army. On a Saturday night, girls with a penchant for the military – known locally as the 'khaki-knicker brigade' – regularly drank themselves out of their skulls on Strongbow before being led away on stumbling feet for a quick knee-trembler between the empty beer kegs at the back of the pub.

The thought did not make him feel any better. In fact, the logic of her argument merely served to infuriate him even further. 'This is the last warning, Mandell. Just keep your sticky fingers out of my things and your snotty little nose out of my life!'

Kelly replied with a sulky shrug. 'I really don't know why you're so worked up.'

'This has nothing to do with logic!' raged Andrew. 'It's a matter of principle!' He lowered his voice and tried to sound reasonable. 'You have violated an intensely personal relationship.'

Kelly laughed. 'I can't believe this. You didn't really think you were sharing a private moment with this woman, did you? Nobody orders just ONE of these things. The recording studios only deal in multiples of ten!'

Realising his position was unsustainable, Andrew decided it was *his* turn to stand on his dignity. 'I don't want to talk about it. Just get this tub of lard out of here.'

Kelly used Andrew's bedside phone to call Room Service. A

155

few moments later, two men in white coveralls and baseball caps appeared at the door with a gurney. Their backs were emblazoned with the words 'LIVE OUT YOUR DREAMS WITH HAPPY-HOUR V-R. GROUP RATES AVAIL-ABLE'.

When they removed the helmet and video-visor and peeled off Vindhook's face mask, his lips were fixed in a frozen smile. The Happy-Hour technicians checked for vital life signs and gave reassuring nods.

'Must have OD'd' said one. 'What did he plug into? A slasher or a throat-gripper?'

'No, just a one-on-one steamer.'

'Is he going to pull through?' asked Andrew.

'He'd better,' said Kelly. 'His cash is locked in the hotel safe.'

Realising there was more to this situation than met the eye, the chief tekkie exchanged a wary glance with his colleague and coughed diplomatically. 'We'll, arrhmm – take him back to his room and give him a kick-start.'

'Good . . .'

'But since you weren't using one of our customer-friendly programmes, we will have to make an extra charge.'

'Put it on the tab,' said Andrew. He helped to heave the unconscious Vindhook off the bed onto the gurney then held the door open as the tekkies wheeled him and the VR power pack out of the suite. He leant his forehead against the door as a wave of tiredness hit him. Come on, laddo, his brain urged. Pull yourself together! He forced his sagging body upright, squared his shoulders and returned to the lounge. Kelly was pouring herself a nightcap from the bar even though dawn was leaking through the curtained windows.

'So . . . this currency swap. What was the deal?'

'I got you two for one.'

'Wha-a-a-att?! The UniBank rate was – '

'Yeah, I know, fifty to one. But he turned that down!'

'That's right! And the bank told him to take it down the street! Sheee! The least you could have done was screw him for twenty! Even a poxy ten to one would have been just about bearable. But no! We mustn't put the squeeze on poor old Lars! Huh! You must really get off on giving my money away!'

Kelly gave him one of those withering, pinched nostril looks you get when some well-intentioned person enters your airspace and discovers you have released an unusually virulent soft-slipper fart.

'Andi – are you always this shitty? I just saved you half a million Cords!'

With tiredness burning through every joint in his body, Andrew no longer had the energy to be unreasonable. 'You're right. Now I'll be able to pay your wages.'

Kelly brightened. 'Oh – so you liked the ship. Gonna buy it?'

'Half of it. In case you've forgotten, I have to play him for the other half.'

'Yeah, that's right. But you don't have to. You've got enough money in the bank to pay the full asking price.'

Andrew managed to quell a feeling of irritation. 'Maybe I have, but you and I both know that tub isn't worth three mil. And besides, I need the rest of that money for, y'know . . . emergencies.'

'So what game have you chosen?'

'Well, I was gonna play five card stud because someone once taught me how to fix the cards, but the crew told me Ganz-wayko's a master at dealing off the bottom.'

'Lucky you found that out.'

'Yeah, and what's more, he's rolled several guys with this stunt before.'

'So what're you going to do?'

'Borrow your idea.' Andrew took the glass from her hand, finished it off and handed it back. 'Gonna challenge him to a sudden death play-off! Mortal combat, best of five!'

'In VR suits? You can't be serious!'

Andrew paused in the doorway to his bedroom and ticked them off. 'Gladiators, Knights of Old, Duel at Dawn, Gun-fighter – '

Kelly dived into her bedroom and slammed the door behind her. Andrew stepped out and put his mouth close to one of the

157

fielded panels. ' – and Thunderstrike Leader versus The Red Eagle!'

☆   ☆   ☆

When Andrew woke, it was mid-afternoon. For a short while he lay back reflecting on everything that had happened since leaving the space station in Randy McRabbit's limo during the early part of the previous evening. It hardly seemed possible that he had not even been on Zhannandor for one whole thirty-hour day. It was as if someone had taken hold of his life and pressed the fast-forward button – and he had the cuts and bruises to prove it.

His mind threw up snapshots of the nightmare ride down the runway clinging to the hatch ladder as the armoured cab swerved in and out of position beneath him. The memory of how close he'd come to getting killed made him shudder. Andrew blanked it out, rolled off the bed onto his feet and took a long, leisurely shower.

Dressed and refreshed, he entered the lounge. A hotel waiter was setting out lunch on the sunlit terrace.

Kelly, as usual, was supervising. Catching sight of Andrew, she dismissed the waiter and poured out two glasses of chilled orange juice. Andrew felt there shouldn't have been oranges on the Rimworld, but then again, if the Atlanteans were using the same computer-controlled bio-genetic programmes they had been running on Earth, citrus fruits were bound to be in there somewhere.

Kelly handed Andrew a glass and raised hers in salute. 'To the Dragon Lady.' They touched glasses and drank. 'So . . . tonight's the night.'

'Yup.'

'You sure you wanna go through with this?'

'That depends on our friend Finnee. I called Sadie Moon's before I hit the sack and left a recorded videogram. I also called the desk downstairs. The night clerk told me the bar has several VR body-booths for clients who prefer to get their kicks down the wires.'

158

Kelly invited Andrew to sit down and take his pick of the food on offer. It didn't include any meat products. She drew the facing chair up to the table. 'Think you can take him?'

'No question about it. When you're on a six-month line patrol – '

Kelly swooped like a hawk. 'Pardon me, did you just say "line patrol"?'

'Uh, yeah, I, err – ' Conflicting voices filled Andrew's mind as he searched for an explanation. 'I was, err – confusing make-believe and reality. Ever since I woke up I've been thinking about this VR challenge and the interactive video games I've played. You know the kind of thing – "Space Patrol! You are the commander of a Navy cruiser tasked with keeping the space-lanes safe from marauding freebooters". It's all been, y'know – whirling around inside my brain and, uh – ' Andrew faltered, unsure of how he was doing. 'I think I should maybe stop talking and eat.'

'Good idea.' Kelly's eyes remained fastened on his. She offered him a plate of mixed salad. 'Know what I find fascinating about you? You're so full of contradictions.'

'Part of my charm,' said Andrew. He busied himself with the food.

'Yes, well, that's totally wasted on me,' said Kelly. 'What is it you're hiding, Andy? I mean we both know you're not Carta-haynyar. Just who exactly are you?'

Andrew chewed through his reply. 'I think we've had this conversation before. My answer's the same now as it was then.'

'But something's bothering you. I know that. Maybe I could help.'

'Really?' The idea made Andrew laugh. 'All you've done so far is help yourself to my money.'

Kelly did not share his amusement. 'That's not how it adds up for me. Okay, I booked into this suite three days before you arrived. In return, I got you out of that fight on the space station, nailed the bag-man, lined up this deal on the Dragon Lady, and got you the unlicensed currency you needed. From where I'm sitting, I'd say that balances the books.'

159

'You forgot to mention I'm also giving you a ride out of here.'

'We're not there yet.'

'No.' Andrew aimed his fork at her. 'And that's what's bothering me. If I manage to sell the idea of a VR play-off, and if I do win – and get my hands on the ship's papers – '

Kelly got there ahead of him. ' – will Finnee and his friends let us walk out of here in one piece?'

'You really irritate me, y'know that?'

'Why? Because I can guess what you're going to say? Or have you got a problem with smart women? Would you rather have me hanging wide-eyed on every word like that dumb-assed Lindy-Lou?'

Andrew carried on eating.

'I'm on your wavelength, Mister Whatever-your-real-name-is. We could make a really great team! You know I'm right. You just won't admit it.'

Andrew laid down his fork, put his elbows on the table and clasped his fingers. 'Let me level with you, Mandell. I don't have a problem with smart women. In fact I get along with them just fine. But I don't like being used or taken advantage of – and that's all I've had from you up to now. As for helping me, you only did that because it fitted in with your own game plan – and don't pretend you haven't got one.

'So let's cut all this "We're a team" crap. It doesn't fool me for one minute and what's more it doesn't make sense. How can you want to work with someone when – as you say – you don't know who they really are?!'

Kelly looked vaguely downcast. A bit like a child who has just had a finger-wagging reprimand for stealing cookies. 'You're right, I don't know exactly who you are – or what *your* game plan is. But I do know you're a man who likes cats.'

'Cats . . .?'

'Yours was called Kelly – remember?'

'Yes, she was,' said Andrew. It seemed a harmless admission. 'What colour?'

'White mainly, with one or two tan and black bits – including the tail. She just wandered in one day, gave my place the once-over and decided to adopt me.'

Kelly stood up. 'Thanks, Andi. That's the closest we've got to the real you. And I was right. We're gonna get along just fine.' She disappeared into her bedroom and returned a short while later with two yellow sleeveless jackets.

Andrew had last seen them when his baggage had been searched by Buena Vista security. Nothing had been said then, but because they had been packed alongside the weapons he had assumed they were flak-jackets.

'Try that on for size.' Kelly tossed him one of the jackets. The waist-length garment proved to be a lot heavier than it looked. It had a V-neck, a one-piece front and back with openings on each side, running down from the armpits. The stitched panels appeared to contain semi-rigid plates.

Andrew slipped the jacket over his head, closed the side openings using the velcro-type strips then pulled the V-straps between his legs and fastened them onto the two quick-release clips on the front.

Kelly, who was now strapped into the second jacket walked over to him and inspected the fit. 'Anyone would think it was made for you.' She pulled open a bulging pocket positioned close to Andrew's left armpit and pulled out a cable that was threaded through two arm straps and linked to a wide leather wrist strap inset with two heavy metal and plastic bracelets.

'This is the magic bit. Normally, you'd wear this under your shirt.' Using the velcro arm straps, Kelly positioned the cable down Andrew's left arm and fastened the bracelet round his wrist.

'Did you steal these from the Navy too?'

'Ask me no questions and I'll tell you no lies.' Kelly completed the installation of Andrew's jacket and quickly attached the lead and bracelet strap to her own left arm.

Something clicked in Andrew's mind. I've worn one of these before, he thought. But it has nothing to do with the equipment

161

simulations I went through with Shalimar or anything 'Carta-haynyar' experienced. It's as if there was someone else inside me. Another life with its own set of memories that is leaking into my own.

'Okay,' said Kelly. 'This is what's called a jump-suit. These bracelets have a twist action. The top one switches the suit on and generates an anti-gravity field. You adjust the amount of negative-g by twisting the bottom bracelet. To achieve zero-g you turn it fully away from you. For a percentage-g setting you twist it back towards you. See the calibrations?'

'Yeah.'

'So if you want to win the long jump, you could select, say . . . point-three-g, but if you really want to fly, you'd go for zero. Like this – '

Kelly hopped up onto Andrew's chair, gave her bracelet a sharp twist then threw herself forward like a diver going off the top board and immediately curled into a ball. Travelling across the lounge midway between floor and ceiling, she performed a triple somersault then uncurled in time to hit the far wall with her feet. Flexing her legs, she launched herself back towards Andrew, fists extended like Captain America.

Realising she was about to sail straight out of the open windows and off the terrace, Andrew threw up an arm. Kelly wrapped both hands around his wrist, swung around his arm like a clapper on a stick, launched her body at the side wall of the lounge, came off at an angle towards the ceiling, soft-landed on her hands then dropped feet first onto the carpet and cut the power.

'Neat, huh? Just the thing for getting out of tight corners.'

'Provided you remember to stay away from open windows.'

'Not a problem,' said Kelly. 'If you're on a tall building and need to reach the street, you just select zero-g, step off and make a controlled descent – '

' – by easing the g back on.'

'That's right. And if you're in a hurry, you can freefall most of the way then pull zero-g when you see the cracks in the pavement.'

Like sky-diving – but without a 'chute . . .

Andrew hoped she was joking. 'I think I'd need a few drinks before trying that.'

'Then we'd better open some bottles, Stanley, cos you've got four hours to push this suit to the limit. When we walk into Sadie Moon's tonight, it's gotta feel like a second skin.' She saw the look on Andrew's face. 'Uh, not that I'm trying to push you around. It's just a suggestion.'

'Good. Just so long as we know who's in charge here.'

'Andi,' said Kelly, 'that was never in doubt.'

Chapter Eleven

Kelly was at the controls of the aircab as it touched down on the roofpad above Sadie Moon's. Andrew looked through the windshield at the four huge bouncers guarding the entrance to the Starlight Lounge and the night club complex below.

'We could have a problem here on the way out.'

Kelly nodded. 'I'll park this on the roof across the street and meet you inside.' She watched him for a moment. 'Listen, it's not too late to call this off. We can always find another ship.'

'Not at this price.' Andrew psyched himself up. 'Okay, let's do it.' He stepped out of the cab carrying Vindhook's bag of money and walked past the bouncers and down the steps into the Starlight Lounge. The heavy background beat rising from the main dance floor below masked the sound of the jet downblast as the aircab headed for a safer perch.

Sadie Moon gave the skin on Andrew's rib cage the thumb and forefinger test as she ushered him into her private parlour. 'Glad to see you dumped the kid.'

Andrew grimaced. 'No such luck. She's parking the cab.'

Sadie pressed the point of her pelvis against the back of his thigh as they went through the door. 'Don't keep me waiting too long, sweetheart. I may go off the boil.'

Finnee Ganzwayko and Lindy-Lou rose to face him across a crimson baize-covered table. The red, black and dark mahogany decor was a glossy Hollywood version of an 1890's New Orleans bordello. The only false note were the neon-lit wall-mounted 'oil lamps'.

Andrew could not help wondering where all these ideas were

164

coming from. He glanced around and feigned admiration. 'Nice place.'

'If you think this is good, you'll love the bedroom,' said Sadie. 'Every piece is an authentic reproduction, made from real wood! Cost a fortune.' She ran a hand lovingly along the top edge of the sideboard. 'The surface is specially treated to attract a light layer of dust which can be instantly removed with a Mister Jiffy Electrostatic Easee-Wipe – now specially formulated to enhance the natural oils in the wood for that just-polished aroma.'

'You've been reading the brochure,' said Andrew.

'Is that the money?' asked Lindy-Lou.

'Yeah.' Andrew heaved the bulging Gladstone bag onto the table. It had a sealed airline-type tag looped around both handles. 'Two million Skandavian Trolls. Counted and certified by the Head Cashier of the Maracariba.'

Ganzwayko checked the seal then tore it off and opened the bag to reveal the tightly-packed wads of notes inside.

Lindy-Lou hugged his arm excitedly. 'Oh, Finnee! Ain't this just marvellous?! I can just see those cute li'l' fluff-balls spread out like a golden carpet, chirpin' and peckin' away, as far as the eye can see!'

Ganzwayko freed his arm, selected a wad of notes from the third layer down, riffled through it to check for blanks then dropped it on top of the others. 'Whaddya think, Sadie?'

Sadie Moon hefted the bag with the easy assurance of someone used to large amounts of money. 'Feels like two million to me. Got the ship's papers?'

Ganzwayko produced a slim wallet containing a mini-CD and passed it over to Andrew. Sadie opened the twin doors of a mahogany wall cabinet and invited him to make use of the reader unit and computer terminal hidden away inside. Andrew scanned the data on the screen relating to past and present ownerships. Ganzwayko and the two previous owners had been operating without the proper paperwork.

'No trading licence,' he observed.

'That's the other reason why she's going for a knockdown

165

price. If you win, you'll be able to afford one with the money you'll have saved. If you lose, it won't be a problem.'

'Fair enough.'

Andrew passed the wallet to Sadie. She unlocked a huge old-fashioned steel safe, stowed the 'ship's papers' and the money inside, shut the door and spun the tumblers.

The die was cast. Andrew put on a confident air. 'Okay. Best of five. You ready to play?'

Ganzwayko shrugged. 'If that's the way you want to do it. We could settle this a lot quicker with a game of cards. Face to face.' He leaned forward with an aggressive sneer. 'Or ain't you man enough for that?'

Andrew weighed up his chances of flooring this overweight beer-barrel and decided some bluff was called for. 'I'm certainly man enough to take you. Would you rather fight for the ship? Is that what you're sayin'? If so, listen carefully.' He kept his voice flat and businesslike. 'I'm going to hit you three times. The first blow will cause a great deal of excruciating pain. The second will leave you crippled for life. But don't worry about becoming a burden to your girlfriend because the third blow is going to kill you.'

Ganzwayko tried to stare Andrew out but couldn't hide the doubt that was now undermining his earlier belligerence. 'Nyaagghh! You're full of shit!'

'Think so?' Before anyone had time to blink, Andrew's arm drove his hand forward at incredible speed. It was a controlled punch that stopped with his fingertips less that two millimetres away from the base of Ganzwayko's nose. The trader didn't even have time to jerk his head back. He just stood there, open-mouthed, like everyone else except Kelly, who made a point of not being impressed.

Using the same, matter-of-fact tone, Andrew said: 'Had that blow landed with full force, it would have shattered the cartilege in your nose and driven a splinter of bone up into your brain. And you'd be dead. That was the demo. You wanna go for the real thing?'

Alarmed at the prospect of losing Ganzwayko and the

chicken farm, Lindy-Lou pulled him back out of range. 'Finnee! Just cool down now! Ain't no sense in windin' up dead just to prove you're a man. We made a fair bet and that's what we should stick to!'

'That's right,' said Sadie. 'Play it smart, Finnee. That temper of yours has brought you down too many times.'

Andrew breathed an inward sigh of relief. 'You were right about one thing. I *was* scared to play you at cards. Y'see I play a pretty good hand myself and with so much at stake, I'd've been tempted to cheat. But you might've caught me and that could have queered the deal. That's why I chose the suits. It's a straight fight – '

' – nobody gets killed. And win or lose, you wind up with a chicken farm.' Sadie patted them both on the shoulders. 'So shake and make up, guys.'

Ganzwayko offered a grudging hand and waved Lindy-Lou towards the door. Sadie pulled Andrew aside as he went to follow. 'The champagne's on ice and there's just two glasses on the tray.'

'Sounds great, Sadie. But I'm not there yet.'

'Doesn't matter. If you go down, come and cry on my shoulder. I'll have you back up in no time.'

☆   ☆   ☆

Kelly watched the VR booth attendant help Andrew into a head-to-toe electro-pneumatic body-sensor suit. Made of a lycra-type stretch material, it was covered with printed circuit patterns and wires that resembled the neural network of the human body. A moulded facepiece went over the the mouth and nose leaving only the eyes exposed.

The final touch was a space-age biker's helmet with a hinged video-visor. When lowered over the eyes, the last portion of uncovered flesh came into contact with soft pads fitted with sensors. His whole body was now wired to receive visual and tactile feedback generated by his opponent's moves and his own reactions and movements were translated into 3-D images within the game space.

167

On the other side of the changing room, another tekkie was wiring up Ganzwayko. Lindy-Lou – who Andrew had assessed as having the brains of a headless chicken – watched and worried from the sidelines, her slim hands dancing about like butterflies in a summer meadow.

Andrew's tekkie helped him step into a VR booth opposite the one Ganzwayko was due to occupy. They were streamlined versions of a fat Pharoah's coffin with a top-hinged lid. The couch inside was angled back at about fifteen degrees from the vertical. As Andrew lay back on the couch, the lining – which was decorated with printed circuit patterns matching those on his suit – inflated around his body. He glanced at Kelly and drew a smiling gesture of support.

The tekkie plugged connector wires into the crown of Andrew's helmet. 'Have you played this particular batch of games before, sir?'

Andrew heard himself say. 'Yeah, but in a float tank.'

Again that voice. What float tank? Where?

'Ah, yes, well – this is the latest hi-definition model with neural scan. It reads the nerve impulses sent by your brain to the muscles throughout your body – '

'And?'

' – it simulates the effect of the desired movement without you actually having to lift a finger.' The tekkie included Kelly in his explanation. 'With these violent games, people tend to thrash around a lot. With the old immersion system, customers were constantly breaking loose – usually when they tried to escape.'

' 'S only natural,' said Kelly. 'Nobody likes being killed.'

The tekkie poured on some oily reassurance. 'In this unit it is absolutely impossible to sustain any physical injury. With interactive feedback, you will feel the impact of all blows delivered by your opponent but any pain is purely imaginary.'

Andrew felt like a boxer listening to the last-minute advice of his trainer just before the bell signalled the first round. 'I'll try to remember that.'

Kelly leant in under the lid of the booth. 'I'm off to the

168

viewing theatre. See you after the show.' She blew Andrew a throwaway kiss and departed.

The tekkie ran a diagnostic check of the suit's connections. 'You will, however, experience fear and all the other reactions associated with danger. This increases the flow of adrenalin necessary to enhance the game situation but the programme is automatically terminated as the winner delivers the killing blow, cut, thrust, bullet or whatever.'

Andrew nodded and tried to compose his mind for the coming fray instead of wishing he was on another planet.

'Okay. We shall, of course, be monitoring your vital signs in case of any unforeseen emergency. So . . . visor down . . . last diagnostic check . . . good . . . closing up and going for countdown. You have twenty seconds before the first game commences!'

The lid came down and the top lining inflated, hugging Andrew's body like a second skin. He was now completely entombed yet there was no suffocating pressure on his body. He was floating in total darkness, breathing through the face-mask.

. . . 19 . . . 18 . . . 17 . . .

As the disembodied digits ticked away in front of him, he became aware that he was standing on a stone floor facing an iron-studded door. A blazing torch of pitch set in an iron wall-socket illuminated a man wearing a loincloth. The man was offering him a round shield and a short sword.

☆　　☆　　☆

The small viewing theatre seated thirty. As Kelly entered, the black screen carried the game logo for *Gladiators*. In the top right hand corner, red digits marked the countdown.

15 . . . 14 . . . 13 . . .

Lindy-Lou was seated two rows from the front with a clutch of Ganzwayko's bar cronies. Participants were given one free guest ticket. Anyone else had to pay the steep entrance fee, which was why there was only a handful of uncommitted spectators. Kelly sat near the end of the row occupied by Lindy-Lou and drew the angry glare she had been hoping for.

169

The excited roar from twenty thousand throats filled the viewing theatre as the darkened screen was suddenly flooded with sunlight and spectacle. Kelly gripped the arms of her seat.

The same blaze of sunlight left Andrew momentarily blinded as the iron-studded door was flung open and he was urged into an arena inspired by the film *Spartacus*. Forget the triangular trees and slab-sided images you've seen in present-day VR trips. This was crisper and clearer than 70mm Panavision.

Ganzwayko, also armed with a shield and short sword, was advancing into the arena from the opposite side. In the middle, on either side, two more guys in loincloths held spears with their points downwards. As Andrew and Ganzwayko reached the edge of a circle drawn in the ground, the two men plunged the spears vertically into the sand and ran for cover.

Andrew took a firmer grip on his sword hilt and advanced to meet Ganzwayko in the centre of the circle.

In the viewing theatre, the audience – thirsting for blood – were already cheering on their favourite. Kelly, finding herself alone, tried to compensate by yelling louder than anyone else – a move which triggered a stream of abuse from Lindy-Lou.

Out in the arena, Andrew's heart thumped wildly against his ribs. Neither he nor Ganzwayko were swordsmen. It was all brute force and wild, grunting swings. The heat of the sun, the smell of the sand, sweat and leather, the roar of the crowd beating against his ears, the ringing clash of steel as he parried blows with his sword and shield, made the experience both thrillingly and terrifyingly real.

Forget Street Fighter Two and the rest of the top-selling Earth-bound RPGs. This was light-years ahead of any game Andrew had ever played before. It was even better than being thrown into the futuristic and sinister world of cyberspace like the hero in *Tron*. This arena might be computer-generated but it was part of a totally believable dimension. Which, in all fairness, was only as it should be. Most of the RPGs available from CyberDreams, the electronic games shop frequented by Andrew in Catford, cost around fifty quid. Andrew's present VR jaunt was costing him twice that much every second. Not having read the small print, he didn't know that yet, nor that the bill would be doubled because he was down to pay for Ganzwayko as well.

Clang! Andrew parried a chopping blow from Ganzwayko. His opponent's sword slid down his blade and crashed against the hilt. As they came nose to nose, Ganzwayko put all his weight on his sword arm to force Andrew's blade down and tried to buffet Andrew with his shield. The bearded face was twisted into a hate-filled snarl. 'You're dead, Carta!'

Andrew resisted the pressure as long as he could then gave ground and side-stepped, causing Ganzwayko to stumble. But despite his bulk, the trader was quick on his feet. He whirled around, deflected Andrew's blow on his shield and came charging in, wielding his sword like a flail. Andrew used his shield to parry the blows raining down upon him but the force of the attack drove him backwards.

Suddenly there was a sharp, high-pitched metallic 'sping' as the blade of Ganzwayko's sword struck the iron rim of Andrew's shield and broke in two a few inches below the hilt.

In the viewing theatre, Kelly leapt to her feet, fists clenched in triumph. 'Yeah! Got 'im!'

The force of the impact drove Andrew's shield downwards, exposing his torso. Ganzwayko immediately hurled what was left of the sword into Andrew's face and rushed past him towards the nearest of the two spears that had been planted on the edge of the circle.

The crowd in the arena rose to their feet and roared.

Lindy-Lou and her friends were now on their feet too. 'Come on, Finnee! Quick! Quick! You can do it!'

Ganzwayko seemed to respond to the urging even though the combatants could only hear the sound effect generated within the game. He yanked the spear out of the sand and returned to the attack, teasing Andrew with short thrusts while he looked for an opening. Andrew used his blade to turn the spear aside and attempted to trap the shaft using the cut-out in his shield but Ganzwayko suddenly reversed his hold on the spear and,

171

using it like a quarterstaff, brought the blunt end down hard on Andrew's wrist. Thwack!!

The sword dropped to the ground.

Lindy-Lou and her supporters yelled with delight. 'That's it!' she shrieked. 'Now kill him! Kill him!'

But Ganzwayko was holding the spear the wrong way round. As he reversed the shaft to bring the point into play, Andrew scooped up some sand with his numbed fingers, flung it into the trader's eyes and raced towards the second spear, shifting the shield to his damaged right arm as he did so.

Ganzwayko drew back his powerful right arm and hurled the spear.

Thwwuunnkk! Andrew felt a hard, sharp object slam between his shoulderblades. The impact expelled all the air from his body. He looked down as he staggered forward. A blood-soaked spear-point was sticking out of his chest.

'Ughh-hhh!' The pain came as he attempted to breathe in. He toppled forward. The sand turned into an all enveloping darkness as it rushed up to meet him.

Kelly leapt to her feet. 'No-oh!'

'Ye-eh-eh-ehhh!!' screamed the Ganzwayko Supporters Club.

The screen went black. Up came the legend: 'Game Over'.

The small tv in Sadie Moon's parlour displayed the score: Ganzwayko 1 – Carta 0. Sadie rose and poured herself another drink. One down, four to go. The boy wasn't beaten yet. She settled down to watch the next contest.

Knights of Old.

The tented stands, set on the greensward below an imposing castle, were full of spectators. This was a smaller, more select crowd but they were all colourfully dressed in medieval finery. Pennants fluttered from tall, striped poles. Young blades with small waists and muscular thighs strutted up and down in doublets and hose drawing admiring glances from groups of young ladies in long, fur-trimmed, high-busted dresses. Their heads, shaven from ears to crown, were topped with hats like tall, thin ice cream cones.

Andrew, now dressed as a tournament knight, sat astride a caparisoned horse whose head and neck were protected by sculpted armour plate. He was positioned at one end of a long, brightly curtained fence. The pointed visor of his helmet was raised, allowing him a good view of Ganzwayko, who was being led into position at the opposite end and on the other side of the fence. Their first act would be to charge along this line in an attempt to unseat each other.

Both were armed with a long tilting lance, a sword, a flail-mace and a shield. Two trumpeters in front of the stands sounded a flourish. Andrew and Ganzwayko dropped their visors. The games marshal, mounted on a black charger opposite the halfway point, raised his sword then brought it down swiftly.

Andrew spurred his charger into a canter as Ganzwayko came thundering in from the other end.

Kelly watched from the edge of her seat.

Further along the row, Lindy-Lou yelled encouragement in a voice already tinged with triumph. 'C'mon, Finnee! Skewer him! Chop his arms off! Beat his brains out!'

The first clash of arms occurred right in front of the main tented enclosure. Both lances glanced off the shields. The impact caused the riders to rock and sway dangerously in their saddles but both remained seated. They turned at the end of the fence and galloped towards each other for a second time. Once again, Andrew diverted Ganzwayko's thrust but his own lance splintered as it struck the trader's shield. The force of the blow angled the shield towards instead of away from his body and, as the moment of collision ran its full course, the long stump of the broken lance ran off the shield, slammed into Ganzwayko's breastplate and lifted him clean out of the saddle.

Lindy-Lou shrieked as the trader hit the ground like a redundant fridge dropped from a tower block. 'Finnee! Fer Prog's sake, shift yer bugle! Quick! He's comin' for ya!'

Ganzwayko lay face up, his forearms waving feebly.

Throwing away his broken lance, Andrew rode to the end of

173

the fence, came back towards the fallen trader and dismounted. Pulling the flail mace from its loop on his saddle, Andrew cast aside his shield and strode towards Ganzwayko.

Kelly was back on her feet. 'C'mon! You've got him! You've got him!'

The trader, badly winded by the fall, was only halfway up on bent knees as Andrew struck the first hammer blow. Grasping the shaft of the mace with both hands, he whirled the heavy spiked ball around on the end of its chain then brought it down on the trader's helmet.

Ganzwayko just managed to deflect the blow with his shield. Sheltering behind it, he backed away unsteadily, trying to free his long sword from its scabbard. Andrew kept up the attack, raining a series of scything blows to the trader's head and body armour.

'Heyyy! That's not fair!' screeched Lindy-Lou.

The trader finally managed to draw his sword, but it was too late. Andrew landed a tremendous blow on the side of Ganz-wayko's helmet. The trader's body toppled backwards in a straight line like a felled tree. Andrew seized the sword from his unresisting hand and stepped astride his opponent. Grasping the hilt with both hands, he raised it high in the air then buried the point in Ganzwayko's chest.

'Yeah! That's *right*!' roared Kelly. The screen went black and signalled 'Game Over'. She turned and gave the stricken bimbolino a one-finger salute.

Up in Sadie's parlour, the score on the tv screen read: Ganzwayko 1 – Carta 1. 'That's better, Andi. Much better . . .' Sadie's well-upholstered body lay like the dressed version of the Naked Maja on an equally sumptuous red plush velvet chaise-longue. The hand which, in the stripped-down portrait, care-fully covered the *mons veneris*, nursed a drink resting on the same spot.

Up came a new logo: *Duel at Dawn*. The titles wiped to reveal a clearing in a wood at dawn. The ground was still shrouded with patches of mist. It was the classic setting in which everyone was wearing clothes that could have come from late 18th century Europe. In the centre of the picture, Andrew and Ganzwayko received their instructions from a referee.

Both combatants wore loose white shirts with frilly cuffs, knee-breeches and boots. Their hair was tied at the nape of the neck with a black bow. Everyone else – the referee, the two pairs of seconds, the doctor, with his first aid bag, wore long black topcoats with high collars and tricorn hats. In the background, amongst the trees, two horse-drawn coaches stood half buried in the drifting mist.

The seconds, who were standing on either side of the referee, raised the lids of the weapon cases they were holding. Andrew and Ganzwayko each lifted out a rapier and a long stiletto with a cross-hilt. Both men stepped back and sliced the air with the rapier to get the feel of the blade.

Kelly, who hated cold steel, covered her face and peeked through her fingers as the two men took up their positions and assumed a fighting stance. The referee raised a white hand-kerchief and let it drop.

Andrew and Ganzwayko immediately set about each other with blood-curdling cries, slashing and thrusting as they circled round, looking for an opening. Having lost the last game, the trader was eager to regain the lead but neither he nor Andrew was any better at fighting with rapiers than they were with swords. Andrew was lighter on his feet, and quick to parry the trader's attacks but when they locked swords and stilettos, Ganzwayko's superior weight threatened to throw his opponent off-balance. It was like trying to stop a bull leaving his pen by pressing on his horns.

Lindy-Lou leapt to her feet as they locked weapons and came nose to nose. 'Trip him up! Finnee! Kick his feet away!'

The trader, as if hearing this, attempted to hook a foot round Andrew's ankle.

'Hey!' cried Kelly. 'That's not allowed.'

'Shyadd-upp!' yelled Lindy. 'He can do what he wants!'

Andrew leapt clear, dodged nimbly behind a tree to avoid another rushing attack, but missed his footing. He felt a searing jab of pain as his dagger arm was sliced open above the elbow.

175

Ganzwayko's supporters rose as one. 'Yeah-heh-hehhh!'

The fighting became savage as both men attacked with mounting desperation. Andrew's left arm hung limply in its blood-soaked sleeve. Baring his teeth, he threw caution to the wind and launched one last ferocious attack –

'Oww-ohh! Holee Molee!' Lindy-Lou clawed at her face. Around her, Ganzwayko's friends sat thunderstruck.

Even Kelly blanched.

Andrew's rapier was buried in the base of the trader's throat. With his eyes popping, and blood bubbling out of his mouth, Ganzwayko clawed at the rapier with trembling fingers.

Game over. Ganzwayko 1 – Carta 2.

Kelly dropped her head into her hands. The coup de grace delivered to the anonymous armoured knight had been bereft of blood and therefore bearable but this was far too gruesome.

What she really meant was it was too real. Like everyone else she had forgotten she was watching lifeless images; mathematical models, made up of coloured dots produced by electron beams.

'Oh, Andi, please!' she pleaded, somehow believing that her words could reach him. 'Win the next one and let's get out of here!'

Up in the red plush and black velvet parlour, Sadie was also addressing the screen. 'Beautiful. Just one more and you're home and dry!'

Up came the fourth logo. *Gunfighter*. It was accompanied by a few bars from a mournful harmonica. The black faded from the screen revealing shades of pale yellow, ochre, brown and bleached white timbers.

Kelly found herself looking down a short deserted street. Both sides were lined with two storied wooden buildings with raised sidewalks. Some had verandahs and side access stairs. The afternoon sun cast long shadows from left to right. Dust swirled across the unmade street. Tumbleweed rolled. Beyond the far end of the street was parched open hill country.

Andrew and Ganzwayko stood at opposite ends of the street. Both were dressed in wide brimmed hats and long open coats, shirt, trousers, leather chaps and spurred boots and they were similarly armed with two six-guns and a pump-action rifle.

They took up their opening positions, feet astride, and worked the pump action of the rifle to put a bullet into the chamber.

The tension in the viewing theatre became almost palpable. Everyone jerked back in their seats as a dog burst out of a building halfway down the street. Barking wildly, he ran to the other side and disappeared down an alleyway.

It was the signal for combat to begin.

Ganzwayko advanced, firing his rifle from the hip. Andrew dived to the ground and rolled sideways. The dirt kicked up around him but he reached the cover of the sidewalk of the end building without being hit. He popped up and took aim at Ganzwayko. The trader was already running for cover, firing wildly as he went.

Andrew's bullets blew chips of wood off the corner of a building on the left hand side of the street as Ganzwayko dived behind it.

Jumping up onto the sidewalk, Andrew ran past the first building then ducked into the alleyway. He checked the other side of the street but there was no sign of any movement. Entering the second building through a side door, he went through to the front room and glanced cautiously out of a ground floor window. The clapboard building was sparsely furnished. A few chairs, tables, stairs but otherwise devoid of life or any objects that might indicate the taste or occupation of the owners. But there weren't any. The whole street was like a film set. Just like the brick and concrete estates on which the British Army practised house-to-house fighting, these structures existed to serve the game that was now in progress.

From the cover of an alleyway, Finnee Ganzwayko saw Andrew emerge onto the roof of the second building. The trader pulled his rifle into his shoulder but Andrew drew back back from the front edge of the building, depriving him of a clear shot. A second or two later, he saw Andrew leap across the narrow alleyway onto the third building and dive out of sight

177

behind the signboard that ran along the frontage. The faded letters on the board read: 'General Store'.

Ganzwayko held his fire. Rather than loose off a shot, it was better that Carta should think he had not been seen.

On the roof of the third building, Andrew raised the skylight and found a ladder placed obligingly beneath. He started down the ladder then saw a stick lying on the roof. Pausing with his head and shoulders out of the skylight, Andrew laid down his rifle, put his hat on the stick and propped it up behind the signboard. Satisfied with the effect, he continued down the ladder – leaving his rifle behind.

Across the street, Ganzwayko grinned and shook his head. To think anyone would fall for such a pathetic ruse. Crouching low, he ran across the street into the alleyway Andrew had just jumped over and opened the side door of the store with infinite care.

Reaching the bottom of the ladder, Andrew surveyed the empty room. Sunlight rayed through the louvred shutters at the front of the building. Motes of dust, disturbed by his entry, drifted lazily through the air, sparkling briefly as they caught the light.

The rifle, thought Andrew. Bugger. I've left it on the roof. As he set foot on the ladder, he heard the creak of floorboards below. He moved swiftly back onto the roof, closed the skylight and recovered his rifle.

Ganzwayko, hearing movement above, exited into the alley on the other side of the store and started up the outside stairs – it being the only way to reach the upper floor. On the way up he kept his eyes and rifle aimed towards the roof just in case Andrew popped into view. Reaching the small outside landing without incident, he used the barrel of his rifle to nudge the door open then took cover against the outside wall and listened.

Silence. He peeked round the edge of the doorway then stepped boldly inside, fanning the room with his rifle. Empty – except for a ladder leading to a skylight. Around it, a thin raised cloud of dust was slowly settling.

'C'mon, Finnee!' yelled Lindy-Lou. You've got him. He's on the roof!'

Once again it was as if the trader could hear the shouts of encouragement. He stared upwards, then carefully laid down his rifle and drew his two six-guns.

Kelly gestured angrily towards the screen. 'Heyy! What is this?!' she demanded. It was Lindy-Lou's turn to deliver a triumphant one-finger salute.

Bam! Bam! Bam-bam-bam! Ganzwayko blazed away with both barrels, shooting a random pattern of holes in the roof. Splinters of wood and dust rained down as the deafening fusillade continued.

The store had a balcony running along the front, below the upper windows. Covered by the noise Ganzwayko was making, Andrew lowered himself and his rifle from the roof onto the side rail then dropped onto the balcony. Chambering another bullet, he ducked under the first shuttered window and moved stealthily towards the twin louvred access doors set in the centre of the balcony.

Inside the room, Ganzwayko was trying to decide whether to go up onto the roof when the striped pattern of sunlight on the floor changed to reveal Andrew's shadow.

The trader spun round and aimed his six-guns at the balcony doors, fingers tightening on the triggers as Andrew, his back to the street, leant against the front rail, kicked the door open and prepared to fire from the hip.

BLAM! Ganzwayko's bullet left the barrel a split-second before Andrew fired, hitting him in the left shoulder. The impact twisted him sideways, sending his own shot wide, and knocked him head first over the balcony.

Kelly, watching the outside view of the action, gnawed her clenched fingers as Andrew hit the ground and lay there unmoving. The Ganzwayko Supporters Club loosed a raucous cheer.

The trader ran onto the balcony and looked over the rail. The crumpled figure of his opponent lay directly below him. The left shoulder of his coat was soaked with blood. Ganzwayko aimed both guns at Andrew's chest and fired. Two dull clicks. Both revolvers were empty. Cursing loudly, he ran inside to fetch his rifle.

Kelly stopped biting her fingers and shouted: 'Quick, Andi! Get up! Please! DO something!'

'Nyahh!' jeered Lindy-Lou. 'He's finished! He's finished!'

Ganzwayko came back and pointed his rifle down over the rail. The street below was empty. Andrew had vanished, leaving behind a bloodstained patch of sand. Swearing even more loudly than before, the trader stepped back inside the room and considered his next move.

Blam! A bullet fired from below blew a hole close to his foot then brought down a shower of dust from the ceiling. The trader leapt to one side. Blam! A second bullet shot up through the floor, missing him by a whisker.

'Mangy shite-sucker!' roared Ganzwayko.

Down on the ground floor, using his good arm, Andrew continued to fire at the ceiling. The cloud of dust shaken loose every time the trader's boots hit the floor gave a good guide to his position. Emptying the first six-gun, Andrew went onto the second.

Upstairs, Ganzywako – trying to avoid getting a bullet up the ass – was performing a comic ballet reminiscent of the hippo-potami in Disney's *Fantasia*. Unable to endure it any longer, he seized a heavy wooden chair and hurled it through one of the back windows.

Andrew, who had slipped off his gunbelt to reload his revolvers more quickly, heard the window break and saw something fall past the ground floor window. He ran towards the back door. Outside lay the wrecked chair. Now it was his turn to curse. He heard the sound of someone heavy leaping down the outside stairs. He ran to the corner of the building in time to see Ganzwayko running out of the alleyway and across the street with his rifle. Andrew raised his six-gun and fired twice. The second bullet hit the trader in the thigh. He staggered then ran on, limping badly. Andrew fired again. Click! He had only had time to load two bullets. Shit! The other gun was still lying empty on the table inside along with the belt of spare ammo.

180

Andrew ran back in, holstered both guns, grabbed his rifle and came back into the alley. Ganzwayko had vanished. Bumholes and buggeration! Deciding to get off the street, he entered the side door of the fourth building whose roof sign announced it to be a saloon and boarding house.

The street had been designed so that the alleyways between the buildings on either side were not directly aligned. Hidden behind an outside stair, Ganzwayko saw Andrew slip into the side door of the saloon. He limped around the back of the next building and reached the alleyway which was directly opposite the swing entrance doors of the saloon. In the alleyway, a covered wagon was parked close to the wall with its empty shafts pointing towards him. Ganzwayko sneaked up to the wagon and hauled himself up as best he could into the driver's seat. The front canvas flaps were closed. Peeking through the flaps, Ganzwayko saw that the back flaps were also closed. The interior of the wagon contained some farm implements and sacks of provisions but there was enough space to lie down amongst them. Two barrels, one of them labelled 'Molasses', were tied to the lowered backboard.

Ganzwayko stayed on the seat while he reloaded both six-guns and his pump-action rifle, then eased through the canvas flaps, laid himself down on the floor of the wagon and pulled a sack of flour across in front of him make a rest for his rifle. Through the five inch gap between the barrels, he was able to see the entire building, and their circular shape allowed him a good field of fire.

All he had to do was wait for Carta to show himself.

Andrew moved cautiously to the side of one of the shuttered ground floor windows and surveyed the opposite side of the street. Seeing nothing, he ducked under the sill and looked again from the other side. His gaze fell upon the covered wagon parked in the alley with two barrels roped to the lowered backboard. The afternoon sun streaming through the slats was hot on his face. His throat was dry with the dust and the tension. He wiped his sweaty hands on his shirt to get a better grip on the rifle.

The oppressive silence was broken by the sudden buzz of an

181

insect close to his head. Andrew swatted it away and, as he followed its zigzag flight across the room, he saw something he hadn't noticed before. A spyglass – lying on one of the saloon tables.

Andrew set down his rifle and picked up the spyglass. Standing back from the shuttered window, he trained it across the street and brought the buildings opposite into focus. The blurred slats across the window reduced his view to a narrow horizontal slice but, by altering his standpoint, he was still able to scan the façades of the buildings opposite.

No movement could be detected at any of the windows. He returned to the covered wagon and surveyed it inch by inch. Bingo. A tiny metallic glint revealed the muzzle of a pump action rifle lying between the two barrels roped to the backboard. The contents of the barrel on the left were unidentified. The barrel on the right was more informative. Red capital letters that Ganzwayko could not see from inside the wagon spelled out the word 'DYNAMITE'.

Andrew set down the spyglass, moved a table closer to the window, knelt down, rested his elbows on the tabletop, drew a bead on the barrel through the window slats and fired –

Kelly leapt to her feet as the viewing theatre was filled with the sound of a thunderous explosion. 'Yeah! Three in a row! That's it!

Cheers from the uncommitted portion of the audience drowned out the protests of Ganzwayko's supporters.

A short while later, when Andrew and a disgruntled Ganzwayko had changed back out of their sensor suits, two club-hostesses escorted them to Sadie Moon's private parlour. A handful of her girls and some male associates had already got the celebrations underway.

'Congratulations,' said Kelly. 'For a moment there you had me worried.'

'Me too,' added Sadie. 'When you went over that balcony I thought it was gonna go right to the wire.'

Andrew nodded. 'Yeah, he almost had me.' He took the drink Kelly offered him. Sadie placed the 'ship's papers' in his other hand.

'Don't lose 'em.'

'If I do, it won't be in a game of chance!'

Sadie took the bag of money from the safe and placed it on the table in front of Ganzwayko. 'Two million Trolls. Better luck next time.'

The trader was clearly very unhappy about losing. The blonde bimbolino was seething.

'Cheer up, Finnee,' laughed one of his cronies from the viewing theatre. 'That's more'n twice what that old wreck is worth!'

Andrew turned to Kelly. 'This always happens to me. The minute I pay for something, some smart-ass always comes out with a line like that.' He drained his glass. 'Let's go.'

Ganzwayko grabbed Andrew's arm. 'Hey! Carta! C'mon. We can't let it go like this. Five hands of stud poker. Winner takes the money *and* the ship. Whaddya say?'

'It's a tempting offer but . . .' Andrew shrugged. 'I think I'd better quit while I'm ahead.'

'Hold on! You can't walk out on me! I'm offering you a chance to scoop the pool!'

'Game's over, Finnee. I won. You lost. End of story.' Andrew steered Kelly towards the door.

Sadie stepped into their path. 'Where you going, sweetheart? I thought you and me had a little private celebration lined up.'

'We still have,' said Andrew. 'I'll be back as soon as I've put the kid to bed.' He planted a suggestive kiss on Sadie's cheek.

She took the opportunity to size up his tool kit with a practised hand and whispered in his ear. 'Don't bother, big boy. You got fifteen minutes to dump the dwarf then I'm coming over to the Maracariba to melt your wires.'

Chapter Twelve

Andrew and Kelly left Sadie Moon's parlour and made their way downstairs. The ground floor bars and dance floors were even more crowded and noisier than before.

'The cab's parked just across the street.' Kelly glanced over her shoulder. 'Uh-oh . . . don't look now but we're being followed.'

Finnee Ganzwayko and three of his drinking friends elbowed their way through the crowd and caught up with them. The trader grabbed Andrew by the shoulder and pulled him round face to face.

'Whassamatter? You frightened of losing a real game?!'

'Yeah,' chimed one of the bar-flies. 'That VR shit is for dildoes!'

Andrew ignored the provocation and calmly assessed his chances. Ganzwayko and his friends were all tanked to the gills but they looked mean, aggressive and there were four of them. He mentally prepared himself to strike the first blow.

'A return match. That's all I'm asking for,' insisted Ganzwayko. 'You may be ace at shuffling the deck but I can take you anytime!'

'Too late, Finnee. You had your chance and you muffed it. Now get outta my face.'

A second bar-fly slammed the palm of his hand into Andrew's chest. 'You don't seem to be listening, friend!'

'On the contrary. It's you guys who don't seem to be getting the message.'

'This is getting tiresome,' said Kelly. She bent the second bar-fly in two with an eye-popping punch in the balls.

184

'Oh, so that's how you wanna play it!' roared Ganzwayko. Before he or the three other men could make a move, two huge bouncers surged out of left field and grabbed all four by the collar.

'That's enough. Cool it!' growled one of the bouncers. He and his companion shook the trader and his friends till their teeth rattled, then let them go.

Andrew looked up towards the central balcony. Sadie Moon was standing at the crowded rail. She held up five fingers three times then blew him a kiss. It was time to make a hasty exit.

Ganzwayko, now alone, followed them through the crowd towards the main entrance door. 'Carta! No offence, huh? That guy was drunk. Out of line. Can we talk about this?'

Andrew brushed the trader aside. A jostling crowd of new thrillseekers pushed between them. He and Kelly were just a few yards from the door when a blunt-featured guy in a black leather jacket and a Wild Ones peaked cap was let through by the bouncers outside.

Andrew – without understanding why – suddenly froze. He knew this man. But from where?

Kelly looked back and found they had become separated. 'What's the matter?'

Andrew pulled her towards him. 'Is there another way out of here?'

She eyed him, then surveyed the crowd around them. 'Your past catching up with you?'

'I'm not sure. It's that guy by the door. Black peaked cap – '

'Studded leather jacket? Coming this way?'

'Yeah. I've got a feeling he's bad news.'

'Head for the roof. I'll get the cab. If you hit trouble, use the suit.' Kelly slipped away towards the main entrance, passing close to the mystery man on her way out.

Andrew turned back and began to work his way through the crowd towards the escalator that led to the upper levels. A hand fell on his shoulder. It was Ganzwayko.

'Ah, great. You changed your mind! I knew you couldn't walk away without taking a crack at that two mil!'

185

'The only thing I'm liable to take a crack at is you,' said Andrew.

As he started to move towards the stairs, Ganzwayako looked past him and broke into a broad smile. 'Hammerhead! Great to see you! When d'you get off the rock?'

'Three months ago. Taken me that long to get here.'

Andrew eased away as casually as he could. Out of the corner of his eye he saw Ganzwayko welcome the returnee with a bear-hug.

'We gotta celebrate, man! Plannin' to stay?'

'No. Lookin' for a fast ride. Still got your ship?'

'Just sold her. But your luck's in. The new captain's right here! Follow me!' Ganzwayko bulldozed his way through the crowd with Hammerhead on his heels. 'Carta! Hey! Carta! Slow down! Got someone here you oughta meet!'

Andrew heard his shouted name but the rest of the message was lost in the general hubbub. He was only a few steps away from the staircase when the trader's heavy hand fell on his shoulder.

'Carta!'

Shit . . . Only thing to do now was brazen it out. But better be safe than sorry. Andrew powered up the jump-suit and turned to face his nemesis. He even knew the man's name now. It was all coming back – memories of another life, threatening to engulf his own.

Ganzwayko made the intros. 'Meet Hammerhead. A good friend of mine. He's just done ten on Alcazar. Andi Carta, owner of The Dragon – '

Their eyes met.

'Andi Carta . . .?' In less than a second, Hammerhead's expression went up through the gears, changing from quizzical appraisal to puzzled recognition, stunned disbelief then turbo-charged anger. He threw out an accusing finger. 'Know who this is?! Daniel Kinsharadeen! This is the rat-fucker who put me away!'

Ganzwayko's jaw dropped. 'Whaa-a-aat?!'

'He's NAVY!' roared Hammerhead.

Ganzwayko appealed to the people nearby. 'Hear that?! The Navy's here! Get him!'

With the music still blasting, not everybody got the message but those that did turned towards Andrew with threatening expressions. He wasted no time. Selecting zero-g on the wrist band, he flexed his knees and performed an amazing back-flip that lifted him up out of the crowd and onto a side balcony above a bar. He landed on his feet but fell back into the arms of four women who were unaware of the reason for the fracas below.

Ganzwayko, Hammerhead and the crowd around them stared at the balcony, jaws agape.

'How in the name of Prog . . .?!'

'The scuzz-ball's got a G-suit!' yelled Hammerhead.

Spotting two people he knew, Ganzwayko shouted up at the balcony. 'Barnee! Gill! Stop that guy!'

The word had spread quickly and now the crowd around Ganzwayko began to chant, pointing at Andrew on the beat. 'NAY-VEE! NAY-VEE! NAY-VEE!'

More and more people joined in. The music faltered and died as the chanting grew in volume. *'Nay-vee! Nay-vee! Nay-vee!'*

Sadie Moon, drawn from her office by the chanting, came out onto the balcony opposite Andrew and watched with mixed feelings as Barney and Gill moved in to make the grab.

Andrew hopped up onto the balcony rail then leapt off towards the right, aiming for the top of the stairway.

Ganzwayko and Hammerhead were already running up the stairs and a knot of men were converging at the top to form a reception committee. But Andrew had not planned on landing. Two slim pillars on either side of the stairway supported the second floor balcony above. Borrowing Kelly's hotel room manoeuvre, Andrew twisted his body sideways in flight, grabbed one of the pillars with both hands, swung around it – eluding the outstretched hands that attempted to seize him from below – and launched himself feet first towards one of the high roof beams that spanned the central well of the building.

Andrew landed safely then realised he had boxed himself in.

187

There was nowhere to go but down. He stood on the beam and steadied himself against one of the uprights. The crowd below was now roaring like an angry lynch mob.

From a second floor balcony, a rope was thrown over the far end of the roof beam and secured. A man started to climb up it. The same thing was happening at the other end of the beam. Andrew kicked the rope off before it was made secure but at the far end the first climber was within arm's length of the beam and others were waiting to follow.

Realising he had to move, Andrew searched again for a way out. There was a tall window off to one side, but from where he was standing, the angle of approach was too narrow to be sure of crashing through it. If he just drifted across, there was not enough framework to hang onto while he tried to kick his way out. The second roof beam offered a better angle – providing the window wasn't shatterproof. It would mean aiming high, then pulling full-g to give him the weight needed to crash through like a projectile then –

No! Too late! A four-man reception committee was clambering onto the second beam!

Ba-boomm-kerrasshh!! The bloodthirsty chanting turned to shouts and screams of panic as the tall window and part of the surrounding wall exploded inwards causing everyone below to duck and run for cover. It was Kelly at the wheel of the aircab, hoverjets roaring. She spun the cab around on its own axis, brought it level with the roof beam and popped open the passenger door.

Andrew dived headfirst into the cab as his pursuers, teetering nervously on the roof beam, made a last, half-hearted grab. The door was still open and his nose was still on the floor carpet as they flew back out of the club and shot between the buildings opposite.

'Watch your feet!' Kelly hit the button to close the cab door.

Andrew untangled himself and slid into the seat. 'You're crazy, y'know that?!'

'Yeah!' laughed Kelly. 'It's the kind of thing they do in the movies. An' you know what? It feels great!'

Andrew reached out to pick up a headset.

'I already called the ship and told 'em we were on our way.'

Andrew bottled his annoyance. 'You speak to Pug?'

'Yeah. Said they'd hit a few problems but hoped to have them sorted by the time we got there and . . . oh, yeah – there's the fuel to pay for plus a few other bits and pieces.'

'Steaming thundermugs! How long's that gonna take? That Finnee Ganzwayko's got half the town out for my blood! And after the way we blew out of Sadie's, they're gonna be comin' after us!'

Kelly fluttered a calming hand. 'Cool down. There are only ten aircabs in town and we've got one of them. There's another one in use, and I booked out the other eight and arranged for them to be sent on auto-pilot to Boot City Field.'

Andrew tried to sound gracious. 'That's pretty clever. When did you arrange all this?'

'I put in a call to the Maracariba when I parked the cab opposite Sadie Moon's.'

'So who's footing the bill?'

'You are.'

'But we checked out of the hotel before we came here.'

'I know. I gave them the PAN-code from your ID card. The charge will be automatically debited to your bank account.'

Andrew clawed the air. 'Kelly! You're doing it *Again*!!'

'Oh, don't fuss! You can afford it – and you said yourself it was a neat idea. If they're gonna come after you, it'll have to be by road. With luck we'll be away by then. But it will mean taking off without running the full pre-flight checks. Could be dangerous.'

'Not any more dangerous than staying here.'

Kelly weighed him up. 'Don't you think you may be over-reacting? I know Ganzwayko's a bad loser but you won the ship fair and square. You saw the way Sadie sent in her bouncers. With her on your side, what's he gonna do?'

'Question is what is *she* gonna do! I've just stood her up on a hot promise and you just wrecked her club!'

'Oh, for Prog's sake! Stop woozzing! I broke a window saving your ass! Things were out of control in there!'

189

'Yeah, but – '

'There are no "buts", Andi. This is Boot City. People torch bars just for serving warm beer!'

'Okay, but suppose they call the spaceport and ask 'em to block the take-off?'

'Of a paying customer? You kidding? In the past eight months they haven't sold enough rocket fuel to start a barbecue and you just put your name down for a hundred and twenty-five thousand litres! Stop you? Huh! Boot City Field's the only part of this dung heap that plays it straight. If word got round that they were seizing ships from people with money, no one would ever land here again!'

'Hadn't thought of it that way . . .'

Realising he was still plagued by guilt, Kelly said, 'If you're still losing sleep a week from now, ask her to send you the bill.'

Andrew thought of the look he had seen on Sadie's face when she came out on the balcony to find the crowd baying for his blood. 'It's a little more complicated than that.'

'Knowing you, it would be.'

'That guy I was trying to avoid . . .'

'The black leather stud?'

'Yeah. He seems to have gotten me mixed up with someone who sent him down for ten on Alcazar.' Andrew saw that hawk-like look again. 'Simple case of mistaken identity, I guess.'

'Seems a strange sort of mistake to make. Ten on the Rock is a pretty indelible experience. I know *I'd* never forget the person who put me there.'

Andrew shrugged. 'What can I tell you? It happens.'

Kelly didn't look convinced. Why should she be? He hadn't even convinced himself. She and Buena Vista had both turned up the Navy connection. And now Hammerhead had supplied a name.

Daniel Kinsharadeen. *Commander* Daniel Kinsharadeen. His alias, 'Andiamo Cartahaynyar', had just been a blind – to mislead him as well as everyone else. This 'Daniel' was the 'real' false persona that Parnassus intended him to assume. But further down the line. Meeting Hammerhead had been not been

190

part of the game plan. But if not now, when? And what diabolical course was he expected to follow? The Fat Man had some explaining to do.

Kelly's voice broke into his reverie. 'So who exactly did he think you were?'

'Just some guy in the Navy. He didn't say who, and . . .' Andrew shrugged again. '. . . I didn't wait to get the full story.'

'And the name of the con?'

The question seemed harmless enough. 'Hammerhead.'

☆   ☆   ☆

As they approached the field, another aircab rose from the roof of the terminal building and headed back towards Boot City. Andrew aimed a silent question at Kelly and was answered with a non-committal shrug. She set the aircab down near the topside hatch. Pug and Aramitz came out and helped them transfer their luggage into the ship.

'Why isn't she up and running?' demanded Andrew.

'We're still taking on fuel,' said Pug. 'Two of their pumps broke down. They didn't have any back-ups. Had to take 'em off-line to repair 'em. I sent Chilli and Gumbo down to help. But it's all fixed now.'

'Well, start the pre-ignition sequence and run the checks for an emergency take-off. Your old pal Finnee is on my tail and breathin' fire.'

'Always was a bad loser.'

'It's worse than that but now's not the time.' He slapped Pug on the shoulder. 'Okay. I just need to square the account and then we're outta here.'

Pug nodded and shambled off. Andrew would have preferred to have seen him depart at the double but then, this was the mate of a beat-up old trader, not a Navy frigate.

Navy frigate? What a strange slip of the mind! He *meant* to say to himself 'this wasn't the Army'.

He banished the confusion with a quick shake of the head and collared Kelly. 'I'm going over to the terminal.'

'Want me to steady your hand?'

191

'No. Send back the cab on autopilot then get up on the bridge and punch up a flight trajectory that'll put us into docking orbit. And don't ask Tarqueen to help. Apparently he's a total bummer at astro-navigation'

'Are we going into Buena Vista?'

'I won't know that until I make contact with a certain party.'

'Okay. Just so long as you're not gonna hand me over to Security.'

Andrew frowned. 'You just saved my life. What kind of a person d'you think I am?'

'Interesting question,' said Kelly. 'I'd say the jury's still out on that one.'

'That's really hurtful.' Andrew set off along the aerial walkway that led from The Dragon Lady to the terminal building.

Kelly cupped her hands. 'Wait till you get to Accounts! Then you'll know what real pain is!'

☆ ☆ ☆

From the duty clerk manning the customer accounts desk in the terminal, Andrew learned that, after applying the bulk discount rate, the rocket fuel ran out at four Cords a litre. Which meant one hundred and twenty-five thousand was going to cost a cool half million. Andrew handed over his remaining cash cards. Fortunately, he'd paid the hotel bill by bank debit.

'And then there's the parking and service fees,' said the clerk. 'I'll just total up the items.' He returned to his computer terminal and began to play a cash sonata on the keyboard.

That was the good thing about *Star Trek*, thought Andrew. Nobody ever mentioned mundane things like money. No Trekkie ever wondered how much Captain Kirk pulled down per year, or what it cost to keep the Enterprise running.

Science fiction was a never-never land where heroes wrestled with intriguing metaphysical concepts, crossed the galactic deeps in the twinkling of an eye, ranged back and forth in time, discovered magical worlds that could only be entered by crawling into a range of domestic appliances, were challenged by haughty female warriors with bejewelled breasts and armour-plated pubes, fought incredibly ferocious alien creatures of every shape and hue (and which, almost always, had one fatal weak point), encountered talking trees, walking sideboards, flying dragons, wise old stones, magic swords, enchanted forests, wizards, witches, benign robots, erratic androids, terminally murderous killing-machines and psychopaths bent on destroying the universe (but who, for some reason, always surround themselves with an army of incompetents), met, conversed with and outsmarted Death in all his many guises yet *never ever ran across an accountant.*

As if on cue, the clerk said: 'Let's see . . . twenty-three weeks and three days at long term rate . . . plus provisioning . . . and departure tax . . . that's . . .' He tapped a few more keys. 'Eighty-four point seven five K.'

Andrew was pleased to have no real notion of what a Cord was worth. It was like playing with Monopoly money. Even so, it still sounded like a fortune. And that niggled him. He had always been careful with money. Even – as in this case – other people's. He passed over his ID card. 'Debit it to my account.'

The clerk slid the card through a reader and eyed the credit balance as it came up on the screen. 'Very good, sir. If you'll just enter your Personal Authentification Number on the counter console.'

Andrew tapped it into the hooded keyboard unit. The transaction was duly processed and the clerk returned his card. 'Thank you for using the services of Boot City Field. You have been automatically cleared with Tower Control and are now free to get underway. Have a good trip.'

Andrew turned on his heel and strode out. Have a good trip . . . Huh! At these rates, it was a mystery how anyone could afford to go anywhere.

☆   ☆   ☆

Returning to The Dragon Lady, Andrew found Pug tinkering with the automatic lock on the top hatch. He climbed down the ladder and watched while the First Mate tried to close it from the control panel. Nothing happened. Pug pounded the panel.

'Is this gonna show up on the main board – or is Tarqueen too polite to tell anyone the ship is falling to pieces?'

Pug continued hitting the panel. 'Worked fine last time I was up here.'

Andrew winced as Pug opened a box on the control panel and gave the contents an experimental poke with his screwdriver. The First Mate ducked his head as sparks fizzed and flew in all directions. 'Hmm, well, the power's on.' He closed the box, hit the panel twice then pressed the button.

The hatch closed and locked itself. The status lights blinked on to indicate the seal was airtight.

'We've gotta do better than this, Pug.'

'Absolutely!' said Pug. 'If you've got the money, we can rebuild her from end to end.'

As they made his way to the bridge they met Aramitz in the passageway that divided the crew's quarters. He indicated an open doorway. 'It's just a temporary arrangement but we, um – put your bags in here with Kelly's. Your cabin's still full of Ganzwayko's gear – most of it unwashed.'

'That's the least of my worries. Where's Kelly now?'

'On the bridge,' said Pug. 'Plotting our take-off trajectory.'

'And Muldoon?'

'Helping her. Besides being able to cook, he's a mathematics wiz. Can crunch numbers faster than a computer. Well – ours, anyway. Tarqueen's livid.'

Andrew cocked his ear then said. 'Shouldn't I be hearing something? Like the comforting sound of pumps pressurizing fuel? Driving it towards the ignition chambers?'

Pug grimaced. 'Yeah, slight hitch in the engine room. Chilli and Gumbo are working on it. Should be fixed any minute now.' He threw an arm across the passageway as Andrew went to move past him. 'They don't like being interrupted when they're busy.'

Andrew looked at the arm, then locked eyes with Pug and in a voice which surprised him by its coldness said: 'I am now the captain of this ship, Mister Shilton, and I will go wherever I

194

please whenever I choose to do so. Your obstruction of this passageway is an act of gross insubordination. If you wish to remain aboard as First Mate, you are never, I repeat *never*, to challenge my authority in this way again! Is that understood?!'

Pug's arm dropped away. He stood aside, back braced, like a squaddie who has just been verbally savaged by a drill instructor.

Andrew strode off towards the engine room, leaving Aramitz and the speechless First Mate staring down the passageway.

'Well, well, well,' murmured Aramitz. 'I never thought I'd hear language like that aboard the Lady. At least not from one of the crew.'

Pug found his voice. 'Yeah, it's like being back in the Navy.' A terrible thought struck him. 'You don't think . . . I mean . . . why us?'

Aramitz shook his head. 'I don't have the answers, Pug. But whatever our feelings, I think we should give our good captain all the help we can to get this ship underway and off this planet.'

'Better call the engine room . . .'

'No, don't,' said Aramitz. 'Let him handle this in his own way.' He smiled. 'But by all means let us go down there and watch.'

☆   ☆   ☆

The door to the engine room was labelled FIRE DEPART-MENT. Andrew paused and took in the scene. The bulkhead around the door was decorated with a wide variety of stolen notices and signs. There were too many to take in at the first viewing but among those that caught his eye were – ADMIT-TANCE BY APPOINTMENT ONLY – KEEP OFF THE GRASS – NO PARKING ZONE – CLOSED THURSDAYS – KNOW THE FUTURE/CONSULT THE TAROT and 24-HOUR ESCORT SERVICE/DISCRETION GUARANTEED.

Andrew – who was still gripped by the strange, vengeful mood that had led him to discipline Pug – clenched his teeth, pushed open the door and was met by a deafening blast of music that almost knocked him off his feet.

195

It was like stepping back into Sadie Moon's.

In contrast to the music, the view from the catwalk around the two large main drive units was reassuring. The engine room was clean and tidy. Not a leaking pipe or shorting power cable anywhere.

Andrew made his way down onto the drive floor. Coverplates had been removed from both units, revealing layers of pipework and sheaves of wiring. Two men were working on one of the drives. The upper part of their bodies was hidden by machinery.

Unable to make himself heard above the bone-shaking beat, Andrew hunted down the source of the noise – a tape-deck loaded with twenty-four-inch diameter reels. Alongside it, a second machine stood loaded, threaded and ready to roll. Both decks were surrounded by a wall of speakers that could have reached every corner of Wembley Stadium. These guys were obviously used to nonstop music while they worked. He reached into the guts of the system and pulled the plug.

The engine room was suddenly filled with a cathedral-like silence which was quickly broken by the ringing clang of dropped spanners and a stream of expletives. Two men, bearing chest tags on their coveralls identifying them as Chilli and Gumbo, slid out from under the drives and rose to confront Andrew.

Chilli was tall, with Abyssinian features and with a skin darker than the usual run of Atlanteans. His long hair was twisted into thin plaits with beads at the bottom. Gumbo, by contrast, was shorter, with broad powerful shoulders, a deep chest, and a shaven head. An aggressive, bull-necked roustabout. Both wore futuristic, wraparound gun-metal shades.

Having attained the rank of captain before leaving the Army, Andrew was used to dealing with disgruntled ORs. 'Pug tells me you have a problem.'

Gumbo squared up to him. 'Problem? Wanna know what the problem is? Some *dude* just walked in here, *un*-invited and *messed* with *my* sound-system!'

'Yeah, I don't like that kind of music – especially when it's played that loud.'

'Oh, is that SO?!'

'Yeah. And here's something else I don't like.' Andrew pushed his face into Gumbo's. '*Being told where I can and cannot go on my own ship! You got that, Mister*?!'

Pug and Aramitz arrived in time to hear this exchange. They looked at each other in dismay. Although he did not show it, Andrew was also badly shaken by this vicious alter ego that had broken loose inside him.

'Uh, Captain, I don't think – '

'Thank you, Mister Shilton. I'm quite capable of handling this. I've tangled with REAL bad-asses. These two are just playing at it.'

Gumbo placed his hand on his hips in a camp gesture. 'Awww! Now how'd he figure that out?'

Andrew bristled. 'Ah, a comedian too. Okay, see if you can come up with a funny answer to this question. Are you going to serve on this ship or are you gonna try and hitch a ride on the next tub that comes through here?!'

Before Gumbo could answer, Andrew turned to Pug. 'Mr Shilton? Call Airport Security and tell them we may need their help to throw two drifters over the wire!'

Chilli stepped forward with a placatory gesture. 'I think we're getting our priorities a little mixed up here, Captain. I understand why you feel the need to come on like Jack the Bear, but why don't we leave all this chain-of-command crap until we got this bird off the ground? That *is* what you want isn't it?'

Andrew managed to insert a mental gag into the overbearing martinet that had invaded his psyche. 'Yes, as fast as we can. You'll have to excuse my irritation. You too, Mr Shilton. The two days I've spent in Boot City have been somewhat stressful. In fact, I shall count myself lucky if I get out of here alive. So . . . just how bad is this breakdown?'

'It's not a mechanical breakdown, Captain. When we landed, we removed several key components to stop the ship bein' hijacked. Know what I mean?'

'Yeah. There are some pretty desperate people out there.'

'In here too, man,' said Gumbo. 'We been grounded for

197

months. It was only when you came through and asked for a burn that we realised we'd forgotten where we'd stashed the parts!'

Chilli saw Andrew's expression. 'S'okay. We found 'em all. Just a few more pieces to pop into place and we'll be ready for lift off. Twenty minutes top.' He paused, then asked, 'Got the ship's papers?'

'On the mini-disc? Yeah. Right here.' Andrew produced the slim wallet.

'Good. 'Cos that's not just proof of ownership. It's the ignition key that makes this turkey fly!'

Andrew frowned. 'I see . . . but as long as Ganzwayko had this, no one could steal the ship. So why . . .?'

Chilli laughed. 'It was Finnee we were scared of, man!'

'But . . . why would he steal his own ship?'

Gumbo broke the news. ' 'Cos he owes us all money, dude! He ain't paid us in over a year!'

'Didn't your partner tell you that?' asked Chilli.

'She's not my partner, and she didn't.' Andrew digested the news and turned to Pug. 'Does this mean . . .?'

The First Mate nodded. 'Yes. When a freelance captain takes over a ship and its crew, he assumes all liabilities.'

'So it looks like it's down to you,' said Chilli.

Gumbo slapped Andrew on the back. 'But don't worry, bro. We's right behind you – all the way to the bank!'

Andrew gritted his teeth together. 'Okay, step on it, guys. If we're not off the ground in twenty minutes, you can kiss goodbye to the money 'cos we won't be going anywhere.'

'He upset some people in town,' explained Pug. 'And they could be here any minute.'

Chilli and Gumbo lost no time in getting back to work.

'See if you can help them, Pug,' said Andrew. As he and Aramitz climbed to the upper catwalk, Gumbo poked his head out from under the port-side drive unit.

'Just one more thing, bro!'

'What's that?' demanded Andrew.

'Nothing moves without the music!'

198

Andrew switched it back on. The noise ceased abruptly as they closed the sound-proofed door.

Aramitz eyed him keenly. 'Do you mind if I ask you a personal question? In my professional capacity, that is.'

'Not at all. Go ahead.'

'Do you have a history of schizophrenia?'

'Uh . . . not that I know of,' said Andrew. He paused, aware of the need for caution. 'But in the last few months . . .'

'Yes . . .?'

'I, uh . . . have been hearing voices – well, one voice. Someone who isn't me.'

'Was he the person who bawled out Pug?'

'Yes.'

'And does it trouble you?'

'Deeply.'

Aramitz nodded. 'I see . . . well, I'm not really the ship's doctor but I'm not without certain skills. If you feel you need help, my door is always open.'

'Thanks, Doc. Stay with me.' Andrew bared his teeth. 'I'm on my way to have a word with a certain party and I may draw blood.'

☆ ☆ ☆

When Andrew entered the bridge, Kelly and Muldoon were still huddled over the holographic display of the planet and the five-hundred mile-high block of space surrounding it. A small point of light indicated the Buena Vista space-station in its solar orbit three hundred miles above the surface.

Kelly punched in a revised set of course coordinates. The projection mechanism drew a thin blue line to simulate the curving flight-path of The Dragon Lady from Zhannandor to Buena Vista. She turned to Muldoon. 'Is that better?'

Andrew swallowed his anger and let them get on with it. He sat down in the captain's chair and inspected the instrumentation. This was his first good look at it, but thanks to the familiarisation sessions in the sim-tank, he knew where and what everything was.

The central overhead computer screen filled with swirls of colour as Tarqueen offered Andrew a velvety greeting. 'Welcome back, Andi. Just knowing you're aboard makes me feel warm and wonderful inside.'

Andrew raised his eyes to the screen. 'Wanna know something, Tarq? You get right up my nose.'

'Oohh, my! Do I sense we're a teensey tad hostile tonight? Has our Miss Kelly been upsetting Mr Grouch again?'

'Right! That's it!' Andrew swivelled his seat towards the navigation area. 'Moses?!'

'Yes, Captain?'

'I want Tarqueen taken off line! Pull the personality module out of the system but leave the voice-activated command and control systems in place.'

'Now?'

'Yes, *now*! Just get this sugar-coated, pink-ribboned scuzz-ball off the air!'

'Right, Captain. But – '

'Just *do* it, Moses!'

Muldoon hurried away.

'I just love it when you're masterful,' said Tarqueen.

Phut! The swirling colours disappeared. The screen turned dull grey for a few moments then came back to life with a diagrammatic status report from the engine room. The space drives were reassembled and the turbo-charged fuel pumps were now delivering fuel to the battery of booster rockets that would lift The Dragon Lady off its pad in the space-park.

Pug hurried back and took his seat on the bridge. Muldoon, Kelly and Andrew were already in their appointed places. Aramitz was strapped into one of the two spare seats at the rear.

'Okay! Final pre-flight check for ETO!' called Andrew.

'Gyros and stabiliser jets running. Booster pumps up to speed and pressure. All systems are Go,' reported Muldoon.

'Go confirmed,' chimed Pug. 'All ground service connections severed. Walkway retracted and clear. Pad free of obstructions. Gear down and locked. No incoming and we have a green from the Tower.'

200

'Navigator?' demanded Andrew.

'Course computed and confirmed. Trajectory lock on!'

'Okay.' Andrew felt strangely at ease – as if he had done this hundreds of times before. 'Initiating emergency take-off sequence! Ignition! Five – four – three – two – one . . . Firing . . . *Lift-off!*'

The Dragon Lady trembled from stem to stern as the eight big rocket boosters mounted under her belly burst into life. The lattice of funnels in the landing pad swallowed the tongues of flame and deflected the blast away from the ship through angled vents.

Mushrooming pillars of black, white and flame orange smoke shot into the air like a salvo from a battery of heavy guns. The glow illuminated the gaunt grey faces of the ragged army of hitchers who had crept out of the darkness to line the electrified fence; to watch another dream slip through their fingers, another hope of salvation fade.

As the ship lifted clear of the terminal buildings, Andrew looked down through the nose view port and saw a speeding group of armoured cabs hugging the last curve on the freeway before the turn-off to Boot City Field. He wondered if Ganzwayko was among them and mentally waved him good-bye.

Sorry, old son. Couldn't wait. Better luck next time.

Forty minutes later, The Dragon Lady slipped smoothly into a parking orbit some three hundred miles above the surface of Zhannandor. As they circled the planet, the Buena Vista station came into view as a bright point of light, grew until they could see the various interconnecting segments and the multiple arrays of solar panels and receiving dishes – even Ffastbukk's floating spaceship lot – then slipped away on their port side creating the illusion that it was moving when, in fact, it was anchored between the planet and the twin suns.

A comparative silence now spread through the bow of the ship, broken only by the background systems hum and the metallic squeaks and groans from the ship's ageing hull. What the First Mate called The Dragon Lady's 'creaking bones'.

'Rocket motors off. Space drive on standby. Internal gravity field, zero point three five.'

'Thanks, Pug,' said Andrew. He patched himself through to Chilli and Gumbo. 'Captain to Engineers. Well done, you guys.'

'Didn't think we'd make it,' confessed Pug. 'I really thought she was going to fall apart.'

'Glad you didn't tell me,' said Andrew. He rose and tapped Kelly on the shoulder. 'I want a word with you. In private.'

She dropped her shoulders and sighed. 'Oh, it's not about money, is it? I don't think I can stand another drama.' She saw his lips tighten. 'Okay, so I didn't tell you about the wages. So what? You cleared half a mil on that currency deal!'

'Yes, I did! And that was exactly what the fuel bill came to! But since you want this out in the open, here it is!' Andrew turned to Aramitz and the others. 'I want to make this clear one last time. Miss Mandell is not my partner in this or any other enterprise. She is not entitled to any privileges beyond those afforded to her as a member of this crew while she is serving alongside you as acting navigator.'

Kelly bristled. 'Acting?! How long for?'

Andrew went nose to nose. 'For as long as it takes to replace you. No further comment. Dismissed!'

'Now wait a min – '

Muldoon stepped in as peacemaker. 'Whoa, now! Why don't we sit down together and discuss this over a sunrise breakfast? I can soon whip us all up a big mug of coffee, eggs over easy, sliced fried potatoes and a big juicy reindeer steak!'

Andrew's eyes widened. 'Reindeer steak? *Reindeer steak*?!'

'Frozen fresh on the bone,' said Muldoon. 'Kelly's friend brought a whole crateful on board.'

Andrew advanced on Kelly. 'You invited that blubbery windbag on board *my ship*?!'

Kelly dodged around the nav display table and took cover

202

behind Pug and Muldoon. 'It was part of the deal I had to do to get the currency! Okay, I didn't tell you back at the hotel because you're so pigheaded, you'd've blown our chances of getting the ship!'

'And we'd've all been sorry about that, wouldn't we, Pug?' Muldoon cued the First Mate with a nudge in the ribs.

'True, yep – absolutely,' said Pug.

Aramitz chimed in. 'She should not have agreed without consulting you, but as I understand it, Miss Mandell believed she was acting in your best interests.'

Andrew's anger waned as he saw the humorous side of the situation although, from where he was standing, it wasn't quite as amusing as everyone else seemed to think. 'Well, at least that solved the problem of where we go from here.'

Kelly emerged from hiding. 'And where's that?'

'Where this nightmare journey with you started. Punch up a docking course with Buena Vista Station.'

'Oh, wonderful!' exclaimed a voice.

'That's where I promised we'd take him.'

Andrew turned to find The Reindeer Man wedged in the doorway to the bridge.'

'How can I ever repay you . . .'

It was a statement, not a question, but Andrew was not in a generous mood. 'You can start with the docking fees.' He turned back to Kelly Mandell. 'And you can start packing. You're getting off there too.'

It was worth all he had been through just to see the expression on her face.

☆   ☆   ☆

Andrew's triumph would have been short-lived if he had known that, not a million miles away (965,897.32 miles to be exact), two Fleet Admirals were preparing to discuss his future.

Boarding a powerful motor launch on The Corporation's home planet of Libra, they sailed out of the marina at the Navy Headquarters at Anchorage into the aquamarine waters of the Western Sea. Their declared intention was to hook a brace of sail-fish but that was merely an excuse to put themselves beyond the range of any eavesdroppers.

The boat was fitted with an electronic screening device which, when switched on, shielded them from cannon-mikes and effectively disabled any transmitter bugs or miniature recording devices that might have been smuggled on board by jealous rivals.

The Admiral's names were Danzigger Korreggidoorian and Jakkaranda Treehausterhaus – the usual Atlantean mouthful – but to their peer-group they were known as Ziggy and Jak.

When the hooks had been baited and the lines paid out, Ziggy and Jak relaxed in their safety seats while the auto-nav system drove the powerboat on its pre-set course.

'Do you remember the Marianna incident?' asked Ziggy.

'Yes . . . unfortunate business.'

'And do you remember me putting an RTA on Daniel Kinsharadeen?'

RTA stood for Record Trace Alert – an instruction to NEPTUNE, the Navy's central computer complex to register any attempt to access a designated file within its massive storage banks.

Jak frowned. 'Don't tell me . . .'

Ziggy nodded. 'A couple of months ago, someone initiated a Deep Seven from an Arkadian spaceliner. The SS Narayana.'

'They can't do that without an input code. Who was it?'

'Sandiego Mandragorian.'

'*Our* Sandiego? Sandy? The weapons designer?'

Ziggy nodded again. 'Except it wasn't him. He never left his workshops. But his daughter took off eight months ago.'

'Again? I see. And you think she . . .?'

'Has to be. That rebellious little kook's been kicking over the traces since she was eight years old. She can also hack into computer systems faster than you can pop your flies.'

'So why didn't you mention this till now?'

'Jak, it's been eleven years since the Marianna disappeared with all hands. You and I both know we acted in the best interests of the Navy but I put RTAs on all the crew so as I could sleep easy. Then suddenly, up pops this trace. Naturally an alarm bell rang, but I didn't see any reason for us to go on Red Alert.'

'So why are we out here with the screen up?'

'The Security Unit on Buena Vista/Zhannandor also launched a Deep Seven on Daniel Kinsharadeen about two weeks ago. The SS Narayana docked there. That's not all. Another was run by TradeCor's security arm – the SID. But Daniel Kinsharadeen was not listed as a passenger on board the Narayana, and no one using that name passed through Buena Vista Immigration Control. You getting the picture?'

Jak looked dumbfounded. 'Could a ringer have . . .?'

'Got hold of his card? Well, the Navy salvaged a stack of debris from the Marianna and a lot of it must still be floating around out there. But the chances of Daniel's ID falling into the hands of someone who looked exactly like him are so astronomical it's not worth considering.'

'So he's alive . . .'

'Alive and kicking,' said Dan. 'A report just came in from one of our contacts on Zhannandor. A Navy type was spotted by an ex-con in a bar in Boot City. Luckily he got away, but it appears the ex-con had ten good long reasons to know Commander Daniel Kinsharadeen'

Having listened with increasing concern, Jak asked: 'So where is he now?'

'I'm not quite sure. But according to our contact, a short while after Daniel broke out of the bar, a tradeship took off from Boot City Field. An old tub called The Dragon Lady. Unlicensed.'

Jak gnawed his lip thoughtfully. 'So our plan wasn't as perfect as we thought.'

'No. This time around, we'll have to take matters into our own hands. You know what they say: "If you want a job done properly, do it yourself."'

'We'll never get away with it, Ziggy.'

'Why not? No one has ever linked us to the Marianna. All we need to do is to move with the same care, pick the right moment – and this time, finish it, once and for all.'

205

'You're forgetting one thing.'

'Yeah? And what's that?'

'Daniel may know, or have guessed, that someone tried to kill him – may even have figured out who it was.'

Ziggy smiled at the thought. 'Then why has he taken so long to stage a comeback?'

'Exactly. Where has he been for the last eleven years? What has he been doing? Better still, who has he been working for? And there's something else. What if he's tied in with Sandiego's daughter?'

It was Ziggy's turn to frown. 'What's she got to do with it?'

'Two reasons,' said Admiral Jak. 'She may – as you suggested – have made the first Deep Seven search. If so, we have to ask "Why?". Second, she knows Daniel's old man. He's still wearing the black ribbon, but suppose Gideon's been stringing us along while he and Daniel piece together the evidence that will nail us to the wall?'

Ziggy mulled this over. 'You may be right, Jak. In which case, our first move should be to take the Dragon Lady out of circulation. These unlicensed and unsafe vessels are a danger to the spaceways.'

Chapter Thirteen

Instead of docking at Buena Vista, Andrew took Pug's advice and sought permission from Honest John T Ffastbukk to moor The Dragon Lady on the outer edge of his floating parking lot. According to Pug, tying-up unlicensed traders to Cor-controlled stations could lead to all kinds of problems.

As ever, Honest John was happy to oblige. Under the arrangement he'd reached with Connie, every helping hand extended to young Andiamo meant another handsome gratuity. And after negotiating a cut of the cabfare, Ffastbukk called in Randy McRabbit to ferry The Dragon Lady's captain and crew across to Buena Vista.

Andrew had expected he would have to drag Kelly ashore kicking and screaming but she proved to be remarkably docile and uncharacteristically silent. A sure sign that she was planning something. Matters weren't helped by the fact that she had somehow managed to enlist the sympathy of the entire crew and that Andrew himself was also regretting the unreasoning anger which had led to her dismissal – if only because it cast him in an unflattering light.

On reaching the main concourse, Lars seized Andrew's hand and pumped it vigorously. His pink chubby face, with its ridiculous pale eyebrows, was split by a beaming smile. The man was so insensitive, so unaware of the animosity he engendered, it was hard not to smile along with him.

'How can I thank you for all you have done? First, you save my life, then you make a generous exchange for my money and make it possible for me to open my first Longship Restaurant!'

207

'A man like you deserves to succeed,' lied Andrew. 'Where are you going to open up – Main City?'

'No! Right here! This space terminal is a potential gold mine! People in transit to and from so many different worlds will be able to enjoy my reindeer steaks and seal cutlets – '

'Right. You'll make a big impression – '

'Just so! People will talk. The news will spread. Ten years from now, the chain of Longship Restaurants will stretch right around the Rimworld!'

'That's a staggering prospect. Best of luck, Lars.' Andrew freed his hand, clapped Vindhook's shoulder then switched his attention to Kelly. 'The next liner isn't due for another couple of weeks. Want some cash to tide you over?'

She eyed him sullenly. 'No thanks. I'd hate to think I still owed you something.'

Andrew feigned indifference. 'Suit yourself.'

The party split into two. Lars and Kelly aimed for the Spaceport Hotel; the others, with Andrew in tow, headed towards the bank. As their new captain, there was nothing to do but look big and pay up. Fortunately, he had had the foresight to leave a hefty balance in his account but by the time Pug, Moses, Chilli and Gumbo had sauntered out of the door with bulging wallets, it felt as if he was haemorrhaging money.

Turning back to the counter, he found Aramitz studying him.

'You must be wondering what you've walked into.'

Andrew gave a dry laugh. 'Yeah, well, it did occur to me that jumping ship might be my best move but the next liner's not due for another two weeks. And now that Lars has decided to stay here, The Dragon Lady is my only means of escape.' He paused then said: 'So . . . what do I owe you, Jean? I shudder to think what a ship's doctor earns but what the heck? Hit me with it anyway.'

'That won't be necessary. I have private means.' He stilled Andrew's protest. 'No. Let me explain. I *am* the ship's doctor but I am not one of the crew. I'm, uhh, well – the truth is I'm a passenger.'

208

Andrew found this hard to believe. 'You actually bought a ticket from Ganzwayko to ride on that tub?'

'Good heavens, no! I've lost count of the captains who have paced that bridge . . .'

'So where exactly are you trying to get to?'

Aramitz spread his hands. 'I have no desire to *go* anywhere in particular. I just like to travel. The ticket came from the Olympic Shipping Agency. It's what they call a PVP – a Perpetual Voyager's Pass. Lasts a lifetime.'

'Olympic Shipping Agency . . .?'

'Run by Constantine Parnassus. A very interesting man.'

'Really?' Andrew's face gave nothing away. 'Now that I'm the captain of The Dragon Lady, shouldn't I be getting a cut of whatever you paid this guy?'

Aramitz shrugged. 'That's not for me to say. But if you put in a claim, I'm sure it would be treated sympathetically.'

'So how do I get in touch with them?'

'With great difficulty. Mr Parnassus operates just within the law but outside the remit of the Corporation. He . . . how shall I put it? He sees himself as the main driving force of the alternative economy.' Aramitz fixed Andrew with a curious stare. 'As a trader yourself, I'm surprised you haven't heard of him.'

'Well, now that you mention it, I may have done business with one of his underlings.'

Aramitz appeared to accept this. 'Anyway – to get back to what I was saying – as a result of his extramural activities, Parnassus likes to keep moving. He says it helps him stay one step ahead of the competition. But you may be able to reach him through Honest John. I believe they have, ah – overlapping interests?'

Andrew nodded. 'Okay. I need to square him for allowing us to use his parking lot, so I'll find out what he knows. Gimme me a couple of hours. I understand there's a restaurant and bar on the first floor of the Galleria called Trixie Treats. Why don't we all meet there?'

☆   ☆   ☆

209

Ffastbukk greeted him like a valued customer, waved him to a seat and went to fix some drinks at the bar. 'So – what did you think of Boot City?'

'It has a certain rough charm,' admitted Andrew.

'And how did you make out with Sadie?'

Andrew took the offered drink and responded to Ffastbukk's toast. 'Pretty well, I think. She brokered the deal on the ship but unfortunately, I was forced to leave town before she could collect her commission.'

Ffastbukk met this with a cheerful laugh: 'Yeah, she's pretty pissed off about that. Mind you, she's not too pleased with me either. Says I should've known better than to send an under-cover Navy man to Boot City.'

'This is gettin' to be a pain, John. I'm not Navy and I'm not working undercover.'

'Look, Andy. I run a strictly legitimate business here. I pay Corporation tax. It's not a problem for me.'

'John, you gotta believe me. That ex-con has gotten me mixed up with someone else.'

'In that case, you'd better get your story straight. The first time we talked, you told me you were A-rated for hyperspace. Only the Navy has those drives.'

Andrew played it off the cuff. 'That's the official line, yeah. But the market's opened up a little.'

'Whoa!' Ffastbukk's hand shot up. 'I don't want to hear about this!'

Andrew downed his drink to steady his nerves. 'So what else did Sadie say?'

'She wants to know who's going to pay for the window. But that's the least of your problems.'

'Oh . . .?'

'Yeah. There appears to be some dispute over who owns The Dragon Lady. This guy Ganzwayko – '

'It's all legal, John. I paid half the selling price in cash and played him for the other half. It was a "Win All or Lose All" deal. Ask Sadie.'

'Yeah, yeah, I know all that. Problem is, you paid him in – '

210

'Skandavian Trolls. Right. He wanted unlicensed currency.'

'Absolutely. But the banknotes were all counterfeit. Forged. Duff. Completely worthless. And he wants his ship back.'

Andrew fell back into the armchair. 'He *what* . . .?!'

Ffastbukk lifted the empty glass from Andrew's unresisting fingers and made a refuelling run to the bar. 'I can't understand how someone with your experience got sucked into buying that heap of shit.'

'What experience? I'm just a beginner, John.'

'Aww, c'mon, Andi! When I tried to sell you that T-40, you came back at me like someone who'd swallowed the Navy maintenance manual!'

'Yeah, well, there were pressures . . . time constraints.'

'So you didn't you check out the others . . .'

'What others?'

'Sadie told me she knew of at least four ships that were on offer.'

'Four? Huh!' Andrew grasped the refill and drank deep. 'John, I flew into Boot City Field. Ganzwayko's ship was the only one still on her feet.'

'I believe you. But that's not the only spaceport west of the Zappalachian Divide. Never mind. The damage is done now.' He laughed at Andrew's crestfallen expression. 'Cheer up. It wouldn't surprise me to learn that Ganzwayko sold you his ship because he was behind with the payments.'

'You mean it wasn't his to sell? But . . . he gave me the ship's papers!'

'Sure. He would have to have those to operate the ship. But they don't confer legal ownership until any forward financing deal is completed. Papers can be doctored. You must know that.'

'This is getting worse by the minute,' said Andrew.

'Relax. I'll have one of my people check it out. Stay right there – won't be a mo'.'

Andrew rose. 'Uh, John – just out of interest – is Imelda still around?'

''Fraid not. She's in hybe, waiting to go back to the lab.

211

Day after you left, I sent her over to our hospitality suite to sweetheart this deal, the client dropped dead with a heart attack, and now his company is suing me for two million Cords.' He waved away the details. 'I can't tell you . . .'

As the door closed, Andrew emptied his glass on the way to the bar and poured himself a second refill. He had time to drink that and pour himself a third shot in the arm before Ffastbukk returned.

'Okay. Here's how it plays. The Dragon Lady is owned by the Olympic Shipping Agency run by a guy called Constantine Parnassus.'

Andrew reacted as if hearing this for the first time.

'It was only leased to Ganzwayko – which means the sale of it to you was illegal.'

'So the fact that I paid him with forged notes is not an issue.'

'Nah. He hasn't a leg to stand on. Problem is, you don't own the ship either. Which is only reasonable seeing as how you paid for it with funny money – but somewhat unfortunate since you have just paid the crew eighteen months back wages.'

Andrew shrugged. 'It wasn't my money. I'm a friend of Connie's too.'

It was Ffastbukk's turn to look surprised. '*Connie* is bank-rolling you?'

'In a manner of speaking.'

Ffastbukk's eyes invited him to enlarge upon his reply.

'We have a deal going down. I really can't say more right now.'

'Sounds intriguing.'

'I couldn't have described it better myself,' agreed Andrew.

Fastbukk chuckled. 'Wish I could be there when you break the news. Connie's going to be thrilled to hear he's just bought back a ship he already owns!'

Andrew shook his head. 'He won't have any cause to complain. The snerf who sold me the fake currency just booked in to the Spaceport Hotel. I plan to go over there right now and jump on his head until he gives me the money back.'

Ffastbukk escorted him past a clutch of big-chested

212

secretaries to the front office that opened onto the main concourse. 'A final word of advice. If you plan to hang around, get yourself a trading licence. If not, move that tub of yours out of here. My sources tell me a Navy ship is due to call here in a few days time. Knowing the way they budget their operations they're obviously not coming especially for you but there's no point in asking for trouble.'

'Thanks, John. I'll bear it in mind.'

☆   ☆   ☆

'Ah! Mr Cartaynyar!'

Andrew looked over his shoulder and saw Captain Krevassar of Spaceport Security heading towards him. Krevassar had been in charge of the brief investigation that had followed the discovery of the guns in Andrew's luggage. He was flanked by two uniformed subordinates.

'Everything going according to plan?' Krevassar's voice had a nudge-nudge wink-wink edge to it.

'More or less,' said Andrew. 'In fact, I'm glad I ran into you.' He drew Krevassar aside. 'Passing counterfeit money – is that regarded as a serious offence?'

'Are we talking about forged Cor-dollars?'

'No. Exchanging fake unlicensed currency for Cords.'

'Well, that's still a fraudulent currency transaction. It would depend on the circumstances and the amount involved – '

'Two million Skandavian Trolls for one and a half mil Cords.'

'Then the perp could spend from five to ten as a tar-baby.'

'Thanks. When I catch up with the guy I'll call you in.'

Krevassar's eyes narrowed. 'He's on station? We'll pick him up for you, Commander – uh, I mean, errrmm, Mister Cartahaynyar! Your word is good enough for me, sir. We can – '

'Slow down, Captain! There's no rush. I have some other business to settle with this guy first. Know what I mean?'

Krevassar's eyes gleamed as he entered into the conspiracy. 'Of course. But just so we don't get our wires crossed, I really should know who this man is.'

213

'He calls himself Lars Vindhook. The last time I saw him he was heading towards the Spaceport Hotel accompanied by a smallish, dark-haired woman by the name of Kelly Mandell. But she's not part of the currency scam.'

'Lars Vindhook?' Captain Krevassar and his two subordinates exchanged loaded glances.

'Do we have some kind of a problem here?' asked Andrew.

'No, more of a coincidence. We're just on our way over to the hotel now.'

'Oh . . .?'

'Yes – to investigate a report by a chambermaid who thought a young woman might be being held under duress in Room 911. The registered occupier is – '

'Lars Vindhook. Right!' Andrew snapped his fingers and prodded Krevassar in the chest. 'This is linked in with my present assignment, Captain – so I want you and your men to stay well back while I assess the situation. I have my own team of specialists ready to go. If I need back-up, I'll call you. Is that understood?'

'Perfectly.' Krevassar could not conceal his disappointment. Feeling a suspect's collar is the highlight of every security man's day.

'By the way,' said Andrew. 'What happened to those four guys you arrested after that fight I was involved in? The gang of muggers – remember?'

'Of course. It was quite entertaining.'

'Not from where I was standing. Were they shipped out – or are you still holding them in the brig?'

'Neither,' answered Krevassar. 'A few days after we pulled them in we were instructed to set them free and drop all charges.'

Andrew looked stunned.

Krevassar hastened to explain. 'We got a call from Trade-Cor's Special Investigation Division.' He smiled as Andrew's bewilderment increased. 'Obviously a case of the right hand not knowing what the left hand is doing.'

'Obviously,' agreed Andrew. He played for time while his

214

brain grappled with this latest revelation. 'The Operational Liaison Unit was set up to prevent this kind of thing. But it looks as if they've screwed up yet again. Thanks for putting me in the picture, Captain.'

'I'll wait for your call.' Krevassar signed off with a salute and led his men back to the Security Unit.

Andrew walked into the nearest coffee-shop and ordered a long, strong black at the counter. He stirred in sweetener and watched the swirling liquid as the thoughts whirled around inside his head.

Lars Vindhook? The wobble-bottom blabbermouth? A Trade-Cor undercover agent? Incredible. What the hell was going on? And – if the report was true – why was he holding Kelly prisoner? Wait . . . the Navy ship. Was that coming to pick her up? Was all this connected with the theft of the guns from her father's design unit? From what little Kelly had told him, Mandell *père* might hit the roof but was unlikely to denounce her. He was used to her frequent disappearances and, so far, she had always returned when the money ran out.

But maybe this time she had overstepped the mark. Lars must have already been on her trail when they were on the SS Narayana. And when she evaded Buena Vista Customs after off-loading the guns, the Reindeer Man had to find some way to stay on the case which, thanks to Kelly, he, Andrew, had been sucked into.

The mugging episode was an elaborate set-piece designed to bolster the deception and to draw Kelly and himself – however unwillingly – into a closer relationship. No wonder they couldn't get rid of the guy. His insane business scheme was another piece of fakery. Whoever Lars was in real life, he deserved top marks for acting.

But now, it was time to bring down the curtain.

☆   ☆   ☆

Entering Trixie Treats, Andrew found Aramitz and the others grouped around one of the tables, enjoying each other's company and celebrating at his expense.

215

Chilli stood up and waved both arms. 'Hey! Skip! Over here!' The directions were entirely superfluous. Had he closed his eyes on reaching the Galleria, Andrew could have found his way to the table just by homing in on the noise.

The remains of an expensive meal, running to several courses, littered the table. Aramitz, who sat back sipping a vintage wine, was the coolest. The others were red-cheeked and bright-eyed but, thankfully, were not rolling drunk. They were just loose enough to go for the scheme he was about to propose – and now, of course, Andrew was quietly pleased they were all Kelly Mandell fans.

He outlined the situation and his proposed plan of action, ending with a warning. 'But I don't want anyone going over-board and wrecking the joint. This has got to be quick, clean, and executed with the minimum of disturbance.'

Everyone nodded. Andrew hoped they meant it. He turned to Aramitz. 'Knocking Vindhook senseless with the minimum of external damage is not a problem, but I want him to remain unconscious until we can get him back to the ship. We'll need a stretcher – '

'The hotel will have one. We can use that.'

'They also have their in-house medical staff.'

'That won't be a problem providing we get to him first.'

'Okay. We also need a knockout drug. D'you have any-thing?'

'Not on me. But I have a collection of rare herbal medicines on board ship that can cure – or simulate – certain medical conditions. A heart attack would be the best.' Aramitz smiled. 'It has a high "alarm" factor. We could then ask the hotel to loan us an oxygen cylinder and a mask – '

'Which will help disguise him. Brilliant, Doc. Find Randy McRabbit. She operates from the SSTV docking bay. If her limo's on station, get her to run you out to the ship, grab whatever you need, and meet us at the Spaceport Hotel. While you're gone, we'll check things out. You'll find one, or all of us, in the ground floor lounge.'

'*Bon. A bientot, mes amis . . .*'

216

Aramitz rose and left, leaving Andrew wondering why none of the crew thought it odd that their travelling companion should be speaking French.

☆　　☆　　☆

'Lars! How're you doing?!' Andrew pumped some bonhomie into his voice as Vindhook's face appeared on the vidiphone screen.

'Andrew . . .' The Reindeer Man did not look overjoyed.

'Lars, listen, I'll be pulling out in a few hours and I didn't want to leave without straightening out a few things between us. I think I owe you an apology.'

'Not necessary,' said Vindhook.

'I think it is,' insisted Andrew. 'I certainly haven't behaved as well as I should. And I haven't thanked you properly for helping me to buy that ship. Your Skandavian Trolls were a real life-saver.'

'Glad to be of help.'

'Well, I'd like to buy you a farewell drink in the Fountain Bar, and to show my appreciation, I talked to some people about your restaurant idea and they just love it. I told 'em you were looking for investors and guess what? They want to meet you!'

Vindhook brightened visibly. 'Really?'

'Yeah. They have a prior appointment but they promised to join us shortly.'

'I'll be right down,' said Vindhook.

'Is Kelly still with you?'

'No. She ran into some men who apparently knew her from somewhere and I haven't seen her since.'

'Okay. I'll set up the drinks.' Andrew cleared the screen and looked across the hotel lobby to where Pug, Moses, Chilli and Gumbo were standing. They acknowledged his signal and moved off.

Andrew went into the Fountain Bar and ordered two Thunderbrew Specials on the rocks.

☆　　☆　　☆

217

Having first arranged for the hotel to cut the power to all the television sets on the ninth floor, Moses Muldoon knocked at the door to Room 911. He was dressed in the coveralls of a hotel repairman, and was carrying an electronic tool kit.

Shades answered the door. 'About time.' He stepped aside to let Moses enter, then locked the door behind him and joined Hot-Roxx and Steel-Eye at a table clogged with drink cans, cards and cash chips. They acknowledged Moses with perfunctory nods then continued their game.

Moses went into the narrow service area behind the wall-screen, opened his toolcase, took out a diagnostic unit, plugged it in, waited a few minutes then emerged into the room. 'Need to get someone here with a spare part. Mind if I make a call?' He produced a mobile handset.

'Sure, go ahead,' grunted Steel-Eye.

'Can I go out onto the balcony? Reception's better out there.'

'Just hurry,' said Hot-Roxx. 'The Rocket Ball Eliminators'll be starting in fifteen minutes.'

Moses unlocked the floor-to-ceiling windows, opened up a small gap and stepped through onto the balcony. Since the hotel was contained in one of the space station towers, there was no real 'outside'; the floors were stacked up the middle of a tube whose walls were landscaped with fibreglass rocks and lush foliage growing on cunningly-arranged hydroponic shelves.

He punched the number that put him through to Pug who was waiting in Room 912 and raised his voice for the card-players' benefit. 'Shannon? Doonlairee. Now listen. I've located the fault in 911, but I need a G-3 Video Repeater. A G-3. Have you got that? Well, hurry up with it. There's some Rocket Ball fans here anxious to see the game an' I don't want to miss it either.'

Moses smiled through the glass at the players then re-entered the room, slid the window shut and pretended to lock it, masking the action with his body. He wandered over to watch the card game. There were a lot of cash chips on the table.

'Sledgehammer or White Diamond?' asked Shades.

'A drink? Oh . . .' Moses, the conscientious employee,

hesitated. 'Ordinarily I shouldn't – bein' at work like – but where's the harm, eh?' He picked up a White Diamond and popped the seal.

There was a knock at the door. Four plus two.

'How's that for service?' Moses put the can down. 'I'll leave that till later.' He put his hand on Shades' shoulder to stop him rising and tapped the fan of cards. 'Get rid of those two . . .'

As Pug exited into the corridor from the room next door, Chilli and Gumbo went out onto the balcony, bridged the six-foot divide with a step-ladder, crossed over to 911 and hid behind the corner of the wall until Chilli caught sight of Moses returning with Pug.

'Hope you brought the right bit,' growled Hot-Roxx.

'I certainly did,' said Pug. Reaching inside his coverall, he pulled out a thirty inch length of heavy duty rubber hose, filled with sand and plugged with a lead spigot at both ends.

Chilli and Gumbo burst in from the balcony as Pug brought the hose down on Shades' head. The flexible hose distributed the force of the blow evenly around his skull without fracturing the bone. He went down and stayed down. Steel-Eye was quick to parry Moses' first piledriver but despite their close-combat skills, neither he nor Hot-Roxx were able to stay on their feet for long. All three were quickly gagged and bound with plastic lock-ties by Chilli and Gumbo, while Pug and Moses searched the other rooms and storage spaces.

Drawing a blank everywhere else, Pug ran across to the master bedroom and threw the door open. Moses, who was close behind, cannoned into his broad back as the First Mate stalled in the doorway.

On the king-sized bed lay a naked female with three pillows under her rear end. Her arms and legs locked around the neck and back of a buffo male whose raised bum was frozen on the back-stroke. Two pairs of eyes stared at Pug and Moses in disbelief. One set belonged to Grey Hair, the man from the bank who had helped to set up Andrew.

For an instant, Pug thought Kelly was being ravished, then

quickly realised the woman in question was being slavishly cooperative. Or had been.

Moses advanced into the room with a placatory gesture. 'Don't mind us! We've just come to check the television!'

Grey-Hair, now over the shock and completely unfazed by his nakedness caught sight of Chilli and Gumbo through the open doorway and dived off the bed towards the clothes he'd left draped over a chair. Pug whacked his ass with the hose to slow him down, grabbed his hand as it reached towards a body holster then put him out with a blow to the head.

The woman seized a heavy ornament from the bedside unit and sent it skimming past Moses' ear. 'Now that's a silly thing to do. You could have killed me, you know that?' he said. He caught both wrists in his left hand and laid her out with a pop on the jaw.

They found Kelly gagged and bound in the walk-in closet and quickly freed her. 'Thanks, guys. If I had had to sit through any more of Moaning Minnie's orgasms, the men in white suits would've been wheeling me out of here.'

'These guys hurt you?' demanded Gumbo.

'No. They just put me in the wrong cupboard.' Kelly massaged her arms and legs as she surveyed the inert faces of Grey-Hair and the woman. After binding their hands and feet, Pug had laid them side by side on the bed and tucked a sheet under their chins.

Moses took out his handset and put a call through to the Fountain Bar.

☆　　☆　　☆

Andrew came back rubbing his hands and resumed his seat next to Vindhook. 'That was your fan club. They'll be here in a few minutes.'

Vindhook beamed. 'Wonderful! I can't thank you enough! My round, I think.' He signalled to the barman.

Aramitz, carrying a medical case, paused at the entrance to the bar. Andrew waved to him. 'Doc! Come and join us!'

Vindhook added a bottle of chilled Campanyard to his order

and when everyone's glass was filled, proposed a toast. 'To future prospects! May they be as rosy as the Doctor's wine!'

'Excuse me,' said a voice. 'Is this a private party, or can anyone join?'

Vindhook choked on his drink as he spotted Kelly standing at his elbow. He slammed the glass down onto the counter and stood there goggled-eyed as Kelly calmly ordered a Shark Bite'n'Lemon chaser.

Andrew took a firm grip on Vindhook's arm in case he made a break for it and camouflaged the move by banging on his back to help him clear his throat. 'You really shouldn't sneak up on people like that.'

'You're right.' Kelly smiled sweetly. 'Sorry, Lars.'

Aramitz used the diversion to spike Vindhook's drink with a small but potent dose of one of his 'herbal remedies'. 'Here . . . sip this gently and take a deep breath in between.'

Vindhook waved the glass away. 'No!' he coughed. 'Gotta, huh – make a, huh – call! Buh-huhh-izzness!'

Aramitz applied a restraining hand. 'Trust me, I'm a doctor.'

'Yeah, you're in no fit state to talk to anybody,' said Andrew. He patted him on the back again. 'Finish your drink.'

Kelly lifted her glass without any sign of rancour. 'Cheers!'

Unable to figure out what Kelly was up to, Vindhook – now sweating profusely – took the spiked drink and glugged it down.

'Gently! Gently!' cried Aramitz.

The non-fatal drug, which was as fast-acting as cyanide, went to work before Reindeer Man placed his empty glass back on the counter. He turned to Andrew and Aramitz with a look of utter disbelief but was unable to utter a word. His throat muscles were already paralysed. Elbowing them aside, he took two faltering steps away from the bar then tripped over Kelly's foot and crashed to the floor before anyone could catch him.

Aramitz and Andrew turned Lars over. His lips had turned blue. Aramitz lifted his eyelids, checked his neck pulse, then shouted to the barman: 'Call the hotel medics! We need a stretcher and oxygen! This man is having a heart attack!'

Opening the medical case, Aramitz pulled out a pre-loaded

221

one-shot syringe and pumped a powerful muscle-relaxant sedative into the Reindeer Man. Andrew quickly searched Lars' pockets and recovered all but one of the cash-cards he had swapped for the counterfeit Trolls . . .

The stretcher and oxygen mask arrived within minutes. And less than three-quarters of an hour later, The Dragon Lady had cast off from Honest John's and was heading clockwise round the chain of planets, along the North Polar trading route.

☆　☆　☆

Aramitz exited from Andrew's cabin, where Vindhook was being interrogated, to find Pug and Moses outside. The First Mate was flexing his heavy-duty persuader.

'How's it going, Doc?' asked Pug. 'Are we gonna have to beat the truth out of him?'

'Relax, gentlemen. He's singing like a man with his codpiece caught in a microwave.'

Pug and Moses exchanged disappointed glances and slouched away. Aramitz crossed the passageway, knocked politely, then opened the door and looked in. Kelly lay sprawled in the bunkspace.

'Don't you want to sit in on this?'

'Uh, no, I think I'd rather stay out of the way.'

Aramitz started to withdraw then stopped. 'Is there a problem you need some help with?'

Kelly sat up. 'Yes. Any minute now, the shit is going to hit the fan. Do you know of some place I can hide?'

Aramitz crooked his finger. 'Come with me . . .'

☆　☆　☆

Andrew was amazed to discover that there was very little difference between Lars, the ebulliently insufferable restauranteur, and Lars, the TradeCor undercover agent. His superiors had probably given him this assignment just to get him out from under their feet.

His real name, it turned out, was Lilleehamma Katzenjamma. Not the most fortunate choice of name for a white-blonde, shambling Mister Blobby but it was just the luck of the draw. Cocooned Atlanteans were all 'christened', sight unseen, by a randomly-generated computer programme called MONIKER.

He had hoped to be called Hamm by the other ERICS in his peer group, but was quickly labelled 'Lillee'. It was this humiliating episode which led the youthful Katzenjamma towards a career in covert operations where he had the freedom to be anyone he liked. The possibility that he could have achieved the same result by going to drama school did not seem to have occurred to him.

When Andrew raised this point, Lars replied, 'It wouldn't have been as satisfying. As an agent, I get to spy on people, betray their trust and get them sent to prison. It satisfies my thirst for revenge.'

'For being called Lillee? Bit extreme isn't it?'

The Reindeer Man sighed. 'There were many other humiliations. I've always been treated as a bit of a buffoon.'

'I thought the whole idea of cocooning was to turn out well-adjusted human beings,' said Andrew.

Lars gave him a sour look. 'That's what they claim. I think some of my wires got crossed. I only really started to be myself when I hit upon the character of Lars Vindhook. It was my section supervisor who came up with the basic cover story – '

'The Longship Restaurants . . .'

Lars eyes lit up. 'Yes! And as I fleshed out the details, I began to realise that it was an absolutely fantastic idea. It just simply couldn't fail! That's why I was so convincing!'

'Well, you certainly fooled me,' said Andrew.

'I fooled everybody!' cried Lars. 'The trouble is, I had this wonderful idea, but no money! The two million Trolls, as you know, were counterfeit. I could hardly believe my luck when Mizz Mandell asked me if I would exchange them for Cor-dollars! The dream was within my grasp! As soon as I handed her over to the Navy, I was going to resign from TradeCor, apply to the ID Register to change my name to Lars Vindhook, and start a new life!'

'With my money . . .'

223

Lars was too caught up in his dream to admit he had been guilty of criminal deception. 'In a few years from now I would have been on the way to becoming the Rimworld's most successful businessman!'

'Somebody has already claimed that title,' said Andrew. 'Can we move on? I think we've pretty well covered the restaurant business in previous conversations.'

'Sure. What d'you want to know?'

'How long have you been trailing Kelly Mandell?'

'About nine months. But I'm just the latest of a whole team of agents assigned to this case. She's been under investigation for some three and a half years.'

'Investigation? What – uh, y'know – I mean, is she engaged in some kind of criminal activity?'

Lars nodded. 'She's believed to be one of the leading organisers of the APF.' He saw Andrew's puzzlement. 'The Animal Proliferation Front. We've been tracking her movements and investigating the backgrounds of everyone she comes into contact with.'

Not having heard of the APF, Andrew was forced to improvise. 'The briefing TradeCor gave you . . . run it by me.'

'Well, this organisation sprang up following the passage of the Hygiene Laws that led to the suppression of animal life forms – '

'Apart from certain approved species – raised in specific locations . . .'

'Correct,' said Lars. 'And after passing the law, the Rimworld Council gave the Corporation the task of policing the regulations. The result being – '

' – there's not an animal or bird, wild or domestic, to be found anywhere,' said Andrew, recalling the complete lack of seagulls above the long honey-white beach on Palladia.

'But they are all stored in the gene banks of LifeCor. They were supposed to be held in secure units, but these maniacs from the APF have infiltrated the system. They have been stealing genetic material and breeding all kinds of animals in underground labs and putting them back into the environment.'

224

'And what is TradeCor's line on this?'

'That we're fighting a bunch of lunatics bent on committing genocide! They see themselves as saviours, restoring the Rim-world to its original state of purity! A lot of gullible people regard them as heroes. They don't realise that the creatures these crazies are letting loose are both the source and carriers of a whole host of fatal and crippling diseases!'

'Sounds dangerous.'

'Draws an automatic life sentence,' said Lars. 'No remission.'

'And you think this was what Mandell was doing?'

'I don't think, I know. She's one of the handful of couriers moving this genetic material around the Rimworld. Must have been through her stuff a hundred times. But I never found anything.'

'So what did you plan to charge her with?'

'Illegal possession of weapons.'

Andrew frowned. 'In that case, why didn't you nail her when we arrived at Buena Vista?'

'Because it's a piddle-shit charge! And with her connections she'd get off with a caution. I was after the big one! That's why I trailed her down to Zhannandor and across to Boot City. It was the only way to establish if there was a network and who was in it.'

'That makes sense. So why arrest her now?'

'To close the books! I had your money and I wanted out! But I needed a result – any result – to justify the expense claims I'd been putting in.'

'Ah, got it – but why keep her in the hotel instead of a holding cell in the Security Unit?'

'A little scam,' explained Vindhook. 'If we had laid charges and put her in the slammer, I'd have had to join the rest of the team in low-budget accommodation. TradeCor really penny-pinch on these field operations. But we didn't actually make a formal arrest.'

'You tied her up and tossed her in a cupboard.'

'True,' admitted Lars. 'But that was the scam. Technically speaking, we had her under observation. Which meant that

225

since *she* was in the hotel, we could all stay there, living it up at the Department's expense, until the Navy arrived. Luxury suite, with all the trimmings – '

'And I came along and ruined everything.'

Vindhook gave a fatalistic shrug. 'Yep. Life's a bitch. Crazy, isn't it? I've been trying to put you and Mandell together since you stepped on board the Narayana but it just didn't make sense. How was I to know she was part of your operation?'

'Operation . . .?'

'Oh, come on, Commander! When I saw you spending time with Mandell, I checked you out! We ran back through your ID then BAM! We hit a brick wall. I don't know who you are, but with the kind of high-level codes you're carrying this gig has got to be a big number!'

'You're right, Lars. It is.' Andrew quickly laid down a verbal smoke-screen. 'I'm on special secondment to Naval Intelligence. Mandell is one of our people. With her background, she was the ideal person to penetrate the APF. Everything she's done has been sanctioned by us. The theft and transportation of the genetic material is a low-level issue as far as we're concerned. What interests us is the linkage between the Animal Proliferation Front and other subversive groups. Mandell is now ideally placed to feed us that information.'

Lars looked impressed. 'Wow! I had no idea! No wonder you wanted her back.'

'It was vital. She has to attend a meeting with representatives of these other organisations. The arguments you've witnessed between us are just a blind to conceal our professional relationship. That's top secret by the way.'

'Of course! Don't worry, Commander. My lips are sealed. Oh, I just love all this intrigue and deception!' Lars sighed heavily. 'Just wish I wasn't leaving the service, but – '

'Do you have to?'

Lars grimaced. 'No choice. The SID team on Buena Vista – '

'The guys who pretended to mug you – '

'Yes. We filed a joint report stating we had Mandell under close observation. Now we have to explain how she slipped through our fingers – which means our little hotel scam will unravel. And on top of that, there's the little matter of trying to short-change you to the tune of one point five million Cords.'

Andrew circled Lars' chair and laid a reassuring hand on his shoulder. 'I don't intend to report that. But you're right. You should post your resignation and push ahead with your plans for those restaurants. Lots of tables, lots of people talking. I've always viewed them as ideal intelligence-gathering centres. You could report back directly to me.'

Vindhook's eyes widened. He started to reinflate. 'Are you saying the Navy would bankroll me?!'

'No, no. I don't think we could find the funds out of any of our operational budgets. But I'm going to introduce you to a man who may be willing to back you. There's no guarantee, you understand? You will have to pitch him your business plan.'

'No problem!' cried Vindhook. 'Oh! This is wonderful! I can't wait!'

Neither can I, thought Andrew. After all Connie has done for me, it's time I started paying him back.

Chapter Fourteen

Andrew found Aramitz in the galley, discussing the finer points of Rimworld gourmet cuisine with Moses Muldoon. Both wore white aprons and the mélange of odours rising from the saucepans was absolutely delicious.

'Doc – '

Aramitz raised a hand to interrupt him. 'Please! It is Jean-Pierre or simply Jean – whichever you prefer.'

'Okay, Jean. I've searched everywhere for Kelly. The only place I haven't checked is your cabin. But the odd thing is, nobody seems to know where that is. Don't you think it's time you showed me?'

'If you insist.' Aramitz. He stirred then sampled a sauce. 'A touch more salt, I think.'

Moses made his own assessment and nodded.

Andrew became impatient. 'I know she's in there.'

'Then you had better follow me.' Untying his apron, he led Andrew out of the galley and down via a service hoist to the lower cargo deck. The trail ended at a round-cornered airlock door set below a flight of metal steps.

Aramitz tapped a pass code into the control panel and unwound the manual wheel lock when the green light came on. As the door opened, a cloud of frozen carbon-dioxide rolled out.

Andrew followed him through the door, which Aramitz then shut before leading the way across a short metal catwalk shrouded in a drifting white curtain of vapour. It was like walking into *Top of the Pops*. Aramitz stopped in front of a circular access hatch, some three feet across, set in the domed

228

end of an enormous pressurised fuel tank plastered with skull and crossbone warning signs. He opened this in a similar manner then put one leg through and ducked inside.

Andrew did the same and found himself standing in a mahogany panelled ante-chamber whose tiled floor ran towards a pair of sculpted bronze doors. They were guarded by two eight foot-high black and gold statues of Horus and Anubis, Egyptian gods whose slim-hipped, skirted bodies bore the head of a falcon and a jackal.

Andrew took in his surroundings as Aramitz sealed the circular hatch. 'How come this didn't show up on the computer layouts of the ship?'

Aramitz responded with an apologetic smile. 'I like my privacy – and it has cost me a great deal to acquire it.' He opened the bronze doors and invited Andrew to precede him.

The area beyond the door bore no relation to the bare functional exterior of the fuel tank. It was like stepping back to Earth and back in time. Andrew took in the scene with growing amazement.

The central section of the room had a vaulted ceiling, twenty to thirty feet high, supported by classical columns. Lower side chambers ran off to the left and right. Many of the wall surfaces were covered with shelves tightly packed with leather bound volumes. There was a balcony lined with even more books and reached by a spiral metal staircase, club armchairs, a partner's desk littered with papers, statues, busts on pedestals, delicate ferns and broad-leafed greenery in brass pots, suits of armour, priceless classical paintings, astrolabes, orreries, old microscopes and other scientific instruments, skulls of animals, several stacks of drawers containing bones and fossils, specimens in jars of formaldehyde. It was a wondrous, spellbinding treasure-trove; the home of a late 18th/early 19th century savant.

Andrew mentally calculated the percentage of his rocket fuel bill that had been spent lifting these goodies into orbit then turned to face his host. 'I can't begin to imagine how you got all this in here.'

'Moving was a problem,' admitted Aramitz. 'But it didn't all come at once. I've been collecting odds and ends for some considerable time.'

'Odds and ends?! Jean, this is like a palace!'

Aramitz gave an apologetic shrug. 'A few home comforts always make a journey more agreeable. You must remember that I have no other home.'

'You must have lived somewhere before you joined The Dragon Lady.'

'True – but it was so long ago, I've forgotten.'

'Do you come from Earth?'

'Earth? Gaia?' Aramitz laughed. 'We all do! The Rimworld was founded by voyagers from Gaia.'

'That was millions of years ago. I mean more recently. Isn't that why you speak French?'

'I speak several Earth languages. It's a hobby of mine.'

'But you have a French name.'

'A private conceit. There is nothing sinister about it, I assure you. It became fashionable to change one's name about four hundred Earth years ago when the Rimworld began its love affair with European languages – English in particular. The ancient Atlantean tongue had become fiendishly complicated and so . . . longwinded.' He shrugged. 'It was getting to the point where it was taking half a day just to say "Good Morning".'

Andrew wasn't completely satisfied. 'What about Muldoon? He claims to be an Irishman from Connemara. The Irish are an Earth race and Connemara is the name of a part of their homeland.'

Aramitz eyed him shrewdly. 'You're remarkably well-informed.'

'It's my business to be,' said Andrew, realising he may have come dangerously close to giving himself away.

'Moses Muldoon is a dekkie.'

'Dekkies' were the third category of Rimworld citizen, born on trading ships, delivered by their biological mothers who had carried them to term like the numberless generations that were

230

born during the Atlantean's long journey to the Rimworld. They were raised from childhood like the Fast-Track Nines – but without the privileges.

'So what's the connection with Ireland?'

'He's a fourth-generation import. His ancestors were among several hundred lifted from coffin-ships and elsewhere to make up for one of the periodic shortfalls in population numbers or skill categories. Have you never heard of "The Blarney Roads"?'

'No . . .'

'Ah, then you still have *something* to learn. Would you care for a glass of port?'

It wasn't Andrew's favourite tipple but it seemed churlish to refuse. Given the decor, it was hardly likely to be cut-price plonk.

Aramitz opened a lacquered Chinese cabinet that would have knocked off the collective socks of the experts on *Antiques Road Show*, and took out a cut-glass decanter and three glasses.

Taking his cue from the third glass, Andrew asked: 'Has she told you the real reason behind this kidnap attempt?'

Aramitz nodded as he carefully filled the glasses with vintage port. 'You won't believe how smooth this is . . .' He raised his voice. 'All right, Kelly! You can come out now! Our gallant captain seems in a remarkably good mood.'

Nothing happened for a moment or two, then Kelly Mandell appeared from the shadowy depths of one of the book-lined alcoves. Her expression was one of sulky defiance. 'So what kind of shit did Vindhook have to peddle?'

'The APF connection. Everything. But then, I suppose you knew you were on the Corporation's hit-list. Must be nice to know somebody wants you. Should have told me, Mandell. Having a known subversive as navigator of The Lady is the last thing I need right now.'

Kelly bristled. 'Oh, well, if that's gonna be a problem, just throw me off at the next stop!'

Andrew put on a puzzled frown. 'Excuse me, but – aren't you the person we just rescued?'

231

She groaned. 'Yeah, yeah, yeah, don't go on about it.'

'A little gratitude wouldn't go amiss. We saved your ass back there.'

'And I saved yours in Boot City. That makes us Even Steven!'

Andrew kept it low key. 'Your father must've been really glad when you left home. Are you always this difficult?'

'Yeah! Hadn't you noticed?! I'm a *bad* girl, Carta. You got me out of a hole. I won't forget that – but don't expect me to roll over and play goo-goo. What you see is what you get.'

'That's okay,' said Andrew. 'We'll work round it.'

'Let's drink to that.' Aramitz handed out the glasses of port and proposed a toast. 'Forward together!'

Jean was right. The port was incredibly smooth. Andrew had to resist quaffing it like ale. He grinned at Kelly. 'Know what I find funny about all this? Every time I tried to dump Lars, you kept on dragging him back in the frame! I'm amazed. No, really! Here you are – one of the top people in the APF and you had no idea this blond bozo was tailing you!'

Kelly gave him a withering look. 'But he didn't find what he was looking for, did he?'

'Were you carrying some of this genetic material?'

'Yeah. But don't lose any sleep over it. It's been delivered to our people on Zhannandor.'

'Did you know he was checking up on everybody you came into contact with?'

Kelly smiled. 'Not everybody. I managed to lose him for two whole days on the way to Boot City.' She sipped her port then asked 'Did he say what they were arresting me for?'

'Illegal transportation and possession of firearms.' Andrew shook his head. 'I thought you were going to sell them?'

'I was,' said Kelly. 'But since you were paying the bills, I didn't need to.'

Andrew appealed to Aramitz. 'See what I mean?'

'Ohh, lighten up, Andi. Or do you have a problem with what the APF is trying to do?'

'I'm not sure . . .'

232

The smile disappeared. 'Did he feed you that garbage about animals being plague-carriers? About how our actions are tantamount to genocide? He did, didn't he? It's lies, Andi – manufactured and spread by the Corporation. They secretly funded the original research into the dangers of animal-borne infection that led to the formulation of the Hygiene Laws. The scientists were in their pocket and the data was faked. Healthy animals were injected with contagious diseases and released into the wild but it didn't stop there. They contaminated food and water supplies – deliberately caused massive outbreaks of skin diseases, nervous and digestive disorders all over the Rimworld – then planted the evidence which showed that it was animals that were to blame. We know they did it, Andi. We've seen the documents.'

It sounded Machiavellian. But then so was the Final Solution; the ultimate Nazi horror hatched in the elegant lakeside palace at Wannsee. 'Why, Mandell? Why would anyone do that?'

'To gain control! It was just one more piece of their master plan! It was so obvious no one guessed what they were doing. First they manufacture the rumours – they already controlled most of the media, so spreading alarmist stories wasn't a problem. Next they call for a programme of research which they manipulate with false data and use the media yet again to call for a legislative response. The Rimworld Council call them as witnesses! Their front men come across as serious, concerned citizens. They even have plans drawn up to deal with the problem. Now they're the experts! The Hygiene Laws are framed with the help of advisers drafted in by the Corporation. Fish, all other marine life and insects were excluded. The Laws banning birds, mammals and amphibious reptiles, except for controlled, approved species, are passed and guess who gets the job of enforcing the legislation and supervising the farming of the approved species?'

'The Corporation. That's pretty neat,' admitted Andrew.

'It was the first big step towards policing every aspect of the Rimworld. It gave their Navy the legitimacy it needed to mount stop and search missions – '

233

'Yeah, but wait a minute. The Navy were trying to drive the pirates and hijackers off the spaceways – '

'Don't be naive, Andi! That was part of their campaign to win popularity! It provided the excuse to harrass the independent shippers – many of whom were driven out of business – allowing TradeCor to step into the breach. The competition was hamstrung by a whole raft of licences and certificates – trading, owner's, navigation, engineering – the list is endless. Then came another masterstroke. The levying of import and export duties on all goods passing through the spacestations. The Corporation sold the idea to the Planetary Councils by offering to split the take, and undercut all the other bids to provide the service. Now, their own Customs officers and Security men are on all stations. The Rimworld is locked tight. There isn't anything or anybody that can move around the system without them knowing about it – and taking a cut. It's incredible to think that so much power could have been amassed by bare-faced deceit and manipulation.' Kelly smiled ruefully. 'Anyway . . . that's my side of the story.'

'Sounds reasonable enough to me,' said Andrew. 'Nobody ever amassed a fortune without exploiting *somebody* along the way. But if you have proof of what happened, why didn't you blow the whistle?'

'It's like I said. They control the media. But even if we did have access, no one would believe our story. That's why we decided on direct action. To acquire the genetic matrices of all the animals that were suppressed, set up secret breeding centres and put them back into the environment. Once we've done that and demonstrated that there is no danger, we may be in a position to expose the Corporation.'

Andrew grimaced. 'That's quite an agenda. Hope you know what you're doing. What about the public? Are they on your side?'

'They will be when they know the truth. It may take years, but we'll win eventually. We have to.'

'Meanwhile, the Corporation is hunting you down.'

Kelly smiled. 'Yeah – but if they're putting people like

Vindhook on our case, we may be in with a chance. What d'you plan to do with him by the way?'

'I've already done it.' Andrew recounted the improvised story he had used to flim-flam Lars.

'Do you think he believed you?'

'Let me put it this way – we did a deal. He wants out of TradeCor. I know it's insane but he's deadly serious about opening up a chain of restaurants. I've promised to put him in touch with a possible investor.'

'Who's that? The mystery man who's bankrolling you?'

'Never mind who it is.'

Kelly appealed to Aramitz. 'You see? He knows everything about me but he won't come clean. That's what worries me.'

'Nobody ever *knows* anybody,' said Andrew. 'As for you, all I've got to work with is what other people have told me, and what you've seen fit to reveal. Which certainly isn't everything.'

'It's more than you've given me. What d'you think he's hiding, Jean?'

'I would rather not be drawn on that, my dear.' Aramitz appraised Andrew and smiled. 'I have no wish to intervene in what is clearly a . . . challenging relationship. However, there is one thing that intrigues me. Where on earth did Vindhook get the idea that you were a commander in the Navy?'

Andrew eyed Kelly. It was clear from her face that she had not voiced her own suspicions on that score.

'That's a good question, Jean. I wish I knew the answer.'

The now-familiar electric tingle ran through Andrew's brain. A sign that the ghost in the machine was stirring.

The signal containing the coordinates for a rendezvous with the SS Mount Olympus came on the following day. Andrew passed them to Kelly. When pressed for an explanation, he told her that Finnee Ganzwayko, the man she had so warmly recommended, had failed to keep up the payments on The Dragon Lady. As a result, ownership had reverted to someone called

235

Constantine Parnassus with whom he now had to negotiate to avoid being hit with a repossession order.

This news came as no surprise to the rest of the crew, but they said nothing now, just as they had said nothing back at Boot City Field, in order not to prejudice the sale which offered a ride into space and the chance to claim eighteen months' back pay from their new captain.

Three weeks later, they reached the rendezvous.

Positioning The Dragon Lady beneath the enormous bulk of the SS Mount Olympus, like a pilot fish under the belly of a shark, Andrew extended the landing pads and passed control of the trader's guidance system to the host ship. The Dragon Lady was coaxed gently onto the extendable docking arms, then lifted up and set down in the cavernous Number Seven hold of Connie's flying head-office.

When the pressurisation cycle was completed, an extending catwalk was lowered onto the trader's top decking, while on the bridge, the lilting voice of 'Maureen', the South London songbird, came over the sound system, inviting 'Mr Cartahaynyar' to attend a meeting with 'a representative of the management'.

'Yukkh!' said Kelly. 'If she looks anything like she sounds – '

Andrew played along. 'My thoughts exactly.'

Exiting through the top hatch, he went up the catwalk two steps at a time. Shalimar, who was waiting in the companionway on the far side of the airlock, welcomed him with a happy laugh and a warm hug. They then embarked on an electric cart ride which took them down a maze of corridors and in and out of several elevators before arriving at the centre of Connie's financial web.

Shalimar led Andrew onto the platform from which Parnassus held sway. Connie greeted him with buoyant good humour then begged a moment's grace while he completed the inspection of a set of accounts presented by one of his diminutive, dark-skinned employees.

Andrew surveyed the lines of desks raying out in all directions, the piles of paper and the numberless army of clerks

236

working abacuses at lightning speed, while others scribbled away, or scurried back and forth along the aisles delivering and collecting documents.

Having approved and signed the accounts, Parnassus despatched the clerk. Andrew watched the man descend from the platform to the floor below. 'Who are these guys?'

'Gujuratis.' Seeing Andrew's blank look, Parnassus explained. 'From the province of Gujurat – part of the Indian subcontinent. Does your grasp of geography stretch that far?'

'I know about Kashmir . . .'

'Gujurat is much further south. Wonderful people. Marvellous accountants. Been with me ages. I brought fifty of them over for a trial run. Turned out very well. Everything was going splendidly then they started to pine away. Couldn't work out what the problem was until one of them plucked up the courage to ask me if they could send for these young girls who they wanted to marry.

'So I shipped them over, then everyone wanted to know if they could bring their immediate family and close dependents. And then they started having children and when they grew up, *they* wanted to get married – but not to anyone who was already here! So back we go for more brides and husbands, which meant a new batch of dependents and it just went on and on! Last time we did a head count, it was seven hundred and fifty thousand, give or take an aunt or two.'

Andrew boggled. 'And they're all on this ship?'

'No, no!' laughed Connie. 'I've got two thousand on board doing the accounts and self-catering. The rest are growing wheat, millet, cotton and rice on Palladia and doing a roaring trade in elaborate woodcarvings. Born businessmen. If I don't watch out, they'll end up taking me over.'

Andrew nodded but remained puzzled. 'Why are you doing all your accounts on paper?'

Connie responded with a vague gesture. 'Call me old-fashioned but I prefer to see things written down. Computers are so . . . how can I put it? Accessible. And vulnerable too. Always remember that when the system crashes all you've got

237

is a heap of very expensive junk. But you can always do bookkeeping by candlelight.'

Andrew pointed to the large terminal sitting on Connie's desk. 'So what's this doing here?'

'Oh, that! We use those for hacking into the Corporation's data banks.' Parnassus rose and extended an inviting arm. 'Let's go and have a quiet little chat. I'm dying to hear what you've been up to.'

☆　　☆　　☆

Seated in a cosy corner of Connie's palatial stateroom, Andrew gave a broad outline of his adventures from the moment he had boarded the SS Narayana. The only bit he left out was his three-day thrash with Imelda.

Shalimar, who knew all about it from the update calls she had received from Honest John, found the omission rather touching.

Parnassus appeared to be pleased by Andrew's account, and made no reference to the fact that his money had been spent buying back something he already owned.

'Congratulations, Andrew. Considering how little time you've spent in the Rimworld, you certainly deserve full marks for resourcefulness. But we never doubted your ability, did we?' The question was directed at Shalimar.

'No.' She gave Andrew a look that said more than just 'Well done'.

'However, there is one small area of concern. That money I put in your bank account. You were supposed to use it to buy a ship. Why did you tell Honest John you only had one point seven five mil to spend?'

'I thought I should put a little aside for a rainy day.'

'Two million cords? What were you expecting? A monsoon?'

'It's a lot less than two million now. There were the crew's wages – Ganzwayko really stiffed me on that one – the fare to Boot City, spacepark fees, the list is endless. People have had their hands in my pockets ever since I stepped off the Narayana.'

238

'You're too kindhearted,' said Connie expansively. 'But then that has always been one of your more attractive qualities.'

'Some people just won't take "No" for an answer.'

Parnassus appeared not to realise he also fell into this category. 'Like our Miz Mandell – except of course, that's not her real name.'

Given her behaviour to date this shouldn't have been at all surprising but it was. 'So who is she?' asked Andrew.

'Her father is Sandiego Mandragorian – the top R&D man at the Corporation's weapon labs. He's based on Libra.'

At least that bit was true. 'And her *real* first name?'

'Kallamazoulou. Her mother died – accident – but her pet name within the family was "Zou-Zou".'

Oh, I'm going to love this, thought Andrew.

'She and her father are very well connected. In fact, she could be very useful to us.'

'Don't count on it. She's been nothing but trouble since I met her,' said Andrew. He had already decided not to mention Kelly's link with the APF.

'Well, let's not be too hasty. You do need a navigator. Rumour has it you're not on speaking terms with the ship-board computer.'

Andrew felt a slight tingle as 'Daniel' surfaced briefly. 'Give me a Series 8 RON and you can send Zou-Zou back to Daddy and feed Tarqueen into the crusher.'

'RON . . .?' Connie looked puzzled.

'It's short for ACRONYM – Advance Computronix Re – '

'Yes, yes, of course! No need to spell it out!'

'You're behind the times,' said Shalimar. 'Advance are installing the 21 Series now, with – '

Parnassus cut her short with a warning glance. 'Let's stick with Miz Mandell. This project is already into overrun.'

Andrew seized the conversational high ground. 'Project, yes. Glad you mentioned that. Before we go any further, I've got some questions that need answering.'

Parnassus exchanged a glance with Shalimar. 'Oh, dear. I hope this is not going to cause any unpleasantness.'

'That depends on whether you've been totally up front with me.' Andrew gave his host a hard, searching look then fixed his eyes on Shalimar.

Parnassus switched into dignified elder statesman mode. 'That really pains me, Andrew. Trust is the most important element in a working relationship. Trust, loyalty, mutual respect, dedication. Once that bond is broken we might as well all pack up and go home.'

Shalimar's eyes remained fixed on Andrew. Calm, unwavering. 'I think he wants to know about Daniel.'

'Yeah, what's he doing inside my head, Connie? We all know he didn't get there by accident.' Andrew's gaze took in both of them. 'Must have slipped in under the wire while I was in the sim-tank. I'm really disappointed you didn't tell me he was part of the programme.'

Shalimar appealed to Parnassus.

Connie shifted uncomfortably and forgot to eat for a moment or two. 'This is awful, Andrew. I'm hugely embarrassed at being caught out like this. I cannot deny I am guilty of holding back certain facts – but only to avoid overloading you *at this stage*. The rest of the story, uh, I mean – plan – was to be revealed on a "Need to know" basis. As an ex-Army man I'm sure you'll understand.'

'Oh, sure, I understand,' replied Andrew. 'But that doesn't give you the right to fuck around with my brain. This guy wasn't on the agenda, Connie! What you did was – '

'Unforgivable? I hope not. In time, I believe you will realise that, in taking these decisions, your best interests have always been uppermost in our minds.'

'My God!' Andrew exploded with laughter. 'I've been fed some twaddle in my time but that beats everything! If you had *my* best interests at heart I'd still be in Catford! C'mon! Admit it! I'm just a pawn in some Byzantine masterplan and *you* are pathologically incapable of telling the truth!'

'Perhaps, but I did promise you adventure and excitement – and there's been plenty of that. Be fair, Andrew. What had life in Catford to offer? A man with your talents? Not to mention

240

intelligence. Working for the tabloids? Newspapers are what people wrap fish and chips in!'

'Newspapers were just one avenue I was exploring. Someone had put me forward for a staff job on *Jane's Defence Review*. Tabloids were just the start. A few years down the line, I might've worked my way up to foreign correspondent on *The Times*.'

'Indeed,' said Parnassus. 'The prospects were so rosy, a week before that little envelope of ours popped through your front door, you were talking about re-enlisting!'

Shalimar supplied the details. 'The Jug and Bucket, Staines. 7.30 p.m. Last Saturday in May. With two of your men from A Company.'

'How the hell d'you know about that?'

'Oh, we've been on your trail for ages,' said Connie.

'Okay, yeah, so it's true. But it would have been *my* choice! *my* decision. It's not being brought here that I object to. So far it's been a weird, wonderful and fairly wacky experience. One I hope I'll be able to look back on fondly when I get home.'

'A hope we all share, Andrew.'

Andrew hadn't finished. 'But what *really* tees me off is being lied to, being deceived by people who then expect me to go out there and put my neck on the line without telling me what the objective is! This is not the way to win hearts and minds, Connie!'

Connie appealed for clemency. 'What can I say?'

'Why don't you go back to the top of page one and take it from there?'

'How much have you discovered about Daniel?'

'I know his name, rank and that he's an overbearing sonofabitch who thinks he's God's gift to the Navy, and that he scares the hell out of me every time he breaks loose. I also know we bear a close physical resemblance to each other.'

Andrew recounted his chance meeting with Hammerhead and his narrow escape from Sadie Moon's and concluded: 'Which is probably why you picked me rather than somebody else.'

241

Parnassus eyed Shalimar briefly then nodded. 'That is certainly one of the reasons, yes. And the physical likeness is not just close, it's uncanny. So, tell me – when this person accused you of being responsible for sending him to prison – did it trigger any memories of that specific event or, err . . . anything else?'

Andrew shook his head. 'No. From the moment I laid eyes on this guy, I was aware of knowing him and could feel a lot of bad vibes but nothing more specific than that – even when he identified me as Kinsharadeen. Up to now, what comes through are not memories. It's his Navy expertise and his abrasive personality.'

Shalimar cut in. 'Do you have any idea what triggers these breakthroughs?'

'Well . . . I have thought about that. I can't predict the time and place but there is a sort of loose connection. They tend to occur when I'm on board ship, or dealing with shipboard matters, and in what I call "control situations".'

'When your authority is being challenged?' ventured Shalimar.

'Exactly. So far, they've been brief, but when he emerges, my own personality is pushed completely into the background. I become a mute bystander. I can hear Daniel talking but I can't stop him – well, that's not quite true. I do consciously try to reassert control – to drive him back into a dark corner – but it's a struggle.'

Shalimar leant forward. 'But you have always won.'

'Up to now,' said Andrew. 'It was Daniel who came through a few minutes ago with that bit about the Series Eight from Advance Computronix. What worries me is that one day I won't be able to get him back in the box.' He smiled uneasily. 'Guess, this is what schizophrenics must feel like.'

Parnassus gave him a fatherly pat on the arm. 'Let me put your mind at rest. The symptoms are similar but you're not schizoid. This is a controlled situation. Let me give you the background on this. Daniel Kinsharadeen was a young, very capable serving officer – rather like yourself. But there is one important difference. Daniel enjoyed an extremely privileged upbringing. His father, Gideon, holds the post of Supreme Fleet Admiral. As the top-ranking Navy officer, he is also a member of the Presidential Executive Board of the Corporation.'

Shalimar broke in. 'And this year he was voted back for another three-year term as the Board President and CEO. Which makes him the most powerful man in the Rimworld.'

The now-familar pained look returned to Parnassus' face. 'Most powerful man in the Corporation, Shalimar, *if* you please. There is a difference.' He turned to Andrew. 'As I was saying – the Kinsharadeen family have served in the Navy for eleven generations and – like the Pharoahs – the post of Supreme Fleet Admiral has passed down the line in dynastic succession. From the day he could walk, Daniel was groomed for the post like his father before him.'

Andrew sensed he was uncovering something within himself. 'You said Daniel *was* – what happened?'

'The Navy frigate he was commanding exploded almost without warning. He and his crew were carrying out an emergency evacuation – they had in fact just launched the spacerafts – when the ship blew to pieces. The crew perished. Daniel was badly injured. My ship, the Mount Olympus, happened to be in the vicinity. There was no Mayday signal from the frigate. Whatever went wrong blocked all communication channels.

'Anyway – we picked up Daniel – did what we could then, when it was clear he was going to die, I arranged for my medical people to perform what's called a "mind-dump". Don't ask me to explain the process. My expertise is confined to high finance, electronic fraud and antiquities. In very crude terms, it's an electronic clone of the brain. You've seen Microsoft's Encarta? The CD-ROM audio-visual version of a well-known encyclopedia?'

'Grolier's,' added Shalimar.

Parnassus acknowledged her input. 'With a mind-dump you end up with something similar. A complete record of a person's life and personality.'

243

To Andrew, the idea of plundering a dead psyche felt vaguely repellent. Like graverobbing. 'When did all this happen?'

Connie gestured vaguely. 'About ten years ago. Fortunately we were able to keep the matrix in pristine condition – '

'Until I came along . . .'

'That, Andrew, was our second stroke of good fortune. Your stunning resemblance to Daniel Kinsharadeen made it possible for me to proceed with my master plan. Operation JERICHO. Years in the planning and fiendishly clever – although I have no wish to blow my own trumpet.' Parnassus squeezed Andrew's arm to give added emphasis to what he was about to say. 'You are the key, Andrew, because you, and you alone, possess Daniel's knowledge and expertise. And – '

' – you want me to impersonate him.'

'We need you to do more, Andrew. If we are to succeed, you will have to go beyond mere pretence. In the final, crucial stage of this operation, you will have to make the conscious decision to release him into your mind. You will – to all intents and purposes – *be* Daniel. And with your help, we are going to shatter the power of the Corporation and free the Rimworld from its grasp – without spilling one drop of blood.'

Andrew nodded. 'I see . . . and in doing this, you are motivated by purely altruistic motives. This is not in order to be able to get your *own* hands round its jugular.'

Connie gave him an 'O, ye of little faith' look, accompanied by a mournful sigh. 'Tell him, Shalimar. He obviously trusts you more than he trusts me.'

Shalimar's eyes radiated reassurance as she expounded Connie's visionary philosophy. 'The Corporation is now so big and so rich, it is only a matter of time before it buys up the entire Rimworld. In Earth terms, try to imagine what would result if the oil giants merged with the global players in construction, chemicals, mining, manufacturing, electronics, food production, processing and retail distribution, consumer products, pharmaceuticals, publishing, film, television, radio telecommunications – and enlisted the Mafia to suppress any competition or protest.'

244

'They had a similar kind of set-up in Italy,' said Andrew. 'Run by a guy called Silvio Berlusconi.'

Shalimar didn't smile. 'What I have just described is The Corporation. Its whole business ethos is based on the bottom line. "Profit before people". Now it is true that Mr Parnassus has amassed a large personal fortune. He had do so in order to fight The Corporation. But despite his enormous wealth, he is the champion of independent traders. He is against the exploitation of the individual by faceless inter-global monopolies. For him, "Small is beautiful". He wants to create a climate that will allow healthy, open competition in trade and industry to flourish. He wants to break down global conglomerates into locally-based enterprises whose only shareholders are its owners and workers – that are responsive to the real needs of their customers, and which will also respect and nurture the environment.'

Andrew chewed his lip and nodded soberly as he took this in. He doubted that the Corporation was the embodiment of all evil, but on the other hand, Hitler's Germany, Stalin's Russia and Ceaucescu's Romania showed what could happen when power was wielded by a single, monolithic organisation led by psychopaths.

Connie's handwoven Harris Tweed vision was certainly a noble one, but given that the man was a self-confessed swindler – albeit of other swindlers – it all sounded like a sanitised PR handout.

Too good to be true.

Or is it? thought Andrew. Perhaps I'm infected with world-weary cynicism. Ten years of untrammelled greed under the Tories culminated in a final frenzied stampede of borrowing and property speculation which had carried the nation over the cliff into a financial abyss like the legendary herd of Gadarene swine.

When you had seen the feelgood factor replaced by the pain of negative equity, it was difficult to swallow Utopian fairy tales without a large dose of salt.

Andrew let his gaze fall upon his Rimworld mentor. Parnassus sat waiting for his response with Buddha-like inscrutability. 'It's

245

strange. Despite what you've done to me since I was foolish enough to accept your lunch invitation, I bear you no ill will, but – '

Connie jumped in. 'Good! We were hoping you'd enter into the spirit of things.'

'After the way you dumped this "Daniel" on me?! Suppose I decide not to play along?'

'Oh, dear . . .' Connie's eyes met Shalimar's briefly. 'We had hoped to enlist your support by appealing to your better nature. If – with your help – our plan meets with success, there would obviously be a handsome reward in any Earth currency of your choice, a free ticket home, and we'd ensure that you never hear from Daniel again.'

'You'd suck him out of my brain . . .'

Connie's plump fingers played an invisible keyboard. 'Urr-roomm-ahh . . . in a manner of speaking.'

Shalimar intervened. 'The process is – '

'Yes, yes, yes!' cried Parnassus. 'I'm sure the clinical details are absolutely riveting but they are not germane to our discussion! It's the big picture that interests me, dear heart! The big picture!'

Shalimar sat back, tight-lipped.

'Where was I?' demanded Parnassus.

'I think you were about to threaten me,' said Andrew.

'Never! Threatening people is such an ugly way to do business. Persuasion is so much better, don't you agree? Of course you do! I've always found if you put your cards on the table, explain things, show people how much they stand to gain, that's half the battle.'

He adopted a matter of fact tone. 'If, on the other hand, you were to abandon your friends and strike out on your own, I'm sure you'd survive – might even do very well – until the pills ran out. And then you'd be marooned here for ever. A moving blur in a world full of statues. Like a ghost in a cemetery – flitting between the gravestones.'

Andrew hadn't considered that.

Parnassus was quick to note his reaction. 'And without our

246

help – even if you did manage to get a new supply of dee-cell – Daniel might take you over completely. Which would be a shame, because the explosion that wrecked his ship wasn't an accident. We know that now.'

Andrew's questioning glance drew an almost imperceptible nod of confirmation from Shalimar.

'Some very important, highly-placed people set out to kill him,' continued Parnassus. 'If they were to discover he was still alive, you would be in constant danger.' He spread his arms as if to welcome a prodigal son. 'Stick with us, Andrew. You know it makes sense.'

Andrew pretended to weigh up the pros and cons but it was obvious he wasn't kidding anybody. His fate had already been decided. But he was not going down without a struggle. 'I want to know everything there is to know about this Operation JERICHO.'

'Of course!' Parnassus gave his arm another fatherly pat followed by a conspiratorial wink. 'All in good time, Andrew. All in good time.' He laid down his empty plate and heaved himself upright. 'And now, if you'll excuse me, I must go and make a few more pennies to help pay for all this.'

'That reminds me!' Andrew held Connie at bay with a pointing finger. 'I met this guy. Lars Vindhook. He has this great business proposition – to do with opening a chain of restaurants. He's looking for a backer.'

'Well . . . I'm always interested in anything to do with food.'

'That's what I told him. He has it all worked out. It really is a very original concept. The guy even has a video presentation.'

'Does he? Hmmm . . .'

Andrew weighed into the pitch. 'Now, of course, I don't have an ounce of your financial savvy, but I really do think that someone with money to invest and with the ability to structure a deal could turn a handsome profit. He's on board my trader. Whaddya say?'

Parnassus nodded. 'Give me an hour then bring him to me.'

☆   ☆   ☆

247

When Andrew had gone to break the good news to Vindhook, Shalimar served Parnassus with another dessert from the overloaded trolley at his elbow, then sat down facing him and slowly sipped a cup of coffee.

Connie set about his dessert like a man who hadn't eaten for a week. 'All things considered, I thought our little chat went rather well. You really did do a magnificient job on our young hero.'

Shalimar accepted the compliment graciously. 'The mind-block is holding a lot better than I thought.'

'But did he swallow the story? That's the question.'

'He will if he doesn't think about it too much. That risk has always been there from the very beginning.'

'I know,' mused Connie. 'But this is the make-or-break phase. I just hope we can get through it before he finds out I've been lying to him yet again.'

Chapter Fifteen

Lars Vindhook returned from his meeting with Parnassus in a buoyant mood. Connie, it seemed, had been greatly taken with the idea of a chain of Longship Restaurants and had invited Vindhook to spend some time on the SS Mount Olympus, honing his master plan and preparing new financial projections with the help of one of Olympic's business managers.

The crew of The Dragon Lady, who were preparing to depart on a salvage mission, found it hard to believe that they were finally going to get rid of Mr Straw-Head. Andrew, in particular, kept his excitement at the prospect damped well down in case there was some unforeseen hitch. But the magic moment finally came. Vindhook's luggage was carried up the catwalk along with the freezer-trunk containing his remaining samples of reindeer steaks and seal cutlets, and it was handshakes all round and apologies for the trouble he'd caused.

Andrew, anxious to speed him on his way, assured him there were no hard feelings.

'Wonderful! I can't tell you what this means to me!' Vindhook looked overcome with emotion and close to tears although – given his past deceits – it was difficult to regard any reaction as completely genuine. 'And please remember, my offer of a free meal still stands! News of our first Grand Opening will be sent to you by Olympic Marketing, so please, come and visit! All of you! I am so looking forward to be sharing my good fortune with old friends!'

'Lars,' began Kelly. 'There's something I've been meaning to tell you. First, the only thing that makes life bearable is the prospect of never seeing you again. Second, I am not your "friend". I never have been. I find you physically repulsive, infantile and incredibly boring, and as for this appalling restaurant you keep wittering on about, you should be utterly ashamed of yourself. It's the most disgusting thing I've ever heard of!'

Vindhook was completely bewildered by this verbal savaging. 'But . . . you said you liked the idea?! You made suggestions!'

'Not the ones I wanted to make!'

'Kelly is a vegetarian,' explained Aramitz.

'Ahhh . . . so *that's* what this is about!' Vindhook turned to Andrew. 'Is that how you feel too?'

'Not exactly. I don't have a problem with reindeer meat, but the idea of having a large tank of baby seals that customers can fish out with a net then send to the kitchen to be clubbed to death *is* a bit offputting.'

Lars responded with a cracked laugh. 'But the baby seals aren't killed! They are put back in the tank when the restaurant closes!'

'Okay. What about your proposal that large parties of ten or more will be able to take home the stuffed and mounted head of the reindeer they've just eaten? Complete with horns.'

'They are going to come from the Corporation deer reserves – after the annual cull! Of course, as yet, I haven't signed the contract.'

Kelly took over. 'Yeah, all right, all right. But *somebody* is killing the animals you're serving up as steaks, ribs and cutlets – and the whole process is completely obscene!'

'But it's not real meat!' exclaimed Lars. 'It's specially textured soya-bean protein extract with simulated flavour additives, chemical preservatives and artificial colouring!'

Andrew was momentarily flummoxed. 'The stuff I saw in the galley certainly looked like real meat!'

'Tasted like it too,' said Muldoon.

'Of course!' cried Lars. 'The new texturising techniques give you a product with an even density, flavour and tenderness plus a satisfying chewability factor. It's *better* than the real thing!'

250

'But Lars!' insisted Andrew. 'The steaks that Moses cooked in the galley – they had pieces of bone attached!'

'That is real,' admitted Vindhook. 'Well, sort of. It's powdered animal bone meal. The shapes are produced by injection moulding.' He shook his head. 'You won't believe the trouble the lab had trying to get the processed soya to adhere to the bone.'

'I give up,' said Kelly. 'Goodbye, Lars. I take back what I said about the food, but the rest stands. You're a pathetic, insensitive, butter-brained creep!'

And with that, she marched back into the ship. Pug, Muldoon and Aramitz followed.

Vindhook's smile remain undented. 'There's no need to apologise. I know she doesn't mean it.'

Andrew bit his tongue. He shared Kelly's feelings but wanted to get the full story.

'So . . . it's all fake. Just like your Skandavian Trolls.'

'On the contrary! It's a top-quality soya-bean product!'

'Yeah, but why bother, Lars?'

'It's called marketing.' Vindhook mopped his brow. 'Have you ever seen untreated soya bean extract? It looks like wet shit on a plate. Tricking it out to look like meat makes it a value-added product. Vegetarian meals are healthy but boring. Meat arouses a primal urge. It's dangerous, exciting. Add in the smoky Longship decor, flaming torches, big-breasted serving wenches, and a chance to get rat-faced on two kells of Kvasir and you're offering people a night to remember!'

'So, basically, the humble soya bean served with a dash of set-dressing and a side-order of razzamatazz equals big bucks.'

'It's the magic formula, Andi! I've spent years studying the market. Watching people eating when I should've been monitoring the movements of subversives. It's not the food that matters. It's *the image* you create *around* the food, and the ambience in which it's served! Get that right, and the customers'll be queuing up to eat whatever junk you put in front of them. Providing it doesn't actually make them sick, they'll keep coming back for more!'

Vindhook had a point. And now it had been brought to his

251

attention, Andrew could think of several fast food chains back on Earth that were using the same formula. He grasped Vindhook's boneless hand and propelled him towards the catwalk with a friendly thump on the back. "Bye, Lars. Hope it all works out for you.'

He could afford to be generous. From here on in, the Reindeer Man would be someone else's problem. And the trick now was to put as much space as possible between the SS Mount Olympus and The Dragon Lady before Connie realised what he had been lumbered with.

☆　　☆　　☆

The salvage operation seemed a relatively straightforward assignment. Connie explained that he had put in the winning bid to collect the Comm-Sat that was in geo-stationary orbit above the mining planet of Nebo – one of a handful of smaller worlds orbiting between the Rimworld chain and the twin suns, Bilharzi and Bengharzi.

Being nearer the suns, the daytime surface temperature never fell below a searing 45° Celsius – far higher than the dryest desert regions of any Rimworld planet. The atmosphere was a dirty yellow; the sky was filled with drifting clouds of sulpurous smoke. There were no oceans, only vast toxic lakes. The hills were volcanic and active. The low lying areas were covered with bubbling pools of molten tar; a scrofulitic landscape whose only vegetation was stunted brown thorn trees and poisonous clumps of porcupine grass.

With facemasks the air was just about breathable; with protective clothing and insulated accommodation units, it was possible to survive in this hellhole. The managers and technicians who ran the mining operation, were rotated every nine months. The workforce, who dredged the tar pits, dug out the sulphur and staffed the processing plants were there for the duration of their sentence.

These unfortunates were known as the 'tar-babies'.

Nebo was the Rimworld equivalent of a debtor's prison. Its population was made up of credit defaulters, swindlers, counterfeiters and individuals convicted of illegal currency speculation. Anyone guilty of financial irregularities and those who could not repay outstanding loans or fines were arrested by the Corporation's Treasury Agents and transported to Nebo to work off their debts on which interest continued to accumulate at 40% APR.

Only those whose debts were paid off by friends or well-wishers ever made it back to the Rimworld.

As the voyage to Nebo proceeded, Andrew was filled with a growing feeling of dread. A premonition of disaster. According to Connie, the mining operation had been closed down after two years of deficit trading. The supervisory staff had been relocated to other sites. The industrial plant, housing and equipment had all been abandoned and without maintenance would not survive long in the corrosive atmosphere.

Nebo . . .

The very name of the planet had a troubling resonance. Andrew felt sure he knew why, and strained to remember. Whatever it was had to be connected with Daniel, but his alter ego – who had been so eager to assert himself when his presence was not required – now stubbornly refused to come out of the shadowy realm of the subconscious.

Andrew sought out Jean-Pierre Aramitz and was invited into his private retreat; the live-in museum of art, science and literature that lay concealed within one of the fuel tanks.

Aramitz would not allow anything but small talk until they were both armed with glasses of a classic red wine, then invited his guest to sit down and unburden himself.

Andrew chose a high-backed wing chair and sank into its comforting embrace. 'It's to do with that brief talk we had a while back. About being in two minds . . .'

Aramitz lowered his glass. 'Yes, I remember.'

'During our last stopover, I asked Connie about you – because of your ticket – and all this.' Andrew indicated their surroundings. 'He told me that you were an old friend – '

'We go back a long way.'

' – and that I could trust you.'

253

Aramitz returned Andrew's challenging gaze. 'If you wish to confide in me, you have my word that nothing you say will reach the ears of anyone outside this room.'

'I'm counting on that. In fact, my life may depend on it.'

Aramitz nodded gravely. 'Where would you like to start?'

Andrew took a deep breath, swallowed some wine then said 'I'm not from the Rimworld. I'm from the other side of the galaxy. From Earth – the planet the Atlanteans once thought of as home.'

Aramitz savoured his wine before replying. 'That is, by any measure, an astounding revelation. You must forgive me if I say that it does not surprise me. I have known for some considerable time that our mutual friend has benefited enormously from his . . . terrestrial connections.' He waved towards a twenty-foot high obelisk engraved with Egyptian hieroglyphs. 'This and the two statues in the hall were brought back by one of his ancestors. Last of a long line of tomb robbers. Claimed he knew Pythagoras.' He broke off apologetically. 'But I digress. Excuse me. Am I to understand that our friend brought you here?'

'Yes . . .'

'Please continue . . .'

Andrew began with a potted bio, then outlined the events between opening his mail on that fateful Tuesday morning in Catford to his first appearance on board The Dragon Lady. He skipped the episodes they had shared, then related his meeting with Parnassus and Shalimar and the dismaying news that someone else's mind had been squirrelled away inside his own.

The mind of Daniel Kinsharadeen.

Aramitz, who knew something of Daniel's background, was visibly shaken by Connie's audacity. He halted any further explanation. 'Let me guess. He intends to use you as a pawn in his private war against the Corporation.'

'Private war?' Andrew laughed. 'In the script I was given, Connie was presented as the White Knight – galloping to the rescue of humankind.'

Aramitz chuckled. 'If you applied an extremely generous

254

interpretation to his motives, I suppose that could, in a limited sense, be true.' He drank some more wine. 'For your own security – and mine – I won't ask you what the plan is.'

'Jean! I don't *know* what the plan is! That's worrying enough, but what scares the hell out of me is that at any moment I may undergo a personality change! I won't be *me* anymore, I'll be – '

'Daniel . . .'

'Yes. You've seen some flashes. But I don't know what it's going to be like if he really takes hold. I may not be able to control it. That's why I had to tell you. I need someone who understands what I'm about to go through and that – if Connie is telling the truth – whatever happens next is all for the best.' He raised his glass.

Aramitz responded to the silent toast. 'Let's hope so . . .'

Some time later, as he was about to leave, Andrew remembered the second reason for calling on Aramitz. 'Tell me, Jean – does your knowledge include an understanding of the difference between the metabolic rates governing life on Earth and here in the Rimworld?'

'I've heard it mentioned but I have no direct experience of it and, as far as I am aware, there is no scientific proof which would support the idea.'

'I was hoping you'd say that.' Andrew took out a bubble pack of pills from his pocket and held them up. 'Connie gave me a supply of these when I got here. They're dee-cell tablets. Designed to slow me down. So far I've been taking them religiously but something doesn't seem quite right. I can't put my finger on it. But it could be another of Connie's scams – '

' – to keep you under control . . .'

'Maybe. If I left these with you – would it be possible for you to find out what's in them? I've got plenty more.'

Aramitz took the pack from him with a reluctant grimace. 'I could try – but I don't have any hi-tech lab equipment. It will take some time.'

'That's okay,' said Andrew. 'We've got a long road ahead of us.'

☆　　☆　　☆

255

On the other side of the Rimworld chain, a signal emanating from their star informant and routed through two intermediaries, reached Admirals Korreggidoorian and Treehausterhaus. It contained the information they had been promised. Daniel Kinsharadeen, aided by half-a-dozen renegades, including the troublesome daughter of Sandiego Mandragorian, was heading towards Nebo aboard a trader called The Dragon Lady. The signal also gave an approximate ETA.

The Admirals, who had made careful and secret preparations to deal with Daniel Kinsharadeen's reappearance, sent a signal of their own to the trusted commander of the NV Korazon. The intercept was put in motion. This time, there would be no mistakes.

☆   ☆   ☆

Sixteen weeks later, after chasing Nebo round the suns, the planet came up on the forward view screens. Another four days went by before Andrew was able to place The Dragon Lady into orbit high above the scummy yellow cloud pattern that overlaid Nebo's dark, pitted surface. The planet looked as if it was suffering from a severe case of acne.

Using the retro rockets and side thrusters, The Dragon Lady was manoeuvred towards the Comm-Sat which was in geostationary orbit, two hundred and fifty miles above the equator on the zero meridian. Since the Comm-Sat always stayed above the same point on the equator, the trader had to adjust its speed to the rotation of the planet and slowly inch closer to its target.

The salvage plan required four of the crew, working in pairs, to don spacesuits and dismantle the large solar panels which powered the Comm-Sat. Once they and the parabolic communications arrays had been removed, the cylindrical body of the Comm-Sat could be guided into one of The Dragon Lady's cargo holds.

The recovery operation involved using jet-packs to cross the thirty yard gap separating the Comm-Sat from the trader. Pug and Moses were the only crewmen with EVA experience. Having performed a simulated spacewalk during his indoctri-

256

nation on Palladia, Andrew found the prospect of doing it for real held no terrors for him. Kelly, who never missed an opportunity to show off, brazened her way into the fourth suit.

The four solar panels – each sixty feet long by fifteen feet wide – were relatively easy to detach. Getting them aboard The Dragon Lady proved a time-consuming task. Once unfolded, the sections that made up each panel locked into place, creating a rigid but delicate structure which – if they were to be recovered without damage – had to be handled with a great deal of patience and skill. While each member of the EVA team possessed these qualities, nobody possessed both to an equal degree. As a result, patience was combined with clumsiness and skill with exasperation. The space around the Comm-Sat was blue with obscenities but, to everyone's amazement, the task was finally completed.

The transmitter aerials were easy, as were the receiver dishes. Even so, Andrew and Kelly managed to lose one when it unexpectedly freed itself when they were trying to force a stripped mounting bolt. The sudden loss of purchase sent Kelly somersaulting backwards away from the Comm-Sat. Faced with losing one or the other, Andrew decided to grab Kelly and was promptly blamed for cocking things up.

They watched the dish sail away like a giant frisbee.

Pug's voice came through on the ship-to-suit link. 'Never mind, five out of six isn't bad.'

It was the last lighthearted moment they were to enjoy for some time. As Andrew and Kelly attached the line that would help to haul the body of the Comm-Sat towards The Dragon Lady, the segment of space above the trader began to shimmer and sparkle with rippling shards of rainbow-coloured light.

A second later, Andrew and Kelly were rocked by an invisible force field. For a brief moment, as it passed through them, it felt as if all their internal organs were about to shake loose. And then it was gone, leaving them clinging to the handholds of the Comm-Sat. They glanced up again and were just in time to see the shards of light coalesce to form the

257

awesome bulk of a Navy cruiser – hovering over them like a dark storm cloud.

The letters along the main hull identified it as the NV Korazon. And what they had just witnessed was its re-entry into the four-dimensional universe after making a jump through hyperspace.

The signal broadcast from the cruiser to The Dragon Lady was relayed through their headsets: 'This is a Navy intercept as authorised under the Prevention of Space Piracy Statues of 233-477/4. If you are not familiar with Stop and Search procedures, you are hereby ordered to obey the following instructions.

'Do not attempt to move your vessel. Deactivate all drives. Keep the Universal Comms channel open. All persons currently outside the ship should return to it immediately. Captain and crew are to assemble on the bridge with all appropriate documentation. To avoid physical damage to your vessel and its occupants you are further ordered to facilitate the arrival of our boarding party.

'You have one minute to confirm compliance. Failure to do so within the time allowed will be interpreted as Hostile Intent and may result in the immediate destruction of your vessel as sanctioned under Article Eight of the above Statute. Response time starts now!'

Pug didn't hesitate. All orders would be complied with. Andrew and Kelly hauled themselves on board using the line attached to the Comm-Sat, and passed through the airlock into the ship. Pug and Aramitz were waiting to help them out of their space-suits.

'Where's Moses?'

'On the bridge, manning the Comms channel,' said Pug. 'What's this all about?'

'Haven't a clue.'Andrew turned to Aramitz. 'That little hideaway of yours . . . anything in there that could give these goons an excuse to make trouble?'

'No. I have stamped Export Licences for everything of value. But don't worry. Previous searches have failed to discover that the fuel tank contains anything other than liquid oxygen. I am confident that this boarding party will reach the same conclusion.'

Kelly read Andrew's look and answered the unspoken question. 'I'm clean. It's all been passed down the line.'

'Good. Okay. I'd better get the ship's papers ready.'

☆　　☆　　☆

A Cor-Navy lieutenant with two ten-year service stripes led the boarding party of ten ratings. They were backed up by a twenty-five-man squad of Space Marines in full combat gear. The boarding party carried sidearms, but that was standard Navy procedure.

Andrew decided that the show of overwhelming force was intended to make it clear who was in charge. Any resistance, or even any disruptive behaviour could result in the application of 'Prejudicial Restraint' – Corporation-speak for a bullet through the brain.

Ten marines mounted guard over the bridge. The Navy lieutenant selected two ratings to stay with him and sent the rest of the joint force to search the ship.

The two ratings collected up the IDs and checked them using a laptop that had a UHF Comms link with the Navy cruiser parked two miles above them. The lieutenant, whose name tag identified him as Moreton Hindermarsh, leant over their shoulders to check the read-outs. The crew's identities were also being scrutinised on board the NV Korazon, and the lieutenant liaised with his shipboard colleagues over the pencil mike attached to his helmet.

'. . . Cartahaynyar and Mandell . . . uhuh . . . he claims to be the captain. Yes, I'll check that out now.'

'Is there a problem?' asked Andrew.

'There could be,' admitted Hindermarsh. 'Central Archives can't make a clean match with your IDs. May be a technical problem. Do you have the ship's papers?'

Andrew handed over the wallet containing the C-D. It was passed to the ratings for processing.

'So . . . what's the story?' demanded Hindermarsh. Seeing

259

the uncertain look on Andrew's face, he elaborated the question. 'What were you planning to do with the Comm-Sat?'

Andrew explained they were on hire to Olympic Shipping who had been awarded the salvage contract by the Corporation.

Hindermarsh took this information on board with a series of 'uh-huh's' that made him sound like a car that wouldn't start. 'Excuse me.' He retired out of earshot and conversed at some length with the NV Korazon.

When he returned, his face bore a puzzled frown. 'More problems, I'm afraid. We ran a check with the Equipment Sales Division and they have no record of awarding a salvage contract for the Nebo Comm-Sat. In fact, it's not even been classified as surplus to requirements. It's still a fully functional part of the Navy's communications net.'

Andrew scanned the faces of his crew. They looked as baffled as he did. 'There must be some mistake.'

'There is,' said Hindermarsh. 'And you guys just made it by letting yourselves be caught redhanded.' His voice changed gear. 'I've been instructed to arrest you on a charge of space piracy – '

'Wha-a-a-at ?!'

'And I must advise you that everything you say is now being recorded and may be used as evidence when you come to trial.'

Andrew turned to Kelly. 'I don't believe this is happening – '

'Under Article Seven, your vessel is automatically confiscated. If it passes a safety inspection, it will be sold at auction. If not, a destruction order will be applied – '

This news triggered a round of anguished protests from Pug, Moses, Chilli, Gumbo and Aramitz.

' – in which case, you will be responsible for the costs of disposal over and above any fines you may incur in respect of this offence.'

'Lieutenant! Listen! Let me put a call through to Olympic Shipping. I guarantee we can sort this out in under five minutes.'

One of the ratings drew Hindermarsh's attention to the screen of the laptop. It was turned away from Andrew. All he could see was Hindermarsh's reaction to what he was reading. The lieutenant's eyebrows rose, stayed up for a while, then fell into a frown. When he reached the end of the data, he uttered a single, ominous, '*uh-huh*'.

He raised his eyes. 'The owner of the Olympic Shipping Agency, Constantine Parnassus – '

'Yes . . .'

'The man you claim hired you to salvage the Comm-Sat . . .'

'Yes. That's right.'

'You are absolutely sure about that?'

'Of course, I am. Are you gonna let me speak to him, or what?!'

'I don't think so. Mr Parnassus filed a Loss Report with Navy Headquarters eighteen weeks ago. It concerns this trading vessel – '

'The Dragon Lady . . .?'

Hindermarsh nodded and indicated the laptop. 'He's the legal owner. The ship's papers you gave me have been doctored. According to this deposition, the vessel was removed from Boot City on Zhannandor after a fraudulent deal involving forged currency – which, of course, will render you liable to further charges – '

'Oh, c'mon! This is getting ridiculous!' cried Andrew.

'You think so? Several people who witnessed the transaction gave a description of the man involved – and so did a number of employees at Boot City Field. Mister Parnassus was kind enough to supply the Navy with an Identi-Pic.'

Hindermarsh nodded to one of the ratings who turned the laptop towards Andrew.

'Who does that remind you of?'

Andrew's face stared at him from the screen. He had been well and truly set up. What the hell was Connie playing at? If this was part of the game plan, it was a bloody dangerous move.

Three Navy men entered the bridge followed by a marine carrying a holdall.

Andrew's heart sank. It belonged to Kelly. He whispered

261

through the side of his mouth. 'I thought you said you were clean!'

'I meant the *other* stuff!' she hissed.

'You might like to look at this, sir.' The senior Navy man took charge of the holdall and brought it over to Hindermarsh. 'This marine found it hidden in a ventilation shaft.'

Andrew fixed a baleful eye on Kelly.

The lieutenant placed it on the navigation table, unzipped it, ran his hands through the loose wadding inside and produced the weapons that had done nothing but cause trouble since Andrew stepped onto the Buena Vista station.

Hindermarsh hefted one of the weapons – a laser rifle – and eyed Andrew with a predatory smile. 'Gun-running as well? My word, Mr Cartahaynyar. This really isn't your day.'

☆　　☆　　☆

After the discovery of the weapons, events moved swiftly. Pug and Moses were ordered to don spacesuits and bring the body of the Nebo Comm-Sat into the cargo hold, then when the doors were sealed, two cutters from the Korazon attached themselves to The Dragon Lady and guided it into the cruiser's main hold.

Since Andrew and Kelly – as captain and navigator and therefore judged to be the principal culprits – were already cuffed and shackled, it was left to Pug and Moses to set The Dragon Lady down on its landing pads. With that task completed, they – along with Chilli and Gumbo – were subjected to the same indignity. Aramitz was the last. As two Marines grabbed hold of his arms, he brushed them aside and confronted Lieutenant Hindermarsh.

'Lieutenant! I must protest!'

Hindermarsh gave him a dull stare. 'Really? What about?'

'Being manacled and placed under arrest! I'm not a member of this crew and not a party to the crimes you allege they have committed. I am a bona fide passenger travelling on a prepaid ticket purchased through a reputable shipping agency – '

'And you have the papers to prove it . . .'

262

'Naturally!' Aramitz produced a document wallet from an inside pocket and held them out.

Hindermarsh made no move to take it.

'I therefore request you accord me the lawful rights and privileges granted to all distressed persons under the Space Conveyancy Act of 118-875. Shall I quote you the relevant section?'

'That won't be necessary, Mister, uh . . .?'

'Aramitz. Jean-Pierre Aramitz. Doctor of Philosophy, Zoology and Astrophysics. Emeritus Fellow of the Interglobal Academy of Sciences.'

'Very impressive,' said Hindermarsh, not looking the least impressed. 'I'd've thought someone with your kind of background would be travelling on a scheduled spaceline instead of bunking down with this bunch of scumbags. But maybe you've also got something to hide.'

Aramitz bristled. 'Take care not to add insult to injury, Lieutenant!

Hindermarsh gave the nod to the Marines. The two soldiers grabbed Aramitz and swiftly applied the wrist restraints.

'Very well! You leave me no choice! I demand to see your commanding officer!'

Hindermarsh swallowed a smile. Taking the document wallet from Aramitz's hand, he stuffed it back into the inside pocket. 'He doesn't want to see you, Doc. So save your breath. Nobody cares. You're finished. Guilty by association. Understand?'

He stood aside and braced himself. 'Mister Kornwallassee!'

A Marine lieutenant jumped to attention. '*Yo!*'

'Escort the prisoners to the holding cells!'

☆   ☆   ☆

A short while later, Andrew, Kelly and Aramitz found themselves behind a set of floor to ceiling bars on one of the lower decks of the NV Korazon. Facing them, across the passageway, in an identical cell, were Pug, Moses, Chilli and Gumbo. There was ample room with eight head-to-the-wall, fold-down bunks on either side, a fixed table and bench (with no back rest), a

263

water-cooler with a supply of paper cups, and a separate washroom with a three-quarter modesty door and a soft trickle of canned music.

Aramitz pulled down one of the beds. It had an integral plastic mattress. He sat down with a resigned sigh. 'I hope you understand that my protest was on behalf of all of us. I thought if I could avoid arrest, I might be able to persuade the captain of this vessel to put me in touch with Constantine Parnassus.' He made an ineffectual gesture. 'This is all very confusing.'

'Seems pretty straightforward to me, Jean.' Andrew glanced up and down the short passageway. There were two more identical cells to his left. The passageway had barred gates at both ends. Beyond them were two sentry kiosks staffed by armed Marines. 'Connie sold us out.'

'I must say I find that hard to believe.'

'Wish I did. Question is – what did he hope to achieve? I know he likes playing games but I've got a feeling these guys are playing for keeps.' Andrew made eye-contact with Kelly. She didn't look at all contrite. 'If you had to keep those guns, why didn't you give 'em to Jean to take care of?!'

'I didn't want to get him into trouble.'

'Oh, so that makes it okay, does it?' Andrew resisted the urge to commit violence upon her person. 'Such concern for other people! But you're quite happy to see *me* go down!'

Kelly gave him a longsuffering look. 'Andi – we're *all* going down. So why don't you give your mouth a rest?'

'Oh, sure! I forgot! When you screw up, no one's allowed to talk about it. It's your way of avoiding responsibility.'

'Andrew,' began Aramitz. 'You have every reason to be upset but I really don't think this is a good time for us to fall out with each other.'

'You're right, Jean. I should've parted company with *Miz* Mandell way back down the line.' He shook his head. 'It's crazy. If I'd started my journey just *one* day later I'd've missed the Narayana, I'd've missed good old Lars and best of all – ' He fixed his eyes on Kelly. ' – I'd've missed you!!'

She nodded. 'Yeah . . . Life's a bitch.'

Andrew turned his back on her, grasped the bars and imagined they were Kelly's neck. He called across the passageway. 'How's it going, guys?'

Pug put his face against the bars. 'Well, we're not about to dance the hornpipe.'

Gumbo joined him. 'You're tellin' me!' He delivered an ear-piercing whistle. 'Hey! Marines! *Yo!* Shift your spit'n polished butts! We got an emergency here!'

A marine guard came out of the left hand kiosk, unlocked the corridor gate and approached the cells. 'What's the problem?'

Gumbo pointed to the wall speaker that was relaying soft, seamless canned music. 'Can you pull the plug on this shit and give us a wall-to-wall blast with a heavy beat? If so, do it fast, 'cos there's two funky brothers about to go cold turkey in here!' He rested his elbows on a crossrail and let his forearms dangle through the bars.

The Marine nodded. 'Got just the thing for you, bro.'

Andrew, who was almost directly behind him, saw the move but had no time to yell a warning before the Marine drew a stun-gun from a quick-draw holster on his hip and jammed it against Gumbo's chest.

The electric charge threw Gumbo's powerful body into a back-flip across the table. His head connected with the bench behind and for an instant he was poised comically with his feet in the air before toppling over and crashing to the floor. Chilli, Moses and Pug moved quickly to turn him face up. Pug began to pump his chest.

The Marine eyed both cells. 'Any more complaints?'

The question was met with silence. It was obviously not a good time to get smart.

Half an hour later, the low-volume steam of canned music was interrupted by a general shipboard alert. There was a high-pitched beep which made Andrew's brain tingle, followed by a disembodied voice. 'Message to all ship's personnel. Stand by for transition to hyperdrive! Remain at your present location until the blue jump light is extinguished and the All Clear signal sounds. Transition in ten seconds . . . nine . . . eight . . . seven

265

. . . six . . . five . . . four . . . three . . . two . . . ONE!'

For a brief instant, the scene in front of Andrew's eyes was washed by rippling pattern of light. Shapes blurred and wavered – like the stones in the bed of a swift-running sunlit stream. A shock wave ran though his body at the same time, making his insides quiver and then . . . nothing.

There were no blue lights in the cells, but he heard the triple bleep of the All Clear. In fact he was expecting it. Buried deep in his mind was the memory of having gone through this process several times and he wondered how far the jump had taken them from Nebo.

One of the paradoxes of hyperspace was that the distance travelled through it bore no relation to the transition time. Distance was determined by the strength of the electromagnetic field generated by the hyperdrive. It was this force – known as the trans-dimensional flux (TDF) – which catapulted the Navy ship out of normal space and hurled it through a dimensionless, timeless void whose nature and properties were still not fully understood.

The scientific principles governing the hyperspace drive had been discovered over twenty-five thousand years ago but it was only in the last thousand that units capable of being installed in Navy ships had been produced. Controlling the distance and direction of the jump – Range and Vectoring – had proved an almost insuperable problem. It was finally solved by throwing huge amounts of money at it for the best part of the last millennium.

Only the Corporation had the financial resources to back such a project and the tenacity to bring it to a successful conclusion just as they had resurrected the concept of space-flight. And succeed they did, but the astronomical costs of the drive units limited their installation to the most prestigious ships of the line; the First and Second Cruiser Squadrons – twenty vessels in all – plus the ten Hunter/Killer Frigates employed on deep space asteroid patrols. Thirty out of a fleet total of twelve hundred ships of all types.

Andrew continued to muse upon the subject. The construction and installation costs of such drives were not the only limiting factor. The energy burned up in each jump was another huge expense, which was why Navy ships didn't go leaping around the Rimworld like Hoppy the Kangaroo.

Captains had to work within tight budgetary controls and were expected to show an operating profit at the end of each annual tour. The Korazon had just made two hyperjumps. The combined cost exceeded the scrap value of The Dragon Lady and the Comm-Sat.

This intercept was already in the red before the Captain made his first move. With the ship's Financial Controller monitoring the cost of everything right down to the last bog brush, he would have known that. So he would not have proceeded without specific orders from a superior officer – at Fleet Headquarters. Only Line Admirals had the authority to sanction a 'deficit' operation.

But why would a Line Admiral at Fleet HQ be interested in the fate of a rusting shit-box like The Dragon Lady? Interested to the point of funding the intercept from the Central Reserve Account?

The Dragon Lady's flight-path towards Nebo would have been tracked by Sector Movement Control. If suspicions had been aroused, it should have been dealt with, at Sector Level, by a run-of-the-mill intercept. But it wasn't. This was a special operation . . .

Andrew was jolted by the sudden realisation that none of these thoughts were his own. It was Daniel who was asking the questions.

The answers weren't long in coming.

Chapter Sixteen

The discharge from the stun gun left Gumbo badly shaken. He was back on his feet within the hour but the spring had gone from his step. The incident had a sobering effect on everyone else, and when twenty armed marines entered the holding cells to re-apply the plastic handcuffs, no one attempted to resist.

A service elevator took the crew to one of the upper decks, where they were quick-marched along a corridor and into a large briefing room.

The front half of the room had been cleared of the usual rows of fold-up chairs. These were stacked on both sides. The large floor-to-ceiling screen on which operational data was displayed during crew briefings was filled with a huge logo enclosing the letters USDC – the United Space Development Corporation. On the dais below, three chairs had been set behind a curtain-front table.

Andrew, Kelly, Aramitz and The Dragon Lady's crew were halted in a line some fifteen feet from the table and ordered to face it. Their individual marine escorts removed the cuffs, then took a noisy pace backwards, slamming the heel of their boots on the floor.

Kornwallassee, the close-cropped marine lieutenant who had escorted Andrew's party from the trader to the cells, commanded the prisoners and escort to stand at ease. He then tilted his head back in order to see under the peak of his field hat and surveyed the line-up. His face had that pinched, disagreeable look that military men reserve for hapless recruits and civilians in general. 'This trial is being held under Navy regulations. When the Presiding Officer and Judicial Panel enter, you will

268

come to attention and remain so until ordered to stand down!'

'Lieutenant!'

Kornwallassee went nose to nose with Aramitz. 'What is it?!'

'If this is a trial, why have we no defence counsel?'

'This is a drumhead court-martial, Mister! Article Four of the Space Piracy Act allows for summary trial and execution of persons apprehended during the commission of a criminal offence. Now pipe down! That goes for all of you! Anyone who attempts to disrupt the proceedings will get their kidneys grilled.'

Kornwallassee caught the signal from the guard on the door. He stepped back and assumed a ramrod stance. 'DEE-faulters! Ah-Ten . . . SHUN!'

Andrew and others jumped to it as the Presiding Officer entered followed by a Navy and a Marine captain. They sat on either side of the Presiding Officer who wore the standard red wide-sleeved gown over his black uniform.

The uniform of a Treasury Agent. The name was something of a misnomer. The Treasury Division was the supreme law enforcement arm of the Corporation: judge, jury and executioner.

Andrew was gripped by a sudden anxiety on realising that he knew the man who now cast his pale, expressionless eyes over the accused. It was Chief Treasury Agent Stagg. Someone whose deeds were etched indelibly on Daniel's psyche.

The shock of seeing Stagg broke the mental barriers inside his mind. The memories came flooding out, sweeping all other thoughts aside. He swayed unsteadily as his brain performed a mental somersault. It felt as if his past life was being sucked into a black hole. Andrew tried to hang on – tried to reassert himself, but it was a losing battle. His brain – his whole body – was being hijacked. They no longer belonged to him. They . . .

. . . belonged to Daniel Kinsharadeen.

Chief Treasury Agent Stagg brought the gavel down. 'This court is now in session. This is a summary trial as laid down under Article Four of the Space Piracy Act. Sub-section Ten of the same Act empowers Treasury Agents to conduct such trials

269

and pass sentence. The charges will be read out, and evidence will be heard from the arresting officers. Under Article Four, the accused are not permitted to make statements and they are denied the right of appeal. The charges will now be read!'

Daniel barely heard the preamble. Stagg's appearance and the bang of the gavel had sent his mind hurtling back into the past.

To the point in time when, as commander of the NV Carolina, he had been ferried across to a sister-ship, the NV Tennessee, to stand trial in front of a five-man Naval Review Board.

The mining planet of Nebo had been his downfall then just as it was now. And Agent Stagg had been at work behind the scenes . . .

The court had been convened in a similar briefing room to the one he stood in now and the Corporation logo had been on the screen behind his five judges. Below the dais, there had been a table for the Prosecutor – Navy Captain Kincaid, who had served alongside Daniel before his promotion to Commander. There was also a table for the Defence Counsel – a role Daniel had chosen to perform himself.

The Navy officer to Stagg's right began to read the charges but it was not his voice that Daniel heard.

It was Kincaid's . . .

'The accused, Commander Daniel Kinsharadeen, is charged with wilful failure to obey a mission order issued by Headquarters, Seventh Fleet on the 7th Quintal, 845-722. The order required him to pick up fifty-three mining supervisors from the planet Nebo and retrieve the Comm-Sat.'

The Presiding Officer interjected 'The operation was being closed down?'

'Yes, sir. Due to adverse geological conditions. The supervisors were high-grade specialists and the Corporation wished to deploy them elsewhere. Commander Kinsharadeen, in direct contravention of this order, landed the Carolina on the surface of the planet and took on board fifteen hundred miners and dependents before allowing the supervisors to embark. And on his departure, he left the Comm-Sat in place.'

Daniel remembered Kincaid's barely disguised unease. They

270

had been reasonably close and now his shipmate was required to nail him to the wall. But that was what the Navy expected.

Duty first, feelings last.

'Nebo is a planet with an extremely hostile environment. The fact that no injuries or serious damage were sustained is testimony to his skills as a captain but in taking the Carolina down to the surface, Comander Kinsharadeen risked losing both ship and its crew. The unauthorised manoeuvre also caused a massive drain in the ship's fuel reserves. As a result, the Carolina's operational budget now shows a negative balance.

'We are therefore asking the court to find the accused guilty on all three counts. One – wilful failure to obey Mission Orders. Two – recklessly endangering his ship and crew. Three – gross financial mismanagement. The prosecution rests.'

Kincaid gave Daniel a regretful glance then resumed his seat. From then on, it had been a duel between Daniel and the Presiding Officer . . .

'Commander Kinsharadeen. You have heard the case for the Prosecution. Does it represent a fair and true account of the actions that have brought you before this court?'

'Yes, sir.'

'Do you have anything to say in your defence?'

'Yes, sir. This just happened to be one of those times when I felt that people had to be put before profit.'

Given the ethos of the Corporation, this was the ultimate heresy. Especially from the mouth of a Navy Officer. The faces of the Review Board had turned to stone. Daniel remembered Kincaid shaking his head in disbelief. After a moment or two, the Presiding Officer regained the power of speech . . .

'Would you like the opportunity to retract that statement – or modify it in anyway?'

'No, sir.'

'Very well. Let it be so recorded. Now answer this. Why did you aggravate the charge of disobedience by leaving the Nebo Comm-Sat behind?'

'The workforce records had gone adrift, sir – so we couldn't be certain we had gotten everyone on board. If we'd taken the satellite, anyone left down there would have had no way to contact the Rimworld. They'd've been marooned with no hope of rescue.'

'Did it ever occur to you that the Corporation might not want these people rescued?'

But they had been. All fifteen hundred and seventy-three miners and partners were being housed and fed in the main hold until arrangements could be made for their transfer.

What Daniel hadn't known, as he stood before the court on board the NV Tennessee was that Stagg and a team of fifty Treasury Agents had crossed the two mile gap separating the two ships. Taking advantage of his absence, they had assumed temporary command of the Carolina and were arranging for the rescued miners to be relocated.

'When the Navy issues a Mission Order, it expects total compliance, not moral judgements. That's Page One of the Training Manual, Commander!'

'Yes, sir!'

'The mineworkers on Nebo weren't there by choice. They were sent there because they had failed to meet their financial obligations. They were bad credit risks, Commander! Workshy welshers who had ducked every chance to straighten things out.'

'I accept that, sir. But since they were working to pay off debt, it occurred to me that they could be deployed elsewhere. That way, the Corporation would get more of its money back.'

'Commander! Don't you think that was taken into consideration? Mission Orders aren't just pulled out of the air! Every factor is fed into the equation. The environment on Nebo is not just unhealthy, it is deadly! After eighteen months your lungs are shot, your blood is poisoned. That's why the supervisors are rotated every quarter.'

'I didn't realise conditions were that bad, sir.'

'It's true the facts aren't widely known. But in your case, ignorance is no excuse. You didn't rescue a viable workforce. Your knee-jerk heroics have saddled the Corporation with fifteen hundred untreatable hospital cases! With no one to pay the bills, the welfare costs would have to be met by the Navy. It's exactly

272

the kind of unrecoverable expenditure that we don't like to see in the annual balance sheet.'

It was at this point that a black-uniformed Treasury Agent had entered the briefing room and approached the Review Board. Kincaid, the Prosecuting Counsel, who was seated just below the dais, heard what was said and told Daniel after the trial.

The Review Board was advised that the Treasury team 'had completed the final audit'. The message had been delivered by Chief Agent Stagg himself. As he straightened up to go, he had fixed his eyes briefly on Daniel. A pale, chilling glance. When he left the room, the Presiding Officer resumed the hearing . . .

'Do you have anything more to add, Commander?'

'Only that I'm sorry I queered things for the accountants. I didn't realise money was that tight.'

'Sit down, Commander. I shall ignore that last remark. Let it be struck from the record. There are too many people who seem to think that the Corporation is run by faceless financiers when, in their view, it should be led by men of vision.

'But it always has been. When the governments of the Home World ran up trillion dollar deficits, it was the global corporations who came to their rescue. It was they who resurrected and funded the space program.

'They realised that money was humankind's salvation. And when the global players came together to form USDC, it was the Corporation which enabled our civilisation to colonise the other planets that made up the Rimworld. We forged the chain! And from many worlds, we made one!

'It was the greatest feat of logistics since the Great Trans-Galactic Migration. And it was made possible by the profits from the trading monopolies created by the Corporation and the licenses fees and taxes paid by millions of smaller enterprises. Our future depends on the continuing success of these commercial interests and it is the Navy's role to protect them – not damage them as you almost succeeded in doing.'

'Yes, sir . . .'

The Presiding Officer had then conferred briefly with his four co-judges. It did not take long to reach a consensus . . .

273

'Accused will rise.'

Daniel remembered the pitying look on the face of his one-time friend, Kincaid.

'The Board finds you guilty on all three charges. Given your previous impeccable record and your family's long and historic connection with the Navy, we are disposed to believe this was a temporary lapse of judgement due, in part, to your relative youth.

'However, we cannot allow your present views to contaminate your fellow officers and crew. You are hereby relieved of your present command and are further sentenced to a loss of three years seniority and a fine of two million dollars suspended for five years. You will also pay the cost of these proceedings.'

'Sir!'

'The Court also warns you that any repetition of this behaviour will attract a much harsher sentence. This also applies to the utterance of the views you have expressed here today. Do you understand?'

'Yes, sir.'

When the court proceedings ended, he had not been allowed to return to the NV Carolina. His Navy kit and personal effects had been collected from his cabin and sent across. His First Officer had been placed in temporary command of the ship.

It was only later, on his return to Fleet HQ on Libra, that he learned from his father what lay behind the phrase 'final audit'. The airlock doors separating the main hold from the rest of the ship had been sealed by Stagg and his agents. The external loading doors had then been opened and the fifteen hundred men and women sheltering inside had been sucked out into space . . .

Daniel's mind jerked back to the present in time to hear Agent Stagg pronounce the verdict. '. . . all guilty as charged. Under the powers granted to me by Article Six of the Space Piracy Act, you are hereby sentenced to death. Termination is to be effected forthwith by whatever means are judged appropriate.' Stagg banged the gavel. 'Court will rise!'

Daniel took one pace forward. 'Just a moment! You have no

right to try a naval officer! Under Article Two of the Disciplinary Code, any officer apprehended on a criminal charge has the right to be tried by his peers or superior officers!'

The heavy hands of his Marine escort fell upon his shoulders and arms. The Marine Captain to Stagg's right signalled them to go easy.

'I am Commander Daniel Kinsharadeen of the NV Marianna. You must declare this a mistrial and grant me a new hearing!'

The Navy Captain exchanged an uneasy look with his Marine colleague behind Stagg's back.

'The Marianna disappeared with all hands eleven years ago,' said the captain.

Eleven years ago? Daniel's mind started to spin.

'There was an explosion. Everyone was killed.'

'Everyone except me.' Daniel tried to master his mental disarray. *Eleven years* . . . ELEVEN YEARS?!

The Marine Captain eyed Stagg then asked: 'So where exactly have you been all this time?'

'I don't know,' replied Daniel. 'And I have no idea how I got here. I must have lost my memory.'

'Very convenient.'

'It was seeing Agent Stagg that brought it all back. The last time our paths crossed was after the final evacuation of Nebo.'

Stagg didn't say anything. He just studied Daniel with those same chilling eyes.

The Navy Captain took up the questioning. 'So are you saying you don't know these people you were arrested with?'

Daniel turned his head to look at them. He pointed to Kelly. 'I've got a feeling I know her from somewhere but, uh . . . I can't recall her name.' He dismissed Aramitz and the others. 'I don't know who the rest of them are.'

Kelly said nothing. She just eyed him and shook her head.

Daniel appealed to the Navy Captain. 'Who is in charge of the Korazon? I need him to send a signal to Fleet HQ informing Admiral Kinsharadeen that his son is alive. If possible, I would like to talk to him myself to explain what has happened here. I also need a complete medical checkup. If I have – as I suspect – been suffering from long-term traumatic amnesia, then I cannot be made legally responsible for my actions.'

Stagg considered this for all of two seconds then laughed it out of court. 'Nice try, Cartahaynyar.'

'Cartahaynyar . . .?'

'That's the name on your ID. You're a two-bit trader from Tyrenia.'

'That's ridiculous!. Why are you pretending you don't know me?! You were in the courtroom on board the Tennessee when I was up before the Review Board.'

'I've been in lots of courtrooms.'

'Well, you should remember this one! You'd just blown away fifteen hundred people I picked up from Nebo!'

The Navy and Marine captains eyed one another. It was clear they were starting to feel uncomfortable about this lengthening exchange.

Daniel tried to enlist their support. 'Why are you stalling on this?! I can give you the access codes that will release my records. Run a DNA test! It will prove I'm telling the truth!'

Stagg went into a brief huddle with his two sidekicks. They both assented to whatever was proposed then the Marine Captain ordered his gung-ho lieutenant into action. 'Mister Kornwallassee! Escort the rest of the prisoners back to the cells. Leave six men here with Chief Agent Stagg.'

Daniel didn't make eye contact with the others as they were marched out.

Stagg produced a powerful handgun, placed it on the table and beckoned Daniel to approach the dias. 'That's far enough!' Stagg waved away the six Marines. 'Wait outside. I'll call you when we're through.'

The room emptied. Daniel, who was still handcuffed, was left facing Chief Agent Stagg.

'So, Mister Cartahaynyar . . .'

'Let's drop the pretence, Stagg. I've told you what the score is. I don't know what's going on here, but you had better think

276

very seriously about your next move. It's not too late to make that call.'

'Oh, yes it is, Danny Boy.'

Stagg stood up, holstered the handgun and stepped off the dais. He was several inches taller than Daniel, with broad shoulders and a craggy face with deep set eyes and a moustache – an unusual feature in the Rimworld. His sheer size made him an intimidating opponent but he also projected a dangerous aura. A simmering threat of murderous violence.

'So you *do* know who I am . . .'

'Of course. I just never expected you to come crawling out of the woodwork. When we wired the Marianna, we thought the Kinsharadeen line was extinguished – permanently.' Stagg shook his head. 'No one should have survived that blast.'

'But I did.'

'Yeah . . . where have you been, Danny Boy?'

'Stagg . . . ordinarily I wouldn't give you the time of day but that is one question I'd give a year's pay to be able to answer. When you walked through that door, a key turned in my brain – unlocking the whole of my past life. I can recall everything up to the moment when the Abandon Ship alarm sounded on the NV Marianna – plus a few disconnected fragments that don't make sense and then – I find myself standing here with no recollection of what happened in between. It's like coming back from the dead.'

Stagg gave a malevolent grin. 'You shouldn't have bothered.'

The meaning was clear. 'Why are you doing this?'

'For the good of the Navy. The Kinsharadeens have been at the helm for too long. It's time for some other men to come through. Strong men – who can keep the Navy on the right course.'

'So who's next – my father?'

Stagg answered with a shrug. 'He was only a threat as long as he was protecting you. Once you're removed from the equation, we can afford to wait. He can't last for ever.'

'It won't work, Stagg. There are too many people involved. Sooner or later, the truth is bound to come out.'

277

'Hah! About what? The arrest and disposal of a bunch of thieving scags? This mission won't even appear in the ship's log! That's why we *are* going to get away with it. Because a *great number* of people from here to Fleet HQ want to make damn sure you never step into the top slot!'

'But those two officers and the Marine escort heard me identify myself. It's bound to slip out somewhere down the line.'

Stagg laughed. 'I'm the guy who pulled the plug on the Nebo miners, Danny. Part of the team who turned the Marianna and her crew into confetti. D'you really think we'd let twenty marines and three officers jeopardise the success of this operation?'

'You won't succeed. Conspiracies always leave a trail. You'll be tracked down eventually.'

'Well, no one's going to be able to track *you* down, Danny Boy.' Stagg raised his right hand. Daniel, expecting the hand to ball into a fist, braced himself for the inevitable blow, but to his surprise, Stagg let him escape with a menacing pat on the cheek.

☆   ☆   ☆

As soon as the crew of The Dragon Lady were returned to the holding cells, Aramitz attempted to explain that their captain's startling transformation was a tactical move designed to obtain a stay of execution.

'Could have fooled me,' grumbled Pug. 'He practically disowned us!'

'Yeah,' agreed Chilli. 'Looked like he was more concerned about saving his own skin.'

'No, no!' said Aramitz. 'You mustn't jump to hasty conclusions. He warned me he might behave strangely. There is more I could tell you, but it's obvious we can't discuss such delicate matters across this passageway. Bear with me. All will become clear later. Meanwhile, let us give him the benefit of the doubt.'

Aramitz stepped back from the bars. Kelly lay sprawled on the bunk she had lowered, hands clasped behind her head. He pulled down the adjoining bunk, sat on the edge and watched her gaze at the ceiling. 'The mind plays such odd tricks. Why did he think he knew you yet failed to recognise the rest of us?'

Kelly shrugged.'You're the doctor. You tell me.'

They didn't see Andrew – or was it Daniel – or both – until they were herded back on board The Dragon Lady and ordered to prepare for launching. Daniel was already on the bridge and had managed to re-activate the shipboard computer's voice function.

Tarqueen greeted them in the entryway. 'The captain wants you all to assemble on the bridge. And my – isn't he masterful?'

They made their way forward and formed themselves into a ragged line while Daniel barked orders at Tarqueen. 'Check the ship is tight! Pressurise to one atmosphere, standard tri-gas mix! Set the grav flux at oh point eight seven five gee then give me a full onscreen systems readout!'

Aramitz watched, listened and marvelled at the transformation which had begun in the courtroom. It was Andrew, yet somehow it wasn't. His whole demeanour, the timbre of his voice, the way he held himself had changed.

Daniel turned his attention from the overhead computer screens onto the crew line-up. 'Straighten yourselves out! Smarten up! Let's show the Navy you've got some pride! Some bearing!'

Gumbo's stance didn't alter. 'The Navy ain't watching, captain.'

'That's why we have to do it, Mister! For each other! To show we still have some self-respect. That we're not just a bunch of dumb-assed snot-pickers! So square up! If we're due to be terminated, I want to feel I'm with a bunch of guys who can take it on the chin!'

Mindful of Aramitz's plea, the crew decided to humour him.

Daniel surveyed the result. 'Okay. That's better. Now for reasons that have yet to be explained to me, it seems I'm captain of this toothless old tramp. Do we have a First Officer on board?'

'Yes, sir. Pug Shilton.'

As Daniel went along the line, everyone announced their name and explained their role on board ship. It seemed a

279

ridiculous game given the time they had been together but they went along with it. When it was the turn of Aramitz, Daniel showed no sign of remembering their private conversation.

Kelly was last. Daniel gazed at her, perplexed. 'We have met, I'm sure of it. I just wish I could think of your name – '

'Kelly.'

'Yes! Kallee Man – '

'Mandell.'

Daniel looked puzzled. 'Not Mandragorian . . .?'

'No.'

'That's amazing. I think you ought to know you've got a twin out there.'

'So have you,' said Kelly. 'And believe me, he's a lot more fun to be with.'

☆ ☆ ☆

The two space tugs which had towed The Dragon Lady into the Korazon's hold, eased her back out through the huge airlock, briefly gathered momentum, then cast off, sending the trader on her way.

Chilli and Gumbo made their way back to their private domain; the others remained on the bridge with Daniel. Through the forward ports they saw the Korazon dissolve into rainbow shards of light then vanish.

Pug grunted. 'Thought they were going to blow us away. Does this mean they've left a bomb on board?'

'No,' said Daniel. 'Nothing so crude as that. They've cast us adrift.'

Chilli's anguished face appeared on the central overhead screen. 'Some cocksuckin' techno-turd has been down here and ripped the guts out of the space drives!'

'Yes,' said Daniel. 'The systems readout indicated we might have a problem. Is it repairable?'

'It might be if we had a workshop! They've wrecked that and stolen all the machine tools! We are seriously fucked, man!'

Daniel gave a dry laugh. 'At both ends. The nav functions are inoperable and we have no external communications. We're dead in the water.'

Kelly moved quickly to the navigation table and hit several keys. The holographic display of the Rimworld failed to appear. She cursed quietly.

'Swearing at it won't help, Kelly. Even if it was working it'd be no use to us. Did any of you notice that moment back in the cells when everything seemed to go sideways for a second or two?'

Daniel's question was aimed at the screen and everybody on the bridge. There was general agreement that something odd had happened. Gumbo said: 'It was over so quick. I thought maybe that was the kicker to push the cruiser up to light speed.'

'Wrong – but there's no reason why any of you could know what was happening. It's called "the ripple effect" and it occurs during the brief moment when a ship travels through hyper-space.' Daniel addressed the centre screen. 'Put up a visual sweep of our surroundings, Tarqueen. Use all the screens. Show us what's out there.'

'Are you sure you want this?'

'Just *do* it!'

The screens went black as Tarqueen wiped the systems info from the screens. And they stayed black. Kelly, Aramitz, Pug and Moses stared at the screens and eventually a thin sprinkling of small stars appeared.

'Have you got an imaging system that gives us some more detail?' enquired Daniel.

'Oh, sure! And what would you like me to do for an encore – walk over hot coals?! This is an over-the-hill trader, not a space observatory and when it comes to star-gazing, I'm One-Eyed Jack!'

'Just do your best. And Tarqueen – '

'Yes?'

'I don't like lippy computers. One more smart remark and you're off line.'

'Really? I think this is where I came in!'

'I mean it, Tarqueen.'

281

Tarq cloaked his petulance with a veneer of unctuous humility. 'Image enhancement coming up. Selecting point from upper first quadrant.'

A blue outline was drawn round one of the faint points of light on the large display. The screen began rebuilding a series of images as the selected point was progressively enlarged.

'Why are the stars so faint?' asked Kelly.

'The answer's on the screen,' replied Daniel.

The selected point of light grew in size. It wasn't a star. It was a spiral galaxy.

'Wait a minute,' began Kelly. 'Are you trying to tell us they are all . . .?'

'Yes. We've been cast adrift in intergalactic space. One of those points of light is the galaxy containing the Rimworld. Unfortunately, we have no way of knowing which one – and even if we did, and this ship was able to travel at light speed – '

'Which it can't – '

'We'd never reach it in our lifetime. But since we have no propulsive power at all, it's not worth talking about.'

'What about the space raft?' asked Moses.

'Removed,' said Tarqueen. 'Doesn't anybody read my screen reports?'

'Is he always like this?' whispered Daniel.

Pug nodded then sat down with a heavy sigh. 'So we're stuck here . . .'

'Until the life-support systems run out. Tarqueen will live to tell the tale – assuming we don't get hit by an asteroid.'

'Thanks,' said Tarqueen. 'It's nice to have something to look foward too.'

Kelly fixed Daniel with a tight-lipped stare. 'I hope you realise this is all your fault.'

'On a simplistic level, I suppose it is. The people behind Chief Agent Stagg certainly want me out of the way. They tried once before. This time it looks as if they've succeeded. But before you blame me for your plight, you might care to speculate on how you all came to be on board this ship in the first place. Then

282

perhaps you can explain how I came to be with you and why we were stealing the Nebo Comm-Sat.'

'We weren't stealing anything. It was a salvage contract.'

Aramitz flashed a warning glance at Pug. 'I really don't think any discussion along these lines will help our present situation.'

'Excuse me interrupting,' said Tarqueen. 'But I think we've got company.'

They all looked towards the big screen. It was a Navy cruiser. But it wasn't the Korazon.

'Give me maximum enlargement and resolution!' commanded Daniel.

Tarqueen obliged. Daniel studied the familiar lines with a mixture of foreboding and excitement. It was the NV Kahsha-thra – his father's flagship.

Chapter Seventeen

The NV Kahshathra was Gideon Kinsharadeen's flagship in name only. Supreme Fleet Admirals only left Navy Headquarters on very rare ceremonial occasions – such as the re-enactment of the First Landings when the entire fleet would assemble in the skies over Dun Roamin, the founding planet, once every two hundred and fifty years, then circle the Rim-world in an impressive show of strength.

Daniel was relieved to discover his father wasn't on board now. It postponed the inevitable meeting for a little while longer. In fact, when he considered the matter, the paternal presence would have been quite extraordinary. He was painfully aware that both his parents had never exhibited any affection or concern for him as a person. They were only interested in whether Daniel had the required strength of character to become a worthy successor. He had never been a child, or a young man – only a perpetual candidate. His whole life had been one long, relentless examination.

The news that the Kahshathra had come to their rescue came as a great relief to the crew of The Dragon Lady. The fact that they were soon to be towed, yet again, into the main hold of a Navy cruiser for the journey home led to some cynical speculation as to where this game of Pass The Parcel was going to end. But they were not ungrateful. At least there were no handcuffs or phaser-happy Marine guards.

Daniel and Kelly were invited to leave the trader and enter the cruiser; the others were warned to prepare for an impending jump through hyperspace.

Before they left, Kelly buttonholed Daniel in his cabin while he was packing the few possessions that had been part of his now-forgotten twilight existence as Andiamo Cartahaynyar.

'There's something I need to tell you.'

'I'm listening . . .'

'I lied about my identity. We do know each other. I'm Kallee Mandragorian.' She saw the look of recognition dawn. 'That's right. Sandiego's daughter. You used to come out to our house at White Sands. But that was when I was five and you were seven.'

Daniel continued his packing. 'Why the deception?'

'I didn't want to advertise my Navy connections. It may help you to know that I've been part of this recovery operation but I'm not at liberty to say more at the moment.'

'I understand.' Daniel closed his zipper-bag and extended his hand. 'Welcome aboard.'

Half an hour later, the warning klaxon sounded. The ripple effect swept through the ship as it entered hyperspace. *Shazzam!* A couple of seconds – plus a prodigious amount of energy – was all it took to neatly sidestep several trillion miles of deep space. They were back in their home galaxy and two days out from the chain of planets that formed the Rimworld.

Daniel, who had been formally welcomed back by the captain of the Kahshathra and given a commander's uniform that almost fitted, was a guest on the bridge when the cruiser dropped out of hyperspace. The main screen showed another vessel nearby – waiting to keep a pre-arranged rendezvous.

It was the SS Mount Olympus. The head office of Constantine Parnassus.

Daniel turned to Kallee. 'I don't get it. Isn't this the outfit that sold us to the bad guys?'

'Yes – but hold your fire.'

The main purpose of the rendezvous was to return The Dragon Lady to its rightful owner. Since two Navy cutters were due to ferry the disabled trader across to Connie's ship, Daniel requested permission to go along for the ride. Kallee asked if she could go too.

285

The Kahshathra's captain agreed without hesitation. Parnassus had already asked for a meeting.

On boarding Mount Olympus, Kallee elected to stay with Aramitz and the crew. The main reason was to share a farewell drink but she added: 'I don't want to have to sit watching that overdressed giraffe go into meltdown every time she looks at you.'

Her remark puzzled Daniel. What business was it of hers? As it turned out, there was no meltdown in evidence when Shalimar ushered him into Connie's private quarters. But the sight of this tall, beautiful, long-necked woman caused a host of conflicting thoughts and emotions to well up inside him.

Parnassus was seated by a large food trolley. He laid down his fork as Daniel entered, extended a plump but powerful hand in greeting then waved his guest to a nearby armchair.

'Are you feeling peckish? Shalimar can easily prepare a plate.'

'I'd rather talk,' said Daniel. 'The captain of the Kahshathra tells me I have you to thank for my rescue.'

'As an honest broker and loyal citizen of the Rimworld . . .' Parnassus paused to mop his bulging lips with the lower end of his huge napkin. '. . . I have always tried to assist the Corporation in anyway I can.'

'By betraying me to the people who are plotting against my father?'

Parnassus aimed a loaded fork. 'A dangerous but necessary ruse to trap the ringleaders and trick them into confessing their involvement with the destruction of the Marianna.'

'I think the commander is a little confused,' said Shalimar.

'One moment.' Parnassus polished off the current plateful and laid it aside regretfully. 'Dare I venture a little informality? May I address you as Daniel?'

'This is not a public occasion. Please do.'

Parnassus eyed Shalimar briefly. As he started to explain, his hands began to perform an aerial ballet around the words. 'The truth is, Daniel, I've been playing both sides of the street. Your father – the Supreme Fleet Admiral – never quite gave up the

286

hope that you might still be alive, while those plotting to bring down the Kinsharadeen family wanted to make certain you were dead.

'Now, although I am a registered taxpayer and model of civic rectitude, I have, quite unjustly, acquired a somewhat dubious reputation – mainly among those who secretly resent my financial success. But I quickly saw that this could work to the Corporation's advantage.

'Because I was seen to be independent and held to be a louche character, it was almost inevitable that others of the same ilk would gravitate towards me in the hope of making common cause. You follow me?'

Daniel nodded. 'I'm beginning to get the picture.'

'That's why I offered myself to the Corporation as an informant. And that is also the reason why they have never sought to drive me off the spaceways. With a finger in every pie of doubtful provenance and a reserved seat in every thieves' kitchen, I quickly became their most valuable agent.'

'Shrewd move . . .'

'I like to think so.' Parnassus motioned Shalimar to pile more of his favourite delicacies onto the next plate then took it from her and started to tuck in. 'And it was because of this arrangement, and as a measure of my reliability and discretion, that I was contacted by two highly-placed officers in the Navy who – through intermediaries – told me they were acting for your father. They asked me to use my widespread contacts amongst the independent traders and illegals to discover if a corpse bearing your ID had been found, or if anyone bearing even the remotest resemblance to you, but using another name, was in circulation.

'Now, obviously, this was a huge and lengthy undertaking. We could not mount a public manhunt. I promised to do what I could. But the first thing I did was set up a direct and very secret line of communication with your father – '

'And found that these officers who claimed to be acting on his behalf had lied to you. They were linked to the group who sabotaged the Marianna.'

287

'Correct. But it took your father some considerable time to find out who these men were.'

'One or both of them must be Fleet Admirals. I've figured that much out for myself.'

'Full marks, Daniel. They are colleagues and ex-classmates of your father. Admiral Korreggidoorian and Admiral Tree-hausterhaus. But their request to me to mount a search was not incriminating in itself. It could be explained away – and was. There was nothing to link them to the Marianna incident. That was why we had to provoke them by sending The Dragon Lady on that salvage mission to Nebo. She was the hook – '

'And I was the bait.'

'Your father approved. You could never be safe unless those trying to kill you were caught. This time, we were pulling the strings. We knew they would use the NV Korazon. And your father made sure the gang's principal hit-man was on board.'

'Chief Treasury Agent Stagg.'

'Correct again.'

Daniel gave a dry laugh. 'He told me enough to get himself indicted for high treason. It's amazing how some people just can't keep their mouths shut.'

'They like to gloat,' said Shalimar. 'I believe it stems from severe feelings of inadequacy.'

'Maybe. It's a pity I wasn't able to record it.'

Shalimar smiled. 'Somebody did.'

'That just leaves two questions. How and where did you find me?'

'One of my contacts happened to be in Boot City – on Zhannandor.'

Daniel looked appalled. 'What in Prog's name was I doing in that sump-hole?!'

Parnassus pulled the empty fork from between his lips and prodded the air. 'Good question. All we heard was that an ex-con called Hammerhead spotted you in a bar called Sadie Moon's. Does that ring a bell?'

'Only the name Hammerhead.' Daniel frowned. 'I seem to recall arresting somebody by that name. Is it important?'

'It was to us,' said Shalimar. 'He identified you as Daniel Kinsharadeen.'

Parnassus took up the story. 'Which at the time, didn't mean a great deal. You had adopted the identity of someone called Andiamo Cartahaynyar – and you had an ID in that name. Do you recall anything about that?'

'No.'

'Well, fortunately my contacts were able to lift you out of there without too much trouble. That's how you got on The Dragon Lady.'

Daniel rubbed his forehead. 'It's really worrying. I remember more or less everything up to the moment when the Marianna blew apart then nothing until I found myself in front of Stagg on the Korazon. That's when I learned that there was an eleven year gap between those two points. What happened to me, Connie?'

Parnassus eyes widened then flicked towards Shalimar.

Daniel clutched his head as his brain started to swim. 'Excuse me. I don't know what prompted that familiarity.'

'All my friends call me Connie. Feel free to do the same. As to your question . . .' Parnassus laid aside his plate and fork and clasped his hands together gravely. When he abandoned his food in order to speak, it was a sure sign that he had an important statement to make.

He began with a heavy sigh. 'I wish I had the answer, Daniel. The truth is we have no idea where you've been. We can only rejoice – along with your father – that you have been found. In time, and with the proper treatment, perhaps those missing years will be returned to you. Personally, I would advise against it. Given the lofty position you will one day hold, it might be better for everyone if they remained buried.'

Daniel took this advice on board with a thoughtful pull at his lip. 'You may be right . . .' He stood up. 'Did you know that the navigator of The Dragon Lady – the woman calling herself Kelly Mandell had Navy connections?'

Parnassus and Shalimar exchanged another look.

'We knew she had been sent to work with us,' said Shalimar.

289

'In a delicate operation like this many of those involved are not what they seem. None of us will know the full story until this is all over.'

'And it's not over yet,' added Parnassus.

'No. Thanks for putting me in the picture.'

Parnassus gave the bracelet on his left wrist a surreptitious twist to reduce the g on his anti-grav harness and rose smoothly from the sofa to shake Daniel's hand. 'Goodbye, Commander. And good luck. Shalimar will take you down to the embarkation deck.'

The journey down was almost silent. Daniel and Shalimar exchanged glances and the odd smile but very little in the way of words until they reached the external airlock to which one of the Navy cutters was attached like a limpet. Both had left the main hold after delivering The Dragon Lady. Its companion had already returned to the flagship.

Daniel turned his back on the two naval ratings who were waiting to see him safely through the airlock and took Shalimar aside.

'Excuse me, but when I look at you I have this strange feeling that we have, or had, a relationship.'

'Of sorts, yes. Once you were found, it was necessary to make certain arrangements before you left for Nebo. We did meet briefly.'

'No. This was more than a brief encounter. But then again, my memory may still be playing tricks.' Daniel paused then asked: 'This question is entirely lacking in finesse but . . . did we have sex?'

Shalimar smiled. 'If we had, I think you'd remember.'

Daniel came through the airlock into the Navy cutter to find Kallee already strapped in and waiting. She gave him a jaundiced glance. 'I'm surprised you managed to tear yourself away.'

'It wasn't a problem,' said Daniel. 'But thanks for mentioning her eyes. They're really beautiful, aren't they?'

It was enough to lower the conversational temperature by several degrees. Kallee maintained a frosty silence during the crossing from SS Mount Olympus to the Kahshathra. Which was fine by Daniel. He needed time to get his head around the latest revelations and to force his mind to uncover the buried memories of the last eleven years.

The cutter docked smoothly in one of the cruiser's many launch bays. The outer doors closed. The ship's retractable airlock engaged with the cutter's exit hatch. The pressure equalised with a smooth hiss. There was a brief pause then the voice of the Navy pilot came over the cabin speaker. 'Stand by to disembark.'

Daniel restarted the conversation as he guided Kallee towards the nearest elevator that would take them to the officer's accommodation deck. The layout of Navy ships was something he hadn't forgotten about. 'Were you recruited by my father?'

'I'll leave him to tell you that.'

'You worried I can't keep a secret?'

'The less you know, the less there is to blow. We're not home and dry yet.'

'That's what, uhh – Parnassus said.' Daniel was going to say 'Shalimar' but decided to avoid that conversational flash point.

Kallee divined the reason for the slight hesitation. 'I don't mind you mentioning her name.'

'Good. Because I don't intend to limit myself to subjects which won't cause you offence. Do you have a problem with this woman? It obviously can't be on my account!' Daniel was struck off by a hideous thought. 'Zigg Zaggurat! Is this related to the eleven-year glitch! Were you and I an item?'

'Given the look on your face, I'd like to say "Yes" just to ruin your day. But No. We never were and are unlikely to be.'

Daniel bristled. 'You'd better watch that tongue of yours. I don't tolerate insolence from the people I work with.'

'I'm not people, commander. I'm someone who's already saved your life on more than one occasion. So keep the stiff neck for your subordinates. If you and I get into another potentially lethal situation, I'd hate to have to think twice.'

She stepped into the elevator as the doors slid open. Daniel

291

joined her. They stared each other out for a moment then, as they started up, Daniel defused the tension with a smile.

And suddenly, for a brief instant, the face belonged to Andrew. Kallee felt relieved. At least he was still in there somewhere.

'What's so funny?' she enquired.

'I was just thinking back to those days at White Sands.'

'Yeah . . .?'

'I didn't like you then either.'

It was Kallee's turn to smile. 'And what I just said was out of order. That's an apology. So make the most of it because they don't come that often.'

'So it wasn't me, just Shalimar.'

Kallee nodded. 'I have an inborn resentment towards women like that. She's too tall, too beautiful, too poised, too perfect in every way.'

'You could always go for a makeover.'

'I prefer the genuine article. When I undress and look in the mirror, what I see may not amount to much but at least it's all mine.'

'Must be a great comfort to you.'

'You know what? It wouldn't surprise me at all if she turned out to be a replicate.'

'A G-Two? So what? They're human beings. They've just been programmed, that's all. Some people regard that as an improvement.'

'Really?' Kallee's eyes and nostrils narrowed. 'And why is that?'

'Because they come with an off-button.'

The elevator's soft voice announced their arrival on the crew deck while Kallee was still trying to assemble a verbal counter-punch. Emerging into the wide corridor, they stepped onto the central moving strip and were carried towards the officer's quarters.

'What's going to happen to The Dragon Lady and her crew?'

'Parnassus has promised a stem-to-stern repair and refit. The Navy have agreed to foot the bill for the damage caused by Stagg's bully boys.'

Daniel turned back to face Kallee and let the travolator carry him along. 'You see? People like to portray us as money-grubbing thugs, but we can still show generosity towards our friends.'

'Just as well, 'cos it's gonna cost a packet. Still – not to worry. I'm sure you're worth every last cent.'

A short while later, after the energy in the hyperdrives had built up to the desired levels, the NV Kahshathra made a third hyperjump towards the Rimworld planet of Libra – headquarters of the Navy and the power centre of the Corporation.

☆   ☆   ☆

Some readers may find it odd that a cost-conscious enterprise such as the Navy should have ground-based headquarters when its remit was the control of the spaceways.

There is a simple explanation.

There *was* a space-borne admin and signals HQ in solar orbit beyond Libra but – like all senior military men throughout the ages – the top echelon of Navy officers liked to enjoy the perks and privileges of the lavish lifestyle to which their rank entitled them.

Our own generals don't like gazing out of their French windows onto a parade ground hemmed in by barrack blocks, and our admirals soon tire of cramped wardrooms and taking a morning constitutional in the teeth of a stiff sou'wester which is dumping large quantities of the North Atlantic on the foredeck. With nothing stiffer than a solar wind, discomforts of this kind are not experienced in space. But you are confined to a sealed environment. The view through the side ports may be spectacular but it quickly becomes mono-tonous and it's not what you could really call scenery.

Watching the almost imperceptible progress of the cloud-patterns across the planet below is nowhere near as inspiring as standing on terra firma beneath the huge sweep of the ever-changing sky with its staggering variety of cloud shapes and colours.

There are no rainbows in space. No green hills, no snowy

293

peaks. And although some of the Navy ships are larger than Heathrow Terminals 1 to 4 laid end to end, there just isn't the room for a decent 18-hole golf course (a game imported from Earth) or a stretch of water large enough to hold the Rimworld equivalent of Cowes Regatta.

A feasibility study was initiated but the accountants quickly ruled in favour of a comunications link between the space fleet and a ground-based HQ surrounded by every conceivable recreational facility. That, in short, is how the senior Admirals and their support staff came to be housed at Shasta Bay on the shores of the Western Ocean. This was where Supreme Fleet Admiral Gideon Kinsharadeen held sway, and at this point in time, he was waiting for a trusted courier to bring word that Daniel and Mandragorian's daughter were descending by space transit vehicle from the NV Kahshathra to a secure and secret location in the desert region one hundred miles north of Fleet Headquarters.

Gideon Kinsharadeen had just come from a meeting at which the long-term strategic requirements of the Navy had been under review. Admiral Korreggidoorian and Admiral Tree-hausterhaus had both been present. Reaching into an inside pocket, he retrieved the secretly-made copies of the latest intercepts of the signal traffic from their fellow-traitors aboard the cruiser Korazon. He read them again with a grim smile.

They suspected nothing.

☆   ☆   ☆

Daniel and Kallee stepped out of the transit vehicle to find themselves on a decaying airstrip in the middle of the desert area known as White Sands. Kallee had recognised where they were heading as they dropped through the low cloud base on the final leg of the computer-controlled glide path.

Daniel had been in the pilot's seat, but at this level of technology he was little more than an observer. He could only override the computer and take control if there was a major systems failure. In the view of most Navy pilots, if all four back-up systems went down, there was fuck all you could do except sit back and whistle the Rimworld equivalent of 'I Wish I was in Dixie' while you waited for the impact.

The airstrip lay inside a huge, fenced-off tract of scrub and shallow dunes that had been a secret weapons testing site – and as such was strictly off-limits. It had been closed when the development programme ended several years ago.

Daniel had been here once – several years before the Marianna incident. He remembered the high chain link fencing with its red and white signs warning that deadly force would be used against any intruders. The sand had already started to encroach on the runway.

Daniel and Kallee pulled their travel bags out of the transit vehicle and shut the hatch. The nearest buildings, an admin block and some hangars, were deserted.

'Do you think they forgot we were coming?' joked Kallee.

The words were no sooner uttered when a jet-copter swept into view from behind the hangers. Hugging the ground, it angled towards them and raised a spiralling cloud of dust as it set down on the runway. Shielding their faces, Daniel and Kallee ran towards it, threw their luggage on board then climbed in.

The jet-copter lifted a few feet into the air, turned in its own length, then headed back towards the hangars. The pilot must have been told to stay low to reduce the risk of being seen from beyond the base. He stayed below roof height all the way, flying down alleyways, twisting and turning until he was back out in open scrub whereupon he dropped down into every gully he could find. The guy was obviously enjoying every minute of it.

Their destination was a large concrete bunker – the underground control and telemetry centre close to the abandoned missile launch pads. The 'copter landed in the shadow that the afternoon sun had obligingly cast over the zigzag ramp leading down to the steel entrance doors. The pilot started switching things off. A Navy lieutenant in blue-grey fatigues came up the ramp as the whine of the jet engines faded.

He greeted Daniel with a snappy salute. 'This way, sir. Leave the bags, I'll get them brought down later.'

Daniel and Kallee followed him down the ramp and into the bunker. The corridor was lit but compared to the brightness outside, it was like walking into a coal mine. Their eyes became adjusted as they reached the door at the far end of the long corridor. It was guarded by a pair of lieutenants cradling compact assault rifles. Despite the widespread use of laser weaponry, the bullet was still highly favoured by the accountants who ran the Navy's procurement programme.

The guards stepped aside and saluted as Daniel approached. As the party reached the door it opened as if by magic. Their escort invited them to go in. Daniel and Kallee paused on the threshold, exchanged supportive looks then stepped into the control room.

The white-haired man behind the door was Kallee's father, Sandiego Mandragorian. He closed the door, gave her a warm hug then pointed to a second door. 'The Admiral and your mother are in there.'

Daniel knocked and entered. His mother Tallamahassee, dressed in outdoor leisure clothes, welcomed him with a wintry smile. Gideon, his father, in Navy fatigues, stood with his back to the door, hands clasped behind his back.

Talla, an elegant Atlantean matron with a finely-boned face and tightly-coiffed silver hair, grasped one of Daniel's hands and patted his shoulder. 'I'm glad you're safe.'

'Thank you, ma'am.' That was as close as it got.

She touched the Admiral's arm. 'Gideon . . .?'

The Supreme Fleet Admiral turned to face his son. Daniel came to attention and saluted.

Six foot six tall, with a powerful athletic frame that belied his age, Gideon possessed the granite-jawed looks and commanding presence that were part of the job-profile. This wasn't a man you'd expect to find cleaning your back yard with a broom and bucket.

Daniel looked straight ahead as Gideon walked slowly round him, making a close inspection.

'What are you planning to do with this hair – grow a pigtail?'

'No, sir!' Daniel had got his hair trimmed while on board the

Kahshathra. The only sailors with shorter hair were the shaven-headed new entrants to the Naval Academy.

Completing his tour, the Admiral returned to face Daniel. 'At ease, Mister!'

Daniel obeyed with the usual response. 'Sir!'

'So . . . how does it feel to be back on board?'

'Very good, sir! I'm looking forward to resuming my duties!'

The Admiral nodded. 'That's something we'll need to think about. Did you speak with Parnassus?'

'Yes, sir!'

'Did he mention that your mother and I refused to accept that you were dead?'

'Yes, sir! I would like to thank you both for restoring me to my rightful position!'

'Eleven years is a long time. Are you sure you can't remember where you've been, or what you've been doing?'

'No, sir! I wish I could.'

His mother spoke. 'I just hope you haven't done anything that would bring discredit upon the Navy.'

'I don't think you need worry on that score, Ma'am. I believe the principles of right and wrong and the sense of honour and duty you both imparted would always prevail whatever the circumstances!'

'I'm glad you think so,' said the Admiral. 'Especially as this is all your fault.'

Daniel faced his father. 'I don't follow, sir.'

'I'm convinced that none of this would have happened if you hadn't gone soft on those miners from Nebo.'

Daniel felt obliged to defend himself. 'Only you can make that judgement, sir. My behaviour may have fallen below the high standards demanded of me, but it did at least serve to expose the traitors in our midst. If the Nebo incident had not taken place, I'm sure they would have found some other excuse to act against you. In that sense, my actions may be thought to have helped preserve the long-term interests of the Kinsharadeen family'

His mother lent Daniel her support. 'That's a good point, Gideon.'

297

The Admiral grunted. 'You always were soft on the boy.'

Daniel said nothing. Stirring within him was the memory of another time, another place. A green, magical place. Broad-leafed trees dappled with sunlight. And beneath those trees, a smiling man and woman embracing – and hugging him within that embrace. A joyous, warm, loving moment to which he longed to return. When? Where? He knew the faces but they did not belong to the couple who faced him now. His mind tried to cling on to the images but they slipped away like a waking dream . . .

The Admiral was speaking '. . . so to maintain total security, you and the Mandragorian girl will remain here incommunicado until the ringleaders have been rounded up. The conditions are not ideal. The original furnishings were all ripped out but you've been provided with all the basic facilities, including some recreational material.'

'Thank you, sir!'

'And your escort will see you are fed. Don't look upon this as a term of imprisonment. Conduct yourself as if you were on a deep space asteroid patrol. I expect disciplined behaviour at all times!'

'Yes, sir.' Daniel came to attention and saluted.

Gideon returned his son's salute. 'We'll be in touch.' He signalled his wife to precede him to the door. Her eyes turned towards Daniel.

'Goodbye, Ma'am. It was good to see you.'

Talla treated him to another brief, wintry smile then was gone. His father didn't look back. There was no reason to. He had said what he came to say and was ready to move on. Lingering regrets were not part of his emotional vocabulary.

Daniel wasn't hurt by any of this. The sentiments expressed towards his mother were completely hollow. He no longer felt anything for these two people, but it came as a shock to realise that he never had. The family had not been held together by love, but by pride – the pride that came from being a Kinsharadeen. Friendship had been replaced by obedience, devotion by duty, compassion by a cruel disregard for those who failed to make the grade.

298

Kallee entered. 'How'd it go?'

Daniel answered with a shrug. 'Okay. And you?'

'Yeah, okay.' She used a finger and thumb to push away the tears from her eyes. 'I always have problems with my pa. I love him like crazy but I hate what he does for a living.' She paused. 'Did your father say how long we were gonna be stuck here?'

'No . . .'

'Well, you'll be glad to hear we've got separate rooms. Wanna come over to my place?'

☆　　☆　　☆

The room had been stripped bare. From the marks on the walls it had once contained several bunks. There was now a makeshift bed, a table with an adjustable lamp, two chairs, a beach lounger and a tv/radio/record unit. The adjacent washroom was still intact.

'Not exactly what we enjoyed at the Maracariba, but I've known worse.' Kallee went over to the bed and opened up her luggage. 'We should thank our lucky stars Jean gave me some booze as a going-away present.' She held up a dark green bottle and two plastic glasses. 'Care to join me? Or should we wait till you come off duty?'

'Don't get smart, just open the bottle.' Daniel watched her fill the glasses with a deep amber liquid. 'Was the Maracariba a hotel we both stayed at?'

'Yeh. In Boot City.' She passed over a glass. 'One of Jean's concoctions.' She read off the label. "Cognac a la mode de Remy Martin" – whatever that means.'

Daniel took a sip and coughed as the fumes came back up. It was strong but not unpleasant. 'These huge gaps in my memory really worry me.'

'You're lucky. There's a few things in my life I would dearly love to forget. Cheers!'

Daniel pointed to the lounger. 'Okay if I sit here?'

'Sure, go ahead.' Kallee sat at the table in order to stay close to the bottle.

299

Daniel made himself comfortable. 'Something strange happened when I met my parents.'

'Did they both give you a great big hug?'

'Hah! No chance. No . . . it was *my* reaction that was strange . . . I recognised them – I mean, I knew who they were – but at the same time there was this voice – inside my my brain – saying "Wait a minute! This is not my mother and father. These are two completely different people! What's going on?".'

Daniel took a bolder sip of the brandy and gestured with his free hand. 'It was as if part of me was standing to one side, listening and watching. And this part could hardly believe what I was saying to these people. It's really very disturbing.'

'I can believe it . . .'

'You'll have to forgive me if I've been short with you. Ever since I surfaced in front of that guy Stagg, I've had the distinct impression I'm not quite right in the head.'

'That's okay. I've been pretty rude to you too.'

Daniel smiled and raised his glass to her. 'Yeah, but you've always been that way. D'you remember at one time the Admiral was thinking of putting you and me together to create the next generation of Kinsharadeens? What a disaster that would have been!'

'Complete and utter.' Kallee emptied her glass and poured herself another brandy. 'Don't know why they bother. I've never understood why your father didn't clone himself. Your family could have done that from way back.'

'They tried but it didn't work. The animals cloned in the labs were of a lower order of intelligence. Being non-verbal, the personality defects and the long-term brain disorders didn't show up. Human beings *are* different. Even the identical twins that were born in the old days were never really identical. And they always had different persona. No . . . Kinsharadeens are moulded and trained from Day One.'

'So was Pavlov's dog.'

'Who . . .?'

'Forget it. Shouldn't have interrupted you.'

'Well, I think what I'm trying to say is that ever since finding myself back here, it's like – ' Daniel broke off to drink some more brandy. ' – well, this is going to sound strange coming from me but . . . it's like waking up to find yourself in Psycho Ward Ten.'

'Yeah, I get that feeling sometimes.'

Daniel grasped the air, searching for the right words as if they were apples on an invisible tree. 'There are moments when . . . when I don't feel I *belong* to the Rimworld. When I get these flashes of being . . . someone else . . . from a different place – a different time!'

Kallee considered the remaining brandy in her glass then asked: 'Is that why you're taking the pills?'

'What pills . . .?'

Kelly got up, went over to her holdall and rummaged around in one of the outside zip pockets. She returned with a pop-sheet of pills. Only two remained out of the original twenty. 'These.'

She dropped them into Daniel's lap. He picked them up and turned them over. The sheet carried no brand name or instructions.

'You asked Jean-Pierre to analyse them. With all the recent dramas he forgot to give you the results.'

'Do you have them?'

'Not written down. Basically they're a placebo. Jean was intrigued by their construction and thinks they were designed to mislead. The outer shell is composed of a harmless inert substance. I can't remember the name but it has no remedial qualities whatsoever. Its sole function is to act as a time-release agent for the substance at its core. You were taking one of these every two weeks – '

'Was I?'

'That's what you told Jean. Anyway, when the outer shell dissolves, it releases a very powerful stimulant. Not all at once, it starts to leak out during the last twenty-four hours then suddenly hits. *Wham!* It's a naturally occurring drug – a plant extract – which was why Jean knew what it was. I've forgotten the name of that too, but the effect is like a turbo-charged adrenalin high – speed with wings. The heart races, and you start to hyperventilate.'

'Uh-huh . . .'

'And Jean thinks that's the trigger which makes you reach for another pill.'

Daniel shrugged. 'I see . . .'

'Only you don't need to. The rush you get from one of these things only lasts for two minutes, three at the most.'

'So why would I be taking them?'

'Good question. This outer coating just gets in the way. If the idea was to get high, why wait fourteen days when you can get an instant hit from a FeelGood Factor-8?'

'Good point. Except that I don't use party drugs.'

'Well, you've been using these. You know what Jean thinks?'

'Do I have to guess, or are you going to tell me?'

'He thinks you were told to take these pills to prevent the feeling you get when the time-release coating wears off.'

Daniel frowned. 'That doesn't make sense, does it?'

'It would if, as Jean suggested, they were designed to mislead. Let me put it another way. Someone makes a similar kind of pill and tells you that they prevent motion-sickness but they must be taken regularly. What they *don't* tell you is that at the core of the pill is an emetic. The coating wears off. The emetic goes to work. You start to feel nauseous – but there's not enough to make you really sick. Only you don't know that because you've been told when you start to feel queasy, you must take another pill and – hey presto! The nausea wears off – and you're convinced it was the pill that cured it!'

'Yes, I see. Neat . . .' Daniel lifted the pop-sheet. 'So what are these designed to make me feel is happening?'

Kallee threw up her hands. 'How should I know? The answer has to be in your mind somewhere. Keep them on you. It may help jog your memory.'

But don't rush back, Andrew.

Daniel still has several very important things to do.

302

SIDELIGHTS ON THE RIMWORLD by 'FIZZ'   No.1922
THE NAVY
A career for men, women and significant others.

Authorities at every level of the Rimworld have always taken a relaxed view of homosexuality. With the new generations cocooned until the age of eighteen, the Rimworld eliminated paedophilia and child abuse at a stroke. Released into the world at the legal age of consent, new adults are free to choose the type of sexual relationship they are most comfortable with.

Even so, the now-historic decision to actively recruit gays and bi-sexuals into the Navy threw up a host of problems and aroused a great deal of unforeseen hostility. To resolve the vexed question of how to maintain good order and discipline, the Corporation was forced to adopt a policy of enlightened segregation; a process that often occurs naturally. There is ample evidence to show that when a bar or club becomes adopted by gays, the straight clientele tend to withdraw – driven out by design or by their own inability to tolerate the counter-culture.

So it was with the Navy. Existing tensions were dramatically heightened on a cruiser with a 50-50 mix when a number of gay officers and ratings began attending parades with the seat cut out of their trousers. This and similar provocations led to heated exchanges; macho posturing by straights, a great deal of hand-on-hip flouncing, some awfully cruel name-calling, smudged eyeliner, wig-throwing and regrettable outbreaks of violence.

Rather than perpetuate this increasingly uneasy mix, the Corporation created two fleets of cruisers, frigates and support vessels; one crewed by straights, the other by gays of both genders. Operational efficiency improved dramatically, morale soared, a spirit of friendly rivalry developed and harmony was restored.

In terms of intercept and arrest rates there is hardly any difference between the two competing fleets but when one takes the deterrent effect into account, the gay Navy has an unrivalled lead.

303

For the majority of unlicensed traders and other law-breakers, an encounter with a gay cruiser is the thing they fear most. Anyone apprehended for even a minor infraction of the Spaceway Code can expect to be comprehensively bum-whacked or invited to a 'Pass The Muffin' party by the arresting crew. Depending on your sexual orientation, this can either be a shimmering or shattering experience but as part of an overall policing strategy it has proved highly effective. Statistics recently issued by the Navy show a significant reduction in the numbers of those re-offending.

The straight Navy is characterised by the outward sobriety of its spacecraft – battleship grey – and emphasis on traditional uniforms of navy blue with red specialist insignia and gold rank stripes. Whereas the 'straight' ships are given historical or mythological names according to the class of vessel, the ships of the gay squadrons sport strident candyfloss colour schemes and are emblazoned with names like *Scarlet Harlots*, *Leather'n Lace*, *Pussy in Boots* and *Bitch-Queen from Camptown*.

Black leather has taken the place of Navy serge, with caps worn at a saucy angle. Gold rank stripes have been abandoned in favour of sequins. Shirts with frilly cuffs, feather boas and dramatic hats are also much in evidence despite the fact that there have been some messy incidents in areas where there is moving machinery.

Recruiting offices can be found in all major cities. The bunks are party-size, the showers are communal, bath time's a hoot and there's a drag night once a week. Bring a significant other.

Chapter Eighteen

The 'Golden E' Award Ceremony at the Supreme Fleet Admiral's official residence on the hilltop above Shasta Bay was a glittering, dress uniform affair held on the eve of the Third Quarter of the Rimworld year.

The top brass of the naval establishment were always in attendance but this was also a gathering of the brightest and the best to which officers and key crewmen from the space fleet were invited. It was a congratulatory affair, the Navy's way of saying 'Well done', an occasion for handing out plaques and prizes for achieving financial targets, raising operational efficiency, for meritorious service and for the honouring of individual endeavour.

The event was held in the luxurious surroundings of the Navy's equivalent to the White House and took place in an atmosphere of dignified razzamatazz. The Admiral's residence – maintained entirely at the Corporation's expense – was a large, graceful mansion with panoramic views of the Western Sea, and the line of hills to the north and east that separated Shasta Bay from the hinterland and the desert area known as White Sands. The mansion itself was surrounded by immaculate formal gardens, paved areas and landscaped open spaces – one of which contained a large transparent pyramid which had been glowing with light and filled with music since sundown.

This was the reception area where guests were welcomed by clean-cut senior classmen from the Naval Academy and served with drinks before engaging in the agreeable task of searching out old comrades and making new contacts. Networking was as important in the Rimworld as it was on Earth.

It was inside the pyramid that Gideon Kinsharadeen, flanked by a coterie of trusted aides, now moved without ceremony or fanfare among the guests, meeting familiar faces, congratulating those about to be honoured, shaking hands and engaging in brief, amiable conversations with a wide range of naval personnel. A host of instantly forgettable people who – like the English Army before Agincourt, experiencing 'a little touch of Harry in the night' – would treasure the memory of meeting him for the rest of their lives.

When the roster of guests had been checked and found to be complete, the Tanzibar bell was struck seven times. The bell – a treasured, carefully-preserved relic of the Atlantean's sea-faring days on Earth – was named in honour of Tanzibar Cremona Panglossian – the child who, at the age of seven, first read the star-signs that led to the discovery of the Rimworld.

Readers with retentive memories may wonder how a bronze bell, over two hundred million years old, could (a) resist corrosion and (b) peal with its original clarity. The answer is simple and comes in two parts.

1 – Progress is not necessarily an improvement as Earth archaeology has shown. Metals aren't what they used to be. Present-day paint pigments fade in months while the Sistine Chapel ceiling and the Lascaux cave paintings continue to glow. Tower blocks fall apart in under three decades but the pyramids at Giza and those of the Incas still reach for the sky.

2 – Molecular stasis – a method of long-term storage devised by Atlanteans before the Trans-Galactic Migration.

The discovery and development of this process by which any artefact or substance, natural or manmade, from Tutankhamun's socks to a Cheesy Wotsit can be preserved indefinitely, is absolutely riveting, but in order not to hold up the narrative it cannot be explained at this or any other juncture. Science graduates will have to be content with the bald statement that it works and the news that King Tut should have worn Odour Eaters.

On the seventh peal, the Supreme Fleet Admiral offered his arm to his wife Talla and led the way out of the pyramid. Setting

306

down their glasses, the guests gradually converged into the traditional column of four and followed them along the canopied path towards the flood-lit facade of the White House and the banqueting hall that lay within.

The main table was composed in the form of a T. Two separate tables lay parallel to the downstroke, and a third lay across its base. Gideon and his wife sat at the centre of the crossstroke. Top Navy brass presided over the three subsidiary tables, but the most important guests sat around the T – 'the Captain's Table' – and their position in the pecking order was reflected in their proximity to the Supreme Admiral.

Sandiego Mandragorian was four seats along to the left of Gideon. His wife having died, he was accompanied by a Navy widow. Admirals Korreggidoorian and Treehausterhaus found themselves seated across the table from Gideon, in the corners formed by the downstroke of the T which was almost wholly occupied by a delegation from the NV Korazon; the captain, section officers from every part of his ship and a party of marines. Chief Agent Stagg had been placed at the bottom end of the T, where he was able to look along the length of the table towards Gideon; the Navy and Marine captain present at Daniel's trial were seated to Stagg's left and right.

When everyone was in place, a small army of white-coated orderlies began serving the meal. These fleet dinners were renowned for their conviviality and the quality of the food and drink on offer and after the first three courses it was clear this was an equally great occasion. Save for one odd feature – noticed by those seated around the top table. There were two unoccupied seats; one to the left of Mandragorian, five places along from Gideon and the other, five places to the right of his wife, Talla.

When the dessert plates had been cleared away, it was time for the award ceremony at which Gideon was expected to officiate – a task he performed with genuine pleasure. The curtains behind the top row of seats parted to reveal a rostrum backed by a huge Navy badge and a stepped table loaded with plaques and prizes. Responding to the invitation from the Chief

307

Master At Arms, Gideon and Talla mounted the rostrum as one of his aides placed the prepared text on the lectern. The assembled guests gave the Kinsharadeens a standing ovation. It was met with a professional smile for a full minute then Gideon silenced the applause with a raised hand.

When his audience had settled into an attentive silence, Gideon launched into the short speech that preceded the announcements of the awards. The white-coated orderlies continued to circulate, replenishing the glasses of the guests. Admiral Korreggidoorian tried to concentrate on what Gideon was saying but his eyes kept returning to the two empty chairs. He could not remember a time when places had been unoccupied. This, in itself, was odd, but his concern arose from the fact that he and Treehausterhaus had been placed facing Kinsharadeen. Although Gideon had conversed amiably with both of them, they should, by established precedent, have all been sitting on the same side of the table.

Korreggidoorian had already asked one of the serving orderlies to check the names on the place cards of the two absentees and had been told that both were blank. A discreet word with the MC – The Chief Master At Arms – had failed to throw any light on the matter. The seating arrangements supplied by the Supreme Admiral's office had placed a guest in all but two of the numbered seats. A last minute choice? Delayed by unforeseen circumstances? Korreggidoorian could not think of a satisfactory answer and, gripped by a strange unease, found himself unable to press his host for an explanation.

The award ceremony, which had begun with the unit citations, continued. Rounds of applause greeted the winners of the various categories who each made brief acceptance speeches. There was some surprise when the Golden E crew award went to the Kahshathra. According to the pre-ceremony scuttlebut, the NV Korazon had been tipped as the winners.

Reacting to his audience, Gideon Kinsharadeen came back to the lectern. 'This unexpected change in the fortunes of the Korazon was also something of a surprise to me. But there are

308

two good reasons why the names of Commander Treffinneeyan and his crew could not go forward.'

Korreggidoorian looked across at Treehausterhaus, then glanced over his shoulder to make eye contact with Treffinneeyan.

'It is why these two chairs have remained empty throughout our celebrations.' Gideon used both hands to signal their location. 'We have traitors in our midst, gentlemen. Traitors who – in an effort to remove me – were determined to make sure these seats were never occupied.'

His word drew growls of disapproval from the crowded tables. These changed to gasps of consternation as Daniel, wearing the dress uniform of a naval commander, and Kallee – almost unrecognisable in an elegant ball gown and plaited hairpiece – stepped from behind the curtains, mounted the rostrum and stood on either side of Gideon Kinsharadeen.

At the far end of the table, Stagg's jaw dropped, and all the way up the table to where the two Fleet Admirals sat, the men from the Korazon who had been directly involved with the 'Nebo incident' reacted with dismay and utter mystification. There was alarm too, as they realised that the white-coated orderlies had exchanged their wine bottles for handguns and were now standing guard over the room.

Filled with dread, Admiral Treehausterhaus caught his colleague's eye. Korregidoorian made a covert gesture for him to sit tight as Gideon continued.

'Some of you may have forgotten who this young man is. It has been a long time since my son, Commander Kinsharadeen, last stood by my side. He went missing after the NV Marianna blew up eleven long years ago. It was listed in the records as an unexplained accident. Unexplained because no one survived to tell us what happened. But now we know it was a deliberate attempt to kill Commander Kinsharadeen – part of a plot to force me aside so that these two men – '

And here, he named and pointed to Korreggidorian and Treehausterhaus.

' – could take control of the Navy!'

This was met by a roar of disapproval mixed with cries of denial.

'But despite the evidence, I never accepted that Commander Kinsharadeen was dead! And neither did these two! They offered rewards and inducements to anyone who could prove he was dead or reveal his whereabouts but they failed to pass on the information they received to me. They did not know they were already under suspicion and that every move was being monitored.

'They were also unaware that their star informant was working for me. It was through him that I received word of someone who might be Commander Kinsharadeen but who appeared to be unaware of his true identity. I was fortunate in having someone else I could trust – '

Gideon indicated Kallee.

'Miss Mandragorian, daughter of the Navy's top weapons designer. Ignoring the danger to herself, she agreed to check out this individual who, I was assured, bore a striking resemblance to Commander Kinsharadeen, with whom she was closely acquainted. She confirmed that he was indeed my son, but suffering from traumatic amnesia . . .'

Daniel looked across at Kallee and connected briefly. Her face gave nothing away but there was a slight hint of mischief in her eyes. He tuned back onto Gideon.

'. . . despite all our enquiries, we still lacked the proof we needed to charge these men with high treason.'

'And you still don't have any!' cried Koreggidorian, half-rising from his seat. 'These are totally unsupported, trumped-up charges against loyal serving officers and agents of the Corporation! What you are trying to do is discredit certain progessive elements within the Navy in the hope of extending the rule of the Kinsharadeens! Well, it will not succeed!'

He pointed accusingly at Daniel. 'That man and this young woman were part of a thieving crew of traders who were arrested as they tried to steal the Nebo Comm-Sat! He may be your son, and he may have survived the accidental loss of the

310

Marianna but he is no longer worthy of the uniform he now wears!'

Gideon responded with a thin smile. 'Wrong again, Danzigger. Your whole plan has been bedevilled by misjudgements since the very beginning.'

He proceeded to lay out the evidence against the plotters and mentioned how they had failed to report that three attempts had been made to access Daniel's Navy records in as many months.

Treehausterhaus rose to interrupt. 'When we put the Record Trace Alert on his records, we did so on your behalf! There was no question of concealment! We believed it was our duty to check out why these Deep-Seven searches were being made before bringing the matter to your notice to avoid raising any false hopes! We were working *for* you, not against you.'

Gideon motioned him to sit down. 'You'll have time to prepare your defence, Jak. But before you tell any more lies, I'd like you to listen to our star witness.'

He signalled to one of his aides. The young officer spoke briefly into a handset.

'The voices you are about to hear in this excerpt are those of Commander Kinsharadeen and Chief Treasury Agent Stagg who presided over the summary trial of the alleged thieves aboard the NV Korazon. Both speakers have been matched to the voiceprints held in our records. Their identities are not in doubt. It was the shock of seeing Agent Stagg that caused Commander Kinsharadeen to regain his memory and it is he who speaks first.'

Stagg started to rise from his chair. Two of the armed orderlies aimed their handguns at his chest. Stagg froze, jaw clenched, face and neck muscles taut, his eyes blazing. For one nail-biting moment it seemed as if he was challenging them to shoot, then he sank back down with a resigned sigh.

Daniel's voice came over the concealed speakers built into all four sides of the banqueting hall. You could hear a pin drop.

'Why are you stalling on this? I can give you the access codes that will release my records. Run a DNA test! It will prove I'm telling the truth!'

311

A voice-over identified the next voice as Marine Captain Gwantannamo.

'Mister Kornwallassee! Escort the rest of the prisoners back to the cells. Leave six men here with Chief Agent Stagg.'

There came the sound of people being marched off. More movement, then Stagg's voice.

'That's far enough! Wait outside. I'll call you when we're through.'

More movement. A door closing. Stagg's voice again.

'So, Mister Cartahaynyar . . .'

'Let's drop the pretence, Stagg. I've told you what the score is. I don't know what's going on here but you had better think very seriously about your next move. It's not too late to make that call.'

'Oh, yes it is, Danny Boy.'

The captain of the Korazon dropped his head into his hands.

'So you DO know who I am . . .'

'Of course. I just never expected you to come crawling out of the woodwork. When we wired the Marianna, we thought the Kinsharadeen line was extinguished – permanently.'

The colour drained from the faces of the two accused Admirals as the incriminating conversation continued, ending on Stagg's last boastful words.

'I'm the guy who pulled the plug on the Nebo miners, Danny. Part of the team that turned the Marianna and her crew into confetti. D'you really think we'd let twenty marines and three officers jeopardise the success of this operation?'

The Navy and Marine Captain who had assisted Stagg at the trial and who were now seated next to him, lunged towards him and had to be physically restrained.

Admiral Korreggidoorian leapt to his feet. 'The Navy was not a willing participant in this act of treason!' He pointed accusingly at Stagg. 'This whole plot was mounted by the Treasury!'

Gideon greeted this with a tired smile. 'Nice try, Ziggy. Commander Bramanti!'

One of the white-coated orderlies snapped to attention. 'Sir?!'

312

'You know who the traitors are. Take them away!'

It was not just the two admirals and the crew of the Korazon; officers and specialists of all ranks and both sexes seated at the three tables were tapped on the shoulder. When they had all been marched off, a third of the seats lay vacant.

The remainder of the guests fell silent, shocked by the charges of treachery and the realisation that the traitors in their midst, had – less than an hour before – been their comrades in arms. Seething too, with anger that this outrage could have been planned by members of the Navy – the arm of the Corporation where unswerving loyalty and unquestioning obedience were the twin articles of faith; the bedrock on which all else rested.

Gideon Kinsharadeen sensed the mood of the gathering and drew strength from it. Daniel, watching him, could only wonder at the blind devotion this man seemed to inspire. At times like this, his presence and the power he radiated was quite awesome. When he spoke, his voice had a timbre that made Daniel's spine tingle.

'We may have cut out the poison within, but Navy is not without its detractors. They envy our power and our achievements. When the news of what has happened here leaks out – and it will – our opponents will try to use it to bring the Navy into disrepute. Their attempts will fail, but we must not let it affect our morale.'

He was interrupted by a prolonged round of applause and table thumping. Gideon held up his hand to indicate there was more.

'I want you to carry these words back to your ships and your stations. "Trust in me, believe in yourselves. We will ride out this storm, this long night will end, the Navy will survive!"'

The guests leapt to their feet and gave him a standing ovation. Once again he appealed for silence.

'There will be music and dancing in the pyramid pavilion as usual. Let us get the celebrations off to a good start with a chorus of the Navy hymn!'

The conductor of the Navy band which had been providing

313

musical accompaniment to the dinner and the award ceremony, struck up the opening bars of the stirring tune. Gideon and Talla led the full throated rendering. Something inside Daniel drove him to join in.

> *'Shoulder to shoulder | Starwards we fly*
> *Onwards to glory | To fight or to die*
> *For Justice and Freedom*
> *On worlds far and near*
> *So rally to the Flag and cry*
> *"THE NAVY'S HERE!"*. . .'

☆   ☆   ☆

Buoyed up by a heart-thumping rendition of the Navy battle-hymn, the guests made their way back to the pyramid to continue the celebrations. In the Navy, the Admiral's wish was their command. Here and there, small knots of people discussed the arrests with worried frowns, but in general the atmosphere recaptured the earlier up-beat mood that had enlivened the reception . . .

Daniel, partnering Kallee on the dance floor, thought the cheerfulness he saw around him was a little forced. The whole atmosphere was surreal. Close to one hundred and fifty people had been plucked from the dinner table and marched off to an uncertain fate and apart from the odd handful with nervous dispositions, everyone who had survived was acting if nothing out of the ordinary had occurred. The phrase 'And the band played on' certainly applied here.

The analogy that came into his mind was provided by Andrew from within. It was like those tv Nature programmes that depicted a pride of lions attacking a vast herd of buffalo. There is a moment of confusion, a brief stampede as the lions race in to select their victim, but once the animal in question goes down and turns into lunch for eight, the stampede ends and the herd carries on grazing. It was over, forgotten – until mealtime came round again.

But not, perhaps, closer to home. As part of Gideon's

314

entourage, Daniel could not help noticing that both his parents were drinking heavily. He could not remember them doing so on similar occasions in the past.

One o'clock came and went and the party showed no sign of ending; spirits, in fact, seemed to be rising. Daniel danced with his mother, Talla – a formal, arms-length affair graced by her frosty smile. Her cheeks were flushed from the alcohol she had consumed but she was perfectly composed and several light-years away from being an incoherent stumbling drunk.

Scarcely a word was spoken, but her eyes never left his face. He felt he was being closely scrutinised – almost as if she suspected he was someone else in disguise. But at the same time he sensed she was trying to express feelings that would never – could never – be put into words. When the dance ended, he bowed politely and expressed his thanks. She thanked him with a gracious nod then, as their hands parted, she held his for a brief moment longer and squeezed them tightly. And that was it.

Make of it what you will, Danny boy . . .

In the middle of the night, a little under two hours before dawn, Daniel and Kallee were tapped by an ensign; one of Gideon's young aides. Would they please accompany the rest of the Admiral's party to the mansion? The only answer was 'Yes'. Kallee cast her eyes over the people in the pavilion but failed to spot her father.

Sandiego Mandragorian was standing inside the open front door as they came up the steps. He had swapped his 'midnight-maroon' party suit for tan chinos and a fleece-lined jacket. Entering, they found Gideon and Talla had exchanged dress uniform and ball gown for blue-grey fatigues. His mother's hair was tightly pinned and tucked under a peaked field cap. Some of the other aides were dressed the same way.

Mandragorian answered his daughter's unspoken question. 'Pack your gown. You're both going back to White Sands.'

Out of the corner of his eye, Daniel saw his mother steal a quick drink from a hip flask which she then slipped inside her tunic. The ensign who had escorted them from the pavilion

315

returned with two sets of fatigues and directed them to the cloakrooms.

When they reached the facing doors, Daniel said: 'Don't ask me why but I've got a bad feeling about this. Why are they putting us back in the bunker?'

'They're not.' The voice belonged to Kallee's father. 'You're going to spend some time with us at Broken Ridge.'

This was the Mandragorian family's desert retreat and the place where Kallee's father came up with some of his best ideas – which, on reflection, is an entirely inappropriate way of describing the process of thinking up new ways to kill people.

'It's your mother's idea,' explained Mandragorian. Noting the effect this had on Daniel he added: 'Don't worry. She's not trying her hand at match-making again. This is just a get-well exercise.'

'Happy now?' enquired Kallee.

'Meet me back here in two minutes,' said Daniel. He banged open the door to the men's cloakroom and went inside.

Mandragorian shook his head. 'Aren't you two ever going to change?'

Kallee pushed open the door to the women's cloakroom and looked back at her father. 'We make a good team, Dad. That's more than enough for me. The rest is just moonshine.'

At the back of the Admiral's mansion, a large jet-copter stood on a floodlit hard-pad with its rotors turning. Camouflaged in jagged patches of grey and blue, with the letters 'NAVY' painted on the tail section, it had a large passenger and cargo section. Both loading doors were slid back, allowing the Admiral's party to board from both sides. Two pilots manned the cockpit. Two winchmen shared the rear compartment with Gideon, Talla, Mandragorian, Daniel and Kallee plus ten aides, half Navy, half Marines. All of them lean and keen with that special, hard, almost robotic look in their eyes that Daniel knew of old.

Andrew, his alter ego, knew that look too . . .

The jet-copter took off and sped towards the black line of hills. Behind them, the sky was beginning to lighten.

As they approached the White Sands missile testing range, the landscape was still shrouded in that special pre-dawn grey that fudged the outlines of everything that lay beneath. Headlights pierced the yellowing gloom. It was a convoy of all-terrain trucks driving away from the range towards the road that led back to Shasta Bay.

The jet-copter lost altitude. Four, small, jeep-type vehicles with open backs were parked outside the main gate with their headlights on. The beams picked out a number of men who appeared to be working on the high, chain-link security fence.

Several of the men came forward to meet the 'copter as it touched down. Everybody got off except Mandragorian. Kallee was supposed to remain on board with him for the flight to Broken Ridge but she elected to stay and follow on with Daniel later.

The jet-copter took off, raising a cloud of choking dust. Daniel, who had stayed at Kallee's side while she waved goodbye, looked to see where the rest of the party had gone and discovered that not all the people he had seen from the air were working on the fence. Some of them were fastened to it.

The disused test site had been turned into a temporary killing ground. The men and the handful of women accused of treason – one hundred and forty-seven in all – had been lined up at intervals on either side of the main gate. Now clad in black prison coveralls, their hands and ankles had been fastened to the fence with plastic kwik-ties, and a steel cable, with loops at both ends, had been passed across the chest, under the armpits, through the links of the fence, and padlocked together at the rear.

Daniel took in the scene, looked at Kallee, then turned back in time to see Gideon and Talla being handed powerful handguns.

Andrew's persona welled up out of his subconscious. 'My God! This is insane!' He rounded on Kallee. 'D'you realise what's happening here?! These people are all going to die

317

because of *me*! Because I *came back!' He clutched his head. 'Jesus Christ Almighty!'*

Kallee reached up and grasped his shoulders. 'We can't stop it happening, Daniel.'

'No? Well, fuck it! I'm not going to stay here and watch!'

He went to walk past. Kallee stepped in front of him. 'You're not expected to watch.' Her voice had a steely edge to it.

Gideon and Talla stepped up onto the back of the lead vehicle with two of their aides. A marine, toting the Rimworld equivalent of an M-16 swung into the seat beside the driver. A second vehicle, with four similarly-armed aides on the back, stood ready to follow.

One of the ensigns who had ridden on the 'copter approached Daniel and Kallee and saluted. 'Sir! The Admiral and his lady are waiting for you to join them.'

Daniel opened his mouth to deliver an abusive reply. Kallee grabbed his upper arm, jabbed her thumb in the nerve centre and squeezed hard. 'Just give him a second or two. The sudden recovery from this amnesia thing has left him with momentary bouts of disorientation.'

The ensign nodded, saluted and returned to the lead vehicle.

Kallee tried to push Daniel forwards.

He dug his heels in. 'Kallee!' he hissed. 'I can't *do* this!'

'You've got to!'

'No! I'm not going to do it. These people are – '

'Innocent?! They killed your crew, Daniel! They tried to kill everyone aboard The Dragon Lady!'

'Yes, but you just can't butcher people like this! This man and woman who are supposed to be my parents are fucking psychopaths!'

'Daniel! They are all going to die whether you like it or not!'

'Maybe they are. But I'm not going to be part of it! I can't believe I'm hearing this from you! You're not part of this madness!'

Kallee took a calculated risk. She stepped in front of Daniel and shook him by the arms. '*Andrew*! Are you listening to me?!'

'Andrew . . .?'

'If you don't go through with this, *you are going to ruin the plan*!'

'Plan? What plan? And why are you calling me, Andrew?'

'Operation JERICHO, Andrew! And don't play games with me. I know you're in there somewhere!'

She hustled him towards the waiting vehicle. Daniel tried to stall her by walking stiff-legged. 'Kallee! Don't you understand. I can't *do it*!'

'Then fake it!' she hissed. 'Throw a fit! I've already given you an out! Just get up there!'

One of the aides extended a hand and pulled him aboard.

'He should be okay now,' said Kallee. She stood back as the jeep moved off. Gideon took a handgun from the same aide, chambered the first round then passed the gun to Daniel. 'I understand you've had a dizzy spell.'

'It's this amnesia thing, sir.' Daniel recycled Kallee's excuse. 'But it'll pass.'

'I hope so, Commander. The eyes of the Navy are on you. Your mother and I expect you to act like a true Kinsharadeen.'

'I intend to, sir!' Daniel dropped his right arm to bring the gun against his thigh where no one could see his thumb push the safety catch back on.

The leading conspirators, Korreggidoorian and Treehausterhaus, were wired either side of the main gate. Their associates were attached to the fence at twelve foot intervals; half to the right of the gate, half to the left. Gideon's jeep turned left and drove to the end of the line. The vehicle carrying the four-man death-squad followed.

Daniel could not believe that he was about to be an accomplice in a mass summary execution without trial but a voice within urged him to stand firm.

Together, they would find a way out of this. They had to. Connie and Shalimar were depending on them. The plan must not be allowed to fail.

The lead jeep began to drive slowly along the line of men and women wired to the chain-link fence. Gideon and Tala scanned the passing faces then, without warning, Gideon raised his gun

319

in a two-handed grip and shot a man through the heart. The victim's legs buckled. The body sagged, head down, supported by the steel cable looped around the chest. Talla then shot the first woman they passed and then the second. It was her task to despatch all the female plotters, a task she performed coolly and without the slightest hesitation.

The jeep, moving at a crawl, carried them past five other men before Gideon raised his gun again and shot the next two. There seemed to be no logic behind his choice. Was it a settling of old scores? These men – anonymous in their black coveralls – may have been close to him. If so, the sense of betrayal would be all the keener.

Gideon shot his fifth victim then turned to Daniel. 'Time to show us what you're made of, Commander.'

The safety catch of his gun was still on. Daniel levelled it at the next man's chest and pulled the trigger.

The gun failed to fire.

'Idiot! You've left the safety catch on! Have you forgotten everything?!'

The second jeep, now some forty yards behind, started to drive along the line of victims. Taking turns to use their automatic weapons, the young aides methodically shot everyone who had been spared so far and pumped several rounds into the slumped bodies of the dead and dying.

The staccato rattle of assault rifle fire caused sudden flashes of Andrew's past life in the army to jump into Daniel's mind. He reeled from the shock then exaggerated the effect for the benefit of those around him. Levelling the handgun at the next victim in the line, he slipped off the safety catch and fired.

Spa-a-aannng! The bullet clipped a link in the fence a centimetre to the right of his target's head and went on through. Daniel let his knees buckle. An aide caught him. Gideon cursed loudly, shot the man his son had failed to kill then turned on Daniel and slapped his face twice. The second blow, a hard-knuckled backhander made his head swim.

'Get on your feet!'

Daniel feigned a valiant attempt to do so and pretended not to know where he was.

Gideon bared his teeth. 'Korreggidoorian was right! You're not fit to wear a Navy uniform! You deserve to be wired to that fence alongside him!'

Daniel realised he had to put on a more convincing show – something that didn't make him look such a pathetic, spineless wretch. Focusing his eyes on the middle distance in an effort to simulate a trance, he began to mumble tonelessly.

'This is the NV Marianna, the NV Marianna, calling all Navy Stations. One of our plasma drives has gone into override and is about to implode. We have lost all main and auxiliary power. Mayday, Mayday, Mayday, Please respond, please respond. This is the NV Marianna, the NV Marianna, calling all – '

Talla left another woman hanging dead on the fence and laid a restraining hand on Gideon as he grasped the collar of Daniel's tunic to haul him to his feet.

'Leave him, Gideon. It's not a beating he needs, it's a doctor.'

Huddled in a corner of the jeep, Daniel continued to mumble the Mayday call with increasing urgency and tried to block out the sound of gunfire. It was no use. The repeated bursts of automatic fire from the execution squad in the second jeep drove into his brain like a hammer drill. When he closed his eyes, a dizzying, kaleidoscopic jumble of images flashed through his mind . . .

Narrow roads, winding through high forested hills – burnt-out villages – bodies lying in neglected gardens, shot, bludgeoned, hacked to death, hands and feet tied with wire – charred corpses frozen in the last movement of a danse macabre – blue-helmeted soldiers – white armoured vehicles driving through falling clouds of earth raised by incoming mortar rounds – a desert landscape – brown-skinned, hollow-cheeked men wearing blankets and waving AK-47s . . .

How strange! thought Daniel, that he should invent a name for a gun he had never seen . . .

Flying in a huge, noisy, ribbed metal tube with other armed men

321

– for endless hours over an endless sea – to a scattering of islands where vast, cloud-filled skies alternated with blankets of mist that clung to the empty hills – moving through those hills – part of a long line of men in green berets, each one overshadowed by the huge packs on their backs – damp, yielding bog underfoot, mud-sucking mile after mile – the flat pointed end of a building on a wet, glistening street filled with strange, huddled, cramped dwellings – the whole wall painted white and on it, the picture of a gunman in green with a black mask and gloves – and above the man, a huge red hand and the letters UVF . . .

The red hand grew larger and larger – blotting out everything else in his mind – and in the palm of the hand, a nose, a mouth, chin, and two eyes began to form – like the face of a swimmer rising to the surface of a dark pool – its blood red features grew out of the skin and became someone he recognised – Chief Treasury Agent Stagg . . .

Stagg . . . that was the answer.

Daniel hauled himself up in time to see Gideon and Talla both pull the trigger on Admiral Treehauseterhaus. Korreggidoorian was already hanging on the wire.

He caught the Admiral's eye. 'I believe I'm okay now, sir. I'd like the chance to do my bit.'

Gideon hesitated then nodded to an aide.

Daniel seized the offered handgun, jumped over the side of the jeep and ran ahead of it, searching the line of tense, resigned and tearful faces. His unsteady run wasn't faked. Strange thoughts, strange visions were running wild inside his head and the mental confusion made his movements erratic.

The twin suns had yet to rise, but the eastern sky was streaked with thin, broken lines of blood-red clouds – heralding the dawn the remaining plotters would never see.

A head taller than the men on either side of him, Stagg was easy to spot. He looked down on Daniel with a contemptuous smile. 'Come do do your bit for the Navy, Danny boy?'

'Screw the Navy,' said Daniel. 'This is for the miners of Nebo.' He placed the handgun against Stagg's chest and fired.

322

Once – twice – three – four times. He was about to fire again when Kallee caught his arms from behind.

'It's enough, Daniel. It's enough.'

He gave her the gun without a struggle and allowed himself to be led away.

Chapter Nineteen

After the 'copter dropped Daniel and Kallee off at Broken Ridge, Daniel spent the next three days as a virtual recluse. He slept for long periods, didn't speak at the few meals he shared with Kallee, and went for long walks across the semi-barren landscape.

Kallee trailed him at a distance to make sure he came to no harm but even when he turned, and must have seen her, he did not react to her watching presence and did not refer to it when she returned to the house to find him staring into the gas-powered log fire.

Sandiego, Kallee's father, spent most of his time in his workshop and design office. He had four resident assistants who were housed in a separate unit and two live-in domestic staff to look after his rambling, split-level home.

The building itself was similar in spirit to Taliesin West, Frank Lloyd Wright's desert home and architecture school in Arizona. Built of local stone, it rose seamlessly from the ridge on which it stood. Even the swimming pool had been constructed to look like a work of Nature and came complete with a hidden 'spring' and cascade.

Rising on the fourth day, Kallee came out onto the wide sundeck to find Daniel swimming in the pool below. She knotted the robe securely round her naked body and walked down the steps. Seeing her, he broke his stroke and raised an arm in greeting. Kallee sat down on the warm stone terrace by the edge of the pool and dipped her feet into the water.

Reaching her, Daniel trod water and wiped both hands over his face and head. 'Hi. How're you doing?'

'I'm okay. Welcome back.'

Daniel smiled. 'Have I been a pain?'

'No more than usual.'

Daniel heaved himself out of the water to sit beside her. He wasn't wearing any swimming trunks but casual nakedness in this kind of setting did not raise any eyebrows on the Rimworld.

He reached for a towel, draped it over his shoulders and used one end to dry his face. 'Do you ever wish you were someone else?'

'Constantly. I got a new ID when they sent me after you. Unfortunately, it was still the same me underneath.'

'So you don't think it's possible for people to change . . .'

Kallee mentally compared 'Andiamo Cartahaynyar' to his double now sitting beside her and smiled. 'Oh yes, I've seen it happen. Who would you like to be?'

'Somebody who isn't part of this crazy set-up.' Daniel dropped the end of the towel. 'This is going to sound odd but ever since that moment on the Korazon when I came back from – well, wherever it was – there's been this feeling, growing inside, that this . . .' He tapped his chest. '. . . isn't the real me.'

'I know the feeling.'

'No, listen, I'm being serious here.' Daniel pressed his fingertips against his temples. 'The weirdest things keep flashing through my mind. Pictures that can only come from some kind of dream world – that is utterly different from this one.' He spread his hands. 'Where do they come from?'

'You tell me . . .'

Daniel turned his head away and studied the distant view. 'It's amazing how the brain can construct these imaginary landscapes – and create this feeling that you've actually *been* there.'

'Yes, it is.' Kallee could have offered a solution there and then but she had been warned by Aramitz not to interfere with the process of self-discovery; Daniel had to find the answer from within. Even so, as their eyes met, she felt obliged to respond. 'There's a good side and a bad side to all of us, Daniel.

Maybe it's time you let the good guy come through. You could make a start trying to relax. You could also try smiling a bit more often.'

'That bad, huh?'

'You're a Kinsharadeen. What d'you expect me to say?'

Daniel studied her for a while. 'It's strange . . .'

'What is?'

'That you, of all people, should have volunteered to come looking for me.'

'Not really. If you took the trouble to know me better, you'd find I was full of surprises.' Kallee stood up, slipped the robe from her slim, trim body and dived into the pool.

Daniel watched as her strong shoulders and thighs powered her towards the far end and wondered why he had become so closely involved with a woman he wasn't remotely attracted to. He decided the answer lay in their childhood when, as he recalled it, she had gone out of her way to annoy him.

A habit she had yet to grow out of.

☆ ☆ ☆

Later that day, a jet-copter came to fly Kallee's father over to the Navy weapons development centre at Thunder Point. As the top man, he spent a large part of his time there, directing the various research programmes and attending meetings with the top brass at Shasta Bay.

On this particular, week-long trip, he took three of his assistants with him, leaving just one in the design studio/workshop. The two domestics continued to look after the house and prepare meals but with the son of the Supreme Admiral in residence they made a point of keeping out of the way except when their presence was required.

All of which meant that Kallee and Daniel were thrown together for most of the day. Which was perfect, because Kallee had a job to do, and so had Daniel – but he didn't know it yet. And what gave the whole thing an extra buzz was that she didn't know what came next. She was back where she liked to be – on the high wire, without a net.

326

'Fancy a day out?' asked Kallee. 'I got Dody to make us up a lunch pack.'

Dody and Dibbs were the domestics.

Daniel practised his smile. 'Sounds good to me.'

'Then pick up that coolbox and walk this way.'

Kallee led him down onto the lower level where the dirt road met the house and used a small infra-red bleeper to raise a wide garage door. Parked inside were two clean, but dented dune-buggies.

'Now does that look like fun?' enquired Kallee.

'It certainly does, Stanley. Which one's yours? The one with the most dents in?'

'No. That's the one you're driving.'

They strapped themselves into their respective vehicles and drove out of the garage. The door closed automatically behind them. They paused side by side, and gunned the motors.

'Where too? yelled Daniel.

'Follow my dust!' Kallee floored the gas pedal, fish-tailed in front of him to raise a blinding white cloud and was three hundred yards down the road before he could see over the bonnet.

For the next ten miles they played a hair-raising game of tag; in and out of gullies, up and down rocky slopes and going four wheels in the air off the crests of rippling white dunes. It was one of those moments when it was good to be alive and still young enough to be fearless. To feel invincible.

They slid to a formation stop on the summit of a bluff. Daniel grabbed the coolbox and followed Kelly to a sandy hollow.

'We can't see the view from here.'

'That's right. And no one can see us.' Kallee opened the coolbox and pulled out some canned drinks. 'Enjoy the ride?'

'Yeah, it was great. A lot better than those stupid computer games we used to play.'

'That's 'cos I used to win all the time.' She popped a can and passed it to him.'

'Yeah, all right, don't rub it in. You almost beat me today too.'

327

'We're only at the halfway mark, Daniel. We have the return trip to look forward to.' She started to set out the food. 'However, I didn't invite you out here to show off my driving skills. I have an ulterior motive.'

'Sounds fascinating. Tell me more.'

'Later. First we eat.'

When the uneaten remnants had been packed away in the coolbox, Kallee produced a portable CD player. 'While we were aboard the Mount Olympus, Aramitz was given two disks by Parnassus with instructions to pass them on to you. Jean asked me to make sure you got them at the right moment. Now seems as good a time as any.'

'To listen to music?'

'The first CD contains music.' Kallee passed him the rigid plastic wallet.

Daniel read off the label. 'The Rimworld Variations, composed by Iggbin Nineberleena, performed by the Jericho Sinfonia.' He passed it back to Kallee. 'Not exactly my kind of music.'

'That doesn't surprise me. But I want you to listen to it very carefully, because you will then understand the importance of this one.'

She offered him the second CD.

The label read: 'The Chikozbar Concerto. Composed by Shadwell Cortz. Performed by the Soho Sextet'. The words struck a chord in Daniel's memory but he couldn't make the link.

'Are you ready?' Kallee pressed the Play button.

The Rimworld Variations turned out to be five full-blooded orchestral works in which the brass section played a leading part. The theme was melodic, martial yet sprightly and, above all, triumphant. And as Daniel listened, he became aware of a staccato thread woven through the music by two trumpets playing in counterpoint.

Like the label on the second CD, the pattern of notes struck a chord within his memory, but this time he made the connection. It was a coded message, skilfully hidden within the music. And

328

Daniel realised he knew what it was – or, to be more precise – part of him knew what it was.

It was a message in Morse code, transmitted by the interplay between the two trumpets. He listened carefully until the music reached its thunderous finale, then said: 'Play it again. From the beginning.'

'Hah! Incredible!' exclaimed Kallee. 'That's exactly what you were supposed to say! Here – use this if you want to write something down.' She pulled an electronic notepad from her shoulder-bag.

'You certainly believe in coming prepared.'

'Someone has to do the thinking round here.'

'Save the jokes. Just play the music.'

This time round, he captured the entire message. He created a file, then recalled it and ran it again across the small screen. He did so twice then, having carefully memorised the key details, he deleted the file along with everything else on the internal disk.

Kallee, from her seat on the opposite side of the hollow, tried to read his face. 'What does it say?'

Daniel held up the second CD. 'This is not a music track. The label's just there to hide the fact that it's a ROM disk. I have to access the FI-COR computer and load this programme into it.

'Oh – is that all? T-hnnhhh! You got as much chance of getting into that as I have of filling a 38D cup!'

FI-COR was the computer division that handled the financial transactions of the Corporation.

'My instructions included my father's very own initial entry code and the authorisation codes to get us past the gate-guardians when making a data input.'

Kallee's eyes narrowed. 'Now *that* does alter the odds somewhat. Would I be right in thinking you intend to screw things up a little?'

'Just a little. Does your father have an input terminal in his design studio?'

'Yes. It's linked to Thunder Point.'

'That's all we need. The costings unit there must be sending figures down the wire to Gold River. We can hack our way in from here.'

'Hold on! Pa and I may not see eye to eye but I don't want him taking the rap for this.'

'He won't. Trust me.'

'Okay. I know my way around computers. If you've got the codes, getting in through Thunder Point won't be a problem.'

'Then let's do it.'

On the return trip, Kallee reached the garage doors and had time to park inside before he reached the finishing line.

All computer viruses are fiendish affairs but Parnassus and his hired guns had been putting the finishing touches to this one for years. It had taken a long time to ferret out the information they needed to build an electronic portrait of the FI-COR computer system, and the destroyer programme had to be reconfigured several times in order to circumvent the new levels of protection that were constantly being introduced by the Corporation.

As soon as the Jericho virus was infiltrated into the system via Thunder Point, it used Gideon's access codes to circumvent the gate-guardians, covering its tracks and concealing its presence as it worked its way into the heart of the system where it began the task of neutralising the array of anti-viral programmes inside FI-COR. When it had invaded the whole system, it made itself completely invisible and settled down to wait. Eventually, when it made its presence felt, the blame for it being there would be spread far and wide.

When the jet-copter carrying Kallee's father and his assistants returned to Broken Ridge, Daniel was waiting by the pad dressed in Naval uniform. An e-mail message, received the previous evening, had informed him that the Admiral wanted to meet with him at Gold River – the headquarters of the Corporation.

Having fed the Jericho virus into FI-COR, Daniel was

understandably cautious as to why he had been summoned. Before leaving, he created a file on Kallee's electronic notepad and entered three words plus Gideon's access codes. 'If, for any reason, I don't return, I want you to hack into FI-COR and enter this file. It's called ENDGAME.'

'You worry too much.'

He smiled. 'Well, one of has to do the worrying around here.'

She stayed on the upper verandah to avoid the dust raised by the 'copter as it took off. She waved as he was carried past and blew a kiss. A brief, half-formed gesture – as if suddenly embarrassed by the thought that he might take it seriously.

☆   ☆   ☆

Given the Corporation's cost-paring approach to its myriad financial enterprises one might have expected its headquarters to have been the Rimworld equivalent of a clutch of Portaka-bins but this was not so. If you lumped together the Carrera-marbled luxury of every financial and business institution from East to West, added in the lavish oil-rich architecture of the Gulf States, then multiplied the result by $(Donald + Ivana)^2$, it might give some idea of the splendiferous surroundings in which the high-rollers who ran the Corporation conducted their business.

You thought the Tyrell Corporation's building in *Blade-runner* was impressive? Forget it. Compared to the black marble, titanium steel and bronze glass ziggurat at Gold River, the Tyrell place was a shack. The 'Zig' was *big*. Built to superhuman scale using the principles so skilfully employed by Albert Speer in the state buildings of Hitler's Third Reich, it radiated power, from its Zeppelin hangar-sized lobby with its hundred-foot-high ceiling to the penthouse with its square mile of carpet.

An ensign greeted Daniel at the helipad, attached a Visitor's Pass to his breast pocket, and rode with him in the elevator to the floor where the Executive Board of the Corporation were about to end one of their regular meetings. They hung around for a few minutes in the lobby area staffed by security men from the Treasury Division, then two massive doors slid open and the twenty-four men who virtually ruled the Rimworld emerged in twos and threes and were immediately surrounded by their support staff.

All the board members were extremely well-groomed, had grey hair, and wore expensive but sober outfits. They had the assurance and authority which came from occupying the seat of power but, close up, there was little to distinguish them from ordinary mortals. If any of them had been standing on their own in the queue waiting to board a spaceliner, you would have been hard put to pick them out.

These were the faceless accountants who had turned existence into a bookkeeping exercise, where the worth of an individual was measured by his contribution to the bottom line.

Only the CEO – this year it was the Supreme Admiral – had a high media profile. He was one of the last to exit. Daniel waited until Gideon's eye fell upon him then crossed the lobby and gave his father a parade-ground salute.

'Morning, sir! Commander Kinsharadeen reporting as ordered!'

The information was entirely superfluous but these formal exchanges had been part of Daniel's upbringing. Even as a child, in the privacy of their home, it would have been unthinkable for him to have used phrases like: 'Hi, Dad. How's it going?'

Gideon returned the simultaneous salutes of Daniel and his escort and ordered the ensign to wait in the lobby while he conferred with 'the Commander'. The ensign was also to order the 'copter to remain on standby to fly back to Broken Ridge.

Daniel felt partly reassured. Unless they were planning to drop him overboard somewhere along the way, the news of the return flight meant that – so far – no one had detected an alien presence inside the FI-COR computer, or that it had been accessed without authorisation via Thunder Point.

'We need to talk,' said Gideon. 'But there's a couple of things I'd like to show you first.' He led the way into a special executive voice-activated elevator and asked for the floor below. The doors slid open to reveal a vast circular room at least fifty feet high. The wall was covered from floor to ceiling with a series of videoscreens that built up into one continuous display right around the room.

Monitoring the screens, from two circular tiers of desks – which each contained several small computer screens – were financial technicians. The overall effect was similar to the flight control center staffed by NASA engineers to monitor space shuttle missions.

The task of the fin-techs manning what Gideon called 'The War Room' was to monitor the financial health of the Corporation's investments in the Rimworld. Every planet and every space-station into which the Corporation's cash had been poured was represented in diagrammatic form around the wall of the War Room together with current details of the various wholly- or partly-owned terrestrial or space-based enterprises.

Even the ships of the Navy and Trade-Cor figured on the display which was in two colours; blue for a positive cash balance, red for a lossmaking situation.

The screens were constantly updated using a never-ending flow of incoming statistics. Whenever an operation went into deficit, its screen image flipped from blue to flashing red and a warning bleeper sounded. The reaction was similar to the Pentagon getting news of an incoming nuclear missile. Management teams instantly bore down on the problem and did everything they could to redress the balance.

Having satisfied himself that Daniel had fully appreciated the scope and importance of the Corporation's activities, Gideon took him back up to the inner sanctum – the boardroom in which the Supreme Executive Council met to plan how to increase their stranglehold on the Rimworld.

The room, which was softly lit, had no windows. The conference table was in the shape of a ring. The CEO's chair – occupied in the current year by Gideon – was marginally larger than the twenty-three other high-backed chairs ranged around the circle. Each seat position was furnished with a computer terminal that could be viewed through a glass plate in the table top. The keyboard was in a slide-out drawer.

At the point directly opposite Gideon, a narrow section of the table had been removed to allow access to a large flat circular screen which carried a diagrammatic representation of the Rimworld system beamed from a projector mounted in the ceiling, directly overhead, and which could be viewed from any of the seats round the table.

Gideon waved his hand around the room. 'This is it, Commander. The future's made right here. Take a seat, see how it feels.'

As Daniel went to take one of the side seats, Gideon laid a hand on his arm. 'No. I want to see you sitting in mine.' He pulled out the big chair.

Daniel sat down at the head of the table. His father took a seat three places to his right.

'How does it feel?'

'Awesome.' Daniel ran his hands over the polished surface.

'That's how I felt when I first took my place in this room – especially when I sat in that chair. But you know what ran through my mind?' The Admiral gave him a long, hard look. His face was tinged with regret. 'I thought "One day, Daniel will head up all this. He'll get to sit . . . right where you are now. He'll build on the work that I, and our forefathers, have put into this enterprise. He'll carry the Kinsharadeen name forward and pass it on down the centuries." But that's not going to happen, Commander. You're not big enough to fill that chair. And let's face it – ' He indicated the room. ' – in your heart of hearts, this is not what you want, is it?'

Daniel tried to hide the mental confusion caused by such a direct question. 'Sir, uh – I'm aware that – for the reasons I attempted to explain earlier I – I did not, uh – I was unable to conduct myself in the manner you expected. And I apologise for that – even though we have a tradition that Navy never seeks to excuse failure. I would simply ask to be given a further chance to prove myself when I am fully recovered. The fact is – '

Gideon cut in. 'I'll tell you what the fact is, Commander.

Even if you had killed your share of those traitors, I would still feel the same way.' Motioning Daniel to remain seated, his father stood up and prowled around the table like a prosecuting counsel. 'Those eleven years which you can't remember have changed you. Things can never be the same. Who knows what skeletons are now lying in the cupboard – what birds will eventually come home to roost?'

'But, sir – who will carry on the family line?'

'A young man called Mark Kinsharadeen.' The Admiral circled round the table towards him.

The news rocked Daniel. 'You have another son?'

'No, not a son. An exact replica of me.' Gideon passed behind the big chair, pushed it sideways to gain access to the slide-out keyboard and entered a single keystroke.

Two panels on the facing wall slid apart to reveal a large computer screen. He entered several more keystrokes. The portrait of a young boy appeared on the screen together with a full length picture of him standing in a garden. He bore a vague resemblance to Daniel.

'That's Mark. He's now ten years old. And this is me at the same age.'

Comparison photos came up on the screen. The two children looked identical. The computer then superimposed the two portraits on each other. They matched exactly.

Daniel sat there – stunned. 'I thought cloning of humans was impossible!'

'That story was put out for public consumption.' Gideon wiped the pictures with another keystroke and closed up the screen. 'But Life-Cor never stopped working on the project.'

'An impressive achievement.' Daniel hoped his insincerity didn't show. 'But now that you have another successor, may I ask what is going to happen to me?'

Gideon resumed his circumnavigation of the table. 'That's something we've given a great deal of thought to, Commander. Your mother has persuaded me that "an honorable retirement" would be our best option.'

'Sounds ominous, sir.'

'Yes. It will mean the death of "Daniel Kinsharadeen" and your rebirth as someone else.'

'"Andiamo Cartahaynyar"?'

'That's for you to decide. But we can arrange the first, and Constantine Parnassus has assured me he can arrange the second – and find you a safe home. But when it's done, we will never see each other again.'

Daniel rose from the Admiral's chair. 'When is this going to happen, sir?'

Gideon passed the halfway mark in his trip around the table. 'I think it should happen as soon as possible, don't you?'

'Yes, sir.' Daniel quickly framed the question he really wanted answered. 'Sir – ?'

'Yes?'

'If you had a new son and heir, why go to all the trouble to find me – and bring me back?'

Gideon met this with a dry laugh. 'You surprise me, Daniel. I'd have thought that was obvious. We needed you – *in person* – to trap and expose the plotters. With so many high-ranking officers believed to be involved, we could not move against them without cast-iron proof.'

'And I was it . . .'

'Exactly. That was why Mark – who will succeed me and be all I ever was – had to be kept hidden away from the day he was born. Now that the traitors have been removed, he can take his rightful place beside me.'

'And if someone is mad enough to try and remove him?'

'There will be another "me" waiting in the wings. And another, and another. The Kinsharadeens will continue to lead the Navy. I shall live for ever.'

This man, decided Daniel, is barking mad.

They were interrupted by a bleeper. The face of one of Gideon's aides appeared on the door screen. 'Sir . . .?'

'What is it?'

'We have a small problem in the War Room. The Director has asked if you will go head to head with him for a few minutes in order to resolve it.'

'On my way.' Gideon turned to Daniel. 'Wait there – and think what might have been.'

Daniel saluted and stayed at attention until the Admiral left the room. He then sat down in the big, high-backed swivel chair and surveyed the room. Given the sensitive nature of the meetings held around this particular table, he doubted there were any surveillance cameras. Not that it really mattered. The entry he was about to make would disappear without trace.

He drew the keyboard towards him and quickly tapped in Gideon's password and access codes. When the screen was ready, he entered the question: What news of Jericho?

The system answered: The city is surrounded.

Daniel typed: Sound the trumpets. And pressed ENTER, then closed down the screen and slid the keyboard out of sight. In forty-eight hours' time, working behind the normal daily activity of the FI-COR system, the virus would start to run its own program.

And the walls would come tumbling down.

☆　　☆　　☆

Back at Broken Ridge, Daniel sought Sandiego's permission to take his daughter for a buggie ride and drove Kallee out to the picnic place on the bluff. When they had settled into the sandy hollow, he started off with the news that he had activated the Jericho virus, and that, in less than forty-three hours, FI-COR – the financial engine of the Corporation – was due to blow its head gasket.

'And you used the CEO's keyboard to do this?'

'While sitting in his chair. Gave me a real buzz.'

'You're crazy. Why risk everything when you could have done it from here?'

'I didn't know if I'd be coming back.' He described his visit to the Gold River complex then told Kallee about the plans his parents had made for his 'retirement'. 'Frankly, after what I saw and heard today, I won't be sorry to leave.'

For some reason, Daniel chose not to reveal he was being replaced by a ten-year-old clone.

337

'So . . . where to from here?'

'They're going to ferry me up to the NV Kahshathra – the ship that saved us – and from there I'll transfer onto the SS Mount Olympus.'

'And after that?'

'I take on a new identity, try and forget about all this and start my life over.' The prospect brought forth a sigh. 'If I can pretend to be Andiamo Cartahaynyar for eleven years, there's no reason why I can't do it again.'

'What happens if you run into someone who knows you?'

'Kallee, there are over a thousand planets in the Rimworld. I'm sure I'll be able to find one where I can settle down and enjoy a quiet life.'

'"A quiet life"? Is that what you want?'

'There's only one thing I want right now – and that's to get away from here.'

Kallee mulled this over then asked: 'Would it be a problem if I came along for the ride?'

The question drew a shrug. 'Don't see why it should. After all, once they hand us over to Parnassus, we'll both be free to do whatever we want. We don't have to stick together, do we?'

'No . . . I suppose not.' For someone who made a point of being up front, Kallee was strangely hesitant. 'I just thought – we might, y'know – join up with The Dragon Lady again.'

'That old shit-bucket? You must be joking.'

'It *is* getting a refit. Well . . . it's supposed to be.'

'Sorry, Kallee. I may be washed up as far as the Navy's concerned but I'm not ready to bunk down with a bunch of raggedy-assed spacers. I spent several years of my life putting guys like that out of business!'

'So what are you going to do?'

Daniel clawed air. 'Kallee! I already told you! It's all up in the air. I don't *have* to make any decisions yet. The Admiral said I'd be leaving here with eleven years' back pay and allowances. That's going to give me plenty of time to look around. How about you?'

It was Kallee's turn to shrug. 'Don't have a lot of choice. I

338

have no money of my own to speak of, and I don't have anywhere to live. Working a trader will provide me with both. The Dragon Lady will suit me fine. I like to move around – see new places, meet new faces.'

'Yeah . . . speaking of places and faces . . . this run-in I had with Hammerhead . . .'

'What about it?'

'What the zagg was I doing in Boot City?'

'You really don't remember?'

'No.' He thought for a while then asked: 'Out at White Sands when I was, uh . . .'

'Yeah . . .?'

'Why did you call me Andrew?'

She gave him a searching glance. 'Don't you know who he is?'

'No. Should I?'

Kallee smiled. 'I think we should save the rest of this conversation until we're out of here.' Seeing his reaction, she said: 'No, I'm not being paranoid, just careful.'

☆   ☆   ☆

When the Admiral arrived home, Tallamahassee, his wife, could see he was not best pleased. She knew him well enough not to ask what had upset him. Throughout supper – served by their resident staff – their conversation was desultory, the subjects innocuous. Talla was content to wait. She would know soon enough.

Retiring to their private quarters, Gideon dropped into his favourite lounge armchair. Talla poured six fluid ounces of a colourless liquid into a glass and tinted it pink with three drops of fruit syrup. The liquid – distilled from a sugar-plant – was 94% pure alcohol, and the resulting mix was called a Brain-Blaster.

She leaned over Gideon, placed the glass in his waiting hand, then began to massage his neck and shoulders. When the drink had smoothed the rough edges of the day, he would unburden himself.

339

'You know what came through today?'

Talla, who knew the routine, kept silent and continued her efforts to relax the bunched muscles at the base of Gideon's neck.

'Trade-Cor sent me over a report that had been filed by one of their agents from their Special Investigation Division. It had been sent in by a man called Vindhook along with a letter of resignation and – don't ask me why – no one bothered to read his last report.'

'Until now.'

'Right.' Gideon took another swallow.

'But why did they send it to you?'

'Because it concerns Mandragorian's daughter. And guess what? She was being kept under surveillance because she was suspected of being a key member of the Animal Proliferation Front!'

Talla's fingers froze momentarily. 'It's not possible!'

'Oh, but it is possible! The SID have had people on her case for the last three years!'

'And they didn't tell you?'

'Of course not! You know what Trade-Cor are like! It's run by people who didn't make it into the Navy. If they can make us look bad, they will – that's why their Special Investigation Division is always trying to prove it's smarter than Navy Intelligence!'

'So do they have proof that Kallee is – ?'

'Guilty? Well, according to Trade-Cor, her SID file contained no hard evidence – despite three years' work – but in his report, this man Vindhook claimed he'd turned up sufficient proof to make an arrest.'

'So why didn't we hear about it?'

'Because she was never arrested. She was taken in for questioning on Buena Vista then released following an intervention by Daniel. According to Vindhook, he claimed to be from Naval Intelligence and that he and Kallee were *both* engaged on an undercover mission! So Vindhook let her go.'

Talla left her husband's locked muscles to look after themselves, poured herself a stiff drink, then sat down facing him. 'But she *was* working undercover – for you.'

'That's right. But why did Daniel say *he* was with the Navy? According to what he told us, he didn't get his memory back until he saw Stagg on board the Korazon! At the time Daniel was on Buena Vista, he was supposed to be this Cartahaynyar character. Kallee was under strict instructions not to reveal she was working for me – and yet here he is, claiming immunity for both of them! And all this took place *before* The Dragon Lady began the voyage to Nebo!'

'I'm confused,' said Talla. She sipped her drink thoughtfully. 'Unless . . .'

'Unless what?'

'He's been lying to us, and she has deceived us. What if she was already involved with the APF when you enlisted her help in our search for Daniel . . .?'

Gideon leapt on to her train of thought. '. . . and what if Daniel's been working with her during the years he's been missing . . .?'

'They both come back. Daniel is restored to a position of trust, her loyalty is beyond question . . .'

'. . . and they are both in an even better position to carry on with their subversive activities.' Gideon finished off the Brain-Blaster. 'The little minx . . .'

'Will you bring her in for questioning?'

'No. It could damage us if any word of this got out.'

The vidiphone bleeper sounded. Gideon set down his glass, reached over the arm of his chair and activated the screen.

The head of one of his aides appeared. 'We have a call from Broken Ridge, sir. Miss Mandragorian has requested to speak with you personally.'

Gideon flashed a glance at his wife. 'Patch her through.'

Kallee's face appeared on screen.

The Admiral put on his good-will act. 'Kallee! Nothing wrong I hope. Is your father okay?'

'He's fine, sir. Thank you for taking this call. I'm hoping you'll grant me a favour.'

341

Gideon smiled. 'In return for services rendered.'

'Not exactly, sir. It would be impertinent of me to put it in those terms. I did what you asked without any thought of reward and would be happy to do so again.'

'I bet you would,' murmured Talla.

'So what is it you want from me?' asked Gideon.

'I would like to be able to leave Libra with Daniel when he, uh – is "retired" from the Navy.'

Gideon smiled again. 'So . . . you two are finally getting together. Are you sure that's what you want?'

'Yes, sir.'

'Then I'll make the necessary arrangements. Good luck to both of you.' Gideon terminated the call and turned to his wife. 'I'd say that proves it, wouldn't you?'

Talla shook her head in disbelief. 'Everything fits. The mystery trips, the unexplained absences – that were all blamed on a difficult childhood – coming to terms with the death of her mother. And all the time she has been working with the APF – right under our noses! How could we have been so blind?!'

'Past history, Talla. It doesn't matter anymore. She's played right into our hands. I've already made arrangements to cut short Daniel's retirement. Now we can kill two birds with one stone.'

☆　☆　☆　☆　☆　☆　☆

SIDELIGHTS ON THE RIMWORLD by 'FIZZ'   No.4793
RIMWORLD JUSTICE
Lawyers no longer have a case to answer.

Although the Navy still tries offenders from its own ranks using the ancient system of courts martial, prosecuting and defence counsels are no longer employed in the rest of the Rimworld. The absence of lawyers is due to the work of one man – Zigg Zaggurat: one of the great Atlanteans.

Born Ziggmundo Zagguratzenberga, he will always be remembered for the reforming zeal which he brought to bear on the social problems that afflicted the Rimworld of yesteryear.

342

It was Zaggurat who postulated that, in an interglobal society, which had the ultimate responsibility for the welfare of all its citizens, the decision to produce children was far too important to be left to the breeding pair.

Zaggurat argued that, since those who lacked the financial means to house, rear and educate their offspring had to be supported by society as a whole, then society, through its governing bodies, should control the process of procreation by a system of permits which (a) cost a great deal of money and (b) involved written and medical examinations and the purchase of health and third party insurance.

The process was likened to the conditions applicants had to fulfil before being allowed to own and drive a ground or air vehicle. Anyone becoming pregnant without a permit faced the threat of sterilisation – a sanction which, as current Earth-dwellers will know, is already being applied in China.

Child licensing was the first move in population control which led to the development of cocooning (described elsewhere) where the new eighteen-year-olds entering Rimworld society were already sterile – which meant they could immediately set about getting their rocks off with nary a second thought. Rimworld medicine had eliminated STDs; the only concern related to sex was the worrying thought that you might not be getting your share.

It was, however, in the field of criminal justice and penal reform that Zaggurat made his greatest contribution – the propositions known as Zigg-One and Zagg-Two.

Proposition One stated that '. . . **human nature being what it was, everyone should be presumed to be guilty until proved innocent**' while Proposition Two declared that '. . . **it was better for an innocent man to languish in jail than for one guilty man to walk free**'.

While this was extremely hard on the innocent few who found themselves banged up, they could at least draw some comfort from the thought that they were playing a key role in the struggle to keep crime off the streets.

Z-One and Z-Two revolutionised the world of jurisprudence

343

but Zaggurat did not stop there. Appointed Chief Justice to the Rimworld Council, he promptly passed a decree which prohibited individuals or partnerships from profiting unduly from the misfortunes of others. Since lawyers fell into this category, it meant they were not allowed to charge an hourly fee higher than the average hourly wage. It was known as 'The Fair Dos Decree'.

Zaggurat believed that too many people were practising law for the wrong reasons. He wanted to turn it from a profession into a vocation and to that end, he decreed that all lawyers who failed to win cases for their clients (a) could not charge for their services and (b) had to compensate their client for any damages awarded against them.

He further ruled that any lawyer entering a defence on behalf of a client with a previous criminal record and who was subsequently convicted by the court of a serious offence, was to be given the same sentence as his client, but with no remission for good behaviour.

Lawyers left the Bar in droves. But Zaggurat had not yet completed his overhaul of the justice system. He posited that lawyers, by their very nature, had always opposed legal reform, had used the adversarial system to line their own pockets, and that, if they retained any sense of natural justice, it was no greater than that possessed by the ordinary man or woman in the street.

The result was a statute which barred all ex-lawyers from taking up posts in any legislative or adminstrative body throughout the Rimworld, on the grounds that they had a vested interest in restoring their previous powers and privileges. The only commercial positions open to them were as private investigators, store detectives and the management of hotels and rented accommodation where they were able to use their litigious skills in framing the house rules.

The classic line – No guests allowed in rooms – reflects their smouldering resentment towards the rest of society.

Having eliminated the middle man, Zaggurat launched upon his greatest work. He poured his prodigious legal mind into a computer programme named LEX. This was the cornerstone of an interglobal system of electronic justice, designed to deal with every imaginable civil and criminal action, and which was accessible to any citizen via the vidiphone network.

Once the complaint and the counter argument has been entered, LEX is usually able to render a verdict in under three minutes. In a civil case, where no damages are awarded, the cost of the action is billed to both parties; appeals attract a higher tariff. Where the verdict requires an arrest, LEX sends the charge sheet and details of the guilty party to the nearest law enforcement agency.

In the area of penal reform, Zaggurat produced calculations to show that, instead of building and staffing prisons, it would be far cheaper to transport criminals and their dependents to island holiday resorts where they would remain in exile for the duration of their sentences. Favourable long-term rates could be negotiated with the hotels, and the offenders would be given a weekly drink, clothing and entertainment allowance.

The scheme – known as 'Sun, Sea and Shangri-lager' – was given a trial on the popular holiday island of Alcazar, located on the planet Zhannandor, and five hundred miles from the nearest land mass. All boats were removed and regular sea and air patrols prevented anyone leaving on homemade rafts.

Even with these precautions it still cost 40% less than the cheapest old-style prison institution and, initially, it proved so successful, the majority of released prisoners immediately re-offended. But it was not long before the more enterprising gangsters formed themselves into syndicates which assumed ownership of the hotels, villas, shops and all other facilities on the island and set up their own criminal justice system.

Although LEX continues to dispense affordable justice and remains the monument to his endeavour, Zaggurat died a disappointed man. His official biographer believed he was haunted by the failure of his holiday prison camps to alter the behaviour of their inmates, although there is no doubt that they saved the Rimworld Exchequer vast sums of money. It was only after several generations of cocoon-reared Erics that the

345

baser criminal tendencies were engineered out of the human psyche.

Alcazar and the other island colonies were closed down when the Corporation took over the task of law enforcement. Their accountants weren't interested in low cost solutions; they were looking to make a profit. They already had their own version of the Gulag Archipelago – the handful of uninhabited mini-planets whose orbits lay between the Rimworld system and the twin suns. It was here that the remaining tanned, gold-medallioned offenders were put to work, alongside the new breed of credit-defaulters in environments that ranged from adverse to extremely hostile.

Nebo for example. Anyone who landed there and saw the twin suns glowing dully through the ever-present clouds of smoke like two baleful red eyes knew at once that the party was over.

They also knew it was a waste of breath asking to see a lawyer.

Chapter Twenty

Daniel did not see his parents again, either in person or over a video-link. The only sign that his Navy career was over was an e-mail message from Central Records granting his application for retirement on the grounds of ill health and confirming that while he did not qualify for a Navy pension, he was entitled to receive eleven years' back pay, subject to approval by the Awards Sub-Committee of the Navy Council.

Details of the award would be forwarded to him via the Olympic Shipping Agency. Travel documents and civilian ID card would be supplied by the Chief Steward of the NV Kahshathra.

A similar e-mail message to Kallee granted her permission to accompany Daniel. A 'copter would take them to the base at White Sands from where a Navy STV would take them up to the waiting cruiser.

When the time came, Kallee's father seemed genuinely upset to see her go – almost as if he did not expect to see her again.

Daniel found it strange that someone whose waking day was spent trying to find more efficient ways to kill people could possess such feelings. It was one of the baffling contradictions of human nature.

Kallee was also close to tears. 'Don't worry, Pops. I'll be back some day. You don't get rid of me that easily.'

'Well, you take care, now – and try to stay out of trouble.'

She laughed. 'Aww, c'mon, Pops, I don't mind putting a clean pair of pants on every day but that's asking too much!'

Daniel and Sandiego exchanged a farewell handshake.

'Goodbye, sir, and thank you. I deeply appreciate the hospitality you have shown me over the last few weeks.'

Even though I did betray your trust by using your computer to hack into the FI-COR network . . .

By accident or design, the 'copter flew a circular route that brought them in low over the main gate of the disused missile testing range. The bodies of the traitors, blackened and swollen through exposure to the sun, were still hanging on the chain-link fence.

It was a grim reminder to Daniel that his return had led to their deaths. They had perished because he was a Kinsharadeen.

That fact, plus the vivid memories of that appalling night, was something he would have to live with for ever. Unless . . .

. . . he could find a way to bury the past.

☆ ☆ ☆

Their reception on boarding the Kahshathra was distinctly low key. For the moment, Daniel was still a Kinsharadeen but he was now a civilian and no longer heir to the Supreme Admiral. He was, in other words, a hasbeen and en route to becoming a non-person – rather like a top Hollywood star falling from grace after a string of turkeys.

A marine lieutenant, backed by a brace of grunts, met them at the airlock and led the way to a cabin on the lower-deck. Daniel and Kallee were left to carry their own luggage.

The lieutenant stepped aside to let them enter. 'I hope you have no objection to sharing.'

Daniel and Kallee dumped their luggage inside and looked around. The cabin contained two bunks and the usual facilities, including what the recruitment ads called 'a small recreational area'.

'Okay with you?'

'Yeah, fine,' said Kallee.

Daniel turned to the lieutenant. 'So what's the drill?'

'Well, sir . . . because of your connections with the Supreme Admiral and in the interests of security, Navy HQ has requested you both be confined to this cabin until we reach the exchange

348

rendezvous. All meals will be served to you here. There is a supply of canned non-alcoholic drinks in the cooler.'

Daniel and Kallee exchanged glances.

'The cabin's intercom facilities have been switched to incoming only. If any sudden emergency occurs, these two marines or their relief will be on duty in the corridor outside.'

Kallee asked. 'When do we get our travel papers?'

'And my ID?' added Daniel.

'They'll be supplied just prior to transfer.'

The lieutenant left the cabin. The door closed and was locked. The mechanism could be accessed from both sides, but only with a keycard – which hadn't been provided. They were now, effectively, prisoners.

Daniel and Kallee sat down facing each other.

'Did the Admiral tell you this was likely to happen?

'No, but I'm sure it makes sense to someone.' He decided this was a good moment to tell Kallee that his father had a new son and heir – a ten-year-old clone named Mark.

'That's not possible.'

'It is now.' Daniel explained why his presence had been kept secret. 'And he won't appear in public until the Admiral calls for him to step forward at my funeral.'

Kallee's eyes widened with alarm.

'Cause of death: a cerebral haemorrhage.' Daniel smiled. 'Don't worry, the coffin will be empty. And it's not due to be staged until after Parnassus has helped me disappear.'

'Why didn't you tell me this before?'

'I was asked not to. But it probably explains all this cloak-and-dagger stuff. Only a trusted handful of people know I've left the Navy. Don't let's forget there have been two attempts on my life. Being locked in here does at least mean no one can get at us.'

'Yeah,' said Kallee. 'It also means that if somebody wanted to harm you, they know exactly where to look.'

Daniel smiled. 'Know what? You keep saying you're not, but I think you really *are* paranoid. C'mon! Cheer up! We're on our way!'

349

Kallee looked disenchanted. 'There are two things you should know about me, Daniel. Despite having circled the Rimworld on several occasions, I'm not all that keen on space travel and I hate being forced to stay behind locked doors.'

'It needn't be a total waste of time. You can tell me what I was doing in Boot City.'

'Don't need to.'

'Why not?'

'Because if everything goes according to plan, it will all come back to you.'

Daniel checked the time. In another nine hours, the Jericho virus was due to begin its attack on the FI-COR computer network.

Reaching the correct departure window, the NV Kahshathra increased its speed to escape velocity and soared out of orbit into deep space. As the planet Libra slowly receded on the viewing screens, the captain sent a signal to the SS Mount Olympus, containing the time and spatial coordinates for the planned rendezvous.

A rendezvous he did not intend to keep.

☆   ☆   ☆

The first sign that their joint futures might be at risk came when the cabin door was unlocked by one of their marine guards. A female naval rating entered carrying two meal trays. The various courses were in containers that fitted into the moulded trays, each of which had a transparent cover.

The rating, whose ID gave her name as Potomaine Potemkeen, handed Kallee her tray with a vague glint of recognition. 'Did we ever meet somewhere? A open-air music-bash perhaps?'

'Been to quite a few. Which one were you thinking of?'

'The Midnight Rain tour.'

Kalle shrugged. 'Can't say I remember.'

'Really? They had that big hit with "Trouble on the Line". Though, personally, I prefer the B-side. "Breakin' Loose". No? Never mind. Enjoy your meal.'

350

When Potemkeen had gone, Daniel asked 'What in Prog's name was all that about?'

'Eat your meal before it gets cold.'

There were two paper napkins tucked under the plastic dish containing the main course. Kallee took them out, tucked them into her top pocket and motioned Daniel to do the same.

When they had finished the meal, she signalled him to follow her into the small washroom where she opened the basin and shower taps to mask the sound of their voices.

'Midnight Rain is not a group of musicians. It was the code name of one of the secret conferences I attended last year. She must be a member of the APF.'

'And the records she mentioned?'

'They're real enough. "Trouble on the Line" was a hit record by Nuclear Confusion. I can't recall what the B-side was but it wasn't "Breakin' Loose". That was by Mammadonna and the Ozmiroids.'

'So what have we got? A coded message from an admirer?'

Kallee carefully unfolded her paper napkins. One of them contained a keycard. The other contained a brief message –
Handover to Parnassus cancelled. At 18:35 Kahshathra will hyperjump to I-G space where you will both be airlocked. Have readied spaceraft 15-B for your escape. Check mattresses. Act quickly.

Daniel unfolded his napkins. One contained the smartcard needed to activate the ignition systems of a Navy spaceraft. The other contained a diagrammatic plan of the cruiser with arrows indicating their cabin and the suggested route to spaceraft 15-B.

'Let's check those mattresses . . .'

Two sets of neatly-folded Marine corps fatigues lay hidden underneath. Stuffed into the body of each mattress, through slits in either side, were a pair of regulation ankle boots. A phaser had been stuffed into the left boot of each pair. Daniel checked them. They were both fully charged.

He led Kallee back into the bathroom where the water was still running. 'We've got forty-five minutes before the jump. What d'you think?'

351

'I think we should go for it. But you're the expert on Navy systems. What's the plan?'

'We don't have many options. The spaceraft is on the deck immediately below us. If we can make it from here to the right docking bay without being detected . . .'

'Yeah . . .?

'Then once we're on board, if this card kicks in the ignition system, then we've got ourselves a ride, but . . .'

'But what . . .?'

'Well, we can't outrun this cruiser, or its cutters – if they were to send one after us. And we can't cast off after the jump because we'd never be able to cross intergalactic space. Which means . . .'

'We have to bail out just before she makes the jump into hyperspace.'

Daniel nodded. 'That's right. But what if the captain changes his mind at the very last minute – before the energy pulse peaks? We could undock, hit the booster button and – surprise, surprise – we look at the retro-vision screen and . . .'

'The Kahshathra's still there . . .'

'Waiting to put a hole through us with a laser cannon – unless, of course, the raft is already rigged to blow.'

Kallee found it hard to accept it was a set-up. 'But the note – the code words "Midnight Rain" – the keycard – the uniforms – '

Daniel gave an exasperated sigh. 'C'mon, Kallee! This is the Navy! We're under close arrest. Are you trying to tell me nobody gave this cabin the once-over before putting us in here? Don't you find that just a little oh-so convenient?'

'But some of our people *are* Navy. That's how we're able to – '

Daniel silenced her. 'Keep your secrets to yourself. They could have latched onto those code words in all kinds of ways. Don't you see what they're doing here? They're pulling both our strings! They've convinced you the note is genuine with this APF connnection. So the pressure is on for us to find a way to get off this ship – in the timeframe *they've* given us. We know the spaceraft to use and – ' he held up the smart card ' – we don't even have to hotwire it.'

'Yeh, well, put like that, I suppose it *is* kind of "on a plate".'

'As for me, I'm Navy and A-rated for hyperspace. They know I *know* we have only one chance of escaping from here in a space-raft. *One* window of opportunity. The splitsecond before they make the jump. 'Cause when they drop out of hyperspace and find us gone, this ship can't jump back until the drives have recharged – which takes at least two hours – and second, it can never return to exactly the same point in the space-time continuum.'

Kallee was not won over. 'That's all well and good – but the note says we're due to enter hyperspace at 18:35. What makes you so sure it's not going to happen?'

'Money.' Daniel gave a dry laugh. 'Back in the glory days, before I spoke out of turn, I used to command one of these cruisers. That meant I had ultimate responsibility for the operational budget. A spaceraft costs six hundred and fifty thousand Cords. Wanna know how much a hyperjump costs? Two and a half million. That's just one way. The round trip will set you back five mil. There's no way the Corporation would sanction that kind of expense just to get rid of us two.'

'So why waste a perfectly good spaceraft? Why not just dump us out of an airlock?'

'Because I'm a Kinsharadeen. The whole Navy knows what happened to the last bunch of guys who tried to kill me. I may be riding off into the sunset but – and I know this sounds conceited – I bet there isn't a man on this boat who'd want the part he played in my death entered into the records.'

'Don't kid yourself. Stagg is not the only psychopath employed by the Treasury.'

'You're right,' admitted Daniel.

'On the other hand, if – as you claim – no one on board wants to terminate us – we don't need to escape. We can just stay here. Which is plainly ridiculous.'

353

'Right again . . .'

'So the threat against our lives is real . . .'

'Yeh, it is. That Midnight Rain bit was their way of telling you they were onto the APF connection. And because you asked to come with me, they must think we're in bed together.' Daniel sighed. 'It also means I've just lost one point five mil in back pay. Which puts us both out on the street.'

'So what do we do – take a chance with the spaceraft?'

'No,' said Daniel. 'I've got a better idea.'

☆   ☆   ☆

At 18:33, as the countdown to the jump was broadcast from stem to stern of the Kahshathra, word reached the bridge that the two prisoners being held on Lower C-Deck had overpowered their marine guards and were now loose somewhere inside the ship. With two minutes to go, search parties were hurriedly despatched in an effort to locate them.

No trace of them was found. All activity had to be halted during the final seconds of the countdown. At 18.34 and 59.75 seconds, spaceraft 15-B dropped away from the Kahshathra, fired all four boosters and soared away to port.

At 18:35, the Kahshathra's commander came on air. The hyperjump had been cancelled. The systems control screens showed a spaceraft was missing. The search for the two prisoners was called off.

Daniel was right. The hyperdrives had never been activated. The bridge crew watched the progress of the stolen spaceraft on the tracking screens and the Fire Control Officer waited impatiently for the order to fire a disabling blast from one of the cruiser's beam weapons. He waited in vain; the Kahshathra's commander had been ordered to do nothing. The 'grey squad' from Navy Intelligence, which had left on the shuttle that brought Cartahaynyar and Mandell up from Libra, had taken care of everything right down to laying the trays that were to be used for the prisoner's one and only meal. They had also ensured that the canteen orderly who would deliver them was word perfect.

354

When the spaceraft was three miles out from the Kahshathra, the white speck on the screens erupted like a mini super-nova.

☆ ☆ ☆

From their hiding place aboard the cruiser, Daniel and Kallee witnessed the fiery end of the fleeing spaceraft on a set of miniature screens he had managed to lock onto the same channel.

Kallee turned away, white-faced. 'That was like watching myself die. Shaggaraymuss! If you hadn't been so clued up we could've been in that thing!'

Daniel switched the screens back to the normal data channels. 'Let's hope they think we were.'

'Well, I don't often hand out compliments – '

'So I've noticed – '

'But putting that raft onto remote was pretty damn clever.'

'That wasn't the clever part. All spacerafts have a remote guidance system in case the escapees are injured. But patching a timing delay into the firing relays was a fairly praiseworthy achievement. But nothing compared to what I am now about to attempt.'

'I can hardly wait.' Kallee surveyed their surroundings.

In Earth terms, it resembled a computerised telephone exchange. A low, background hum came from row after row of floor-to-ceiling units. Banks of status lights flickered on and off like regimented fireflies. It was the kind of place where you spoke in whispers.

'How come nobody's here?

'They don't need to be. All the data that's being monitored here is displayed on the bridge and in other control centres all over the ship.'

Kallee followed Daniel as he walked up and down the rows of units, checking the numbered panels. 'But supposing somebody comes in and finds us?'

'Then we'll use the weapons in that bag of yours to subdue them and tie them up.' Daniel eyed her and shook his head. 'I can't believe they let you walk onto the Kahshathra with that stuff.'

355

Kallee grinned. 'That's why I didn't rush to buy your idea that the Navy was bound to have checked that cabin before they put us in it.'

'I suppose they're stolen.'

'Of course.'

'From your father?'

'Just let's say it's a long story.'

The bag in question contained the same items which had been causing trouble for Andrew from the moment he had presented his luggage for Customs inspection on Buena Vista. With the sudden mental flip-over to Daniel, he had forgotten the discovery of the guns by the search party from the NV Korazon along with everything else prior to the moment when Stagg re-entered his life.

Recognising them as prototype weapons, the Korazon's Master at Arms had taken the guns back to Libra when selected members of the crew had shuttled down to attend the award ceremony – from which they did not return.

The bag had been handed over to Sandiego Mandragorian who had taken it back to his workshop at Broken Ridge. Kallee, challenged to explain the theft on her return, had won over her father with her usual well-honed act of contrition then, prior to leaving, had stolen the same bundle of goodies from his experimental armory in order to have something she could raise money on.

Daniel stopped in front of the unit he had been looking for. 'Let me have that little tool kit of yours.'

Kallee handed him a toilet bag. 'So much more useful than make-up and skin conditioner.' She watched him use a pressure tool to unloosen an inspection panel. 'So what goes on in here?'

Daniel checked the numbered boards inside then slid one out and examined it closely. 'This is the Damage Control Centre. These units monitor all the onboard systems a thousand times a second to make sure everything is functioning properly. They also monitor the loading on the ship's structure and the air pressure on every square inch of its hull.'

'In case a meteorite gets past the radar and – '

356

'Blows a hole in it. Correct.' Daniel produced several jumper leads from the toilet bag, connected them to various parts of the board, then plugged in a mini-electronic notepad. He smiled at Kallee. 'I can't believe you've got all this gear. Just possessing this could get you – '

'Yeah, I know. Spare me the lecture. Go on with what you were saying.'

'Ah, well, naturally, the Navy has all kinds of drills to cover every type of emergency. Generator fires, radiation leaks, problems with the air supply, major systems breakdowns. But of course, this being a Navy ship and not The Dragon Lady, regular maintenance ensures that none of these things happen.'

'I think I can guess what's coming.'

'Just pipe down and listen. Hand me that red lead.'

Kallee passed it up and watched him make the connection.

'But we *still* do the drills to check the crew's reaction times. And to make sure nobody cheats, the emergency drills are not called by the ship's captain. The timing and type of emergency is decided by Fleet Headquarters at Shasta Bay – and *they* send a signal direct to this little box of tricks, telling it to run a simulation.'

'And you're about to do the same thing.'

'Major disaster. You're gonna love it.'

'Mind if I mention one tiny little . . .?'

'What?!'

'The top clip on the red lead. I think it's about to fall off.'

Daniel gritted his teeth and reset the clip. He then used the mini-notepad to input the code numbers of the desired simulation routine, keyed in a start time and replaced the panel. 'Okay, it's up and running. We've got five minutes to get to the bridge. The quickest and safest way is through the air ducts. Break out the anti-grav jackets.'

☆ ☆ ☆

The Kahshathra's commander and his executives were caught completely by surprise as the electronic klaxon blared five times. A robotic voice issued from the ship's speaker system.

'Emergency Drill! Emergency Drill. Meteor strike! Major Systems Failure. Losing air pressure. Abandon ship! Abandon ship! Go to your evacuation stations immediately and prepare to launch spacerafts!'

Commander Billbow Briggadoonray turned angrily to his chief exec. 'Are they crazy? What in the name of Tanzibar does Fleet HQ think it's doing?!'

'I don't know, sir – but if we're going to hit the target time we'd better get moving. We can complain later.'

'You're right. Shut down the drives. Maintain all other systems!' Briggadoonray swept his eyes across the expectant faces of his subordinates. 'Report to your evacuation points! Move! Move! *MOVE*!'

Ninety seconds after the evacuation order, spacerafts and Navy cutters began to cast off from both sides of the huge cruiser and head out towards the assembly points laid down in the drill manual. Another two minutes elapsed before the last cutter – carrying Briggadoonray and the execs tasked with shutting down the ship – undocked and sped away to port.

☆   ☆   ☆

Daniel peered through the ventilation grille and inspected what he could see of the bridge. It appeared to be deserted. Empty swivel seats had been swung away from the abandoned consoles. Status lights continued to flicker. The video screens were still displaying data.

He swivelled his head around in the confined space and looked down the length of his body to Kallee who lay in the duct behind him. 'Know something? I've got a feeling this is actually gonna work.'

Using the butt of one of the stolen carbines, Daniel knocked out the grille, switched his anti-grav jacket to zero, hauled himself out of the trunking and floated gently to the floor. Kallee followed.

On the line of vision screens that ran around the bridge, they could see the fleet of spacerafts and cutters continuing to fan out from the Kahshathra.

Daniel dropped into the captain's chair and slid his hands along the moulded arms. It felt like coming home. He surveyed the controls available to him. When the bridge was fully staffed, the task of piloting the ship was divided among the crew but, in an emergency, the basic manoeuvres could be handled by a single individual – provided the occupant of the captain's chair knew what he was doing.

Kallee watched Daniel bring the drive units back to life. 'Want any help?'

'Depends on how much you know about Navy cruisers.'

'Hnnhh! Where d'you think I learned to be a navigator? A school for bakers?'

Daniel almost hit the wrong button. 'You . . . were in the NAVY?'

'Ninth Fleet. Two and a half years. Ship of the line. The NV Zarathusa.'

Daniel took this in with a shake of the head. 'You never cease to amaze me.'

'That's what makes me so exciting to be with.' She slapped her hands together. 'What's the first move?'

'Close all the doors to the launch bays. You'll find a set of yellow buttons on the third console to the right of the centre screen. And sit tight. The drives will be cutting in any second now.'

☆   ☆   ☆

Aboard the captain's cutter, Briggadoonray tapped the shoulder of the Navy pilot. 'How long till we hit the ten-mile marker?'

'Another sixty-five seconds, sir.'

Briggadoonray checked his watch and turned to his chief exec with a satisfied smile. 'We're going to be inside our best time yet!' The frown returned. 'But I'm still going to memo Fleet HQ I mean – two evacuation drills in five weeks – that's really jerking us around!'

359

The cutter slowed and joined a gaggle of spacerafts which had collected around one of the six designated assembly points.

The pilot of the cutter turned to Briggadoonray. 'We have all the units on line, sir.'

Briggadoonray donned a headset and mike. 'Kahshathra SunRay One to all rescue units. Congratulations on an excellent response. We cut seventy-two seconds off our best previous evacuation time and I expect that to earn us a commendation from Fleet HQ. Okay. Let's get back to work. Return to your docking stations!'

His chief exec, who had been watching the cruiser through a viewport, turned to Briggadoonray in alarm. 'Sir! The ship!'

The Kahshathra's captain turned in time to see his cruiser moving from right to left, revealing a ragged line of bright dots – the scattered groups of spacerafts positioned twenty miles to starboard. The outlines of the cruiser blurred then dissolved into rainbow shards of light as it vanished into hyperspace.

The SS Mount Olympus, with its state-of-the-art communications array, was one of the first to pick up the distress signal sent out on the open Mayday channel by the Kahshathra's dispossessed crew.

Parnassus had been marking time, waiting to receive the coordinates of the promised rendezvous. Since the signal – aimed at all Navy ships – merely asked for help, Parnassus could not guess that Daniel and Kallee were not among those waiting to be rescued. The Navy would send ships, of course, but appearing on the scene would earn Olympic Shipping a few more brownie points.

And they would be especially useful in view of what was about to happen.

On Libra, it was to be a night to remember. Beginning at twelve, the Jericho virus sprang into action inside the FI-COR computer system and went on the rampage for the next five hours. None of the duty staff were aware that anything was amiss. Jericho's genius lay in its ability to mask what it was doing. The monitor screens continued to display their usual array of information and reports of financial movements, but behind this façade of normality, huge amounts of money were being shifted around the banking system in tens of millions of transactions.

By four o'clock on the following morning, all the cash reserves of the Corporation had been transferred into the accounts of its customers. The transfer had been accompanied by a printed notice faxed to each customer's home address informing them that, through its Bank-Cor subsidiary, the Supreme Executive Council of The Corporation had decided to issue a Bonus Dividend to celebrate a millenium of trading and, in a further celebration of this anniversary, the balance of all outstanding loans had been cancelled.

Once this notice had been despatched, the Jericho virus proceeded to destroy all the file directories within the FI-COR system, making it impossible for operators to access any of the records. It also corrupted its mathematical functions, rendering it incapable of performing even the simplest calculations.

The best was yet to come.

Haunted by the destruction of Atlantean civilisation on Earth by a rogue asteroid, the primal fear of a further un-solicited visitation still lurked within the psyche of the descendants of the voyagers who crossed the galaxy and colonised the Rimworld. It was this ever-present fear that had led the Corporation to store its gold reserves on four 'Treasury' planets.

Libra was one, the other three were at roughly ninety-degree intervals around the chain. But the gold was not stored in subterranean vaults. Each of the four 'Treasury planets' was pitted with clusters of underground silos, each one housing a missile as large as the Saturn rocket used by NASA to launch the moon missions.

There was one important difference. The payload of these rockets was solid gold. If Libra, the key planet of Rimworld, was ever to be threatened by a giant asteroid, the Corporation's

361

wealth would be sent into a safe solar orbit. Its power would be preserved, enabling it to lead the task of reconstruction.

At half-past four, the guards stationed outside the unmanned missile silos on Libra were woken by a deep rumble within the earth as the Jericho virus tricked the FI-COR computer into triggering the ignition sequence. They rushed outside. Through the high security fence they could see the silo covers opening up like clam shells. Huge clouds of smoke and orange fire shot out of the exhaust vents around each silo. The rumbling became an unbearable, teeth-jarring crescendo of sound that punctured eardrums and shattered glass as a hundred huge rockets lifted clear of the ground and roared into the sky.

But it didn't end there. The thunderous barrage washed back and became a rolling wave that threatened to engulf the entire region as fleet after fleet of shining rockets rose into the morning air on plumes of white smoke.

The same scenario was being played out before a startled audience of security guards on the three other 'Treasury' planets.

Alerted by calls from the various rocket sites, the night shift at Fleet HQ could do little more than gather on the forecourt and follow the trails left by the nearest launching. The Supreme Admiral, roused from his bed, sped over to Shasta Bay in time to receive a summons to attend a crisis meeting at Gold River.

Gideon lingered long enough to organise a mass intercept of the bullion rockets once they had settled into solar orbit. He was also given the news that Cartahaynyar and Mandell were believed to have perished aboard a spacecraft after escaping from the NV Kahshathra. A second signal from Briggadoonray contained the bald announcement that, following an evacuation exercise initiated from Fleet HQ, the unmanned cruiser had vanished into hyperspace.

On checking the outgoing signals log, it became clear that no evacuation exercise had been mounted by Fleet HQ. Gideon said nothing. Having made sure a rescue mission was being mounted, he boarded a 'copter for Gold River. As the journey proceeded, he turned this latest news over in his mind and sought an explanation. By the time Gold River came into view, he had begun to toy with the idea that Cartahaynyar and Mandell might *not* have perished. In which case, Daniel was far cleverer than he had suspected. And a great deal more dangerous.

There was no time to lose. He made an air-to-ground call to Shasta Bay and ordered them to put out a General Fleet Alert. The NV Kahshathra was to be intercepted ASAP. Anyone found on board was to be apprehended. No effort was to be spared in finding her.

Coming on top of the urgent signal to intercept and retrieve the fleet of bullion rockets, Gideon's order was ill-timed and, because of his failure to prioritize the conflicting missions, caused a considerable amount of delay and confusion. Matters were not helped when, following his arrival at Gold River, the Supreme Executive Council went into secret session making it impossible for Shasta Bay to obtain the clarification it needed for several hours.

Out in space, parked around the chain of planets that made up the Rimworld, there were others who had made their preparations well in advance. Alerted to the possibility of a 'golden handshake', a veritable armada of trade ships of every size and condition was now lying in wait, like a fleet of French tuna fishermen in the Bay of Biscay.

Jockeying for position, they waited to give chase as the payload stage of the rockets came sailing past. Twenty thousand of them, split into four golden shoals. The crew of a trader only needed to get their hooks into one and they were instant millionaires.

☆   ☆   ☆

Gideon and the other Council members listened, grim-faced, as Varrago Sveedennbork, the executive director of FI-COR explained the situation.

'We have been unable to trace where this rogue program was put into the computer. When we interrogated the system, it pointed the finger at over two hundred terminals – three of them around this table.'

This caused a rustle of consternation.

'We can return to the how and when later,' said Gideon. 'What's the bottom line?'

'The entire central account has been siphoned off and we've received final confirmation that the gold reserves from all four Treasury planets are now in orbit.' Sveedennbork eyed Gideon. 'How much we recover from space will depend on the Navy. The task would be made easier if we were to enlist the help of Trade-Cor.'

'No!' Gideon banged his fist on the table. 'If that bunch of bargees and scowmongers get their grubby hands on any of that gold, that's the last we'll see of it!'

Sveedennbork looked suitably chastened. 'Very well. Your view on this matter is noted. May I, ah – proceed?'

'By all means.'

'As of six thirty this morning, the bank does not have any money it can call its own. All the central records have been wiped, only the account files in branches seem to be be intact.'

Kraftvon Zeppellinneka, a council exec, leaned forward. 'Wait a minute! Let's put the question of the gold to one side. We know where that is. We're not talking about a bank heist. This is electronic fraud. But we own all the banks and major credit facilities in the Rimworld! FI-COR and BANK-COR are running the only game in town – which means the money must be still inside the system!'

'It is. We're still trying to piece together the full extent of the damage.' Sveedennbork produced a sheaf of papers, took one and passed the rest on to be distributed to everyone around the table. 'This is a copy of an e-fax sent to a customer in Gold River. It was timed at four a.m. this morning. As you can see, it confirms the transfer of a considerable sum of money into his account. Knowing I was an early riser, he called me at six-fifteen to say thank you.'

Council Exec Wallazee Gammajeez read from his copy. "Millennial Bonus Dividend"?!'

' "Declared, authorised and distributed by order of the Supreme Executive Council",' added Sveedennbork. He didn't need to read from the text. The words were burned into his brain.

Tarantorino, another exec, saw a way out. 'It's simple. All we have to do is issue another notice saying the first one was a fake, forgery, mistake, whatever – and claw the money back.'

'We can't do that,' said Sveedennbork. 'Have you any idea of the size of our customer base?' He waved the notice. 'Supposing they've all been sent one of these? The money will have been credited to their accounts! The Corporation's reputation was built on the concept of sound money. We have always been the model of financial rectitude! If we were to renege on this or reveal we are the victim of a massive fraud, it would totally destroy our credibility.'

His words drew a measure of agreement from those around the table.

Tarantorino came back with another solution. 'Okay, let's say this "Dividend" stands. The money that is now in our customer's accounts is still *in* the bank. So it's ours to use whenever we want to.'

'What happens if they all decide to draw it out?' asked Gammajeez.

'All of them – all at once?' Tarantorino laughed. 'Unlikely, wouldn't you say? Sure, some of them are going to go on a spending spree. But what would the rest do with the money? Hide it under the floor? We own the bank, Wallazee!'

'I know! But in the past, branch acccounts have always been covered by the central reserve!'

'Wallazee! It's simple! We just don't tell anybody the money's not there. The Navy will bring back the gold. FI-COR will rebuild its computer system, and we can cover our losses by quadrupling our bank charges and raising the interest rate on all existing loans from 33% to 55% APR.'

'Take a look at the second paragraph,' said Gideon.

Tarantorino scanned the text and discovered that all existing loans had been cancelled. The third paragraph was even worse.

It passed control and ownership of the Corporation's subsidiary enterprises to the individual managers and workers.

'But this is crazy!' he exclaimed. 'They're going to have to come to us to get the money to keep these companies running! All we have to do is provide working capital, stiff them on the interest rates, call in the loan and repo the assets. A couple of years from now, it will all be back on the books and we'll be home and dry!'

'Unless they get their money from someone else.'

Tarantorino looked at Gideon. 'Like who for instance?'

'Our customers,' said Sveedenberg. 'They are the ones with all the money.'

'True,' riposted Tarantorino. 'But we're holding the bag.'

At ten a.m., BANK-COR branches were instructed to post notices about the dramatic increase in bank charges and interest rates.

At twelve a.m, the wraps came off newly-furnished business units all across the Rimworld, revealing them to be branches of a new corporate entity. Calling itself the INTERGLOBAL TRADING TRUST, and backed by Constantine Parnassus and a consortium of the leading independent traders (most of whom were currently roving the space lanes, garnering a further fortune), IGTT offered prospective customers five years' guaranteed free banking and long-term loans at a very competitive 11% APR.

The trickle of new customers that crossed the threshhold in the first few days was to become a flood in the following weeks as mutinous clients of Bank-Cor grabbed their money and ran, leaving the Corporation facing the prospect of having to lay off half their employees and cut the salaries of those still lucky to have a job.

But that crisis was still some way down the road.

On the afternoon of that first dreadful day as the full extent of the damage to the FI-COR computer network became clear, Gideon sat in the big chair, musing on past and present events.

He had the analytical frame of mind and the requisite degree of paranoia needed to assemble labyrinthine plots from the flimsiest material.

Gradually a picture formed. A plausible scenario of breathtaking audacity. A grand plan hatched with infinite care, whose preparations stretched back over the years and which involved Daniel, Kallee Mandragorian and Parnassus who – at that moment – was performing his civic duty by rescuing the stranded crew of the NV Kahshathra.

Without extracting confessions from Daniel and Kallee, he could not move against Parnassus. And if the Corporation foundered through lack of money, he would no longer have the means to impose his authority – to obtain the proof he needed – and bring Parnassus to trial.

Never mind. There were other ways of getting even. The game was not over yet.

Chapter Twenty-One

The game was also far from over for Daniel and Kallee. Dropping out of hyperspace near Palladia, they scanned the signal bands, picked up the constantly repeated General Fleet Alert and realised they were now top of the Wanted list.

Either side of the common channel, the wavebands were swamped with traffic. Every Navy ship seemed to have been mustered to pursue them or a swarm of runaway bullion rockets whose present ownership appeared to be in dispute.

'Okay, here's what we're gonna do,' said Daniel. 'We'll put the Kahshathra on autopilot, send it into a solar orbit and bail out. With luck, we . . .' He lapsed into a puzzled silence.

Seeing he looked totally lost, Kallee said: 'Have you just realised we've outsmarted ourselves? There are no spacerafts or cutters left. They all disappeared when you ran that evacuation exercise. We're stuck here!'

'That is something of a problem,' admitted Daniel. 'But that wasn't what stopped me in my tracks.' He frowned. 'Why did we come to Palladia?'

'You don't remember? This is where Parnassus lives. He owns an island here!'

'Does he?'

'Well, that's what you told me.'

'Did I? Oh – you mean when I was Cartahaynyar?' Daniel massaged his forehead again. It was becomg a habit. 'I keep getting flashes of . . . this other life. It's very confusing. All I know is we have to find a way to get down there.'

'Well, we'd better do it fast, otherwise we're dead meat.'

Kallee glanced at the vision screens. 'Oh-oh . . . something's coming our way!'

Daniel locked one of the Kahshathra's scanners onto the distant object and checked the resulting radar image. 'It's not a Navy ship. No ID pulse. Can you give me maximum resolution?'

'Yehh, hang on.' Kallee went to one of the consoles on the tier below where Daniel was sitting and hit several keys.

The mystery ship was enlarged in several steps with brief pauses in between each one while the picture was rebuilt, line by line, on the big centre screen.

Kallee studied the outlines of the rusting hull. 'I don't believe it,' she breathed. 'It's The Dragon Lady!'

Faced with the threatening bulk of the Navy cruiser, the crew of The Dragon Lady capitulated meekly and obeyed the order to heave to. The rocketload of bullion they had fished from the deeps of space had been squirrelled away in Aramitz's quarters and – with luck – would not be discovered. Nevertheless, it was with some trepidation that they steered the battered trader through the rear clamshell doors of the NV Kahshathra and set down on the vast cargo deck.

The doors did not close.

The next transmission from the cruiser ordered them to activate the dorsal airlock and prepare to receive a boarding party.

Tarqueen issued an electronic gurgle. 'O, frabjous day! I'd recognise that masterful voice anywhere!'

He did not elaborate, and The Dragon Lady's crew were taken completely by surprise when the two spacesuited figures who emerged from the airlock turned out to be their former captain and navigator.

'This calls for a celebration!' cried Aramitz.

'Nice idea – but I'm afraid there isn't time, Jean,' said Kallee. 'The Navy's after our blood.'

'Oh – is this the ship they're all looking for?' asked Muldoon.

'Yep.' Daniel turned to Pug. 'Can you move The Lady out of here – but like *now*?! The Kashatra's on auto-pilot and she's powering up to make a hyper-jump.'

'*She's what*?!'

The double shout came from Chilli and Gumbo, wedged in the door to the bridge.

'This mother has hyperdrive?!' cried Chilli.

'And you are the *sole* owner?!' yelled Gumbo.

'I really don't have time to discuss this,' said Daniel. 'Kallee and I need a ride down to Palladia. Fast!' He appealed to Pug and Moses. 'C'mon, guys! We've gotta get out of here!'

Pug wavered, his eyes switching from Daniel to Chilli and Gumbo. 'How long do we have before the hyperdrive kicks in?'

'Twenty minutes, half an hour. What are you getting at?' Daniel turned to find Chilli and Gumbo struggling into the spacesuits. 'What in Zagg's name are you doing?!'

'Take the cutter!' cried Pug. 'We'll look after things here!'

Daniel gazed at Pug and Moses in disbelief. 'You . . .? Steal this cruiser? You'll never get away with it!'

Moses chuckled. 'That's what you think. We'll find somewhere nice and safe to park, then rip the best bits out and sell what we don't need. Parnassus has been dyin' to get his hands on a hyperdrive. We'll all be able to retire ten times over on what he'll pay us for it!'

Chilli and Gumbo locked their gold visored helmets into place. Moses left the bridge to see them through the airlock.

Daniel shook his head. 'I hope you guys know what you're doing.'

'Let us worry about that,' said Pug.

Kallee gazed around the bridge. 'I thought you were getting a refit.'

'There was a sudden demand for our services so we just replaced the missing parts.' Pug smiled as he thought of the neat piles of gold bars hidden in Aramitz's quarters. 'Next time you see us, things will be different.' He ushered them off the bridge. 'I'll show you to the cutter.'

'Thanks . . .'

Pug paused in the doorway. 'And I wonder – as you're going to Palladia – could you drop something off at Star-Point for me?'

Star Point was the spacestation that served the planet.

Pug noted their hesitation. 'It won't take long – and you can bill the docking fee to Olympic's account.'

'It's not the money I'm worried about,' said Daniel. 'There may be a General Alert out for us as well as the ship.'

'You don't have to identify yourselves – or even get off the cutter. Just say you're from The Dragon Lady.'

'Yeah, well, I hope you're right,' grunted Daniel. 'After coming this far . . .'

'I'm sure it'll be okay,' said Kallee. 'Let's go, Pug. It's time we were on our way.'

Pug led them down to the crew's quarters, paused outside a cabin door, produced a keycard, opened it and addressed the occupant. 'Okay. You're free to go.'

'About time too!' said a pained, familiar voice.

Daniel's head started to spin as Lars Vindhook hove into view. 'Five days you've kept me in here! Without any explanation! I shall compain to – '

Vindhook broke off as his eyes lighted upon his old travelling companions. 'Andrew! Kelly! Ohh! But what a wonderful surprise!'

Daniel clutched at the door to steady himself as his mind started to slip away. His consciousness shrank within his skull with the suddenness of a pricked balloon and as his psyche was sucked into the void . . .

. . . Andrew burst through to take vacant possession. His eyes fastened on Vindhook and froze in astonishment. 'What the fuck is *he* doing here?!'

'Connie asked us to run him to Star-Point. We were on our way there when you turned up.'

Lars beamed at them both. 'I'm opening a restaurant!'

'I think this is where we came in,' said Kallee.

'The first of a chain of Longship – '

Andrew cut him short with a wave. 'Great news, Lars. But you already gave us the sales pitch. And right now, we've got

371

more pressing business to attend to! So bring your bags. You're coming with us.'

'Marvellous! You must come to the Grand Opening. I promised you a free meal, remember?'

Kallee rolled her eyes at Andrew. 'How could we ever forget?'

The Dragon Lady's cutter was housed in a dorsal recess. Entry was through an airlock in the floor. The goodbyes were brief.

'You'll be able to contact us through Parnassus,' said Pug. 'We haven't forgotten you're still the captain of this tub.'

'That's good to know.' Andrew prodded Pug's chest. 'If you're lucky enough to pick up some of this bullion that's supposed to be floating around, don't forget I'm due an equal share.'

Tarqueen's voice came out of a nearby speaker. 'You see? I told you!'

'Pipe down! Blabbermouth!' Pug composed himself and smiled at Kallee. 'If The Queen of the Seas is still with us when we next meet, we'll need a qualified navigator too.'

'You got yourself a deal.' She entered the airlock. Vindhook was already inside, waiting to go through.

'Bye, Pug,' said Andrew. 'Don't hang around. I've stirred up a lot of shit. I'd hate any of it to fall on you.'

'Don't worry. We're old hands at this game.' Pug patted Andrew's shoulder. 'Good to have you back.'

Seconds after the cutter eased out of the Kahshathra, the clamshell doors closed. Andrew fired the main boosters. As they sped towards the distant spacestation, the Navy cruiser vanished into hyperspace.

'Do you wish you'd gone with them?' asked Andrew.

'Part of me does.'

'And the other part?'

'The other part wants to make sure you get out of this mess in one piece.' Kallee looked at him curiously. 'Something happened back there on The Dragon Lady, didn't it.'

'Yeah. I got my memory back.'

'Which memory is that?'

372

'The one I started out with.'

'As Andiamo Cartahaynyar? Or d'you mean before that?'

'Before that . . .?'

'As Andrew Webber.'

Andrew's jaw dropped.

Kallee quickly reassured him. 'Don't blame Jean-Pierre. He did not betray your confidence. I eavesdropped on your conversation.'

'I see . . .' Andrew checked the instrument read-outs. They were still on course for Star-Point. It would soon be time to make contact and ask for permission to dock.

'Does this mean you've forgotten everything that happened from the trial aboard the Korazon until now?'

'No. That's the strange thing.' Andrew searched for the best way to explain his present state of mind. 'It's all still there, but it no longer seems "real". Although the threat to our lives is real enough. It's as if I've woken up from a bad dream with that hanging over me – like a premonition of disaster.'

It was the cue for Lars Vindhook to appear from the small cabin. He laid his arms along the back of their seats. 'You can't know what this means to me! It's good to have such friends!'

'You've been a great help too, Lars.' Andrew locked eyes with Kallee. 'If it wasn't for you, who knows who I'd be?'

Vindhook frowned as he tried to work that out.

Andrew switched on the voice-comms channel and handed the mike to the Reindeer Man. 'This is your big moment, Lars. Call up Star Point control and request permission to disembark. This is Dragon Lady X-One. We need clearance for a Set-Down and Go. There's no need to mention us.'

'Or that you're planning to open a restaurant.' It was Kallee's turn to look at Andrew.

Vindhook looked genuinely disappointed. 'Does this mean you won't be coming to the opening?'

''Fraid not, Lars. Duty calls.'

'Yeh,' said Kallee. 'We'll catch you next time around.'

☆   ☆   ☆

373

Pug was right. There was no trouble and no hitches at Star Point. Andrew berthed The Dragon Lady's cutter in one of the small docking bays, offloaded Lars and his luggage without emerging from the cutter himself and told the Reindeer Man to take care of the fees. Twenty minutes later, they received clearance to undock. They gave their forward destination as the Dragon Lady en route for Ozzymandias – the name of the first Rimworld planet that found itself on the tip of Andrew's tongue – and eased back out into space.

The timing was fortuitous. An hour later, the Corporation sent out a further alert to the Navy and all its Security and Customs units on the spacestations around the Rimworld, ordering the interception of The Dragon Lady and the arrest of its crew. Unable to move against the big fish, Gideon Kinsharadeen had decided to net as many minnows as he could.

The only minnow to be found on Star Point was its newest resident – Lars Vindhook. Alerted to his arrival, a squad of security goons swooped on the Immigration Office where his application for a work permit was being processed. Vindhook was frogmarched back to the security unit protesting his innocence every step of the way. He was, he claimed, a business entrepreneur and an ex-member of Trade-Cor's Special Investigation Division.

Security checked this assertion and found that 'ex-' was very much the operative word.

It was at this point that Fate dealt a mortal blow to Vindhook's long-cherished dream of a chain of Longship restaurants. In the rush to unload Lars and his luggage, Andrew had mistakenly passed him one of Kallee's bags. It was only now, when security conducted the standard search through his belongings that the error came to light.

Unable to explain how he came to be in possession of such a deadly arsenal, Vindhook was promptly thrown into jug. This was, by any measure, an act of gross injustice, but it might also be argued that the Rimworld's collective digestion was marginally improved by keeping The Reindeer Man out of circulation.

By this time, of course, the cutter was no longer 'on-station',

374

but Star Point traffic control – whose operators tracked the movements of all vessels in their sector – were able to inform Star Point Security that Dragon Lady X-One appeared to be heading for a landing on Palladia.

They, in turn, contacted a wholly-owned subsidiary of the Corporation on Palladia which, under the cover of a front-office selling a range of electronic alarm devices, specialised in covert surveillance and abuction. The planet was one of a number where the Corporation only had minority holdings and this outfit was employed to help them gain a greater foothold.

Andrew and Kallee braced themselves as the cutter encountered the upper layer of Palladia's atmosphere. The buffeting began, announcing the start of a juddering, teeth-rattling ride. A red glow appeared along the bottom edge of the side view-ports and crept slowly upwards.

Kallee pulled her seat harness as tight as it would go. 'Is this thing gonna make it?!'

Andrew raised his voice over the constant creaking and rattling. 'This is the only way to find out!' He wrestled with the yaw and pitch controls. 'I've never flown anything this old before.'

'Neither have I!' yelled Kallee. She steadied herself as they rolled violently to port. 'You sure you know what you're doing?!'

'No,' shouted Andrew. 'But Daniel does!'

The fiery transition from space to atmospheric flight left both of them wrung out – mentally and physically. The cabin atmospheric controls proved as temperamental as the top hatch of the Dragon Lady that Pug was always promising to repair. The air was hot, humid and fetid. Andrew used the side thrusters to alter their course towards the southern hemisphere and peered anxiously out of his view-port.

'What are we looking for?' cried Kallee.

'An archipelago. Luckily I flew over it several times while I was here, and rode an STV from there up to Star Point.'

'Where you met the Narayana – and me.'

'A moment I am not likely to forget.' He surveyed the surface again. They were still high above the cloud cover – which fortunately was not too dense. 'It's a long curving chain running parallel to a land mass with over a hundred islands in it. We have to set down on the last one.'

Kallee searched the ocean on her side. 'What's that over there?'

'Where?'

'There!' She watched his eyes search in every direction but the right one. 'THERE!! What are you – blind or something?'

Andrew saw the slender, curving line of dots in the viridian ocean. From this height it looked like shot silk. 'You're right! That's it! *That's it*! We're gonna make it!'

He used the side thrusters to steer towards it then checked their height and speed. The cutter could not be manoeuvred like an aeroplane. It could only turn in a gentle curve, and it could only lose height. The nose had be pointed down to keep its speed above two hundred miles an hour. Below that, the cutter would simply fall out of the sky. There was a battery of downward-pointing jets mounted in its belly but they only had a short burn and had to be saved to control the landing at the very last minute.

Andrew tried to contain his mounting excitement. Already in a high state of tension, his hands were trembling. He willed himself to concentrate on the job in hand but his mind kept leaping forward to what came after the landing. The possibility of escaping the vengeance of Daniel's father by leaping across space and time . . .

The prospect of going home . . .

The offices of Cerberus Security happened – by sheer chance – to be in the principal city of the continent closest to the Hedjukhayteen Archipelago where Connie had his private retreat. That city also prided itself on having the best and busiest spaceport as well as possessing an airport handling normal fixed-wing traffic.

A contact of Cerberus working in spacetraffic control was able to tell them that a small STV had been tracked entering the atmosphere and on being requested to identify itself, had replied with a code sign employed by Navy Intelligence. The contact was able to suggest the region where the STV was likely to land.

The region included the island archipelago towards which the cutter was now descending. Cerberus Security knew that Parnassus owned many of the islands. They were also aware that the tradeship known as the Dragon Lady was owned by the Olympic Shipping Agency. Since the cutter had come from the tradeship it was not difficult to make the connection between it, Parnassus and Hesperides, his private hideway.

Boarding a hurriedly chartered supersonic mini-jet, a five-man team from Cerberus headed south towards a coastal airport lying across the water from the southernmost tip of the island chain. Once there, they would be within helicopter range of Hesperides.

☆　　☆　　☆

Cursing under his breath, Andrew pressed an array of buttons repeatedly and checked and re-checked a section of the instrument panel before giving voice to his frustration. 'Shit! Shit! *Shit*!!'

Kallee glanced at the instrument read-out. Speed was okay, altitude was now seven thousand and falling. The island of Hesperides was dead ahead. 'What's the problem?'

Andrew jabbed at a cluster of dials. 'There's no fucking fuel in the retro rockets! Can you believe that?!'

'Does that mean we can't make a soft landing?'

'How can we?! If we can't fire the belly pack, we can't hover!'

'Shaggeraymus! Has this thing got any wheels?'

'No! Just landing pads. Wheels wouldn't help. Hesperides hasn't got a runway! SHIT!' Andrew pounded the instrument panel with the heel of his hand. 'We're just gonna have to go belly up.'

'Where? You just said this place doesn't have a runway!'

'I know! But it does have a long beach right where we need to be . . .' Andrew fired a short burst on the starboard thruster and over-corrected. '*Fuck it*!' He pressed the button to fire the port-side booster to bring the cutter back on course.

Nothing happened. The pressurised tank was empty.

Andrew took out his frustration on the control panel again. 'What a bunch of arseholes! How could they leave a ship in a state like this?!'

Kallee tried to inject some calm. 'I don't think this was ever meant to be used as an STV. It's only thanks to you that we've gotten this far. Do we have any control thrusters left?'

Andrew read off the fuel states. 'There's a few seconds of burn in the under-nose units. But we're not lined up with the beach any more. We're gonna have to ditch in the sea.' He tried to figure the odds. 'We've got a flat underside, that's something in our favour. Question is . . . will this thing stay in one piece when we hit the water?'

As they dropped below two thousand feet the smooth expanse of green silk resolved itself into a real life ocean scored with endless lines of rippling waves. Luckily, there were no lines of spray being whipped off the crests – an indication there was little or no surface wind. The cutter was on a more or less parallel course with the beach – which lay some way to the right. Provided they could get out before the cutter sank and took them down to the bottom, they would be able to reach the shore.

With a few judicious bursts on the under-nose thrusters, Andrew flattened their angle of descent. He was attempting to perform what pilots call 'the flare-out' – the final manoeuvre before touchdown when a jet-liner stops losing height and appears to float along the runway before its main wheels make contact.

The plan Andrew had in mind was to play 'Ducks and Drakes', lifting the nose of the cutter as its belly hit the water in the hope that it would bounce across the surface like a rounded stone, gradually losing speed. If the cutter nosed in before they lost most of their speed, it would be sent cartwheel-

378

ing across the surface like Campbell's record-breaking Bluebird on Coniston Water – and with the same fatal consequences.

It worked. In the split-second before the cutter bellied onto the surface, Andrew lifted the nose with a puff of thrust then lifted it again as they landed on the second bounce, and the third and the fourth. The force of each impact threatened to drive the base of their spines down through the seat cushions. The intervals between the bounces shortened dramatically until it became one continuous boneshaking ride.

In the cabin behind them, seats tore loose and crashed from side to side and from floor to ceiling. Around them, in the cockpit, panels – and anything else that could come loose – sprang into malevolent life like maddened kitchen utensils in a Spielberg movie.

Kallee and Andrew spent a nightmare thirty seconds trying to shield their faces then with dramatic suddenness, the flying debris glued itself to the instrument panel and viewports as the cutter went nose down into the sea, then flipped over onto its back and sank. It should have been completely airtight, but the landing had split several of the hull seams and water was spurting in on all sides.

Andrew and Kallee quickly threw off their safety harness and made their way into the cabin – walking on the ceiling, which was now knee deep in water. They had entered the cutter through the airlock in the floor. But now it wouldn't budge.

'It must have been welded shut with the heat of re-entry!' yelled Andrew. 'I'll try the dorsal hatch!' He plunged into the rising water, found the manual release for the airlock, wound it open then resurfaced, choking for lack of air. 'Okay, out you go!'

Instead of obeying, Kallee tried to gather some of the floating luggage. Andrew grabbed her by the scruff of the neck and pulled her under – down towards the airlock.

It seemed as if they would never make it to the surface, but just as it seemed their lungs would burst, their heads bobbed clear of the water.

Andrew wiped the water from his eyes and looked shorewards.

He was able to see the line of pale golden sand and the cluster of white buildings one of which was the domed taverna. 'I reckon we must be a good half mile off shore. Think you'll be able to make it?'

'Yes. When I get rid of these.' Kallee trod water and began to wriggle out of her clothes.

Andrew followed suit. They both stripped down to their briefs and set off. Using a powerful crawl stroke, Kallee soon pulled ahead.

'Hey! Wait for me!' yelled Andrew. 'I'm the one who could be in trouble here!'

Fate, which had cruelly dashed Vindhook's dreams, showed a more benign face to Andrew and Kallee. Being forced to land in the sea proved to be their salvation. With the cutter now resting in two hundred fathoms of water, it was no longer visible to prying eyes.

The twin suns were setting as Andrew and Kallee reached shallow water and started to wade towards the beach. It was then that Andrew spotted the jet-copter coming in low from the west – along the shoreline.

From his stay on the island, he knew it wasn't based there. His sixth sense warned him that its arrival could mean trouble. As they reached the water's edge, he grabbed Kallee, pulled her to the ground, and locked her body into a 'From Here to Eternity' embrace with the water lapping round their ankles.

The jet-copter swept overhead and carried on down the beach.

Kallee wrenched her mouth away from his. 'I don't really want to do this.'

'Neither do I!' hissed Andrew. 'But I think that 'copter may be looking for us.' He silenced her protest. 'Yeah, I know! That may sound crazy but I've got a feeling that those guys up there could be from the Corporation.'

'Don't you think you might be imagining things? They couldn't have got onto us this quickly!'

'Don't underestimate them. You thought you'd pulled the

wool over their eyes, and Trade-Cor had Vindhook sitting on your tail!'

Kallee glanced along the beach. 'They're coming back.'

'Okay. I'm gonna roll off you. Sit up and wave as they fly by, then join me in the water.'

The 'copter approached. Kallee waved excitedly then ran into the breakers. Andrew was already wading out to where the water was chest deep.

The 'copter flew in a wide circle round them.

'Start splashing!' said Andrew. He swept several handfuls of water towards her, then grappled with her playfully and took her under as the 'copter swooped even lower. They burst out of the water and both waved.

It seemed to work. The 'copter flew off northwards towards the island's interior.

Andrew led Kallee into the taverna to find the waiters playing cards around a table loaded with wine bottles and wreathed in smoke.

Seeing they were both wet and almost naked, one of the waiters gallantly provided each of them with tablecloths. A second went to fetch towels from the washroom, and a third filled new glasses with wine.

After the many meals he'd shared with Shalimar, Andrew was no stranger. There was no time to explain how they came to be there and, in fact, there was no need to. Because of the interest in the card game, no one had witnessed their spectacular arrival. They might as well have stepped off the legendary Clapham omnibus. The presence of the jet-copter *had* been noticed by some of the kitchen staff who thought it odd. Parnassus had gone to great lengths to secure a legal ban on overflights of the island because of the frequent comings and goings of his own private spaceshuttle.

Andrew explained that the jet-copter was probably looking for him and his companion and that their continued presence on the island posed a danger to everyone and – for that reason alone – it was vital that he left Hesperides immediately by the door through which he had arrived.

The waiters, anxious to continue their card game and their relatively peaceful existence, agreed and directed him to the offices under the colonnade.

Wrapped in the tablecloths and towels, Andrew and Kallee ran barefoot along the terrace and into the colonnade where they found the two shuttle technicians locking the doors. They had overseen his transfer from Shadwell Street and he had gained a nodding acquaintance with both of them during the time he had spent learning about the Rimworld with Shalimar.

Andrew gave them a brief rundown on the situation and learned that Connie and Shalimar were both on board the SS Mount Olympus. No one knew their exact whereabouts but it was believed they were engaged in an operation which could have far-reaching consequences.

'I know,' said Andrew. 'We're part of it – and they were supposed to meet us! Which they failed to do – '

'Leaving us to get here under our own steam,' added Kallee – who hated being sidelined at moments of crisis.

'And as for far-reaching consequences, if the people in that helicopter come back and find us here, you're gonna have shit coming through the roof – and Connie will not be best pleased!'

'That's right!' Kallee cocked an ear to the sky. 'Is that it now?'

The lead technician became nervous. 'I think we'd better discuss this inside.'

They entered the reception area. The technician locked the door behind them, and pressed the switch that made the window glass opaque. 'The thing is, I'm not authorised to operate the shuttle without the express consent of Mister Parnassus.'

'If he was here, he'd give it,' said Andrew. 'Do you still have my clothes by the way? The ones I came in?'

The junior technician went off to look for them.

Andrew called after him. 'And do you have anything for my friend here? An overall or something?' He turned back to find the lead technician looking worried. 'Is there a problem here?'

'Well, yes. Didn't Shalimar explain? I just can't send you

382

through just as you are. There have to be . . . certain preparations.'

Andrew felt Kallee tugging at his arm.

'Can we have a word?'

'Sure.' Andrew turned to the technician. 'Look, do whatever you have to do to get this thing up and running and I'll come back to you.'

The junior technician returned with Andrew's clothes and a set of green coveralls for Kallee, then went off with his colleague.

Andrew started to dress. 'What is it?'

'I keep hearing you say we've got to get out of here – are you actually intending to go back to Earth?'

'Yeah. It's the safest place for us to be.'

'But how? I mean, how do we get from here to there?'

'Weren't you supposed to be listening when I explained this to Jean? What did you do – drop off in the middle of it? It doesn't matter how!' Andrew tapped his chest. 'It was never explained to me! It just *works*, okay?!'

'But . . . what will I *do* there?!'

'I haven't the faintest idea. We'll work out something. If Connie keeps his promise, he'll get in touch with us.'

'But what is it *like*?!'

'Well, strangely enough, in many ways it's very like the Rimworld except there's more rubbish. We don't go swanning around in space, there is only one sun and one planet worth speaking of but – as you can see from me – the people are no different, and the ones who live where we're going absolutely *love* animals!'

Kallee's face brightened. 'Really?'

'Yes! So get out of that tablecloth and put this on.'

She held up the coveralls. 'This is far too big.'

'Then roll up the legs and sleeves.' Andrew checked the inside pocket of his jacket. His wallet was still there. He opened it and found his bank and credit cards – along with three ten pound notes. Great.

The head technician returned. He still looked worried. 'I

383

really think you should wait until we can make contact with Mister Parnassus. I don't think you understand the danger to yourselves of going through without compensating for the differential.'

'Are we talking metabolic rates here?' demanded Andrew.

'That is part of it,' admitted the technician.

Andrew laughed. 'C'mon, let's stop playing games! All that stuff about metabolic differentials is a load of garbage. Those pills that Connie gave me were just a clever piece of fakery! I stopped taking them weeks ago and *nothing happened*! Look at me! I'm perfectly normal!'

'No! You don't understand – '

'Oh, don't worry! I understand perfectly. It was all part of the plan to trick me into going along with Connie's master plan. But it's okay. I don't mind about that.'

'But – '

'*No!*' cried Andrew. 'No more "Buts" and no more talk! *We have to go*! There are people on our trail. And if they find us, they are going to kill us – and they'll probably kill you too!'

'It's coming back! I can hear it!' shouted Kallee. She was standing by the locked entrance door. 'I'm not joking! Come and listen!'

Sweat beads formed on the technician's forehead. 'Follow me.'

☆   ☆   ☆

When the the floor-to-ceilings rays surrounding them vanished, Kallee surveyed the circular chamber and said: 'What's happened? We didn't move!'

'That's what you think.' Andrew slid open the curving glass door and stepped into the outer office. The computer on 'Maureen's desk' was still switched on. The screen saver program spread its coloured patterns. The slats of the venetian blinds were horizontal. It was getting dark outside. Andrew caught a glimpse of lighted windows. Down in nearby Piccadilly and Leicester Square, the nightly pursuit of pleasure in all its guises would be gathering pace.

384

'Welcome to London.' He saw her blank look. 'It's the capital city of the country I live in. After all your travelling around the Rimworld, you may find it a little cramped.'

'But there will be animals.'

'Oh, yes . . .' Andrew searched the drawers of the desk and found a set of keys labelled 'Street & Office Door'. He beckoned Kallee. 'This way. We've got to find ourselves a hotel for the night. Somewhere nearby. We'll come back tomorrow and see if there's been any messages.'

Andrew led the way down the stairs, opened the street door, stepped out onto the pavement, then recoiled violently as a dark shape streaked past just in front of him. He bumped into Kallee who was just behind him in the doorway.

'What happened?'

'I'm not sure . . .' Andrew took a tentative step onto the pavement and looked up and down Shadwell Court.

Sheee-onnnggg! With a high pitched blast of sound, another dark shape shot down the middle of the street, leaving two lingering streaks of white light. They disappeared and were replaced by two brief wavy streaks of red as the moving blur turned right into Godbold Street.

Andrew suddenly felt very frightened. This was crazy! Motioning Kallee to remain where she was, he edged along the wall towards the window of Chico's Bar. Light poured out into the pavement. He screwed up his courage, took another step and looked into the bar. It was empty.

No! It wasn't empty! He could hear a meaningless gabble of high pitched chatter. Like a Chipmunk record played at triple speed. And he glimpsed bright moving blurs in front and behind the counter.

Everything was speeded up. It was exactly the reverse of what he had encountered on stepping out onto the verandah where Shalimar had been standing motionless. Looking at the motionless sea. Then *he* had been a moving blur and now . . .

Now . . .

Andrew returned to the doorway and pushed Kallee inside. She scanned his face anxiously. 'Something's wrong, isn't it?'

385

'Yes – and I don't know why.' He shut the street door and led her back into the first floor office. He locked that door too then altered the angle of the blinds so as he could look down into the street. 'Everything's moving too fast. The thing that flashed down the street was a motor car. It wasn't going at more than fifteen miles an hour but it looked as if it was travelling at Mach 3!' Andrew gestured towards Chico's Sandwich Bar. 'The shop next door – there are people inside, I can hear them – *but I can't see them properly*!' He slapped both sides of his head. 'I don't understand what's happening!'

Kallee sat down at the desk. 'Maybe Parnassus was telling the truth. Maybe time, or metabolism, or whatever the X-factor is *does* move at a faster rate here.'

'But the pills were fakes!' cried Andrew. 'Aramitz gave you the results of his tests! They weren't slowing me down – and anyway I stopped taking them after Daniel came through!' He stopped to wrestle with the problem then tried again. 'Okay . . . let's suppose there *was* a difference between here and the Rimworld. It would make sense if you stepped out of the shuttle and went down to the street and found the people and the traffic a moving blur but *it shouldn't be happening to me*! Unless . . .'

Kallee got there ahead of him. 'Unless you . . . are from the Rimworld too.'

Andrew's head started to spin. He sat down on the nearest chair and laughed weakly. 'No, no, that's impossible! It doesn't make sense! I mean . . . how could it? I was born here, in England – in a town called Amersham. My mother wrote articles for magazines. My father was a pilot in the Royal Air Force then when he quit flying, he went into civil aviation and became a Senior Air Traffic Controller at Manchester! I went to Cambridge to study English and History – started flying with the University Air Squadron then – oh God . . .' Andrew leaned forward and buried his face in his hands. He drew them slowly down towards his chin and looked across at Kallee. 'I don't know what to believe any more.'

The room darkened. Kallee was lit by the glow from the

computer screen. The slats of the venetian blinds picked up the yellow light from the street lamps outside.

There was a series of high-pitched beeps as the terminal came to life. The slowly gyrating coloured shapes vanished and a message appeared. Andrew read it over Kallee's shoulder.

STAY INSIDE THE OFFICE. HELP IS ON THE WAY. IF YOU NEED FOOD AND DRINK, PHONE CHICO'S BAR. IDENTIFY YOURSELVES AS OLYMPIC MARKETING AND ASK THEM TO LEAVE THE TRAY AT THE TOP OF THE STAIRS. ORDER WHATEVER YOU LIKE. WE HAVE AN ACCOUNT THERE. PHONE NUMBER IS ON PAD IN TOP LEFT HAND DRAWER. PILLOWS AND SLEEPING BAGS IN BOTTOM OF STATIONERY CUPBOARD.

LOVE, M.

PLEASE ACKNOWLEDGE COMPLIANCE WITH THIS MESSAGE BY PRESSING 'A' THEN 'ENTER'.

PS: YOU HAVE PERFORMED SPLENDIDLY. CONGRATULATIONS.
CONNIE.

Kelly responded as instructed. Andrew walked over to the only cupboard, opened it and found the pillows and sleeping bags. Good old Connie. He never missed a trick.

'I've been thinking,' said Kallee.

'Yeah?'

'Mmmm. Since you've gone back to calling yourself Andrew, I'd like to be Kelly Mandell again. Her life was always a lot more exciting than mine. And she doesn't have to worry about hurting her father.'

Andrew unrolled the sleeping bags. 'Oh, why's that?'

''Cos when I was writing her life story, I made her an orphan at an early age. I think it makes me more appealing. More vulnerable.'

Andrew dropped the pillows into place. 'Amazing, isn't it? The way people see themselves. If I was asked to describe you, those two words would never have occurred to me.'

Chapter Twenty-Two

The next day, they awoke to the sound of an insistent high-pitched beep from the computer. Stifling a yawn, Kelly shambled blearily over to the desk in her bikini briefs and pressed 'Cancel'. The alarm fell silent and the screen saver pattern was replaced by a new set of instructions.

'Want me to read you what it says?'

Andrew poked his head out of his sleeping bag, nodded, then shifted onto his back and stared at the ceiling.

'"At 11.25 a.m., please lie down on the floor of the front office, face upwards, with your arms by your sides. At 11.30, two paramedics will transfer you onto stretchers, administer a tranquiliser, and take you in a private ambulance to a clinic owned by Olympic Enterprises. Once there, a simple but crucial operation will be performed that will synchronise your metabolic rate with your present environment. Do not eat or drink anything while awaiting collection. If you are very thirsty, you may take a small sip of water. Please acknowledge compliance with this instruction by pressing 'A' then 'Enter'. Love, M."'

It was then 08.45.

'Do we want to go along with that?'

'Do we have any choice?' replied Andrew.

'Who's this "M" person?'

'Search me . . .'

Kelly hit the response keys then tottered into the washroom. The smell of freshly ground coffee and warm toast was already wafting up the stairs and under the door. Andrew sloughed off his sleeping bag, padded over to the front windows and peeked

388

down through the blinds. In the half-shadowed street below, a steady procession of moving blurs marked the passage of nearby office workers collecting their breakfast from Chico's Sandwich Bar.

Kelly came out of the washroom, towelling her head. 'How d'you feel?'

'That depends on which one of us you're talking to.'

Kelly eyed him and shook her head. 'I really don't understand why it should be such a problem. I've always got a kick out of being somebody else.' She looked down at the street then let her gaze wander across the buildings on the other side of Shadwell Court. 'This certainly is a Stone-Age City. The smell . . . and the noise! How many people live here?'

'About fifteen million.'

'Shagga-raymuss! That's more than half the total population of Libra! Is the rest of the world like this?'

'Some places are even worse. In cities like Cairo and Calcutta there are times when you can hardly move.'

'But how do people breathe?!' exclaimed Kelly.

'With difficulty. But things are better away from the cities.'

'Can we go there?'

Andrew shrugged. 'Depends on what happens next. We certainly can't go anywhere like this.' He folded the sleeping bags carefully, and placed them, military style, with the pillows on top in the stationery cupboard. Satisfied he was leaving the place in good order, he took his turn in the washroom.

At 11.25, having tilted the venetian blinds upwards to allow them a view of the hazy blue sky, they lay down side by side by the window, with their feet facing the entrance door. Andrew tried to let his mind go blank. The next five minutes seemed to extend for ever. Kelly's hand reached out to touch his. He didn't resist as their fingers entwined.

'Nervous?'

'Just a little,' she said. 'Do you mind?'

389

"Course not. Just relax. Compared to what we've been through, this'll be a cakewalk.'

☆   ☆   ☆

Cakewalk or not, it proved to be remarkably painless. The last thing they remembered were blurred figures passing around them. When they woke up, within minutes of each other, they found themselves sharing a sunlit room decorated with vases of flowers and framed pictures of animals. The only sign of the operation was an adhesive bandage stuck to the right side of their abdomens.

From their hospital beds, they could see green lawns fringed with trees and an immaculate, winding gravel drive. A few hours after they sat up and began to take notice of what was going on around them, a gleaming black, top-of-the-range Ford Transit turned into the drive and scrunched to a halt not far from their window. It had ominously dark smoked-glass windows like the black vans in the Hollywood movie 'Slither' starring James Caan.

The cab door opened and a pair of unmistakable long legs preceded the rest of Shalimar. Adjusting her dark glasses, she slid back the side loading door and helped Constantine Parnassus step down from the luxuriously-appointed interior.

Andrew had a sudden memory flash. Of years ago . . . at his aunt's home in Shropshire when he . . . had been recovering from a near-fatal motor-cycle accident . . . some months after the death of his parents. The deep laughter of a visitor that had awoken him from a drugged sleep . . . coming from downstairs . . . the sound of the front door closing.

The feeling of curiosity that had overcome his drowsiness and propelled him out of bed . . . sent him hobbling towards the window trailing bandages like Christopher Lee in *The Curse of The Mummy*.

A similar kind of van, but a much earlier model, had been parked outside the green-painted, double wooden gate . . . framed by the neatly-clipped hedges on either side. Andrew

390

had caught a fleeting glimpse of an enormous well-tailored bum as it disappeared through the side door . . . a door which was closed by a tall, slim woman in a long skirt . . . who then entered the cab without looking back at the house.

Parnassus and Shalimar . . . they had visited his aunt's house in Shropshire . . . all those years ago. When he had asked his aunt who the callers were, she had told him they were from a firm trying to sell spray-on loft insulation. Aunt Jessie? Involved with Parnassus? It didn't seem possible, unless . . .

His mind-searchings were interrupted as the door was thrown open and Parnassus entered the room, bearing a bouquet of red roses. The arch-manipulator looked immensely pleased with himself, fizzing with zest, and bubbling over with good humour. In a word, ebullient.

'Andrew! Kelly! My heart rejoices to find you both looking so well.' He tut-tutted. 'You caused us great deal of needless worry . . . rushing off like that.'

Shalimar, his elegant shadow, closed the door. She was carrying a large, gift-wrapped box.

Parnassus presented the roses to Kelly with a courtly flourish then snapped his fingers. Shalimar placed the gift-wrapped box on Kelly's bed.

'Belgian chocolates,' said Parnassus. 'Handmade, of course!' He passed between the beds and spread his bulk over a two-seat sofa.

Shalimar picked up the house phone by Andrew's bed and eyed him tantalisingly while she keyed a number.

Parnassus drummed his fingers on the armchair. 'Shalimar! This room is utterly bereft of food! What's happened to the lunch I ordered!'

She brandished the phone. 'I'm ringing the kitchens now.'

'Fancy a chocolate while you're waiting?' asked Kelly

'No, thank you. I ate several boxes on the way here.' Parnassus waved towards the black Transit and sighed. 'I hate travelling in these stupid little tinpot cars. The cooking facilities are so limited.'

391

Andrew exchanged a smile with Shalimar, then said: 'Should've bought a Winnebago and hired yourself a chef.'

'A Winne-what?'

Andrew ticked off the plus points of a Winnebago motorhome. Parnassus aimed sharp glances at Shalimar as the specifications were unveiled. 'I hope you're listening to this.'

'I don't need to. I already have the brochure on file.'

'Then let's get one for the return journey.'

'Can't be done,' said Shalimar firmly. 'All the arrangements are already made. There just isn't time.'

'Hmmphhh!' Connie, a man used to having every wish instantly fulfilled by underlings, pouted angrily. 'I must say this is all *very* disappointing, Shalimar!'

The tension was dissipated by the arrival of three trolleys loaded with *hors-d'oeuvres*, entrees and desserts. Parnassus tucked the table-sized napkin under his chin and eyed the goodies on offer.

'You'll have to excuse that minor burst of irritation. I suffer from a rare brain disease. When I'm not ingesting food, I start to feel physically and mentally threatened . . .' He began munching the first *hors d'oeuvre*. 'Okay, fire away. Ask whatever you want. It's cards-on-the-table time.'

'How about starting with this operation?' said Andrew.

'Okay. It's as good a place as any.' Connie aimed a loaded fork. 'You were right about the pills. They were a blind – an extra control mechanism if you like. But a necessary part of the deception. We had to trick you into thinking you were from Earth until all the other parts of the plan had fallen into place.'

Shalimar passed Parnassus a new *hors d'oeuvre*. 'We also had to make sure the mind-blocks we had inserted would continue to hold once you had returned to the Rimworld.'

'The first trick was when you arrived and stepped out onto the verandah and saw Shalimar. Nothing was moving – but you couldn't help noticing the drink on the table with the note underneath.'

'Which I read, then emptied the glass,' said Andrew.

392

'And woke up a few minutes later – and then we had lunch.'

'Aha! That's where you're wrong! You *thought* it was a few minutes. What you said was '. . . it's just not possible to be in Soho at five to one and on a world with two suns at quarter past. Remember?'

'Yeah, I think so.'

'Well, you were right about the time it took to get to us. You walked out of the transmitter room on Hesperides two minutes after entering the chamber in Shadwell Court. But our lunch date was two weeks later!'

Andrew sought confirmation from Shalimar.

'It's true. We had to remove the accelerator unit and gradually bring you down to Rimworld speed.' Shalimar delved into her bag and produced a small, squashy object about the size of a Zippo lighter, with connector tubes at each end. 'This is what you've just had put back inside you.' She passed it to Andrew then smiled at Kelly. 'You were meant to be given these before you left but – '

'Wonder-Boy thought he had it all figured out.' Kelly caught the unit as it arced across from Andrew's bed and inspected it closely. 'Neat . . .'

'A marvel of bio-engineering,' chomped Parnassus. 'It extracts chemical agents naturally present in the body and reformulates them to produce a constant supply of the elements needed to raise your metabolic rate to Earth speed. And it's completely transparent to X-rays.'

'And I suppose the Gujuratis you shipped to the Rimworld were all given something similar – but working in reverse?'

Parnassus aimed another forkful of food at Andrew. 'Very good! That's why I built this clinic!'

With money stolen from fat cats in the City, no doubt. But this was not the time for recriminations.

'So who am I, Connie?'

'Who indeed?' Parnassus spread his left hand. His right hand was busy shovelling food into his mouth. 'That is a profoundly interesting, deeply philosophical question – and one that only you can answer. By all accounts, Andrew Webber was a fine

393

young man whose life was cut tragically short a few months after his parents died on Tenerife.'

'So there really was an air-crash.'

'Oh, yes. You took it very badly. And one night, you got very drunk at a party in London, set off back to Cambridge, and had the most ghastly accident on the M something.'

'The M11,' said Shalimar. 'Just a few miles from here. There was nothing anyone could do to save him. Andrew had extensive injuries which – apart from anything else would have left him paralysed from the neck down and in a wheelchair for the rest of his life – '

'But he was also in an irreversible coma,' interjected Connie. 'Had we not intervened he would have been pronounced brain-dead.'

'Sounds like you got there just in time,' said Kelly.

Parnassus eyed her mischievously. 'We like to think so.'

Shalimar took up the story. 'Daniel had already been brought through Shadwell Court. It was too dangerous to leave him in the Rimworld. He was here, in the clinic's Intensive Care Unit – badly injured, but his condition had stabilised. It was then we heard a police radio broadcast about a serious accident involving a young motorcyclist – '

'Me – I mean, Andrew . . .'

'All we knew at that point was that his injuries might prove fatal and that he had been rushed to a general hospital on the other side of the motorway which had a specialist unit handling road traffic victims. We contacted them and explained we were acting on behalf of his sole surviving relative – '

'Aunt Jessie . . .'

Shalimar nodded. 'Yes, and they gave us a clinical assessment of the injuries. It didn't make happy reading. Anyway, we monitored your progress – or rather, the lack of it – over the next four days, by which time the accident unit had decided that your coma was irreversible. They were prepared to give you another week before beginning the administrative process which would allow them to pull the plug on your life support systems.'

394

'And that's when you decided to ride to the rescue,' said Kelly.

Andrew bridled at her tone. 'Hey! Don't start trying to stir things up! This has nothing to do with you.'

Shalimar was unfazed. Kelly's carping attitude did not reflect any deep concern about the moral issues involved. It arose from the fact that she was tall, beautiful and impeccably dressed whilst Kelly was, by Atlantean standards, a dwarfish, Plain Miss Prudence who wanted Andrew to desire her above all others.

Some chance.

Shalimar resumed her account. 'Before the week was out, we went back to the hospital, posing once more as agents for your family – who wanted us to take over your long-term care. Needless to say, the NHS did not need much persuading. They were happy to be relieved of the financial burden.'

'So I was brought here and that was when you performed the mind-dump.'

'Yes.'

'Only it was Andrew's mind which was transferred into Daniel, and not the other way around. The very opposite, in fact, of what you've been telling me.'

'That's right. But now you know the circumstances, perhaps you will not judge us too harshly. Bringing your minds together was a very delicate balancing act. We had to push Daniel completely into the background but – despite all the odds – it worked out amazingly well.

Kelly, unable to keep silent for long, sounded another sour note. 'Not for Andrew. He ended up dead.'

'I disagree,' said Shalimar. 'The essential Andrew is alive and well and with us in this room.'

Kelly threw up her hands. 'Oh, well – if you're gonna start hiding behind philosophical concepts!'

'Hey!' Andrew tapped his chest. 'This is not some goddam philosophical concept sitting in this bed! This is *me*! I'm *here*! So just pipe down and let her get on with the story!'

'When Daniel had reached the convalescent stage, we moved

you to Shropshire. To a house near the village where Andrew's father was born.'

'Aunt Jessie's . . .'

'That's right. 'Only of course you didn't recognise her. On top of all the other problems, you had traumatic amnesia. It lasted about three months but it allowed us to manipulate the past. We put pictures of Daniel's parents through a computer and combined them with the photos Andrew was carrying at the time of the accident. Even when your memory came back, you accepted them without question.'

Connie had time to interject while swapping plates. 'You were a real find, Andrew. Most people were awash with family. But not you. All your mother's relatives were in India. Your father's parents were both dead. He had two older brothers, one in America, the other in New Zealand.'

'And Aunt Jessie?'

Connie grimaced. 'You're not related. She's an employee of mine.'

'Ahhh . . . pity. I liked her.'

'She liked you too. And looked after you very well indeed.'

'Yeah . . . is she still in Shropshire?'

'Uh, no. She's now the housekeeper at this villa I own in Switzerland. Shalimar will give you the address. Any time you want to go there for a holiday, feel free.'

'Thanks. One more question. All that stuff about me not being your first choice was just a wind-up wasn't it? My battalion commander was never on the list and those three other people you said were killed in transit – that didn't happen either, did it?'

'No. It was all part of the plan to win you over. A little mild deception that didn't hurt anyone. And it worked. You swallowed it completely.'

'Yes, I did. So . . . what happens now?'

Connie frowned as he chewed. 'In relation to what?'

'I'm a schizoid, Connie. You've saddled me with a split personality. Back in the Rimworld, you made me a promise – '

'Yes! I know.' Parnassus toyed briefly with his food then

buoyed himself up with another mouthful. 'You'll have to forgive me. I'm a compulsive liar. I've sought help from countless experts but I'm told it's something to do with my genetic make-up. I shall, of course be eternally penitent – '

'Like hell, you will – '

'You're right. That's not true either – ' Connie broke off and prodded the air with his fork, as if trying to spear the right words. 'I'm afraid unravelling your twin personae is not as easy as I made it sound. In fact, it's impossible because, well – it's *you*, Andrew, who doesn't have a home to go to.'

'So what're we gonna do?'

'Why *do* anything? You've both been rubbing along for ten years now. It's a wonderful example of symbiosis. I don't think you realise the influence you've had on each other. Daniel's natural ability to command certainly helped your Army career, Andrew, and you, in turn, helped make him into a much nicer person.'

'Thank you,' said Andrew's alter-ego.

'Had to be said, Daniel. With your background, you couldn't have become anything other than totally excremental.'

'I think you'll find there is no such a word,' said Shalimar.

'There is now!' snapped Parnassus.

'Okay, okay! The thing is – what do I call myself?'

Parnassus turned his attention to the dessert trolley. 'It's simple. You call yourself Andrew Webber. Daniel Kinsharadeen is not going to cut much ice in the Rimworld. After the stunt you just pulled, the knives are out with a vengeance.'

Shalimar stepped in as Connie fed his face. 'You were right to worry about that helicopter. It was looking for you. We checked out the firm it belonged to. The people who hired it were linked with the Corporation.'

'But they won't be able to throw their weight around for much longer. If things go on as they are, the Corporation will run out of money. They'll have to start laying people off.' Connie launched into a brief but detailed account of the problems which had beset the Corporation following the insertion of the program containing the Jericho virus. 'Of

397

course, my team of developers did most of the work, but it was my concept so I deserve most of the credit. On the other hand, it could never had succeeded without you two. Well done!'

'Thanks,' said Kelly.

'I meant Andrew and Daniel,' said Connie. 'But I'm aware that you also played a key role in all this. And I look forward to working with you again in the future.' He sighed wistfully. '"So much to do, so little time". But we'll talk about that after your holiday.'

Andrew frowned. 'Holiday?'

'A much-needed break, a well-earned rest, sabbatical – a period of reflection, a chance to take stock of your life before embarking on a new adventure.'

'Here – or in the Rimworld?'

Connie drew the fork from his mouth with a flourish. 'The Rimworld, of course!'

Andrew tried to gauge Kelly's reaction then asked: 'Why would we want to go back when we're joint-top of the Corporation's hit list?'

'Oh, don't worry about that. That will all die down. Trust me, Andrew. I have your best interests at heart.' Connie cocked his head to one side and sized him up. 'With a little plastic surgery – '

'Oh, sure! Why not? You've already given me a brain transplant! Why stop there?!' Andrew waved dismissively. 'No. Sorry. Count me out. Kelly might have good reasons to go back, but I've had enough of the Rimworld to last me a lifetime.'

Parnassus started on his first bowl of dessert. 'Okay. Fine. As you wish. We didn't come here to pressurise you, did we Shalimar?'

'No. Just to make sure you were all right.'

'And to express our appreciation. After all, you are a very special person, Andrew – an Earth-being who also belongs to the Rimworld and – '

'Correction. "Who used to". I've seen all I want to see of it. I've decided to become a very "down-to-Earth person" now.'

Parnassus shrugged. 'For now perhaps. But people change. Life is full of unexpected surprises. How does that song go, Shalimar?'

'*Que sera, sera.*'

'Precisely. You've tasted the future, Andrew. You've helped change it! What is there here to compare with that? There are one thousand, four hundred and seventy-six planets in the Rimworld. Your adventures have barely begun!'

'Four hundred and seventy-eight,' said Shalimar.

'What . . .?'

'You forgot Fantazmagoria and Nebulon.'

Connie eyed her with disdain. 'I was referring to the number of worlds whose existence is not in dispute – planets whose presence can be proved empirically!'

Shalimar checked her watch. 'We'll have to leave in five minutes if you want to catch that plane.'

Parnassus set down his plate, threw aside his napkin and levered himself off the sofa with Shalimar's assistance. 'The briefcase!'

She passed it to him with a longsuffering look.

'Call the kitchen. Have them pack the rest of that food. I'll eat it in the car.' Parnassus lumbered over to Andrew's bed, plonked the case down and turned to Kelly. 'Stop sulking and listen. This concerns you both.'

Shalimar positioned the food trolleys by the door, then used Andrew's phone to call the kitchen.

Connie produced a set of car keys from the briefcase. 'When you leave, you'll find a vehicle parked out front. A V-6 Turbo Izuzu Trooper. Wide-track, tinted glass, charcoal metallic finish.'

'Oh, great! I've always wanted one of those.'

Shalimar covered the phone. 'I know.'

'The documents are all in the case, plus a motoring atlas and the address of the house in Shropshire, plus two sets of door-keys.'

'Does this place have a name?' asked Kelly.

Andrew nodded. 'Meadowcrest Farm. You'll love it.'

'Can we move on?' demanded Connie. 'The deeds are held in your name by a local solicitor. Details are all in here.' He dropped the car keys into the case and glanced at the contents. 'And what else? Oh, yes! Some folding money to tide you over, plus information relating to your Swiss bank account.' He snapped the case shut and laid it against Andrew's chest. 'I do keep some promises.'

'Thanks, Connie.'

Shalimar answered a knock at the door. Three kitchen orderlies entered, seized the depleted food trolleys and made a speedy exit.

'Are they going to have that packed and ready in time?!'

'Don't worry,' said Shalimar. 'If it isn't, we'll stop at a Little Chef.'

'If that's a joke, it's in very bad taste.' Parnassus turned back to Andrew. 'Where was I? Oh, yes! Forget Catford and your career in the tabloids – '

'But what about my flat? All my belongings?'

'The lease on your flat has been sold, Andrew. Your worldly goods have been moved to Shropshire – where you will both be able to get plenty of fresh air and exercise. I can't force you, of course, but if you were to spend the next six months at Meadowcrest reflecting on the recent past and considering what you'd like to do next, I am sure you would find it extremely beneficial.'

'Does this place have a garden?' asked Kelly. 'With space to keep a few animals?'

'It has a garden, a small orchard and one hundred and fifty acres of paddock and pasture.'

'An acre . . . is that a big piece of land?'

'It is if you have to mow it,' said Andrew. 'On the other hand, we could always get some sheep.'

'Oh, yes!' cried Kelly. 'And some dogs – and horses too!' Her eyes sought out Parnassus. 'Can we do that?'

'Of course!' Connie treated her to a benign smile. 'Just don't plant anything that takes a long time to grow.' He caught Shalimar's warning glance and switched from cuddly uncle to brisk tycoon. 'Time to leave!' He blew a kiss to Kelly and gripped Andrew's hand. 'Just popping over to Switzerland for a few days, then it's back to Shadwell Court and home.'

'Give my love to Aunt Jessie.'

Parnassus was halfway out of the door. 'I will!'

Shalimar supplied the final details. 'If there are no problems with your next check-up, you'll be released from here the day after tomorrow.' She nodded to Kelly and gave Andrew a lingering glance as she left the room. 'We'll call you before we travel home to make sure everything's okay.'

As the door closed, Andrew hugged the briefcase and looked across at Kelly.

She sampled the chocolates. 'Think you can stand being with me for another six months?'

Andrew shrugged. 'Yeah . . . reckon I could just about manage that.'

A pillow, thrown with considerable force, winged its way across the room. Andrew fended it off with the briefcase.

☆   ☆   ☆

Four days later, at around quarter past six in the evening, Kelly knocked on the door of the downstairs loo of the house in Shropshire. 'Andy! Quick! Parnassus and Shalimar are on television!'

Andrew, who was in the process of wiping his bum, cursed loudly then lurched out of the lavatory, clutching his trousers loosely about his person.

Reaching the door of the lounge, he was in time to hear the newscaster recounting the arrest of '. . . the Greek financier, Constantine Parnassus and his female companion . . . both of whom are believed to be implicated in several multi-million dollar electronic banking frauds in Britain, Europe and the USA'.

The cameras showed Connie and Shalimar being escorted by uniformed police officers from an executive Learjet and being eased into the back of a stretched Mercedes limo – probably the only vehicle that could be found to house Connie's huge bulk with a modicum of dignity.

In the afternoon of the next day, Shalimar called from Brown's Hotel in Dover Street to announce that she had been released without charge. Connie was still being interviewed by senior officers of the Fraud Squad and was due to meet with representatives from the various banks he was alleged to have swindled. Some were already in London, others were jetting in from the four corners of the globe.

Andrew voiced his concern.

Shalimar had not called just to explain what was happening; she wanted to know if Andrew could come down to London and lend her moral support until Connie managed to extricate himself.

The words 'Yes, of course' burst from Andrew's lips before she was halfway through the question.

☆   ☆   ☆

Shalimar met Andrew in the lobby of Brown's Hotel. She hugged him briefly then led him to the desk to sign in. 'We have an entire suite but this just makes it official. Is that okay with you?'

'Are you kidding?'

Andrew picked up his hotel pass. They headed for the elevator.

'How's Kelly getting along with the animals?'

'She's still making lists,' replied Andrew. 'We only got there a few days ago.'

'Did she mind you coming?'

'Didn't ask. Just said I had some business to attend to.'

The 'Do Not Disturb' sign was already hanging outside the door to the suite. She had also drawn the curtains in the master bedroom. She slipped off her shoes, unpinned her imposing coiffure then shook it loose and fluffed it out into a lustrous cascade that fell across her shoulders and halfway down her back.

They came together in an unhurried embrace, kissed then got undressed. In bare feet and with her hair down, she was only

402

four inches taller than he was. I can live with that, he thought. When they slid into the bed and lay in each other's arms, the difference ceased to matter.

'At last,' he breathed.

Shalimar kissed and caressed his face then pulled her head back and searched his eyes worriedly. 'You do know this won't be anything like it was in the sim-tank?'

Andrew drew her close to him. 'I don't care. All I ever wanted was the real you.'

And, as sometimes happens, the real thing turned out to be far better than either could have hoped for. But the idyll was shortlived. They spent the next two days walking hand-in-hand through the green spaces of Central London. They gazed into each other's eyes, elbow to elbow across the tables of small, dark, cosy restaurants, and spent several precious, restlessly passionate hours in each other's arms.

And they were so engaged when the telephone rang and rang – demanding to be answered.

It was Parnassus – announcing his unpublicised release through a little known back door to the Judge's Chambers at the Central Criminal Court at the top of Fleet Street. The same private ambulance which had carried Andrew and Kelly to the clinic would be conveying him to Chico's Sandwich Bar in Shadwell Court. Could Shalimar book out of the hotel and meet him there in forty-five minutes?

There was only one answer expected. 'Yes, of course. I'll be there.'

'Good – and if Andrew's with you, bring him along.'

When the hotel staff had loaded the luggage into the brand-spanking new V-6 Trooper, Andrew drove Shalimar to Shadwell Court and parked in the garage entrance. A 'CLOSED' sign hung on the door to Chico's but Connie could be seen inside, his ample rear spread across three bar stools. He waved and signalled them to enter.

'Andrew! Just talking about you.' He introduced the beaming proprietor. 'Chico Nikkoleides. That's Anna, his wife and Mamma.'

The blackclad woman by the expresso machine flashed a gold-toothed smile. Her square, lined, weathered face reminded Andrew of the women in the Oklahoma dust-bowl photos of Dorothea Lange.

'They look after me when I'm in town,' explained Connie. He ordered two more coffees and another whole chocolate fudge cake for himself.

When the cups were placed on the counter, Andrew asked: 'So, is it serious? Is there going to be a trial?'

Connie burst into laughter, causing his body to wobble like a blancmange perched on a spin-drier. 'My dear boy! I haven't been released on bail! I've been released, period! There was insufficient evidence to mount a case against me!'

'I don't get it. If they can't prove you took the money, why were you arrested?'

Connie set about the fudge cake. 'Because they cobbled together enough evidence to have me charged, but it was all circumstantial and very tenuous. It seems that after I had conducted perfectly bona fide transactions with all these banks, they discovered that several more millions were missing from the till.'

'I see . . .'

'What they really wanted to know was how I did it. Naturally I declined to say anything except protest my innocence.'

'Naturally . . .'

'I also warned them that if I was forced to stand trial, the subsequent revelations could plunge the global banking network into a crisis from which it might not recover.'

'So they backed off . . .'

'All except the Bank of England. The Governor wanted to call my bluff so I suggested that – in his own interests – he should call in the Attorney-General and the Director of Public Prosecutions.' Connie carved another twenty-minute slice of fudge cake. 'When they arrived, I showed them my Swiss and Greek passports – I enjoy dual nationality – then outlined the situation, the gravity and complexity of the charges and explained that this was likely to become the biggest and longest fraud case to come before the English Courts.'

'And . . .?'

Connie spread his hands and shrugged like Marlon Brando in *The Godfather*. 'I made them an offer. I said if they could persuade the Bank to drop all charges, I wouldn't apply for legal aid.'

Shalimar clapped her hands in delight.

Andrew laughed too, then shook his head in disbelief. 'You should get a medal, Connie.'

'They awarded me something better than that. An out-of-court settlement of one million pounds. Compensation for wrongful arrest! Not a bad week's work, eh?'

'Not bad at all . . .'

'Mind you, the collapse of the case against me has caused a certain amount of disappointment around the Inns of Court. I heard that several leading barristers were salivating at the prospect of six-figure fees. When the news gets out, I imagine a few of them will feel like throwing themselves off the roof.'

'Won't happen,' said Andrew. 'But it's a nice thought.'

Parnassus turned to Chico. 'Do you have that spare key?'

Chico produced it from a drawer under the counter.

Parnassus passed it to Andrew. 'Key to the office. If you ever want to get in touch, use the computer.'

'Type five capital Os, then Enter. That will bring up the Help Menu,' said Shalimar.

Andrew shook his head. 'I still can't believe any of this. I know that first telephone call was routed through the computer but that still doesn't explain anything. Scientifically speaking, it's just not possible to send a signal – let alone a body – from here to the Rimworld in the same instant.'

Parnassus chuckled. 'Well, I can understand it might be a problem for the editorial staff of *Nature*, but Earth sciences are still in their infancy. You are living proof that it can be done, Andrew.'

'I know . . .'

And when you were on the Rimworld, did you imagine, for one moment that you would be sharing a cup of coffee with Shalimar and myself in Soho?'

'No . . .'

Connie spread his hands. 'Yet here we are. All things are possible, Andrew. Always keep an open mind. And remember this. Before the universe was created, it first had to be conceived by the supreme being that you call God and whom we refer to as The Programmer. We, and everything around us, from this empty plate to the farthest star in the most distant galaxy, spring from and are sustained by that one, single, all-embracing thought.

'Never underestimate the power of the imagination, Andrew. When we let it roam free, we tap into the cosmic overmind. It's the source of all our ideas – the energy that drives our creativity.'

Andrew walked with them to the street door of the office. The farewells, with handshakes and hugs all round were brief and over all too quickly. The door shut of its own accord. He didn't linger.

☆   ☆   ☆

Kelly came to meet Andrew at the front door as he parked the car. 'You had a caller while you were away.'

'Oh? Who?'

Kelly opened the door a few inches. Kelly the cat emerged, rubbed her cheek against the door frame, then allowed herself to be gathered into Andrew's arms. She pushed her face into Andrew's chin and purred with pleasure.

'I'm amazed she remembers me.'

'Yes. Some men have that effect on women. She was delivered by an outfit called Securicor. Just walked in and made herself at home.'

'Yeah, some women are like that.'

'It's gonna be a bit confusing us having the same name.'

'I could always call you Zou-Zou.'

Her face hardened. 'I wouldn't recommend it.'

Andrew set his cat down and watched her pad off to explore the garden. A lot of small furry and feathered creatures would have cause to regret her arrival. He pulled his overnight bag from the car.

406

'Has he gone?'

'Parnassus? Yes.'

'Dilly-dally Longlegs too?'

'Yes.'

Kelly invited him to enter the house and followed him through to the kitchen. 'I suppose she was all over you.'

Andrew leaned against the rail of the Aga. 'What makes you think that?'

'Women can read the signs better than men can. So . . . where do we go from here?'

'Not sure. Thought I might try my hand at writing a book about all this. *Tales of Adventure from the Rimworld.* Could make a packet. What d'you think?'

'I think you should write it first. You can fantasise about the fame and fortune later.' Kelly lifted her behind up onto the kitchen table and sat facing him, ankles together, legs swinging.

Andrew leaned back against the Aga and ran his hands along the warm rail. 'There's something I've been meaning to ask you.'

'Ask away.'

'When my father hired you to check me out – which is probably why we both happened to run into each other on the Narayana – '

'Yeah – '

'Why did you give me so much grief? I mean like . . . dumping those guns on me when we landed at Buena Vista?'

'You got away with it, didn't you?'

'Yeah! But – '

'It's simple. Back on the Rimworld, when we were young, you were very mean to me.'

'Yeah – 'cause you were such a little squirt.'

'And you were a pompous fart. But at least you knew I was around. The guns and all the rest of that stuff was just a bit of fun, Andy. I get a real kick out of giving you a hard time. It keeps you on your toes. Relationships that become boring and predictable never last. When you look back on all this, you'll thank me.'

'I see. Well, if you feel the Rimworld calling, don't let me stop you.'

'Kelly laughed. 'No dice, Andy. You don't get out of it that easily. You brought me here. I'll go back when you do!'

Andrew considered the prospect and decided he needed a drink. He walked over to the fridge and took out a bottle of Pilsner Export. 'I don't feel like cooking tonight. Why don't we drive over to that pub outside Ludlow?'

'Great. Means I don't have to dress up.' She fisted his arm. 'Don't take what I said too much to heart. It's good to see you back. I'll just put a comb through my hair.'

Kelly went upstairs, changed her muddy jeans for a clean pair and decided she also needed a fresh shirt. She slipped her feet into a pair of thick-soled cowboy boots with three inch heels, straightened out her hair with her fingers and wondered briefly how long it would take for it to grow down to her shoulders.

Forever, probably – and even then it wouldn't make any difference. Nor would the three inch heels.

As they walked out to the car, Andrew paused and took a critical look at Kelly's tightly-clad rear end. 'You forgot to take the label off.'

☆   ☆   ☆

Parnassus swept out of his private taverna with the last flavours of another gargantuan meal still fizzing on his taste buds. Shalimar's arm was linked in his. He stopped, inhaled several litres of sea air then glanced fondly at his faithful assistant.

'Do you miss him?'

'Not as much as he's missing me,' said Shalimar. 'Wasn't that why you asked me to invite him back to London?'

Parnassus patted her hand. 'You're a good girl. I don't know what I'd do without you.'

They strolled along the sidewalk towards the colonnaded verandah and paused to survey the huge sweep of white-gold sand. A series of faint shrill cries from seaward drew Connie's attention to the sky. Above the breaking turquoise waves, several dozen white, slim-bodied creatures with V-shaped wings wheeled and dived.

Connie frowned. 'What on earth are they?!'

'Seagulls . . .'

'Seagulls? Hhmmmhh! Whatever next?'

They descended the steps that led to the beach. One of the gulls drifted gracefully over their heads and settled on the white dome of the taverna.

Shalimar smiled to herself. Unbeknown to Kelly Mandell, she was also member of the APF. And she knew that the gulls, along with all the other seabirds, were just the beginning.